Copy

First Edition July 2012

ISBN-13: 978-1477590102
ISBN-10: 1477590102

Dedication

To Kellie, who has been there with me from the very beginning when I started Superstars. Your love and support has been monumental. Thank you.

Acknowledgements

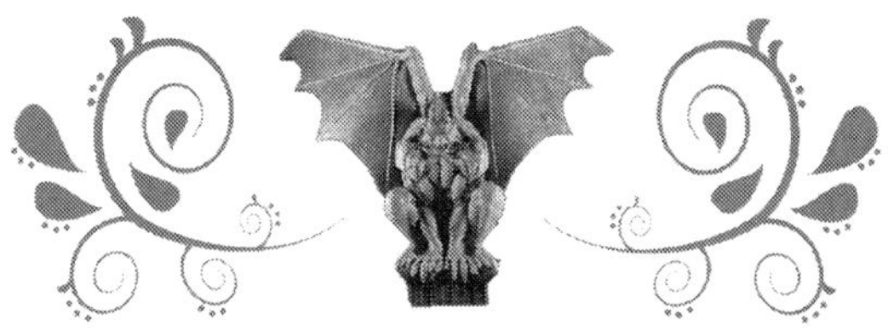

There are so many people I am grateful for in their support of me while I pursued my dream of becoming a writer.

My editor Peter Enman had his work cut out for him when he took me on but he did so with class and patience. To Allie Brown who between university exams and work found time to proof and add valued critiques of my writing.

My mentor Mirella Patzer, an accomplished writer and publisher of women's historical fiction, took me under her wing and showed me the ropes. I hope to someday pay it forward. Thank you, Mirella.

To my close friends, Don & Christine, Brett & Debbie, Blair & Ruby to name a few who listened to my stories for the past two years and easily could have been skeptical but instead chose to be supportive and positive. They are true friends.

My good friend Louie whose patience is always tested in our friendship helped create my cover page and I am thankful for that.

My mother, Alice, an avid reader of fiction of all types never wavered in her support of a son who was never short of ideas but sometimes short on execution. Thank you so much for everything you have done for me. I cannot forget my brothers Gord and Shaun and sisters Karen and Lorraine. I hope you like the book.

My children, Kayla, Kale, Katon and Keenan. My grandchildren Lyric and Cooper, step grandchildren Robbie and Matthew and my son-in-law Cliff. Always supportive of their big dreaming dad and grandfather. Kellie's son Griffin who always makes me laugh.

Prologue

Part 1

Tiridates the Great, heated by lust and driven by passion, thrust into his wife, Queen Bitus. Even at the age of sixty-eight, he was as virile as when he was a young soldier schooling himself in Roman war tactics. Grunting as he reached climax, feeling the oncoming rush reach his genitals, his euphoria interrupted by a blood curdling scream from Bitus underneath him. Aroused by the pleasure he was giving his wife, he thrust harder into her causing her screams to continue. Sweat reaching his eyes, stinging, he looked down at Bitus, her screams piercing. As much as he would like to think it was him, her screams were not from his lovemaking. Something was wrong.

Turning to look back in the direction of his wife's gaze, he was shocked to see a man standing at the foot of their bed. A large man, a commoner, dressed plainly. He held no weapon. Rolling off his wife to face the stranger, he thrust himself up out of the bed and with a flash of tremendous speed and agility retrieved his sword. A sword he kept in its sheath he had custom built into the headboard, and confronted the brave but foolish commoner.

"I do not know how you made it past my guards, and into my bedroom, but I promise you one thing, your death will not be swift. Instead, I will carve you up piece by piece and feed it to my dogs," bellowed Tiridates.

Suddenly the commoner standing in front of the naked King began to morph into a beast. The man's arms bulged and lengthened, tearing the fabric as it did, the skin turning milky white and slimy. A menacing claw grew out of the end of the arm, where a hand once appeared. Horrified at what he was witnessing, Tiridates, cringed as he heard snapping sounds from the creatures morphing body. The beast's neck bulged and widened.

Queen Bitus screamed, alerting the guards out in the hallway. Finding it locked they shouted and banged on the door but found it impenetrable. Turning to face the screaming Queen, the beast bellowed, "Silence" causing the Queen to scream even more. This resulted in more shouting and pounding from the hallway as the soldiers tried to axe their way through the thick wooden door. The beast flew into the Queen. The force flung her against the bedroom wall with such force, her head took the brunt of the blow. With an audible crack, the Queen collapsed unconscious to the floor. The candles lighting the room extinguished and the room became dark and cold.

"The Devil fights in the dark to hide like a coward. Show yourself so I can drive this sword through your soulless chest," King Tiridates shouted.

A light illuminated the creature, revealing a repulsive monster whose hideous head revealed a mouthful of fangs dripping in hatred. The King thrust his menacing sword at the beast. Snapping its massive claw-like hand, the beast grabbed the King's sword arm and threw the King over the bed. Tiridates crashed onto the floor on the other side of the room. The beast turned his attention back to the unconscious Queen. He grabbed her by the neck with a vise-like claw and lifted her high into the air. "Armenia will not adopt Christianity," he hissed in a menacing, demonic voice. The beast then crushed the Queen's neck with a flick of its massive claw. The blow severed the Queen's head and struck the floor with a sickening thud.

Tiridates let out a blood-curdling scream and attacked the

beast with his bare hands. He jumped onto the bed and with the weight of his entire body, slammed into the beast before it could even react. Tiridates rolled off the beast narrowly escaping the powerful claw that sliced past him. Tiridates reached for his sword. He lifted it high in the air to deliver a devastating blow. The beast with speed that was no match for a mortal slammed him into the wall pinning his arms with his enormous body. Tiridates could smell the creature's vile breath as it shoved his huge head close to his. Its eyes burned a bright crimson red as it opened its mouth to speak, "You are the King of a small worthless country. I am Satan, the King of Death who will wipe this country and its people off the face of this earth if you do not stop this declaration towards Christianity. I will start with your seven sons and kill each one, slowly and painfully. I will hang their seven heads on poles in front of this palace. Your people will see how weak and powerless you are. Your Queen died easily, your sons will not be so fortunate." He lifted his huge claw-like and drove its talon right through Tiridates shoulder. Impaled, he bellowed in pain.

"Do as you have been commanded or I will be back. Your seven sons will wish they were never born. Then I will wipe out every man, woman and child in this country." the beast then dropped the King to the floor.

The door to the bedchamber finally came crashing open and a dozen soldiers poured into the room. The commander rushed to Tiridates, "Your Majesty!"

"Get him you fool, kill him" the King cried out.

"Get who your majesty?" the commander asked, as his gaze swept over the dead Queen. Tiridates lifted his head from the floor. To his horror, he realized there was no one in the room but the soldiers. The beast was gone. Vaporized like mist.

****

So it began from there. Boldly, Tiridates defied the threats from the evil that threatened him and led his country to embrace the religion Christianity. His people entered into a viscous civil war in defiance of his plans to adopt a religion they wanted nothing to do with. He pushed ahead and fought their resistance at every turn, his armies led by his fierce and brave sons. For the next two years, Tiridates, warred with his own people. Rebels from other neighboring countries soon joined the resistance. His seven sons became the targets of assassins, narrowly escaping death on numerous occasions, no doubt dispatched by the devil himself.

Tiridates, exhausted, knelt beside his bed as he readied for a night's sleep. His country ravaged by civil war, he prayed to the God of his country's newfound religion, for His guidance, and His wisdom, to help lead his country out of this turmoil. "Father, why do they resist your love so fervently? I am tired Lord, and so is my army. I am worried about how much longer they can fight. My sons are great warriors, but I worry about them Lord, our enemy Satan attacks them relentlessly, and I fear it's a matter of time before he succeeds," prayed the King.

Eyes closed, the King continued to pray for God's guidance. Suddenly, a bright light appeared above him and over top of his bed. He shielded his eyes against the intense brightness. The heat from the light warmed him. A deep and powerful voice came from within the light, "Do not be afraid, King Tiridates, for I am with you. Be prepared for your country to suffer even more, much more than they ever have. The price for my love and salvation will be worth it. Do as I am about to command you King. Have your seven sons leave this country to be hidden until I give the sign for their return. Their return will signal your triumph over the evil forces that command your enemies. Prepare King and obey." The voice from the light began to fade.

"Wait my Lord. Wait! How will I know when my sons can return?"

He watched the light continue to fade, but before it disappeared, the voice spoke one last time. "You will know. Now go and prepare."

Just as the Lord commanded, under complete secrecy, Tiridates moved his seven sons far from Armenia. His oldest son,

Abgar was defiant and refused to back down from his enemies and hide in a foreign country. Tiridates took Abgar out into the forest behind his palace, where the Queen was buried. They stood before her grave. "Abgar, I never told you the truth on how your mother died because if I did I knew you would seek revenge. That would have been the death of you my son," Tiridates said.

"I am not afraid of anyone or anything father, you know that. All I know is when I returned from battle mother was dead. What happened to her father?" asked Abgar.

"Abgar, you and your brothers are in grave danger. The whole country is in danger," Tiridates replied.

Abgar's stare burrowed into his father, "Father what happened to mother?"

"She was murdered son. Her head was cut off in front of me in our own bedroom," Tiridates said solemnly.

"What! Where were the guards? Where was your sword father?"

"I share your grief my son. I am sorry I could not protect your mother."

"This is madness, my mother the Queen was murdered. I will cut the head off of this traitor and murderer after my brothers and I torture him first," a red-hot Abgar fumed at his father.

"There will be no vengeance son, only survival. It was no man that entered our bedroom but a Beast. The Prince of Darkness, Satan himself, son, bent on stopping me from leading this country to Christianity."

"I can't believe what I am hearing father! I will kill him. He killed my mother, your wife and this country's Queen father."

"If it was just a man Abgar, he would have been dead the second he appeared by my bed. The future of this country lies in your hands and those of your brothers. We are not negotiating Abgar. God has spoken to me. He has commanded me and I have listened and so will you. You and your brothers are in unimaginable danger. All of you will leave at once and remain in exile. I will signal for you when it is safe to return. You are not to return until I send for you do you understand me."

"I understand, father, but I swear I will revenge mother`s death upon my return."

"Your brothers are to never know the truth Abgar. I told you only because you are my oldest son and will someday very soon sit in this throne and lead this country. The truth will get your brothers killed."

Within days, Abgar and his six brothers Abyssal, Babken, Davit, Edil, Gamar and Maxim disappeared from Armenia without a trace. Considered deserters and cowards amongst the King's army, Tiridates heard their whispers. He was the only person who knew why they left, but no one would know where they had gone. Tiridates hoped the Beast would never know where they were because even he did not know.

****

Over the next two years, Tiridates, watched as his beloved Armenia, was pushed to the brink of annihilation from a combination of civil war, starvation and disease. The plague that fell upon his people threatened to wipe out every man woman and child in his kingdom. Tiridates now faced mass desertions from within the ranks of his own army, soldiers fleeing to neighboring countries with their families to survive the famine and war. Through it all, he continued to pray to his God for His compassion and salvation. Satan was destroying his kingdom just like he promised. He needed God's protection now more than ever or else all would be lost.

Alone in his bedchamber, Tiridates knelt on one knee beside his bed, his usual position when he prayed. Suddenly an incredibly white light emerged from the expansive ceiling above his bed. He shielded his eyes against the intense illumination. Startled and about to clamor to his feet, Tiridates heard a voice call out to him from within the light. The voice was the God he knew. The Lord had returned to him. Overpowered with a sense of wonder, Tiridates fell to his knees. With his arms spread wide to the light to embrace its warmth and love, he let it course through his body like a radiant blast of sunlight. Then the Lord spoke to him in a deep and magnificent voice, "Do as I command King Tiridates. Prepare for the return of your sons to wage battle against the evil one that plagues your country. Satan will unleash his final fury on your country and your people once and for all for your sacrifice to Me. I have not forsaken you, nor have I forgotten you through your struggles. It is time."

"What will I do my Lord? How will I fight an enemy I cannot see, an enemy who fights not with armies of soldiers but with storms, drought that destroy crops and starves my people, cold winters that isolate and cause despair?"

"Summon your sevens sons back from where they hide in exile to confront what is coming your way. Satan is amassing your enemies from the north in Iberia and to the south in the Parthian Empire. Position your seven sons with a full division along the Atropatene, Adiabene and Nisibis borders to the south and Sophene border to the west. Also the Pontus border to the northwest and the Albania border to the northeast. I want your bravest and fiercest son Abgar to the south on the Parthian border. Do this as I command Tiridates, and do it quickly. Satan`s armies are amassing as we speak to crush your Kingdom." So Tiridates sent word out to his commanders as he knew word would travel fast and would reach his sons in their hiding place for their return to Armenia. Aware of the massive movement of troops around their borders the seven sons slipped back into Armenia under the cover of darkness and protection of the King's commanders and made their way back to the Kingdom.

Meeting with their father in the palace over a fire, the flames flickered shadows around the room and on the faces of the seven sons as they spoke. Abgar, his rugged good looks framed by long wavy black hair, separated into chunks with beads and a bushy beard to mask his many battle scars spoke first, "Father, what is going on? We are about to be invaded by armies so huge in numbers we don't stand a chance. Why were we not summoned sooner?"

"Have no fear, Abgar. The sword of the Lord God Almighty will be with you. He has spoken to me and has instructions for each of you."

Abyssal, second oldest to Abgar, a wicked scar running from the corner of his left eye down his cheek to his mouth spoke next "Father, our armies are depleted from starvation and sickness. We would be lucky to muster up four divisions certainly not seven, that's impossible, father."

"The men fight against you, father. They don`t believe in your declaration. We will never be able to gather an army! "`stated Gamar, his massive bulk inflating as he spoke, was the youngest of the seven brothers.

Maxim, who at age seventeen was dispatched to Rome to be educated added, "The men think we`re cowards father, because we disappeared. They will not fight for us!"

"Will this God give us the powers to harness the lightning in the sky to throw at our enemies as spears?" Babken, his shaved head revealed a brutal scar that ran from his eyebrow to his crown, giving him a maniac's look that defied his thoughtful personality. Babken was not as gifted a swordsman as his brothers but his heart more than made up for it.

Edil was the most gifted swordsman in the entire Kingdom. Many times he represented the royal family in competitions, easily defeating anyone that challenged him. "You can count on my sword father. I will wipe out an entire enemy division with my sword alone."

Davit grunted when he heard Edil boast. His brother was such a braggart, but there wasn't another sword in the Kingdom he would rather fight beside.

"They will go to the battlefields that I promise you, as I have pledged the treasures of this Kingdom to every man that fights for his country. How they fight will be up to you my sons. The survival of this country is in the hands of you Abgar and your six brothers. Now go all of you and prepare quickly. May the light of God shine through you."

Over the next several days, Tiridates sons summoned every soldier, even the sick or physically incapable of fighting, to defend their country. The great battle to come required all men, not just enlisted soldiers. With the promise of great financial gain for their families, farmers left their fields; blacksmiths dropped their tools, all to defend their King and country. His sons gathered with their armies and massed at strategic points along the southern, western and northern borders. The brothers were aghast at the condition of their men. They were in no condition to fight a bloody battle that awaited them. Tiridates knew it was sheer madness. He had ordered these men to almost certain death. Many did not even have proper weapons, carrying crude tools masquerading as some sort of weapon. It did not matter because the enemy would be upon them within day's maybe even hours and certain death awaited them all.

****

Abgar, heir to the throne, prepared his division of over 20,000 soldiers. Their numbers spread out over a vast expanse on the southern border of the Adiabene, of the Parthian Empire. A messenger was brought before him by an officer, "General, there is a message from the King." The officer handed him a dispatch.

He read the message from his father and was stunned at what his father commanded. It was pure madness! His father instructed him to send half of his division west to join the division assembled by his brother Davit at Arsamosata that bordered Sophene. The scroll instructed him to send to Arsamosata the weakest and sickest of the division leaving behind the strongest and most skilled soldiers. Abgar could not afford to lose one soldier, but to send off over 10,000 soldiers was insanity. The army he faced across the Tigris would crush him without even breaking a sweat. His scouts had reported the Parthian's were over 50,000 strong including 5,000 horsebacks. What was his father thinking? He could not and would not order half of his army to march to Arsamosata. He would have the messenger killed and report to his father after the fact if they survived, that he never received the dispatch.

"General there is one more message from the King," the officer stated handing Abgar the second scroll. Unfurling the scroll Abgar read the second set of instructions. Its contents left him aghast. His father wanted him to march his remaining soldiers around the Tigris to the west where it ends and then south straight into the mouth of his enemy. The enemy soldiers would be marching towards Armenia not expecting to see Abgar's army for days. They would be unprepared and caught off guard giving Abgar and his men an opportunity to inflict heavy losses. They would be on the high ground when they confronted the armies from Parthian. The 50,000 soldiers would be vulnerable to the arrows that would rain down on them from above. His father had instructed the division headed by his son Davit to march east towards Abgar. He would then turn south into Parthian at Nisibis and flank the under siege and retreating Parthian army, trapping them in the crossfire of Abgar and Davit's archers.

Abgar was to send the weakest soldiers not to meet up with Davit's division, but to march at once northwest to fortify the fort at Tigranocerta. There the soldiers would have the protection of the castle walls while they regained their strength. Once the victory was achieved against the Parthians, Abgar and Davit's soldiers would march directly north across Armenia to join his brother Maxim and his armies positioned along the Iberia border. All of the other brothers and their armies if they survived their battles were to join the rest of the divisions gathering on the Iberian border. The mother of all battles would take place on Armenia's northern border.

Prologue

Part 2

As he prepared to go to bed for the night, King Tiridates, knew he would not be able to get any rest tonight. His sons, all great warriors, were likely to die over the next several days and weeks. He had led his country into a war they could not win. His people, starving and in despair, punished by his zealous quest to embrace a God they never asked for, to believe in Jesus Christ, the Son of God they knew nothing about. Kneeling before a majestic cross hanging on his bedroom wall, he prayed for God's power and grace to embolden and strengthen his weakened soldiers, to fight, against an enemy driven by an unspeakable evil. He raised his hands to the cross, his eyes welling in tears and said, "My Lord, my God. May your sword reach down from the heavens, and touch the tips of the swords of my sons. We are fighting Your enemy my Lord. Fight through us and with us my Lord. Let us defeat the evilness that plagues my country. He believed in His maker and he knew that His God would not fail him or his country. Finding comfort in that knowledge, sleep finally found him.

****

Moving across the land that would host the massive battle like a dark cloud, Lucifer surveyed what was to be. He moved around this earth in the shadows, in the mist and in the darkness and in these shadows that hid his persona, he was overjoyed. The energy of evil and wickedness filled his body like the blood of man. Soon he would sit at a throne with God's treasured mankind at his feet, the spirit of The Creator gone forever.

As he pondered the battlefields in front of him, the Dark Prince knew the advancement in the belief of Jesus Christ would receive a mighty blow over the upcoming days. The fear to convert to the word of Christ would be too high for man to overcome. For any country, that considered Christianity, they would only have to remember what happened to Armenia, if they tried. He would use this example, to send a message to other countries considering this declaration. Invite Jesus Christ into your country and you will invite certain death.

He would crush Armenia and hand it over to its enemies on a silver platter. Years of inflicting disease, famine, drought and chaos set the table for what would happen here on this battlefield. Victory over God, and His people would be his.

****

The battles began and Armenia's enemies attacked her borders, its soldiers bent on crushing the Kingdom, that embraced a religion they feared would spread to their countries someday. Tiridates, safe in his castle, stood on a lookout at the highest perch, where he could see for miles, but not far enough. He knew the great battles had begun, and he wished with every fiber in his body, he could be there on the fields. He was confident in his sons that they would prevail, despite the great odds against them. He thought of the massive Parthian army to the south, their soldiers were huge and strong, capable of swinging heavy weaponry, for long periods without tire. They had now mobilized to cross the Tigris and into Armenia. Here Tiridates had planned an unexpected attack, led by the great Abgar. Flanking the Parthian army to the south, Tiridates son Davit, and his division, trapped them, with the Tigris blocking any escape route. Crashing down the riverbanks by the thousands, they engaged the Parthians and their heavy weaponry. Tiridates army, lighter and quicker, entered the shallow waters to do battle. The sound of leather and metal was everywhere. Grunting like wild beasts, sweat making their leather armor greasy, they swung their blades over and over. The smell of blood filled their nostrils. Their bowels loosened by fear, the Parthians, weighed down by their weaponry, and the water, didn't stand a chance. Davit's men and their swords cut into their flesh, getting past their shields, goring their stomachs and chests. Within a few days the great Parthian army was defeated. Thousands of Parthian soldiers lay dead in the water like rocks sticking up, and on the fields and riverbanks leading into the mighty Tigris River.

Abgar allowed the men to rest, regain their strength, and get ready to march north. He prepared a fire outside of his tent to cook food and to feel the warmth. The night was clear but chilly as he observed his men, thousands of them, moving about below him in the fields surrounding the Tigris, preparing for sleep. Davit joined his brother by his fire, his body free from the heavy armor, accepted Abgar's offer of a plate of food. Abgar asked his brother, "How are your men? Are they finding rest?"

"Their spirits are high brother after their great victory. I think our father's God was fighting alongside us today Abgar. The men feel something, there is allot of talk among the men."

"Humph, we'll see how our father's God feels when he sees what will be waiting for us in the north brother. He may just turn and run like a frightened animal," Abgar laughed uproariously, causing some of the men that were nearby to stop and look at them, curious as to why their leaders would be laughing so joyously.

Word reached Tiridates of the success of Abgar and Davit against the Parthians. This was great news for him. He returned to his bedroom, knelt in front of his cross on the wall, that he has prayed so many times before, "Heavenly Father, I give thanks to you for our victory in the south. You are with us Lord and that gives me great hope and strength. May you continue to embolden my sons in their battles in the east."

Along the southeastern and eastern borders of Armenia, their enemies moved in. Each time Tiridates's weakened, and depleted divisions led by Abyssal, Gamar and Babken battled back with heroic and miraculous strength and courage, thwarting their enemies at every turn. Taking their place on the front lines to the amazement of their armies, they swung their swords like men possessed, cutting a swath through the enemy lines as they did. Their bravery inspired their men to even greater heights. Wounded soldiers re-gripped their swords with renewed strength, some swinging with only one arm, but they fought with everything they had.

Word of his son's bravery and success on the battlefield spread throughout the country. People from all over travelled to the Kingdom to show their appreciation to the King.

King Tiridates knew that the spirit of God, was with his sons, right beside them, on the battlefields. He continued to pray to the Lord, thanking him for His spirit that flowed through his sons, but the real battle was yet to come. The armies of Iberia would be led by the evilness of Satan himself, and Tiridates shuddered at the thought.

****

The weary soldiers, commanded by the seven brothers, continued to arrive along the northern borders of Armenia, to face the great armies from Iberia. A dark and stormy mist blew over them as they gathered. Satan, sensing that the spirit of God, was flowing through the seven warrior sons of King Tiridates, did not cause him to reconsider his adversary before him. He knew the King foolishly prayed for His intervention. The success the sons had so far, was because they were damn good soldiers, and leaders, not because of some divine act by God himself. Satan knew, that the spirit in the mist that carried him, also carried the spirit of God. He also knew the Lord, did not understand the magnitude, the loss of this war would mean, to the advancement of the teaching of His Son Jesus. Satan would use this victory, to stamp out any future Christian uprisings, and that this victory, would spell the death of the memory of Jesus Christ forever. The number of soldiers in the Iberian army was staggering, numbering in the hundreds of thousands. Bolstered by tens of thousands of soldiers from neighboring Albania, with promise of a piece of the spoils, of a conquered nation as payment, the great victory here today over the Armenians, would propel them across Europe, defeating one army after another. Stamping out any uprising in the name of Jesus Christ, and making Iberia, and its kingdom, the most powerful country in the world, was intoxicating to the Iberian King. The Iberian army, buoyed by his wickedly evil spirit, was eager to lift their swords in the air, to rush the front lines of the puny Armenian army, crashing their swords down on top of their heads as they did so.

****

The northern border of Armenia that bordered Iberia and Albania was strife with unforgiving mountain passes and deep forestry in the lower areas that favored the Iberians, masking their army's movements. The valley where the battle would be fought opened up on the edge of the Iberian side of the border, allowing the Iberians to use the cover of the trees to hide their troop movements. On the Armenian side it was wide-open valley, for miles and miles, the odd random cluster of a small forest the only thing to break up the openness of the valley. Abgar knew this exposed his armies greatly to their enemy. He could not see their movements, yet they could see all of his. He gathered his brothers on a lookout high above their divisions on a valley ridge, giving them an ample view of their men below, as they prepared for certain death, "Our blood will flow here on these fields brothers. You have fought like true warriors, and I am proud to be your brother."

Abyssal, the badly scarred side of his face gave him credence when he spoke, "We have made it this far Abgar, and we will prevail here today."

"Our men will fight these cowards like heroes. Their superior training will overcome their numbers," boldly stated Maxim.

"I will show our brother Edil what a true swordsman can do today," smirked Davit.

"When my men and I are finished killing our enemies, we will turn our swords to the overmatched Davit, and help him out of his mess," smiled Edil.

The soft spoken, but menacing looking Babken spoke out, "Our victory here brothers will be spoken about for generations. It will be our children's children who will claim it was them that fought this battle. Let's not disappoint them."

Abgar spoke again, "Lead these men into battle brothers, for our King, and for our country. May the Lord our God shine down on us this day."

"Here! Here! To the King! To Armenia! To the Lord Our God!" shouted Gamar as the brothers lifted their swords high in the air in unison.

Departing after many hugs, handshakes and well wishes the brothers turned their horses about and rode away to join their divisions, for the final battle, and most certainly, the final days of their lives.

****

The Iberian army, its soldiers drunk on thoughts of bloodshed and carnage on the battlefield and the spoils of war after their great victory prepared to attack. Pillaging the towns and villages of their women and riches is all they talked about. To the man, they knew nothing as to why they were fighting this war. It was their duty and they would be rewarded for it, which is all they cared about. That is exactly what Abgar and his brothers were hoping for. They knew that if a soldier did not fight for a cause, they were weak and vulnerable. When the call came down the line from the Iberian commanders, ordering the first wave of infantry to advance across the border, and engage the enemy, tens of thousands of Iberian soldiers marched across the fields like a pack of wild dogs, sensing the bloodshed that was about to happen, driving them crazy. Rushing like raving lunatics towards Edil and Davit's battle weary divisions, their rage and recklessness made them easy prey for the ready swords of Edil and Davit's men. They chopped down the Iberian and Albanian soldiers like sheep.

Abgar knew the Iberian commanders would be sitting on their horses far behind the front lines watching in horror as thousands of their soldiers fell to the ground like leaves falling from trees. Not wasting anytime they sent in the second wave of infantry towards Abgar's division. Like birds flying out of the tops of trees, the Iberians poured out of the forest by the thousands, shaking their shields and swords like madmen, angered even more by the slaughter of their comrades. Their commanders also ordered a full strike by the archers. The arrows of the Iberian archers cascaded down on Abgar's division like rain falling from the sky. Crouching down, holding their shields, to the sky, to protect them as best they could, from the wooden daggers falling all around them. Wave after wave of arrows, darkened the sky as they launched upwards from the snap of the Iberian bows, then arching down, gathering speed as gravity helped pull them down, on top of the soldiers. With his horse turned into a pincushion, Abgar stood in front of his men, commanding them to prepare for the soldiers racing towards them, their swords drawn and cocked. Facing death, the heavily outnumbered front line standing behind him moved about nervously. Abgar held out his sword, high in the air in front of him, and yelled at the top of his lungs, "I do not fear my enemy for the Lord God in Heaven is on my side. I will strike you down with my sword."

Suddenly a bright light opened in the sky above them, a light so bright, soldiers, paused to shield their eyes. The light came down from the sky in a flash, hitting the top of Abgar's sword like a lightning bolt. Without even thinking, Abgar, swung his mighty sword in an arc towards the advancing Iberians. The white light leapt off the tip of his sword like fire, cutting a devastating swath of destruction into the Iberian army, vaporizing thousands of them, with one fell swoop. Feeling the power of God course through his veins, Abgar, swung his mighty sword from left to right, in another arcing motion, causing the explosive white light to wipe out the remainder of the infantry that were moving towards them.

The soft breeze, blowing across the faces of the stunned Armenian soldiers, witnessing the miracles of the God, their King, that had fought so hard to embrace, was in stark contrast to what the Iberian army was feeling. A stinging howling wind, was blowing across their ranks, like a whip being snapped by an imaginary chariot.

The ground began to shake as the notorious Albanian cavalry, came pouring over the far hillside, on the eastern tip of the battlefield. Thousands of horseback, carrying sword wielding, and armored soldiers, bent on finishing what the infantry couldn't, raced towards the Armenian army. Maxim's division, supported by the divisions of Abken, and Gamar, prepared for the hell coming their way. Their armies gasped, at the sight of so many mounted men racing towards them and began to panic. Ranks broke down, and men turned to run.

Out of nowhere, Abgar saw a white horse carrying his father, swathed in a white robe topped with a blazingly bright gold helmet, burst through the ranks of the front lines. Galloping towards the massive sea of Albanian horseback that were stampeding towards him, the King drew his massive gleaming steel sword from his scabbard, and raised it to the sky, in honor of his God. Tiridates then swung it down, towards the ground. Pulling on the reins with his right hand, Abgar watched his father change directions, cutting across the front of the stampeding Albanian soldiers. As he did so, his sword began to release a powerful beam of light that opened up the ground in front of it. What happened next was just one of the many miracles performed that day. The bottomless pit in the ground, that

Tiridates sword was opening as he raced his horse across the front of the Albanians, swallowed them up like boulders tumbling over the edge of a cliff. Thousands of Albanian soldiers on horseback could not corral them in time, disappeared into the crevice opening beneath them.

The power of the Lord would not be denied on this day. He and his brothers, their soldiers strengthened by the miracles around them, rushed their divisions into the retreating armies of the Iberians and Albanians, cutting them down, before they could reach the safety of the hillsides. Soon the fields were littered, as far as the eye could see, with tens of thousands of dead or wounded Iberian soldiers. The few that were alive, collapsed in surrender. In just a few hours the power of the Lord, revealed itself in a glorious and triumphant way, crushing the evil intentions of his enemy, and its armies.

Still on their horses, Tiridates, and his sons, gathered together in triumph on the battlefield. The men and their horses, seeming to bask in the glory of victory along with the men they carried, lined up side by side, overlooking the carnage before them, and paid homage to their God through prayer. Thanking Him, for the miracles this day that saved their beloved country.

The fading sun cast long shadows over the rocks and trees of the battlefield, immersing the corpses strewn across the hillsides, in coming darkness. The shadows however, carried a dark and angry spirit, when under the cover of the darkness projected by these shadows, a beast like form materialized. Stunned by the intervention by God he did not expect, nor anticipate, Satan seethed at what the Lord had done. Baffled as to why he could not detect the Lord's intentions, from His spirit, that flowed in the same wind he did, but yet had hidden his intentions so masterfully. Instead ending the spread of Christianity for good, he had inspired it to even greater heights. The victory here today, by the Armenian King, and the miracles of God, would spread like wildfire throughout the region. Countries would embrace Him, without question. His plan to use this battle to defeat his enemy, and His forsaken Son, had failed.

He would learn to mask his spirit, to hide his intentions, from the Lord, like He had done to him so cleverly. He would destroy mankind someday. He knew it will be generations before he has the chance again. The anger flowed through his spirit like a tidal wave. He could sense the spirit of God dancing around him, and all over his beast like body, celebrating His love and grace for His beloved mankind. It made his anger swell inside of him that was so powerful the Beast looked up into the heavens in a furious rage, and screamed.

King Tiridates, his sons, along with the thousands of surrounding soldiers in the battlefield, were drawn to the roar of thunder coming from beyond the hillside. It sounded like a raging storm was coming upon them, but Tiridates knew better. Looking at his sons, he said, "Come, let`s get your men back home to their families."

Chapter 1

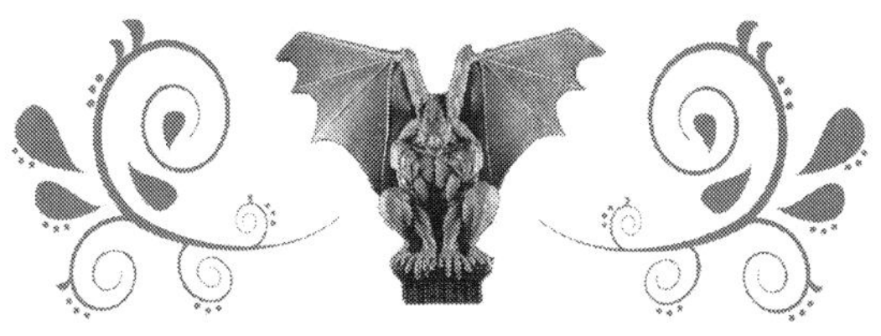

It was another spectacular September evening in Maracaibo, Venezuela. The warm breezes off beautiful Lake Maracaibo, carrying. the fragrance of driftwood mixed with the unpleasant fresh scent of oil from anchored tankers nearby, reached the neighborhoods of hard-working Venezuelans. Venezuela's second largest city, with two million people, Maracaibo was a hustle-and-bustle metropolis, with a combination of factories and academia boasting Venezuela's largest university. The city was also famous for producing top players for Major League Baseball. The country was on a real upswing with its burgeoning oil industry, and Maracaibo had benefitted greatly with many new infrastructure projects. People were working in Venezuela, and Maracaibo was at the hub of it all.

Rafael Jimenez made his way through the dense traffic, from his factory job at the state-run sugar processing plant, Central Cumanacoa. He couldn't wait to get home to his wife Marie, who would be waiting for him, he hoped, with another satisfying dinner. They were trying to start a family, with little luck. He refused to let Marie take a job, even though they needed the money, thinking the stress of a job would further complicate Marie's getting pregnant. His job at the sugar factory was hard, with long hours, but he enjoyed the work. Promoted to plant supervisor, he was now paid well compared to other jobs—well enough that, with some cutting back in other areas, Marie could remain at home. He was very happy with his life to this point. He no longer made himself miserable dwelling on what could have been. He had been a can't-miss, first round draft pick in the major league baseball draft.. One scout for the Boston Red Sox commented, "With a Rafael Jimenez patrolling the infield, his range and quickness, and cannon for an arm, teams would have no need for any other infield position players, as he can cover the whole damn infield by himself!" Unfortunately, a bone defect in his shoulder meant that it could never hold up to the rigors of an everyday professional baseball career, and forced him into retirement. He never had the chance to taste the riches that accompany life in the big leagues. Now, instead, he chose to think of baseball as the reason he met his wife. She was his life, and she had transformed the memories of what could have been on the diamond into pleasant ones.

Before he met Marie, he would spend many a night after work, and Saturdays, at the local ball diamond, playing pickup with a bunch of guys from the neighborhood. He was twenty-five years old then, and it was during one of these games that he noticed this beautiful girl in the stands. She had long brown hair, pulled back from her face in a ponytail. He could tell she wore very little makeup. She didn't have to, she was naturally beautiful. He couldn't keep his eyes off her, so when it was time for him to bat, he handed his bat to the next guy waiting, just so he could continue to stare at her. She was hanging out with some other girls, watching the game. He wondered if she knew he was the great Rafael Jimenez. Turning to the guys he said, "Play without me today," and decided then and there that he would ask her out on a date. Mustering his courage, he approached the girls, wondering what he would say to this beautiful creature.

"Hi. I am Rafael Jimenez. I am sure you have heard of me, but I wanted to come over and say hello," he mumbled, reaching his hand out.

Not taking his hand, Marie was quick to reply, "Well, if it isn't the great Rafael Jimenez, the best shortstop to ever play the game of baseball! Nice to meet you. My name is Marie, and no, I have never heard of you, till now, when my friends informed me who you were. Speaking of my friends, have you met Joella?" Picking up her sweater, she turned to her friends and motioned them to join her, leaving the ogling Joella alone with him.

He was blowing this, he knew, and he tried to recover. "Let me help you off of these bleachers. They're not very safe. They should really be torn down."

"Tear them down? Forcing us girls to sit on our sweaters in the grass? These stands are solid, no?" Marie stamped her foot on the stand to prove her point. She turned to leave, brushing past him as she walked down the bleacher steps.

Gathering his wits, he set out after Marie, who was leaving the ballpark with her friends, catching her as they gathered at the bus stop. He glanced at the other girls, then looked at Marie and said, "Ummm, that didn't go so well back there. I'm better at throwing a baseball, I think, than I am speaking to a pretty girl. Would you like to grab a milkshake with me before you leave?"

She glanced at her friends, then said to him, "Because you said my favorite word, milkshake, I will take you up on that. I don't have much time though, my momma will send out the search party if I'm late for dinner." She said goodbye to her friends, and walked with Rafael over to the burger stand, a dilapidated old bus parked on the grass along the third base line, the smell of grease permeating the air as they approached. He ordered them each a chocolate shake. They sat down on an old bench in front of the bus, enjoying the shakes, and he asked, "Do you like baseball?"

"Not really. Too slow. I like watching soccer, much more exciting."

"Then why are you here watching a boring game of pickup baseball?"

"My friends insisted I come, something about a cute ball player who hangs out here all the time."

"Oh, really," was all he could say, when he realized she was talking about him. "Marie, would you like to see a movie on Saturday night?"

"Hmm, I'm not sure. Tell you what. Get on the bus, ride home with me, and you can ask my momma if that would be okay," replied Marie.

He did as he was told, got on the bus and sat beside Marie, the most beautiful woman he had ever seen. The bus blew smoke, wheezed and coughed, as it chugged along a crumbling road with potholes so cavernous they threatened to swallow the bus itself. He thought to himself, what am I doing? Marie's mother doesn't know me, and if she had, then she would know he was just a washed-up ball player, like a thousand other Venezuelan kids. He looked at Marie as the bus bumped up and down like a ship on the high seas, thinking she would be late for dinner, and wondered if her mother would use a rolling pin or a frying pan on the side of his head. He could feel Marie lean in closer to him, ever so slightly, as they sat, making his heart soar. The bus eventually groaned to a stop in a neighborhood he had never been to. Marie reached over and picked up his hand, then said, "Come on, Mr. Casanova, it's time for you to meet my momma." Following her lead, they got off the smelly bus, and walked together down the street, and surprisingly, Marie was still holding his hand. Hers felt like soft baby skin, he thought. He didn't ever want to let it go, she was making his heart melt. They walked a short distance when Marie stopped in front of a house. More like a shack. It was very small, the paint all but worn away. Small porthole windows, evenly spaced, running along the top of the walls.

"This is where I live. Me, my three little brothers and momma. My dad left us when my youngest brother was born. He was a drunk, and anyway, he beat us. Momma is a tough lady, but she had to be. You get my momma to like you, and it's a date Saturday," she smiled.

He put on a brave face and followed her up the walk to the house. He looked at the small yard, a broken bike lying on its side, random toys everywhere, all making the house seem smaller as they got closer. The front door was hanging by only one hinge at the top. The bottom hinge had pulled right out of the frame, leaving a hole in the wood. He found himself looking at Marie again. He could sense strength in her, making her appear even more beautiful. The smell of deep-fried empanadas filled the air as she opened the door. He was instantly hungry, and hoped her mother would like him enough to ask him for dinner. He noticed right away that the inside of the house was nothing like the outside. There was no man of the house to do the repairs outside, it seemed, but inside it definitely showed a woman's touch—warm, inviting, nicely decorated, and that heavenly scent of empanada's.

She dropped his hand as they entered the house, and he instantly missed her touch, wanting to reach out and hold her hand some more. She shouted, "Momma come here please! I have someone I want you to meet!"

Walking from the kitchen into the front room, he was greeted by Marie's momma, a portly but pleasant-looking woman, weathered and worn by years of hard work. Her hair tied at the back of her head in a bun, she wore no makeup, wearing a simple green dress covered mostly by an apron. He shook her hand, noticing how large it was, like a man's. Her smile filled the room when she spoke, "Marie, my dear, he is very handsome! Is this young man with you, or is he here to take me away?!" Her laugh was infectious, as she led him into the kitchen, Marie following close behind. "I insist you stay for dinner. My empanadas, and arepas, are the best in Maracaibo!"

He got Momma's approval that day, to go along with the stomach ache from too many arepas and empanadas, winning Marie's heart, and access to the best cook in the country. He and Marie became inseparable, and married six months later.

****

Rafael and Marie Jimenez both loved to sit on the front porch of their modest home after Rafael arrived from a hard day at work. He worked long hours, allowing him and Marie to save enough to purchase their little house in the Bolivar district of the city.

Small and square like a box, white stucco exterior, with a red, aluminum roof and a small veranda in front, it wasn't much, but it was brand new and theirs. If you didn't know their exact address you would never be able find it, sandwiched as it was amid a sea of identical-looking dwelling. Tonight she had prepared Rafael's favorite appetizer, arepas, a lightly oiled, and fried, round corn flour tortilla filled with cheese. She used a special pan, called a budare, to lightly brown them, and finished cooking them in the oven. Much crispier that way. She watched him as he dived right in, grabbing three arepas. "Honey, slow down, they are called appetizers for a reason! I want you to enjoy dinner, not fill up on the arepas."

"I know I know, just three, I promise."

He watched her return to the kitchen to finish preparing dinner. He couldn't stop marveling at her, he loved her so much. They had been married for five years now, and yet, that first bus trip together, to her momma's, felt like yesterday. They both longed to start a family, but so far she had been unable to conceive. This bothered her greatly, he knew. She longed to have her family well on its way before she reached thirty. They could not afford to see a fertility specialist, so she was acutely aware of her cycles. When she would enter her fertility 'zone', he had better be rested.

She returned to the dinner table carrying his absolute favorite, pabellón criollo. The dish was a treasure containing seasoned shredded beef, fried plantains, black beans and rice. The meat was slow cooked until tender, shredded and then cooked again in a tasty sauce that included onions, garlic, peppers, tomato and spices. She could cook this famous dish better than anyone.

After filling his plate with the criollo, she turned to return to the kitchen.

"Marie, please sit down, you are making me feel guilty serving me all this food."

"Sit and enjoy, sweetheart. I will be right back, I am just grabbing us some wine." She returned to the table a few seconds later carrying two wine glasses and a bottle of French Pernod Ricard Cabernet, their favorite, and affordable.

He now realized what Marie was up to, and it brought a smile to his face. She was getting him in the mood, because she was ovulating. He knew better than to protest. Great food, wine and a beautiful woman: did it get any better?

Thirty minutes later, after five arepas and a very generous portion of the criollo, he slowly made his way to the living room.

"I am so full, I could burst. Honey, that was really, really good. Thank you. I need to stretch!" he cried as he flopped like a beached whale on the loveseat.

Joining him, she said, "I have satisfied one appetite, no? What about the other appetite?" she purred, sliding her hand down his leg, stopping on the inside of his thigh as she snuggled close to him on the worn rattan loveseat.

He needed time to recover from dinner, he was that stuffed. "That appetite will have to wait. Don't you see honey, it will take all night just for me to get the strength to get off this couch!" he protested.

"Blame it on the cook. If I did not feed you so well, you would never sleep with me, just for punishment," she teased.

He reached for her, pulling her close, "I tell you what, honey. Tomorrow, when I get home from the plant, we will mess the bed up, before you try to kill me by stuffing me with your spicy and artery-clogging, but very scrumptious meal," he teased Marie.

"Not a chance, mister. I didn't bust my butt cooking all this food for you, and change into my sexiest blouse, so you could avoid your husbandly duties! If I don't get pregnant soon, then you know I will have to go and get work." Taking a deep breath, she declared, "My friend Lucia needs another cleaner for her night crew at the university."

"No, Marie, no. You are already tired cleaning and cooking for me. Working nights, you will be worn out completely, and in no mood to make love to a randy husband. He began to undo his belt buckle as he said, "We decided we were going to try to have kids now, before we get too old. I think now is a good time to start," he announced, as he leaned in close to her, desperately trying to maneuver his hand under her blouse.

"I thought you were too stuffed, Rafael? So my cooking isn't as satisfying as you claim? You're such a liar," she giggled.

He stood up, stretched and looked down, with a mischievous look in his eyes, and said, "Do I need to pick you up and throw you over my shoulder like a sack of rice, or would prefer that I drop to my knees right here in front of you and beg."

"Okay, move it, buster, to the bedroom, and I will show you what you are getting for dessert."

He began to walk to the bedroom when he suddenly felt an intense wave of heat hit him, with such force that it knocked him back against the living room wall, pinning him, unable to move. There was some unseen force squeezing his throat. His eyes were watering and he couldn't breathe. He was barely able to move his head to the right, towards the couch, to Marie. He looked at Marie. She was staring at him, her eyes wide in terror. *What the hell was going on?!*

Chapter 2

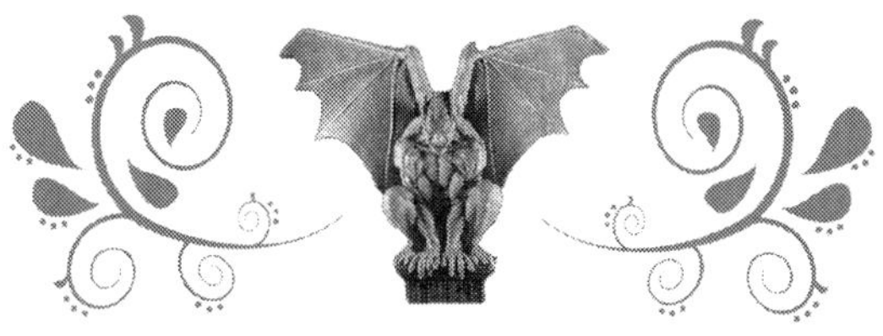

Twenty-nine-year-old music producer Avery Johnson, sitting in the plush office of his hugely successful recording studio on Santa Monica Boulevard in Hollywood, was pissed.

Pissed because his client was late. Again. As per usual. The studio session players were all ready to go, the backup singers were in place, but no J 'Tick Tock' DBL J, or Tick Tock to anyone in the industry. Only to his mama was he known as Dwayne Benjamin Loxley.

Whatever Tick Tock wanted to be called, or whatever his mama called him, Johnson didn't care: he just wanted to call him 'fired'. He had sworn his studio would never sign a rapper to a contract. They were too difficult to manage. However, even he couldn't ignore the enormous popularity of hip-hop music today, and against his better judgment, he had signed the unknown and unproven Tick Tock to a record deal. It turned out to be one of the best decisions he'd ever made. Although Tick Tock treated Alive Records as if he owned it, and his lack of respect and immaturity towards people in the industry aside, Tick Tock was a gold mine. His records were a money-making juggernaut that swept the music industry by storm; selling more records than any other hip-hop recording artist in the business. His last album, *Beware Out There*, reached number 1 on the Billboard Top 100, and went multi-platinum in sales faster than any other hip hop album in history.

For this reason, Tick Tock was still in the Alive Records stable of recording artists, but he was still a pain in the ass. These singers and session players were some of the best in the business, and did not come cheap. They would be here all day, and into the evening, laying down tracks to Tick Tock's follow-up to *Beware Out There.*

He punched his secretary's extension.

"Jen, get Tick on his cell, and find out where he is. He's late and I need him here yesterday. If he doesn't answer his cell, then call his manager, his girlfriend, his mother, his masseuse, whomever, okay?"

"Do you want me to send a driver to his hotel if I don't reach him? I'll bet he's still sleeping off last night's party at The Cave," offered his always-thinking secret weapon.

"Good thinking. Do that and let me know. Thanks."

Managing some of these stars, he thought, was like working with preschoolers at a daycare center: controlled chaos at the best of times. That was the nature of the beast. Some of these artists were a whisker away from living on the street one day, millionaires the next. Crazy, but he had to admit he loved every minute of this business. He ate, slept and breathed the music business. Building Alive Records to one of the top record labels before the age of thirty gave him credibility amongst his veteran peers, and a reputation that attracted new artists in droves. Established artists were also moving to Alive Records and its marketing power, as a way to re-energize their careers. To ensure Alive Records was always on top of their game, he outfitted the studio with the very latest and best sound and recording equipment money could buy. Musicians and producers marveled when they entered his recording studio. He also spared no expense in the interior decorating of the studio. The reception area was large, resplendent with contemporary leather furniture. His extensive memorabilia collection adorned the walls in the reception area and the hallways leading into the studio. Jen's reception desk area was slightly elevated, making visitors look up when they entered. The huge, round desk area stood like a pedestal, loaded with state-of-the-art computers, phone system and built-in filing cabinets. On the wall behind Jen was the Alive Records logo in stainless steel, about four feet in diameter, embedded with LED lights, giving it a sparkling look. The studio also had a large, beautifully decorated, and well-stocked lounge area, with plush leather chairs, tables, a bar and kitchen. There were days when he and his clients would work all day and into the evening, so it was important to him they were comfortable. There were many nights when the leather couches would have clients sleeping on them, rather than return to their hotel rooms.

His quick ascent to the top of the music business still made him pause now and then to reflect on his good fortune. No question, he had worked very hard in the last five years getting Alive off the ground, but he also knew he'd got lucky, and more than once. He thought back to when he'd been a 20-year-old, up-and-coming musician with a breakout album, and how his record label had treated him. The contract his manager signed with the record label at the time was all smoke and mirrors, leaving him with virtually nothing from an album that was hugely successful, going all the way to platinum. The record company's reasoning was that the first album is to prove yourself, and the second album is where you make your money. He fired his manager, sued Starfire Records and won. He made it his mission to start a record company that gave new artists the same opportunity as established recording artists. With his settlement from the lawsuit, and some family inheritance, he started Alive Records in West Hollywood, just down the street from some of the industry's biggest recording studios, including Paramount, Village and Ocean Way.

His first big break came in the first month he opened his studio, and it was a gift from another successful recording artist, a good friend of his, who referred a young, beautiful, and talented singer with the voice of an angel. Stephanie Newcombe was going to be a bona fide star. He convinced her to change her name to Stephanie Chalice, and changed her look completely, from her hair color and style to the clothes she wore. The result was, she not only sang like a star, she looked and felt like one. She had since released three albums, all multi-platinum, and become one of his biggest stars. He fell in love with Stephanie right from the beginning, and they shared a wonderful three years together, before the pressure of their careers, and time away from each other, eroded their relationship. They called it quits, but remained the best of friends. He had a knack for finding and identifying talent, and he knew how to bring out the very best in his clients, so having full creative control was critical. It was a frantic pace, but he was young, ambitious and felt he could conquer the world. When Stephanie won the Grammy for Best New Artist, for *Capture Me*, her debut album, she dedicated the award to her manager, producer and record label owner Avery Johnson. He was the talk of the music world, and the new top talent came looking for him.

His own musical career was put on hold while he got Alive Records off the ground. He continued to write music, but mostly as a contributor to his clients' albums. Alive Records had a well-rounded mix of artists, including rap, hip hop, rock and country. Working with some of the most creative minds in the industry was the juice that made him go, and he drank it down as if he were dying of thirst.

He snapped back into reality when he heard a knock on his door.

"Come in!" he shouted, knowing full well it was Jen, because she was the only one who ever entered his office. He believed there was no one better than Jen Steinart to run an office. She was beautiful, razor-sharp smart, worked incredibly hard, and if she ever left Alive Records it would devastate his business. That is why he paid her extremely well.

"Big Bob is dressing Tick as we speak, in his hotel room, after throwing him in the shower," Jen said. "Avery, he's a mess. Big Bob says he looks and feels like shit. You want me to send everyone home for the day?"

"No bloody way. I will squeeze every ounce out of him today. Trust me. Then I will stay here all night fixing it in the

Cube." He called his mixing room the cube because it was like an isolation chamber, a small, soundproof room where he would spend hours at a time fine-tuning the music, never leaving until he got it just right. "Get him in here!"

Son of a bitch, he thought. There was a limit to his patience. It was time to tune Tick Tock's clock. First, he needed these tracks completed. He would wind up Tick when he arrived.

Leaning back in his chair, he grabbed the latest edition of *Music Talks* magazine that Jen had placed on his desk earlier that morning. On the front cover was a picture of Tick Tock, in all his glory, sitting on top of a grandfather clock, with his legs dangling down the side. Of course, Tick had no shirt on, and if he did it was usually so big and unbuttoned he might as well left it in his closet. Tick liked to show the bling and the tats. He was covered in both. Most of them were tattoos of girlfriends in some uncompromising position. If he actually got married someday, he would tattoo a shrine on his body.

He flipped through the magazine to read the article, and to see how much of the print would have Alive Records in it. He opened the magazine to read when he noticed the picture of *Music Talks* writer Bentley Paxton. Wow, she was a looker. She would be granted interviews by most of his sleaze ball competitors only because they thought they could get some action with the hot interviewer.

As he reached the article on Tick, he noticed the writer of the article was Bentley Paxton. He was sure Tick would try his hardest to charm Paxton; that would be his style. After the usual intro banter, the first question Bentley asked Tick was:

"So tell me J, what makes you Tick!?" He loved this. He knew that Tick would be pissed with that question, as it referenced his name in a negative way, but he would keep it inside, because he was in charm mode all the way with this interview. The interview was predictable, though Bentley did press Tick on his reputation for hard partying. He knew that Tick would eat that up because he could care less what anyone thought of him, especially regarding his well-publicized partying that would occasionally get him in trouble. Tick wanted people to think of him as an out-of-control party freak who slept with hundreds of women, a modern-day Mick Jagger.

He was not happy that the article did not mention Tick's record label, or who his producer or manager was. No press for Alive Records or himself. That was not good for company business. Why would the editor not have included important information like who is behind the career of Tick Tock? Poor writing and a lousy article, he thought, as he tossed the magazine across the room, banging it off the window that looked out onto the rest of the office.

There was a tap on the door, Jen leaned her head in to say, "Everything okay, boss?"

"No. Make sure Tick comes into my office before he heads into the studio. Oh, and get me the number to the editor of *Music Talks.*"

"He just got here. Do you want me to send him in?"

"Damn right. Tell Big Bob to wait outside."

The day was not starting well. Tick's lateness and the article had him in a bad mood. The door opened and Tick walked in. Dressed in a 1970s maroon velour sweat suit, with white stripes running down the arms and legs, he looked like a gangster from Mod Squad. Covered in bling, wearing his trademark dark sunglasses, he plopped himself in a chair and smiled. His smile was like looking at the kitchen sink. Too much metal.

"What's up, Ave?"

"What's up? You're kidding me, right? Do you know what time it is?"

"Time to get started?"

"No, that was an hour and a half ago. You want to stay up all night and party, that's your business. But when you come in here late and hung-over then it's my business. The session players were ready to go home for the day. We almost lost a full day of recording time because of you. Do you understand what I'm saying, Dwayne?"

"Whoa, boss, take it easy. It's all cool."

"Like hell it is. I don't have time to fuck around. You got me? Now get in there and make it happen before I decide to cancel this fucking album altogether."

Rising up out of his chair like a deflated balloon, Tick looked at Avery through his dark glasses, "Sorry boss. Won't happen again, promise. Please don't call me Dwayne. Only my momma calls me that."

"Then don't be late next time. And don't call me 'Ave'. Not even my momma calls me that."

Chapter 3

Twenty-seven-year-old James Campbell loved September. It was his favorite time of the year. It was 1998, and the New England Patriots were kicking off their football season, the Boston Bruins training camp was in full swing, and the Red Sox were gearing up for the playoffs and a likely showdown with the Yankees.

He was a sports fanatic; he knew it and he loved it. Who couldn't be, growing up and living in Boston, the sports mecca of America! The best thing of all: his beautiful bride of just seven months was as fanatical about Boston's sports teams as he was. She says it's why we married, he thought, but that's not entirely true. He had been madly in love with Nancy since he first laid eyes on her in seventh grade, growing up in Littleton.

Nancy had moved to Littleton from California that summer, and when he discovered this new student was in his homeroom class wearing a Red Sox cap on the first day of school, he was smitten. The homeroom teacher was quick to enforce her rules, including no headwear allowed. Forced to take off her cap, he watched her tie her long blond hair into a pony tail. His crush on the new student was complete.

While other girls were discovering makeup, short skirts, and whatever else they could get away with from their parents and the school, she would tuck her long blond hair behind her ears and put on her navy blue ball cap with the Red Sox logo on the front. She would wear jeans and a t-shirt to school, and with the clanging of the bell at the end of the school day, she'd fish that cap out of her backpack and stuff it back on her head. A living, breathing tomboy.

That's how school went for him the next two years at Littleton Middle School—in la la land. When he wasn't tearing it up in every school sport he could get into, he would hang around the gym or the field where the girl's sports teams would play, just to get a glimpse of her. She was easy to spot because not only was she beautiful, but she was the best athlete out there. She was taller than the other girls and her longer legs made her much faster. One day after school James stopped by the gym to see if the girls' basketball team was practicing. They were, and he was able to watch Nancy tear it up on the court. He doubted if she noticed him watching but he was amazed at how good she was. She would drive to the net for a layup and the other girls were defenseless to stop her.

It wasn't till the school graduation ceremony at the end of grade eight that he finally had the courage to ask her to the dance. When she told him that she had already been asked by Tommy Skinner, he was crushed. Tommy and Nancy dated all summer, and he was always spotting them at the mall holding hands or bumping into them at the movies. His friends took great pleasure in reminding him that Tommy was dating his girl. He hated that summer, and he was determined that when he entered high school that fall, he would not make the same mistake of being too shy again, Tommy or no Tommy.

When he made the senior basketball team as a freshman at Littleton High School, everyone in the school knew who James Campbell was—including Nancy, he hoped. But she was Tommy's girl, and likely never gave him a moment's thought.

His father was a sales executive for an ad agency in Boston, and was sometimes able to score Red Sox tickets in their corporate box and had them to the game on Saturday at Fenway versus the Orioles.

It was Sunday afternoon, and the Red Sox were on the road playing the Rangers. James and his Dad—who would have a Red

Sox logo tattooed on his forehead if Mom would let him—were sitting in the family room watching the game.

Taking a deep breath to steady his nerves, James turned to his father.

"Hey Dad. I need to ask you a favour."

His father turned his head and looked at him, then returned his gaze to the television.

"Let me guess. You have a practice this Saturday and can't come to the game."

James fidgeted in his chair.

"Not exactly." He paused. "Umm—" his father looked at him again. "Would you mind if I used the tickets to bring a friend to the game instead?"

"Really?" his father looked, not angry, but a little hurt. "James, this is our thing. I only get a few games a year, and you know, it's our thing."

"I know," James blurted, feeling guilty as he spoke. "And I love going to the games with you, I really do—but this is important to me. Do you mind?" he added, knowing that his father really did.

"Who is the friend, son?" his father asked dryly, "and why is it so important to you that you wouldn't want your old dad to go?"

James stared at the carpet, trying not to blush.

"A friend." he said, embarrassment rising. "Can we leave it at that, Dad?"

He heard his father chuckle.

"Okay, I get it son. It's a girl. You want to impress some hot chick from school by taking her to Fenway. I get it."

There was no helping it. Blood rushed to his face. He turned back to his father, wrapping his arms around his own stomach as he spoke.

"To answer your question," he said, "it would impress her." Some hot chick! His father didn't understand as much as he thought he did. As though he would miss going to the game with his dad for just 'some hot chick'! "She is a bigger Sox fan than you and I combined."

His father shook his head with an expression of mild disbelief. James looked down at his hands in an agony of suspense.

"Well, I doubt that." his dad said at last. "But no problem, son. You need me to take you guys to the game?"

James beamed back at him with gratitude and relief. His father might not quite believe him about this girl—but wait till he met her!

"That would be great!", James said. "And we can take the bus back home." "*I have the best dad in the world!*" he thought to himself.

"Geez, thanks Dad, this means a lot." He felt his body start to relax.

"You owe me," his father warned good naturedly. "You can start with raking the leaves." His dad looked at him, amused, as James's eyes widened with panic and he glanced from his father's face to the television screen. "After the game," his father reassured him.

James settled back into his chair. Now he could enjoy the game. One down, one to go—now he had to ask *her.*

Little did his Dad know, but he hadn't asked Nancy to the game yet. He didn't even know if she'd say yes. Now that he had secured the tickets, the next step was inviting Nancy tomorrow at school. Settling in to watch the rest of the game with his Dad, James felt his mind drift away from the action on the TV to Nancy, and how infatuated he was with her. Girls were never something he'd cared about until she came to town. It was as though his whole world had changed from that point. The next day he found her by her locker at the first break, wearing her trademark Red Sox cap.

"Hi Nancy. Wow, you look great today! Umm, how was your first class?" he fumbled.

"Well. The great James Campbell, the Tiger's star basketball player, stopping to chat with the common folk," she teased.

"You forgot about football. Star football player too, you

know." God, I'm bragging, I must sound like an idiot, he thought.

"Oh yes, I forgot, Mr. Multi Sports Star. What's on your mind, Mr. Campbell?" asked Nancy, her voice lightly tinged with sarcasm.

"Well, if you're not doing anything Saturday, the Red Sox play the Orioles, and I have tickets. I mean, if you would like to. But I understand if you are still with Tommy and…"

"Shut up already! Been waiting since junior high for you to come to my locker, dummy, and ask me out. Besides, even if I was dating Johnny Depp, I would dump him if I had to choose between him and a Sox game".

He felt his face flush. He couldn't believe she had been waiting for him to ask her out. "Great ... umm ... my Dad will take us to the game and drop us off, and we can bus it back, is that okay?" He was babbling.

"Sure, it will be fun. See you Saturday." She turned and headed to her next class, leaving James unable to move. As she was about to turn the corner she looked back at him and said, "By the way, I broke up with Tommy during the summer. Where have you been?"

Leaning back into her locker, so nervous a few minutes ago, he now felt like he could slay the biggest, fiercest dragon in the world. He was feeling numb, and people were looking at him strangely as he walked to his next class, because he had this big-ass smile on his face, as if he was laughing at his own joke or something.

On the Saturday of the game, James and his Dad drove over to Nancy's place to pick her up. Pulling up in front, waiting for Nancy to come out, his Dad said, "Hey, stud, I think it would be the right thing to do if you went up to her door, and escorted her back to the car." He gave his dad a strange look. "Hey, ask your Mom, I did it. Show her the fine gentleman you are," he teased. Knowing his dad was probably right, James climbed out of the car and went to her door. He was about to ring the doorbell, when it opened, and there she was. Dressed in tight jeans, a Red

Sox hoodie, and her Red Sox cap with her ponytail pulled through the back, she looked beautiful. He could only stand and stare until Nancy broke the silence. "Come on, James, let's go before your dad gets tired of waiting and decides to drive off without us."

The rest was history, as they say. After that first time together at the Red Sox game in grade nine, they were inseparable through the rest of high school. They got along so well, and were together so constantly, that they both endured regular speeches from their parents and friends warning that they were spending too much time together. They didn't care what other people said about them, they just fit together like the legs on a fine pair of jeans. Both of them graduated with honors, and they both accepted athletic scholarships to Boston College. Over the next few years, they both excelled in school. Nancy breezed through her major in Environmental Sciences and was completing her Masters in Environmental Geosciences. He completed his degree in Economics, and found his place in the professional world of sales, making serious money with a technological firm, Ametak Process Instruments in Providence, specializing in manufacturing instrumentation panels for the aeronautical industry.

Getting married was never an 'if' with them; it was a 'when'. That 'when' had been last February, on Valentine's Day. They were married on the Cayman Islands, accompanied by their immediate families. It was the exclamation point on a love affair that had no boundaries, no walls, no schedule or agenda— just a love that was real and beautiful. A month later, they were spending a week in Fort Myers, home of the Red Sox spring training facility, watching the Red Sox retool for the upcoming season.Seven months later, driving his modest BMW sedan, he turned on to his block after another productive day at the office, to their new house in the highly desirable district of College Hill in Providence. Life could not be better for Nancy and him. He continued to excel in his career at Ametek, he was making big money, and his success already had him earmarked for bigger and better things within the company. They talked about how great it would be to have children someday, but with her school and career, it would be a long time before they were ready for that. He could not wait for that next chapter in their lives: bringing a child into this world.

As he pulled up the driveway and into their garage, he couldn't help but think how fortunate they were. They were happy, successful and in love. His high school and college buddies were mostly still single, still partying like there was no tomorrow, still chasing women. Thank God I have Nancy, he thought to himself. He climbed out of his car, hitting the door opener to close the garage door. He couldn't wait to grab Nancy and pull her close, maybe take it a step further and carry her upstairs to the bedroom. He was just in one of those moods. His love for his wife occupied all of his thoughts as he opened the door into the house. The ungodly smell hit him like a sledgehammer. The pungent odor was awful, indescribable. He felt his stomach grow weak instantly, feeling the bile rise within him.

He entered the home and straight into hell. A monster, serpent-like, hideous-looking beyond belief, standing at least seven feet tall, hovered over his battered and bruised wife. Its eyes were burning bright red. Looking at him, as he stood there at the entrance, it hissed and moved towards him.

Chapter 4

Marie tried to move towards Rafael, who was trying to pull himself off the wall, struggling against an invisible force. *Why could he not move?* A tide of intense heat washed over Marie, almost burning her skin. Pinned to the couch, she realized that she too was being pulled back by a force she could not see.

Terrified, she reached behind to try to pull herself over the back of the couch so she could get on the floor and crawl to Rafael. *Oh my God, the house must be on fire*, she thought. Straining, she slowly inched away from the couch, sweating profusely. It was like moving in drying cement.

She struggled towards him, reaching out for anything she could use as leverage to drag herself along. She suddenly heard a loud thump, as if like something had fallen heavily to the floor, and looked up to see that Rafael had been peeled off the wall by invisible hands, then thrown back against it with such velocity that she heard his bad shoulder snap on impact with the wall. Rafael grimaced in pain from the terrible blow, and Marie pushed herself even harder to get to her husband. *What the hell was happening here?*

As Marie struggled, the house became like a blast furnace. She knew they did not have much time before they would be burned to death in their own home. Why was there no smoke? Marie needed to stand up and find out where the hell all this heat was coming from.

Reaching for the table behind the couch to prop herself up, Marie was unprepared for what she now witnessed. Fear took over like ice freezing in her veins, as she found herself staring directly into the fiery red eyes of the Devil himself. As Marie's mind began to shut down, she felt herself slipping into unconsciousness, thinking of Rafael and what this beast was about to do them.

The creature moved towards Rafael, only a few feet away from where she stood frozen, unable to move. Tears flowed down her cheeks as this horrible beast hovered over her husband. She could do nothing, she could not even scream. She could only watch her helpless husband struggle to get away, crying out in agony from his mangled shoulder. As the creature bore down on him, she could see it clearly, and the sight was horrifying. The serpent-like creature had talon-like claws, scaly, slimy arms and legs, and a mouth full of enormous, razor-sharp teeth, dripping in drool, anticipating the kill. The rank stench of the beast and her own terror made bile rise up into her throat. Marie bent over, wretching and sweating, horrified at what was happening. *My God, she silently prayed, what have we done to deserve this nightmare.*

Struggling to stay conscious, Marie blurrily saw the monster move in for the kill. At the sickening sight of this monstrosity, she mustered up as much strength as she could and screamed, "WHO ARE YOU?! WHAT THE HELL ARE YOU?! WHAT DO YOU WANT WITH US?!"

The beast ignored her. With its eyes blazing bright red, it reached down and grabbed Rafael, lifting him high in the air as if he were a doll, then reared its ugly head back, its mouth open wide, and bellowed with a guttural voice so evil, it could only have come from Lucifer himself. "DO NOT RESIST ME! I WILL SHRED YOU INTO TINY STRIPS AND TURN YOU INTO A WINDOW BLIND IF YOU SO MUCH AS MOVE!"

Marie watched as this ... thing ... flung Rafael to the floor with such force on his broken shoulder that he cried out, gasping for breath. Just before he slipped into unconsciousness, she heard him whisper, "Marie," then watched as his head lolled to the side, his eyes closing.

"Rafael! Rafael!" Gathering all her strength, she rushed towards her husband. As she knelt beside him, she felt a searing, white-hot pain in her back, as the beast sunk its talons into her shoulder, piercing it like a meat hook, yanking her off Rafael and flinging her across the room. She slammed against the wall so hard that the shelf above her fell on her, bringing with it a cascade of ornaments and framed pictures. Dazed and in pain, Marie looked up at the hellish bright eyes of the beast as it moved to finish her off. Wanting this nightmare to end, Marie curled up, expecting death, when the monster let out a hideous, blood-curdling scream. When she saw why the beast was recoiling backwards away from her, it snapped her back to reality.

Rafael, with his left arm hanging uselessly at his side, had driven the long blades of the garden shears into the back of the beast before collapsing to the floor. The blades pierced the chest of the creature, causing it to fall backwards. She watched it stumble and drop to one knee. Rafael, grimacing in pain, pulled himself up off the floor and yanked the shears out of the beast's back. Standing behind the wounded beast, he raised the shears high above his head for another strike.

Stunned and disoriented, the beast begins to rise. Marie saw its eyes glowing a dim yellow color. Rafael had wounded it! It grunted like a wounded animal caught in a trap, not noticing the steel blades now bearing down on the back of its head as Rafael aimed to end this nightmare once and for all.

Suddenly, and with such speed it was a blur, the beast thrust his claw straight backwards, piercing Rafael's leg just above the knee. Screaming, Rafael fell to one knee and the beast began pulling his claw out, twisting the talon sideways as he did so, slicing Rafael's leg off above the knee. Rafael screamed in agony, his blood spurting everywhere. Marie watched in horror as the monster drove its claw through Rafael's throat and with a flick of its wrist sliced Rafael's head cleanly off. With her husband's headless body falling to the floor, Marie let the blackness take her.

****

She awoke a few minutes later, thinking she had just experienced a terrible nightmare. But no. She found herself staring once more into those fiery eyes, eyes reflecting a deadly hate. She turned away from those eyes, hoping they would disappear. The beast bent over, moved closer to Marie and spoke with a voice not guttural or menacing, but the voice of a human. The change in the sound of his voice startled her.

"If you want to live, do exactly as I say. If you resist, your death will not be as quick as your worthless husband's. I will kill you slowly, and I promise, you will not pass out. You will feel every second of what I will do to you. Do you understand? Now get up."

"Go back to the hell you came from," she hissed and spat in the beast's deformed face. At the same moment Marie spun away from the beast, turning her body towards the wall. Finding strength she thought she no longer had, she stood up and looked for a way out and away from the monster. The archway into the kitchen and out the back door was just a few feet away. Hope filled her as she made her move. She never got the chance.

The man-beast's hand was on Marie's throat before she even saw him move. He picked her up as if Marie was a doll in his hand. He held her out and screamed with such hatred his voice no longer contained any resemblance to that of a human. "You have been chosen! Resist any further and you will die!" He threw Marie to the floor with a sickening thud.

Pain flashed throughout her body, as she tried to absorb what this creature had just said. *I've been chosen…chosen for what?*

God, please just let me die, Marie pleaded silently.

She glanced at the headless corpse of Rafael only a few feet away, the scene causing her to flinch and wretch. She vomited, and then began to sob uncontrollably. She had made him his favorite meal, just a few minutes ago, and now he lay dead and mutilated. Their dreams of starting a family together were gone. *Why was this happening?* A sickening sound brought her attention back to the beast.

The beast had moved into the center of the room. She gaped in horror as the beast began to transform, revealing hell itself.

The glow surrounding the beast became brighter, as its repulsive body began to reshape itself. Its bent and muscular reptilian hind legs straightened out, thinned and lengthened, forcing the beast to stand even taller, but changed. The scales were disappearing. With a hissing sound, the beast grew smaller, arms extending, head smaller, the skin turning white.

The metamorphosis was complete. The beast was now transformed into a human being. *How was that possible?*

The entire room darkened except for a soft glow surrounding the creature, terrifying her as she now beheld it standing on its hind legs with its arms extended to the ceiling. The temperature dropped to almost freezing, chilling her to the bone. With its head reared backwards, the beast began to speak almost in a whisper; steam escaped its nostrils as it spoke, barely audibly and in a language she did not recognize. *It almost sounded ... Latin?*

"Vos es sperma of Vorago meus hostilis. Progenies of suus memoria ends iam." (You are the seed of Abyssal my enemy. The lineage of his memory ends now.) The beast spoke in a soft, human voice that sounded eerily familiar to Marie.

"EGO sum verus vinco of universum quod vir. Meus sperma mos iam grow inside vestrum." (I am the true master of the universe and man. My seed will now grow inside of you.)

Straightening up, completely naked, the man-beast approached Marie. Its eyes. *They were glowing crimson red again!*

The man-beast's muscled body towered over Marie, its manhood fully erect, its eyes burning into her soul. "The Prince of Darkness, Master of the Universe, Ruler of the Ages now commands you! You will not resist or you will die. Your destiny was decided centuries ago by the mistakes of your bloodline."

Sobbing uncontrollably, now fully aware of what was about

to happen to her, Marie began to pray. "Our Father, which art in heaven, Hallowed be thy Name..."

"Quiet!" he shouted, then slapped Marie so hard in the face that her head hit the wall with such force it punched a hole. Everything went black.

Coming to seconds later, she realized he was on top of her, pinning her down. Marie tried to move, to resist, but the pain from her shoulder, where the beast had earlier ravaged it with its talons, immobilized her. She saw stars from the blow to her face, blood ran from her broken nose. Marie knew she was trapped. Then she felt it. *He was entering her! Oh my God! Help me!*

His physical size causing her excruciating pain, Marie prayed for God to take her, to end this hell. His body pressed down hard on her pelvis with such force Marie thought she would be crushed. His seed entered her like molten lava, filling what seemed like the entire inside of her. Marie turned her face aside and vomited.

Standing above her once again, its body surrounded by a soft glow, its eyes burning red as the sun, the beast spoke: "Your body is with child now. You will protect this pregnancy and this child. If any harm comes to the baby you will die. Your family, and the family of your dead husband will all die horrible deaths. The Master will always be watching. Don't ever forget that. He is always watching...."

She stared at him, wanting to kill him. But she could not move. The reality she had been raped by this monster became too much for her to bear. This was no nightmare.

Mercifully, darkness came to her.

Chapter 5

It was not the best of times in Ireland. The economy was in ruins, unemployment was rampant and the distrust in the government was palpable. The Irish were not a happy bunch, and Grew McClosky was one of them. A switch had been flipped to 'off' on the economy; one minute everyone seemed to be prospering, and the next everybody was out of work. Markets were at record lows, the unemployment rate had risen from a low of 4.6% to as high as 13.7% recently. The opposition has been calling for an election since last year, when the government was forced to accept a humiliating bailout from the EU and the IMF to deal with an unprecedented economic crisis.

Grew was a few years away from his thirtieth birthday, and he and his wife Katherine continued to live with his parents in a cramped flat in Balbriggan, a seaside town located 32 km north of Dublin City Centre in North County Dublin. Depending on who you talked to, the name of the town in Irish is either Baile Bricín, meaning Town of the Small Trout, or Baile Brigín, meaning Town of the Small Hills.

Grew and Katherine dreamed of a flat of their own in Dublin, but it seemed like a pipe dream for now, until things turned around for the out-of-work Irish. Grew worked part-time as a waiter at a local pub at nights and spent his days looking for real work, seemingly impossible to find. Katherine studied in school towards her nursing degree. Katherine had never really thought of being a nurse, but one thing she and Grew felt was that nursing was recession proof. Hospitals will always need nurses and doctors. Or so they hoped. She rode the transit into Dublin five days a week, getting up at 4:30 a.m. to get ready, and out the door in order to make it the School of Nursing at Dublin City University morning classes at 9:00 a.m. Thankfully she had done very well in high school, and so received some much-needed financial aid through bursaries and grants; otherwise they would never have been able to afford nursing school.

Grew's father Shamus was barely able to keep things together on his salary, having worked over thirty years with Iarnród Éireann, or Irish Rail, which operated the DART system (Dublin Area Rapid Transit). Shamus, a shift superintendent for the past twelve years, would thankfully, reach his pension without the threat of a layoff. That was the result of a very hard negotiation between the union and the government two years earlier that had brought the DART system to a standstill for over three weeks; the resulting pressure from the travelling commuters had forced the two parties to get a settlement done. It was always a struggle for the McClosky family, but somehow they managed, as it was no different for anyone else in Ireland.

To make matters worse, when Grew and Katherine were dating, she became very sick and was diagnosed with a severe case of endometriosis. The bleeding and scarring, plus the pain, forced them to decide to have her undergo a hysterectomy. Unable to bear children at the age of 21, Katherine took the devastating news hard. Feeling guilty for being unable to give him a family, she avoided Grew's desire to marry. Sitting in their tiny bedroom one evening, where they often retreated after dinner to be alone, sipping tea, Grew reached for Katherine's hand and held it.

"I love you, Katherine. You know that."

She knew what he wanted to talk about; he always wanted to talk about it. Marriage. She pulled her hand away and curled up under the quilt she'd wrapped herself in.

"You say that now, but in five years, or ten years, when you know you will never have children, you'll not say that."

He looked into her eyes and held her gaze, not allowing her to turn away.

"We will adopt if we want children. I want to marry you and spend the rest of my life with you. We are shaming my parents by living together without marriage."

She shifted in her chair abruptly and leaned towards Grew. Her eyes pooled with tears as she spoke.

"The shame they feel knowing that the McClosky name ends with you, if we were to be married, will be worse."

He was adamant with her that it made no difference to him or his parents that she could not conceive. He was losing her, he could feel it.

"Let's talk about this more with Father O'Sullivan. Will you do that?"

Wiping a tear away, and then reaching for Grew's hand, Katherine smiled. "I do love you Grew, more than anything. I am so sorry that I cannot give you children. I do need Father O'Sullivan's council. We both do. Thank you."

They met with Father O'Sullivan soon after, and he was able to help Katherine understand it was not her fault; there was nothing that she or anyone else could do to change her medical condition. God's love for her was real, and even though He had taken away her ability to conceive He had other plans for her. Most importantly, Father O'Sullivan was able to show her that Grew truly did love her, and wanted her as his wife, children or no children. What mattered most was the love they shared for each other. Grew and Katherine were married soon after by Father O'Sullivan in a beautiful ceremony attended by just about everyone in the tiny village of Balbriggan.

The McClosky lore had been told to Grew at a very young age, instilling family pride early, resulting, more than a few times through school, in his defending the McClosky name. Usually with fast fists, another McClosky trademark. Grew, like his father Shamus, was not very big, but he was as tough as nails and never ever backed down from anyone.

The glue, though, that had kept this family together over the years, passed down from Grew's father Shamus and from his father before him, was their unwavering faith in God and their deep Catholic beliefs. It was a foundation as strong as the brick their home was built on. It was ingrained in Grew that no matter what was going on in your life you always, always, made Sunday morning mass unless you were sick in a hospital. The McClosky family priest, Father Thomas O'Sullivan of the St. Colmcille's Parish Church about twenty minutes drive away in Swords County, had been a mainstay and close family friend since Grew was just a boy. Often Father O'Sullivan would come to the McClosky home Sunday afternoon after mass for tea, and most times, Father would stay for Patricia McClosky's scrumptious stew and potatoes. Father O'Sullivan had shared many a Sunday dinner with them. He loved Pat's stew, but mostly he enjoyed the company of the McClosky's.

This Sunday would be no different. Father O'Sullivan was in the mood for Pat's stew.

Grew and Katherine, along with Shamus and Patricia, enjoyed another passionate sermon by Father O'Sullivan before a packed congregation. After the service, Grew watched, as they made their way out of church, Father O'Sullivan mingle with the parishioners as was his custom, shaking hands and offering lots of hugs. Grew and his family, along with the people of Balbriggan, loved this man; he had been a godsend during these tough economic times as people turned to their faith for answers, guidance and support to get by. Father O'Sullivan spent countless hours in the homes of the people suffering the most, keeping their faith strong and offering much-needed emotional support.

While Grew's parents spent a minute with Father O'Sullivan before they exited the church, likely confirming dinner plans, Grew and Katherine spent a few minutes with Katherine's parents, Kenneth and Joanie Kearney. After small talk and promises to get together during the coming week, they made their way to join his parents and say goodbye to Father

O'Sullivan. As they approached, they could not help but notice the troubled look on Father O'Sullivan's face. As he looked up and saw them approaching, he seemed to make a concerted effort to gather himself. Something was troubling him.

Grew accepted Father O'Sullivan's outstretched hand, surprised by the strength of his grip.

"Good morning, Grew. Morning, Katherine. Great to see you both. Did you enjoy the service? I hope it wasn't morning coffee that kept you awake through it, but the message itself," smiled Father O'Sullivan.

Grew, after the handshake, wrapped his arm around Katherine's waist.

"I only drink decaf, Father," laughed Katherine.

"That works for me, child. It was great seeing you both this morning, and I will see you later, when I come to devour your mother`s stew," nodded Father O`Sullivan, as he fought an overwhelming sense of dread that had inexplicably come over him.

Saying goodbye, Father O'Sullivan pumped Grew's hand so hard again, that he thought Father O`Sullivan would tear it off. There was definitely something was troubling him. As Grew and Katherine caught up with his parents outside the church and climbed into the car, he asked, "What`s up with Father O`Sullivan? I thought my hand was in a vise when he shook my hand—and the look on his face when he looked at Katherine!"

Shamus glanced in the rear-view mirror at Grew with a look of concern on his face.

"We felt the same vibe as you did, something is really bothering him today. I could feel something was up with him all morning during his sermon. I guess we will find out tonight when he comes by."

****

As he watched the McClosky's leave the church, Father O'Sullivan could not shake off the sense of dread building in his soul. Something was gnawing at his soul and he couldn't shake it. *What is going on with me?* He wished he did not have to attend the meeting this afternoon with the deacons. He wanted to get over to the McClosky's and try and make sense of this weird feeling he was having. Discussing the church's budget was not his favourite thing to do, but they had to decide how much they would commit to this year's Christmas production, plus make some decisions on monies to aid a few of the families in real need this Christmas. They shouldn't be deciding this on a Sunday, but getting the deacons all in one room during the week was difficult. Besides, the deacons would want to get back to their families as quickly as possible, so everyone would be focused on the task at hand.

****

Grew and Katherine, along with Shamus and Patricia, arrived back at their townhouse on Clonard Street, in one of the oldest residential areas of Balbriggan, after the 20-mile drive from church. Pat and Katherine made their way to the kitchen to put lunch on the table. Shamus asked his son to join him in the den. Sitting down in his favourite chair, Shamus turned the TV on to search for the soccer match between his beloved Bohemian FC of Dublin versus Dundalk. Watching soccer after Mass while the women prepared lunch was what Grew and his father did almost every Sunday. Grew knew that his father liked to use this time alone to get caught up on what had gone on during the past week in his and Katherine`s lives. Today would be no different. Finding the game well into the twelfth minute already, Shamus turned to his son and asked, "Tell me Grew, how is everything between you and Katherine?"

"Fine pops, why ya ask?"

Grew noticed the creases in his father`s forehead were deeper than usual. Today could get heavy.

"No reason in particular. Been thinking about Katherine and I know it's not easy starting a marriage, and having to live with your husband's parents. Not exactly a fairytale way to start a new life with the one you love."

Glued to the match on the television as Dundalk kicked one past the Bohemian goalkeeper, thankfully bouncing off of the post, Grew distractedly glanced back at his father.

"I know, but she's a trooper, pops, she really is, and she knows it's temporary. With her school, and me not being able to find some decent work, without you and Mom helping us out, it would be a lot worse. We are thankful for that, pops. Hopefully this bailout by the EU will create some real jobs soon."

Turning the TV down to almost mute, Grew`s father turned towards him. "I don't want to get your hopes up, Grew, but there is a real chance that the DART will lift the hiring freeze very soon. If that happens I can pull some strings and get you in at some level. How does that sound, son?"

"That sounds great; it would be a miracle, really. Let's hope—" Grew was interrupted by a loud scream coming from the kitchen. The scream was Katherine, and it sounded like she had seen a monster. Her scream was followed immediately by a horrific scream from Grew's mother. Both Grew and his father jumped from their chairs and bounded into the kitchen.

Running down the hall towards the kitchen, there came a roar so loud and so demonic it chilled Grew to the bone. Reaching the kitchen right on the heels of his father, he was confronted by the most horrible sight imaginable. Even though it was mid-afternoon with the sun blazing through the windows, the kitchen was almost pitch-black. The blackness was illuminated by a faint glow, and the air was very cold. Looking to his left, Grew was jolted by what he saw before him.

The decapitated body of his mom was impaled on the kitchen wall by a butcher knife through her chest. Then Grew saw the beast. Then he saw Katherine. *Oh my God! Help us!*

Chapter 6

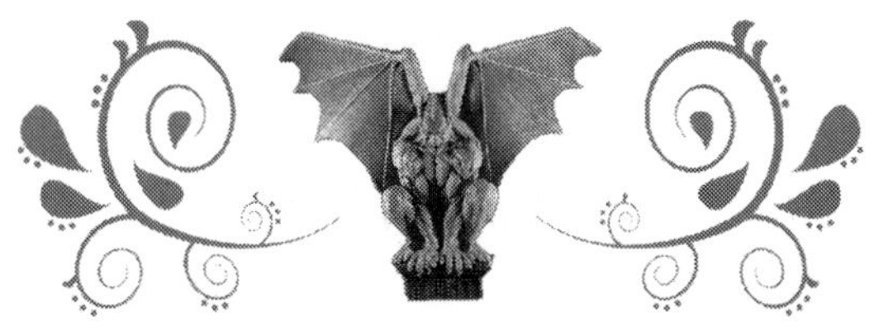

It was almost midnight when Avery finally left the office at Alive Records. What a day, thought Avery. He was exhausted. Once he got Tick Tock into the studio, it all kicked in with precision. For all his faults, Tick Tock was still a professional when it came to his music. He worked his tail off, redoing the takes over and over, overwhelming the studio musicians, but between him and Avery's associate producer, Jake Joyce, they made it work. The album was in the bag and ready for final editing and production. The first single, 'Hunted', featuring Spanish singing sensation Adora, would be released for radio airplay within a few weeks. He and Tick Tock would begin shooting of the "Hunted" video shortly after that.

He guided his BMW down Santa Monica Boulevard towards his modest condo on North Havenhurst Boulevard in West Hollywood, only five minutes away from Alive Records. He was thinking about his phone call with the editor of *Music Talks* magazine. To appease Avery—to whom he made it very clear he had zero obligations to—he would grant Avery and his record company an exclusive interview for the magazine, showcasing Alive Records as one of the most significant record labels and music producers in the industry today. It was an article already being planned, so Avery would have gotten a call from them regardless. Yes, today was a good day; the smile on his face was drawing stares from other motorists.

Avery was 29 years old and still single, which was hard to pull off in this industry, being surrounded by beautiful women almost on a daily basis, from the usual record business groupies to musicians, singers, agents, etc. This business was a rat race, and he'd decided that the less he intertwined his personal life in it the better it was for his health and mental state. He'd had girlfriends but nothing serious. He was too busy and focused for a relationship right now in his life. Someday he would be open to a relationship, but now it certainly was not a priority.

Feeling more energized, Avery decided to stop at a club for a drink to relax and take the edge off some of that exhaustion. Hell with it, he thought, he would head to the Vanguard Nightclub. The lineup would be huge this time of night, but he was considered VIP and would be let in pronto. He would stay for one drink; check out the crowd and leave, as he had another big day at the office tomorrow. Pulling off Santa Monica at North Fairfax Avenue to get turned around to head back onto Hollywood Boulevard, it was no more than ten minutes before he pulled up to the front of the Vanguard. Handing his keys to the car attendant along with a $20 tip, Avery was escorted to the entrance and then into the club, past the young mob, dressed to the nines, standing in line. Once he was inside, the music hit him like a slap in the face, instantly assaulting all his faculties with an extremely loud, bass-filled hip-hop extended dance version of Jay-Z's "Can I Get A." The lights were pulsating right along to the beat of the song. The massive dance floor at the Vanguard was packed. Girls virtually naked, rubbing themselves up against guys wearing tight jeans and tight shirts that showcased muscles amped by steroids. Thursday night at the Vanguard was the biggest night of the week, and it was rockin' tonight. He almost felt like joining the mass of sweaty, gyrating youth on the dance floor, when a Tick Tock song started up, putting the kybosh on that thought in a hurry.

Finishing up his dry martini and preparing to leave, Avery thought he heard his name being called through the din of the loud music. He looked around but didn't notice anyone looking at him. Turning to leave he almost bumped into a man standing right in his path. Excusing himself, Avery swerved to walk around the guy when he heard, "Are you Avery Johnson of Alive Records?"

Eyeing this guy with suspicion, as he did with everyone he didn't know, Avery replied, "Well, that depends on who wants to know!" almost screaming to be heard above the loud music.

"Let me introduce myself. My name is Robert Best. I am a music producer and manager." The man extended his hand towards Avery.

Great, another wannabe producer trying to get face time with someone who actually is a producer. With a sting of sarcasm in his voice, Avery, fighting the noise of the dance floor, yelled, "Nice to meet you, Robert! Sorry I have never heard of you, have you produced anything recently? Any clients I might know?" just wanting to get past him and be on his way home. Obviously this guy was new and trying to make a name for himself. Accepting the handshake as he spoke, Avery felt the man's grip. It was like a vice and was so cold, it felt like the guy had it tucked into a bag of ice before he shook his hand.

"Whoa, easy on the grip, there, fella. You want to make an impression on people in this industry; you may want to consider warming up those hands considerably, before shaking someone's hand. It's as cold as ice, buddy," scolded Avery.

Best was staring directly into Avery's eyes as he spoke. Avery was momentarily drawn to them, something spooky about those eyes, he felt, a chill beginning to form down his spine. When Best spoke it seemed he was not yelling at all to be heard over the music, yet Avery heard every word he said.

"My apologies, Mr. Johnson. I have been gripping too many ice-cold martinis tonight. To answer your question, I must admit I am quite new to the industry, but I hope not for long. Currently I am managing the career of a new rap artist by the name of Devon Devine. Just trying to get his debut album some airtime. You remember what that's like, don't you?"

"Never heard of him, but I'm sure I will soon. Good luck

with your client, Mr. Best, and I hope things work out for you. Now if you don't mind, I have to leave. I have a very busy day tomorrow." With that, Avery pushed past Best, giving him a reassuring pat on his shoulder as he did so.

"Oh, things will work out for me. That I can guarantee you, Mr. Johnson."

The tone of Best's voice, sinister and dark, heard clearly over the drone of the club, startled Avery.

"Excuse me—what did you say? With the music I didn't quite hear you."

Stepping towards Avery and getting in his space, within inches of his face, Best stated, "You will hear a lot about me in the years to come, Mr. Johnson. We may even be negotiating a record deal someday for one of my clients."

This guy was getting weird, thought Avery, time to go. "Good luck, Robert, but something tells me you won't need it!"

As he turned to walk away, Avery swore Robert Best's eyes turned crimson red for a split second. That was downright freaky, he thought. *Did his eyes just turn fluorescent red right in front of me?* I must have imagined it, he thought, because it was just for an instant, probably one of the lights from the dance floor reflecting off his eyes. I'm not so sure, though. *The way he looked at me when they turned red.* Almost evil-looking. I need to go home and get some sleep.

Waiting for the car attendant to retrieve his BMW, Avery was more than a little creeped out by his encounter with Best. Something about that guy didn't add up. He made a mental note to do some research on this guy and his client, Devon Devine.

He arrived at his condo twenty minutes after he left the Vanguard, exhausted and tired. Barely getting out of his clothes, he slumped into his king-sized bed, not even making it under the covers, and was fast asleep before his head even hit the pillow.

The next morning, in a deep sleep, he was awakened suddenly by his Motorola StarTac cell phone ringtone chirping away on his dresser. Glancing at his watch, he was startled to see that it was already 9:45 in the morning. Putting the StarTac out of its misery, he answered his phone. It was Jen, and she was panicking. "Avery, where are you? I have been calling you for over two hours. Your 9:00 a.m. appointment is still waiting. Are you sick or something"?

Looking around his bedroom at his clothes strewn all over the place, his head pounded. Probably someone at the club had dropped a hit of ecstasy in his drink, then watched as he began to make a fool of himself.

"Shit, Jen, I overslept and never heard my phone ring. Reschedule this 9:00 a.m. appointment with my sincere apologies," thought Avery, hanging up. *Jesus, I never sleep in.*

The aggravating chirp of the cell phone started in once again. It was Jen again. He had to change that bloody ringtone, he reminded himself for the millionth time.

"Yeah, what now?"

"Hung over and cranky. Nice. Anyway, I already tried to reschedule him but he insists on waiting. He says that you made him promise last night that he would bring his client in first thing this morning to meet with you."

Avery's stomach began to clench. "Who is my 9:00 a.m. appointment, Jen? I don't remember asking some guy last night to bring his client into the office the next morning for a meeting."

"He says his name is Robert Best and his client is a pop/rapper musician named Devon Devine. Just what you need, Avery, is another rapper," replied Jen with a touch of sarcasm.

"Alright, alright. I'm on my way in, should be there in half an hour. I want a complete and thorough background on Best and his client sitting on my desk when I get there. Call everyone and anyone in the industry until you find someone who knows or has any information on this guy. I want to know as much as I can on him. Thanks, Jen, see you soon."

Jesus, this Best is a character, that's for sure, Avery mused. He had one drink last night and, yes, he was dead tired, but he would've remembered inviting Best back to his office this morning. He'll get rid of him and his rapper client when he gets into the office.

He dressed quickly in jeans and a button-down shirt, and gave his hair a quick brush. He grabbed his electronic shaver and ran out the door. Arriving at Alive Records twenty minutes after speaking with Jen, he found Best looking as fresh as if he had come from fifteen hours of sleep and a pampered massage, not the seven hours ago in the Vanguard.

He was accompanied by a tall, skinny black kid, obviously the Devon Devine Avery had heard about last night. The kid screamed "rapper." Two-piece Nike red sweats with matching white and red Nike running shoes, and the industry standard gold chain outside his shirt. He wore dark sunglasses and a white hat sideways on his head, with the Nike red swoosh on the front of it. *Jeepers, was this kid sponsored by Nike,* thought Avery?

Normally, Avery would greet his clients warmly, especially if he was late. Not this time. He was pissed, to say the least.

"Robert Best, if my memory serves me correctly. It's been such a long time," Avery commented with light sarcasm in his voice.

Best raised himself effortlessly from the deep and plush leather reception room chair, extending his hand towards Avery. Avery ignored it.

"Good morning, Mr. Johnson, and thank you for agreeing to see my client so soon. May I introduce you to Devon Devine, the next Usher, if I may be so bold," stated Best, pointing at Devine who popped out of his chair as if he' been jolted with 10,000 volts of electricity. Offering his hand to Avery and smiling, exposing the other industry standard with rappers, gold-capped teeth. *Unbelievable, these rappers, they're all the same*, thought Avery.

"Your manager told me you're good. We'll see about that. Have a seat, both of you. As far as that invite to my office this morning, we need to talk about that. First, I need ten minutes in my office to clear some matters, then I'll be ready for you. Can Jen get you something to drink? Coffee? Juice, maybe?"

Leaving them in the capable hands of Jen, Avery made his

way into his spacious office and closed the door. Reviewing quickly the rest of his day's agenda, Avery noticed that there was nothing from Jen for Avery to review on Best. He was about to buzz her when there was a knock on his door. Jen walked in, closing the door behind her.

"There is absolutely nothing out there that I could find on this guy or his client Devine. No one has heard of either one. The only thing I found was Best is a member of the Association of Music Producers. He's definitely new to the industry or else has had no clients show any promise. You want me to send them on their way, boss?"

Quickly absorbing what Jen had just told him, and somehow not surprised there was nothing on Best, he looked up at her and said, "No. Send them in now. I'll have a talk with this guy. Then I'll get rid of him".

Two minutes later, Jen led Robert Best and Devon Devine into his office. Offered chairs around a reception table at the opposite side of Avery's office, they sat down.

"Very impressive office, Mr. Johnson. You have done extremely well in this industry at such a young age. Congratulations on your success—which is why Devon and I are very excited to talk to you about recording his debut album with Alive Records."

Clearly annoyed, Avery decided he would put a stop to this meeting.

"Let me get right to the point, Mr. Best. You come into my office without an appointment, with a story to my secretary that I personally invited you this morning, which I did not. I have never heard of you, and in fact, from what I can tell, no one has ever heard of you. I am not looking at this point to sign any new artists for Alive Records of the genre Devon represents. I hope you can appreciate that."

Not showing any signs of taking Avery's rebuke poorly, Best continued: "My apologies, Mr. Johnson, or may I call you Avery? Thank you. You did indeed invite me here this morning. In fact you followed me outside to the valet, handing me your business card, which I have right here with me, to personally invite me this morning, and if possible to bring Devon in as well. I am surprised and disappointed that you do not have any recollection of that conversation. I know the Vanguard was a happening place last night. Maybe you had one too many martinis and do not remember."

Avery's annoyance with Best was turning to anger. He struggled to control it. This idiot was clearly playing him, and he didn't like it.

"I can tell you with some certainty Mr. Best, or may I call you Robert, that I did not have too many martinis last night. In fact, I stopped in at the club on the way home from a very busy day at the office, and had one martini, so I think I would remember approaching you about Devon. Regardless, Robert, the fact remains: I am not looking to sign any new rap artists."

Best displayed a confidence that bordered on pure arrogance. He pretended to be listening when he spoke, but Avery knew he wasn't.

"Fair enough, but do me the honor of at least taking the time to listen to Devon's demo recordings of three of his songs. I am sure you will hear enough to have us come back. Thank you for your time, Avery, and my apologies for any confusion about our appointment." Looking at Devon, motioning to him that it was time to leave, Best turned to Avery, reached into the inside of his suit jacket, and produced a CD, handing it to Avery.

What a strange pair. Not even sure if Devon Devine could sing or not—Avery could care less—but one thing for sure, he couldn't talk, as he hadn't said one word the whole time he was here. Bizarre. Holding the disc in his hand, Avery watched the two of them leave his office and enter the elevator. As they turned back towards the office and before the elevator doors closed, Avery swore he saw Best's eyes instantly, for a millisecond, flash crimson red. Just like last night. It was so quick, Avery couldn't be sure of what he seen.

Tossing the CD into the garbage can beside his desk, Avery hoped he'd never see or hear from this pair ever again.

Chapter 7

Finishing up Sunday Mass was difficult for Father Thomas O'Sullivan. He could not shake the dread that had overcome him when Grew and Katherine McClosky arrived at church. It just kept getting worse as the morning went on. And then he had this distinct feeling that they were in imminent danger when he said goodbye to them after mass. It was weird, he thought. His spirit was heavy, and he rushed to get through the meeting with the deacons and the church business, so he could get over to the McClosky home.

At fifty-eight years of age, as a Catholic priest, he had seen it all over the years. Being a man of the cloth certainly has its ups and downs. He had seen more pain, counseled more broken hearts than he could remember. Witnessed some of the most tragic and outrageous confessions from people over the years, including confessions to rape, armed robbery, even an accidental killing that led the tortured soul, three months later, to take his own life, awash in guilt and sorrow. That left Father O'Sullivan terribly pained for a very long time, knowing that he had failed that man, not being able to reach through to him to exorcise the demons that ravaged his soul.

Born and raised in a very strong Catholic environment, Thomas knew early on that his faith and relationship with God would always be a big part of his life, though not necessarily that he would eventually turn to the priesthood. Especially, he thought to himself, growing up dirt poor with two sisters and an alcoholic father and a mother who turned a blind eye to the abuse his father would inflict on him and his sisters. His father was mean who hated everyone, including his own family, especially his own family. Working long hard days in the textile factory, he came home a broken and miserable man, who would quote biblical passages as he beat his children to a pulp. Visits to the home by the parish priest were just a drinking session with Father Christy and his father. When Father Christy was too drunk to stand, his mother would make him comfortable on the couch with a blanket and pillow. His father would then beat the hell out of us before he would pass out in his bed. Mother would dutifully drape blankets over him, making sure he was comfortable and not even checking on us, even though she could hear our cries.

When Thomas decided to become a priest at the age of eighteen after completing high school, he made a promise to himself that he would spend as much time with his parishioners, individually or as a family away from the church environment, as possible. He felt it was important to get to know the people in their own surroundings, plus he felt he could better understand their issues, and identify potential problems within a family structure before they escalated. To realize his dream, he enrolled in the University of Dublin in 1958, obtaining his Bachelor's Degree of Arts with a Major in Psychology four years later. He continued his education and four years later obtained his Masters Degree in Psychology.

Thomas, when he left home for school, kept in touch with his sisters, but no longer communicated with his mother or father, nor did they communicate with him. It was if he had died in their eyes. Thomas supported himself and paid for his schooling by working two jobs. He bagged groceries at the local mart from 3:30 p.m. to 6:30 p.m. Monday to Friday and then 9:00 a.m. to 4:00 p.m. on Saturdays and Sundays. Thomas also worked 8:00 p.m. to 2:00 a.m. Monday to Friday stocking shelves and running a forklift at a large inventory warehouse. The work was not that difficult, but it was a lot of hours, and combined with the hours needed to attend classes and study time, it was grueling.

When he entered All Hallows Seminary College in Dublin at the age of twenty-six, armed with a Masters degree in Psychology, his passion to become a priest, to serve God and his fellow man, was as strong as ever. Four years later, he had completed his studies, graduating from All Hallows with an expectation that Father Thomas O'Sullivan would do great things for the Catholic Church, and the people he was so eager to serve.

Dispatched to the small Church of the Immaculate Conception & St. Patrick in the Diocese of Cork and Ross in the south part of Ireland, in the township of Bandon, he was thrilled to finally break away from the drone of studies spanning almost twelve years. He was joining a church in need of help, as the congregations across Ireland were swelling with new members, and this church was no exception.

Thomas began his six months' tutelage as a church deacon under the guidance and watchful eye of Father James O'Malley. Father O'Malley was seventy-one years old, frail with diabetes, soon to be retired with this, his last mission for the church, being to prepare Thomas for his vows. In the six months working with Father O'Malley, Thomas was amazed at the energy of his mentor, even though he was very sick. Father O'Malley worked tirelessly, putting in long hours, served his people with compassion and a purpose that truly inspired Thomas.

One Sunday evening after all the services had been completed for the day, Father O'Malley and Thomas sat down in the elderly priest's cramped office and shared a cup of tea. Sensing that Father O'Malley had something important he wanted to talk about, Thomas sat quietly, waiting for him to speak.

Once the tea had steeped, he watched as Father O'Malley went through his usual ritual of dropping four heaping spoons of powdered cream into his tea. Once Thomas had asked him why he used so much powdered cream in his tea, whereupon he'd received a jovial reply, "I like a little tea with my cream." And then Thomas asked him why he used powder and not regular cream, whereupon he received the reply, "I like how the powder sits on top of the tea, then slowly dissolves, turning it white." Thomas made a mental note to himself to never ask silly questions again.

Father O'Malley looked at Thomas over the cup of tea that he held up to his lips and asked him, "Do you still feel you want to be a priest, Thomas?"

It was a question he'd been expecting from Father O'Malley for a while now. The church took the vows very seriously, so it was up to Father O'Malley to determine if he was ready for the priesthood.

"I do, Father. This has been my dream since I was a boy. I feel I am ready to serve the Lord in every way I can."

"You are a good-looking, athletic and highly educated young man. There are many great opportunities outside of the church for you. Do you understand that, Thomas?"

"I want only to serve my Lord, Father, with all my heart and soul. To carry out His purpose for me, in whatever way He decides to use me as a messenger and servant of His word. I want to help people, Father, reach out into the community and make a difference. To even come close to the service you have given this church, and to God, would bring joy and satisfaction to my heart a thousand times over."

Father O'Malley looked intently at him before he replied.

"Thank you, Thomas, for those kind words, but I see in you a much greater purpose. I believe you have been chosen for something incredibly important that will have an indelible impact on mankind. I am sure of it."

He poured Father O'Malley another cup of tea as they continued to discuss his vows. Thomas was flattered that his mentor would speak so highly of him, even thinking that he would have an impact on mankind.

"I don't know about impacting mankind, Father, but it is

my hope that I can help the people of my church and community, navigate the rough seas of life that come their way."

Thomas watched as Father O'Malley shifted in his seat so he could face him. His brow furrowed and he hesitated slightly as his eyes bore into Thomas before he spoke.

"Listen to me, Thomas. The church feels you are a very special young man and has asked me to explain to you where they want you to go from here."

Taken completely off guard by Father O'Malley's comments, Thomas struggled to maintain his composure. The Church of the Immaculate Conception meant everything to him. It was where he wanted to belong.

"Father, I am expecting to take over for you right here at Immaculate Conception when you retire. This is where I belong."

"I know, son. The people of this community would be truly blessed to have you serve them, but you have a greater purpose that our Lord has in store for you. This is an order that came from the Vatican and has been decided. You will leave for Rome in the morning."

He was shocked at what he had just heard.

"The Vatican?! Father O'Malley, I entered the priesthood to serve the people of this wonderful country, in the homes of the people, at mass, to bring people closer to our Lord, to experience the love He has in store for them."

Father O'Malley reached over and placed his frail hand on top of Thomas's.

"You may very well get that opportunity, Thomas, but the Church has plans for you right now, which I am not privy to, but you must understand, Thomas, your life of servitude is not determined by you alone. It is decided by God Himself. Now go and prepare for your trip. You will be gone for many months. May God be with you, Thomas, always."

****

He set down the letter from the Archbishop of Dublin on his lap as the plane climbed farther away from the country he loved so dearly. Thomas was at a loss as to explain why he'd been chosen to journey to Rome immediately after his vows. Reflecting back to this morning, his disappointment at being dispatched to the Vatican had been obvious as he said goodbye to Father O'Malley.

He had stood at the doorway of the church office holding his two suitcases, about to descend the stairs and into the waiting car of the church deacon who would take him to the airport, struggling to find the words to say goodbye to Father O'Malley. A profound sense of sadness, that he would be leaving this church so suddenly weighed down his soul. There was no joy in his heart at being dispatched to Rome. Father O'Malley placed his hands on either side of his shoulders, squeezing them in reassurance, and regarded Thomas with a sense of pride before he spoke.

"Do not be discouraged, Thomas. Whatever that letter contains, or whatever the purpose for summoning you to Rome is, I am sure it is God's will. The Church needs you, Thomas, for a great purpose. Serve your Lord, Thomas, with your complete heart, mind and soul. I look forward to the day when you will come back here to this humble church and visit an old retired priest. Will you do that for me?" Father O'Malley smiled as he embraced Thomas, giving him a final hug.

"I will, Father. You have taught me well, and I will take your passion to serve with me, and instill it into whatever plan God has for me. You are a great man, Father, you've been like a real father to me. I look forward to the day of my return, to sharing a cup of tea, and making you laugh at the many stories I'll be able to tell of adventures in our beloved Rome."

Feeling his eyes grow heavy as the direct flight from Dublin to Rome reached its cruising altitude, Thomas drifted off to sleep full of questions and apprehension about his new life journey.

He snapped out of his deep slumber when the Boeing 707s wheels made contact with the runway at Fiumicino Airport in Rome. Thomas could not believe he'd slept through the entire three and a half hour flight. Passengers were busy getting out of their seatbelts and up out of their chairs, retrieving their carry-on luggage. Thomas was in no hurry, so he would wait for the line to clear before he got up and departed.

Suddenly, seemingly out of nowhere, he heard a voice addressing him.

"You should not look so glum, Father. I would think coming to the motherland would bring great excitement," commented a passenger somewhere behind him.

Hearing this comment startled Thomas, and he was at first unsure if the comment was directed at him. Maybe there was another priest sitting nearby. No, the man couldn't be talking to him. No one knew who he was, and he wasn't wearing clerical clothing, just khakis and a sweater. Looking up, Thomas spotted a man a few rows back, standing in the aisle waiting to depart, looking directly at him.

Motioning to the man with his hand, Thomas asked, "Excuse me, were you speaking to me?"

"Please, come grab your bag," the man replied, pointing in front of him down the aisle, gesturing for Thomas to slide out of his row, grab his carry-on and deplane.

Thomas was slightly annoyed by the stranger's suggestion, as he just wanted to sit and wait for everyone else to deplane first.

"It's okay, thank you anyway. I am in no hurry. I prefer to wait," replied Thomas.

The passenger smiled back at him but did not move.

"I insist, Father. Come on, you are holding up the rest of the passengers, Father. I'm sure you have some important people waiting for you."

Shifting his body across the three seats and into the aisle, Thomas smiled at the passenger, nodding his head at the same time.

"Alright, thank you. By the way, do I know you?" asked Thomas as he retrieved his briefcase and windbreaker from the overhead storage.

The passenger glanced over his shoulder at the crush of

impatient passengers behind him and then looked at Thomas.

"I doubt it, unless you've heard of the American band The Impressions. I'm their manager and producer. My name is Robert Best," his hand extended to Thomas. "We'd better get moving or we might become part of the fabric of this carpet," chuckled Best as he glanced back behind him.

With no one in front of him, Thomas was able to quickly make his way off the plane, stopping at the entrance to the gangway, out of the way of the departing passengers, and continuing his conversation with the American music producer.

"Can't say that I've heard of that band, I have never followed the American music craze, sorry, but if they were a blues band I very much might have. I love your blues music. In Dublin, American blues musicians are extremely popular. My name is Thomas. Thomas O'Sullivan—and, yes, a freshly minted clergyman. How did you know? Is it that obvious?" Thomas smiled, as he shook Robert Best's hand. He was instantly taken aback at the intensity of the handshake from Best. It was powerful, and way over the top. He was about to protest when Best jerked his arm forcibly towards him, bringing Thomas's face only inches away from his.

Best's demeanor completely changed. His face lost all expression and color. It was blank, and the grip on his hand was like cold steel.

"I know why you are here in Rome and what your mission is at the Vatican. I also know that we will meet again someday. I look forward to that day very much, Father O'Sullivan." A sinister smile crossed Best's face. As Best released his vise-like grip on Thomas's hand, his eyes flashed a deep crimson red and seemed to burrow right into the soul of Thomas, startling him. "Good luck in your training, Father. You will need it. You will need much more than that," Best muttered as he leaned into Thomas, his eyes flashing that deep red. With those final words, he turned and walked swiftly away, up the last few feet of the gangway, and disappeared among the swarm of passengers making their way through the terminal.

Leaning against the gangway wall, sweating profusely, Thomas tried to gather himself and wrap his head around what just happened to him. *Who was this guy, and how did he know who I was? How did he know what I was doing in Rome and the training I'm about to take at the Vatican?*

Thomas could feel the fear begin to build inside of him. Those eyes sent a cold shudder down his spine. What is going on?

Chapter 8

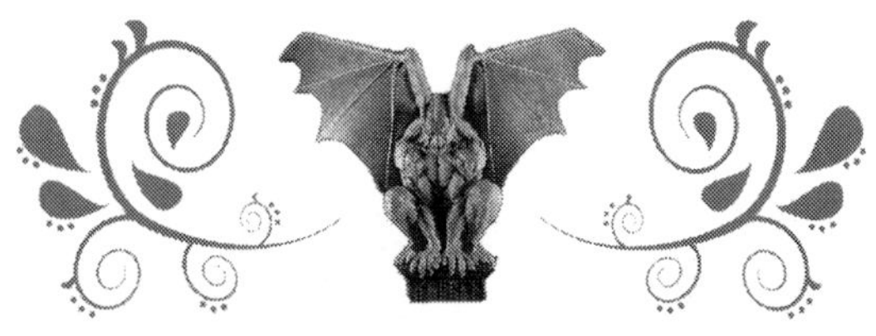

James's mind was racing out of control. What the hell is going on? What is this thing? My God, that smell was so bad it was burning his eyes.

James looked at this thing and could not believe his eyes. It was almost half man and half prehistoric Tyrannosaurus Rex. Its legs were massive, with large muscles bulging everywhere, glistening in a slime covering its greenish-brown body. Bent slightly forward, the creature had armour-like plates running down its back from its head to the tip of its ten-foot tail. The arms were almost human in their size and shape, the arms of a bodybuilder, very muscled. Long, talon-like nails protruded at the end of its fingers. Its head had the look of a deranged human encased in a demonic monster shell. Its mass was so big it literally filled the entire space of both the kitchen and the dining room area. James was unable to move, frozen at the entranceway from the garage, unwilling to step into the pit of hell.

Nancy's scream snapped James out of his temporary state of shock.

He knew he needed to act now. There wasn't much time, and this creature was going to kill Nancy. Backing up the few feet to open the door to the garage, he reached with his hand to grab the shovel he kept on a hook on the wall beside the door. Fortunately, the shovel was a spade with sharp edges. The eyes of this monster were burning bright red, watching him almost in a curious state. Without taking his eyes off the beast creature, he could see Nancy out of the corner of his eye leaning back on her hands and beginning to slowly and quietly backpedal away from the monster, and into the living room. As he met her eyes and saw the look of horror in them, she indicated, with a slight nod to reassure him, that she was using the distraction to try to escape.

He mustered as much courage as he could, hoisted the shovel above his head, and approached the creature from hell. Cocking the shovel, he prepared to take its head off. Screaming at the top of his lungs, a primal sound he did not recognize, he swung the shovel as hard as he possibly could, striking the creature flush across the face, surprising it somehow, and it fell backwards a few feet, but quickly recovered. He watched in horror as it swung its massive tail towards him, taking out two kitchen cupboards while doing so with incredible speed and power, the cupboards collapsing like matchsticks. Ducking in the nick of time, he gaped as the tail swooshed above his head and crashed into the fridge, cutting it in half. Issuing a guttural roar full of rage and hatred, the beast turned to face him and move in for the kill, snapping out its long, powerful arms towards him. James leapt to the right, into the kitchen where its tail had just raked the cupboards. Grabbing nothing but air, the beast screamed in rage and moved once again towards him, its eyes burning as red as the sun.

Sweating profusely, adrenaline coursing through his veins, he spotted the knife rack on the kitchen countertop, still intact. The creature was preparing for another strike, so he needed to make his move, and quickly. Launching himself towards the knife rack on the counter, he reached for the one with the biggest blade, grabbing it, then using all of his strength to whip it around with lightning speed towards the beast, slicing the right arm of the creature almost clean off. Clutching its wounded arm, the beast tilted its grotesque head backwards and let out a scream so piercing that James found himself covering his ears as he scrambled past the beast and into the dining room. He saw that

Nancy was standing at the front door, frozen in fear and unable to move.

"For Christ's sake, Nancy, get out of here! Move it. Now!" bellowed James.

He could see the expression on Nancy's face suddenly crumple in horror.

"James!! Look out!"

Too late. The beast, recovered from the blows James had inflicted with the shovel and the knife, now was closing in behind him, reaching out with its deadly claws. Reacting too late, James felt the beast clutch onto his back, its claws ripping through his skin. Then it flung him with such force against the dining room wall that it sent him crashing through it and into the living room on the other side. Dazed from the pain coursing through his body, James looked up to see the beast crashing through the remainder of the dining room wall, its eyes burning bright red with a fierce hatred, its wounded arm dangling uselessly at its side. It turned its attention to Nancy. Too weak to even get up off the floor, James watched helplessly as the beast whipped its tail 180 degrees towards Nancy, catching her in the chest, sending her flying into the living room where she landed with a crash against the large-screen TV. The blow rendered Nancy unconscious, and she slumped in a heap on the floor in front of the mangled TV stand.

"Nooo!!" cried James after seeing Nancy flung across the house like a rag doll. *My God, what was happening to us?*

Distracted by the sight of Nancy, he did not see the beast had moved towards him.

With incredible speed that caught him off guard, the beast shot its undamaged, half-reptile, half-human arm towards him, grabbing hold of his left leg in a vise-like grip that James desperately tried to break away from. But his efforts were futile, the beast had him. Squeezing his upper thigh in its grip, the beast lifted James in the air, hanging him upside down, rotating him so that his face was inches away from the battered face of the beast. The smell of its breath coming out in blasts from its nostrils was nauseating. Staring into its beastly mouth, full of razor-sharp teeth, terrified to the core, James flinched as the beast screamed at him..

"Do not resist me or you will die! I only want the woman!"

He needed to do something, or he and Nancy would die. With his dangling arms almost reaching the floor, James spotted a splintered piece of wood that was about eighteen inches long, and he strained to reach it. Still maintaining eye contact with the beast's red pits of hell, he grabbed the stake and with one sweeping motion brought the dagger up over his head and, hoisting his body with as much force as he could muster, he drove the stake deep into the neck of the beast. He caught the beast off guard and unprepared for the blow. The wound erupting in a splash of blood, drenching him, the smell so foul he thought he would vomit, James pushed the stake further into the neck of the creature.

The beast screamed—a piercing, demonic wail—dropping James to the floor as its massive bulk reeled backwards onto the rubble from the dining room wall. It suddenly became still and did not move.

He killed it, thought James. The monster was dead. Their nightmare was over. Forcing himself up off of the floor, he had to get to Nancy. Standing on weak legs, he turned towards Nancy, and saw the look of horror on her face as she stared at something beyond him. Then she screamed.

****

Nancy screamed in horror, watching as the beast pulled the wooden stake from its neck and crept up behind James. She could only watch as James reacted to the look on her face and began to turn around towards the beast. The stake the beast pulled from its neck was now coming down towards James like an axe. The beast drove the stake down on the crown of James head, crushing his skull like a smashed watermelon. She sat frozen in terror as James's lifeless body fell to the floor. Then the beast turned its attention towards her.

Seeing her beloved James murdered and his head crushed by this demonic monster was too much for her, and her mind began to shut down, the light started to dim, and darkness was coming fast. She just wanted to die and be taken from this nightmare. Just as she was about to slip into the abyss, she felt a steel-like grip around her throat choking the breath from her. She opened her eyes to see a man, completely naked, lifting her off the ground with his grip tightening around her throat. *What the hell happened to the creature?* She could not breathe, gasped for air and thrashed her arms and legs to try and free herself from the death grip that held her. Loosening its grip on her, the beast dropped her to the floor, where she landed with a sickening thud. With pain and exhaustion overtaking her, she waited for this monster, or whatever the hell it was now, to finish her off.

Closing her eyes, knowing that she was about to die, Nancy began to pray. "Dear Lord, I don't know why this is happening but take me now, to be with you and James, in Heaven. Forgive my sins, Lord. Give James and me the chance to be with you in Heaven. Thank you, Lord. Amen," whispered Nancy. She waited for the blow that would take her to James. She was not afraid.

Instead, she opened her eyes to the sound of laughter. She looked up to see this—thing—laughing hysterically, with his eyes burning that frighteningly bright red. He spoke, "He doesn't hear you, never has, and never will. He does not exist. You humans are pathetic, praying to a God that has never existed, but yet you continue to gather, celebrate His existence and pray for forgiveness. Man's weakness, clinging to this myth you call Jesus, will be its apocalypse!" boomed this evil creation.

"Who are you? What do you want with me?!" cried Nancy.

Just as Nancy spoke, the room turned dark and became very cold. The beast's eyes continued to burn red, glowing like beacons. He bellowed down to Nancy, "I am the true ruler of this world and every other world in this universe! The time is near for mankind to make a decision. You have been chosen by the true Master of this universe, through your lineage to the fallen warrior Maxim. The time to serve your true Master has arrived!"

Suddenly the man-beast began to rise in the air, levitating about a foot off the ground. With a glow surrounding his body in the cold darkness, he seemed to be meditating. He was silent, but then he began to speak in a language she had never heard before.

"Consilium meum regi ultionem meam perdere humanum genus est Tiridates" (My plan to destroy mankind includes my revenge on King Tiridates).

"De familia Tiridates semen meum terminetur in ipsum. In regula mea lux mundi incipit" (The lineage of Tiridates ends with my seed in this bitch. The dawn of my rule on this world begins).

In a flash the man-beast was on top of her, pushing her down flat on the living room floor with such force she felt like she was being pinned underneath a truck. The beast ripped off her pants with one pull, tearing away as if they were attached by Velcro.

She screamed so loudly the beast smashed her across the face hard; she could feel the bones in her nose snap.

The full reality of what was about to happen to her hit Nancy with a force more powerful than any physical blow he could have hit her with. *She was going to be raped by this monster.* Why? Why her? Why did James have to die? What was he talking about, lineage to Maxim. This is madness! *What the hell is happening? Please God don't let this happen, help me, she prayed.*

Blood poured out of her nose from the blow, filling her mouth. She thrashed at the beast, fought it with all the strength she had. Suddenly this thing was directly on top of her, pinning her, forcing him on her with such pressure the pain was unbearable, she thought she would pass out, silently praying she would. She just wanted to die, there was no reason to live after this horror. When he entered her, the size of him, she thought would rip her apart. He made no sound as his pelvis crashed into hers, over and over, till finally he released his evilness into her. It seemed he was on top of her for hours, but it was only a few minutes. It felt like hot, volcanic lava was spewing into her. His body was sweating, yet he was cold and clammy on top of her, just as death would feel like, she thought.

She leaned to her left and vomited.

Then the darkness came. Finally, the death she prayed for arrived.

Chapter 9

Nine-year-old Bentley Paxton just knew she wanted to be an actress. So bad, in fact, that when she informed her teacher that she wanted the role of Cinderella in her grade school's play, "The Glass Slipper," it became an obsession. She fretted and worried day and night, and could barely sleep until her teacher, Ms. Cranston, made her decision on who would get the coveted role. Bentley knew she was competing against Jessica Williams, the spoiled and most popular kid in Red Oak Elementary School.

Bentley's mother, seeing her daughter so emotionally involved, suggested that Bentley ask her teacher to allow her and Jessica to audition for the role to make it fair, and allow Bentley to show her teacher that she was best suited to be Cinderella. That is exactly what she did. She asked Ms. Cranston to consider an audition for her and Jessica, expecting her to say no and then deny her the role for even suggesting such a thing. But she was wrong. Ms. Cranston thought it was a great idea, and selected a scene in the play where Cinderella is all alone in her room, crying over her plight of not being able to go to the ball because of her wicked stepmother. There would be no advance time to allow for practice. They were told of the scene and had thirty minutes to learn the lines and act it out.

Bentley pulled off the scene like a seasoned professional and got what she wanted fair and square. Jessica stumbled over her lines, the pressure too much for her. Getting the coveted role of

Cinderella was just the first of many personal accomplishments for Bentley as she grew up in the affluent Highland Park suburb of Chicago. Her dream of being an actress always burned bright as she played in school productions all through junior high and high school. When she was sixteen, in grade eleven, stunningly beautiful and with honor roll marks, she was offered the position of school newspaper editor at Highland Park High School. She took on the work with a passion, soon discovering her love for journalism, writing and using her creative talents in this medium. Turning down drama scholarships to various universities, Bentley applied to the University of Missouri School of Journalism Undergraduate Program in Columbia upon her graduation from high school. She was determined to make journalism her career path.

Bentley's looks and obvious talent were opening doors for her early on in her newspaper career. At nineteen, she landed a job as a part-time reporter for the entertainment section of the *Columbia Daily Tribune*. Covering local concerts, festivals and various other small-town happenings kept Bentley busy along with her studies and deepened her passion for journalism.

As the pretty reporter from the *Daily Tribune*, Bentley had many guys asking her out on dates. She went out on a few but found herself too focused on her school and her job to take it any further than one or two dates. Bentley's parents would visit often, making the seven-hour drive one way to spend time with their only child. Most of the weekends, when they would come to visit, Bentley had to work covering some event, but she would try to have her parents join her. It was a great way to spend time with them and they usually had a blast. They even liked the rock concerts, but they drew a line at heavy metal bands, choosing to stay firmly planted in country music instead. One weekend they had planned to visit but then chose to stay at home when they learned she was covering the Splendid Seven concert. They'd take a rain check, they said. The Splendid Seven was certainly over the top, but concert goers loved them. When Bentley interviewed the band the afternoon of the concert, then again after the concert backstage, she was more intrigued with their manager, Avery Johnson, who wasn't much older than she was. *He is awfully young to be managing such a top act*, she thought. She made a mental note to herself that he might be a good subject for a future interview.

She went on to complete her Bachelors Degree by the age of twenty-two and then was accepted into the Berkeley School of Journalism to complete her two-year Masters Degree. Soon after arriving on campus in the fall, Bentley secured another part-time job as a reporter for the music magazine *Vibe*, covering the concert scene. It was a great opportunity for her to pad her resume covering and interviewing some of the best musicians in the industry coming through San Francisco and the rest of the Bay area.

Finding a small apartment in Emeryville just a few minutes south of the Berkeley campus, Bentley was getting settled before classes began in a few weeks. The upcoming weekend she would be working her first concert for *Vibe*, a new Top 40 band called Watermark, with a hit new single, "Balanced," getting a lot of the airplay on the radio. She loved these gigs because the new bands were yet to be spoiled by their own success, not full of attitude yet and still giddy at their rise up the musical charts. On Saturday, the afternoon of the concert, she would conduct a full interview with the band and their manager, Robert Best.

As it was only Wednesday, Bentley took advantage of some free time to finish off an article for *Vibe*. After she had finished her article, she snuck away from her apartment to do some much needed grocery shopping. Her parents had raised her in an environment that encouraged proper nutrition and lots of physical activity. Both of her parents, now in their mid-fifties, were in excellent physical shape and looked like they were in their early forties. They both had great skin and boundless supplies of energy, that thankfully, thought Bentley, had been passed down to her.

Moving through the local Safeway, Bentley stocked her cart with fresh foods. She did, however, sneak a carton of Häagen-

Dazs Rocky Road ice cream into her cart for those weak moments that she allowed herself from time to time. Plus, she was not expecting her parents for a visit for a month or two anyway. Bentley tried to avoid the lectures on food choices with her parents if she could. Making her way to the checkout, she noticed that the music magazine *Spin* had a tagline on the front cover featuring an article on the inside on the next up-and-coming music producer, Avery Johnson, and his move into the recording industry with the startup of Alive Records. Wow, she thought to herself. This Johnson dude was a mover and a shaker, having coming a long way since she'd met him at the Splendid Seven concert a few years back while working for the *Daily Tribune. He is also a pretty good-looking guy*, she thought. Funny she'd never noticed that back in Columbia. Too focused on my job, she laughed to herself.

Saturday morning found Bentley eagerly getting ready to head off to the local ladies-only gym. Too much Rocky Road the night before, watching reruns of Law and Order. She'd put the necessary time on the treadmill this morning, that was certain. Then back home after the gym to finish off her notes she had put together for her interview with Watermark. She made sure she was always prepared for her interviews. Doing research on her subjects included full background workups on each of the band members. She liked to know as much as she could about them—their likes and dislikes, marriages, girlfriends, favorite sports teams, etc. The inspiration for their music was also a good topic for the article. She was surprised that she could not find any information on their manager, Robert Best. That's weird, she thought, unusual in this business, as typically the Web is full of information on anyone in this industry. Previous bands or musicians he had managed, previous articles that linked Best were nowhere to be found on her searches. He obviously avoided the spotlight, again unusual for this industry. She checked the website of the IAMA, the International Artists Managers' Association, and found Best was not a member, which was mandatory for any manager, or management company managing the career of a recording artist. Bentley would check into that during her interview with Best.

After showering and doing her hair and makeup, Bentley took a moment to take stock of herself in the mirror. She was a pretty hot chic, she had to admit. Great bloodlines. Wearing a black leather skirt bordering on too revealing, a white blouse that fell down past one shoulder, revealing the proper amount of her ample cleavage, Bentley completed her wardrobe with knee high black leather boots. She tried to match her wardrobe to the nature of the concert, careful not to overdress or under dress.

Grabbing her media credentials off her dresser, she headed out the door as she discovered after consulting her watch that she was running late. The concert was maybe thirty minutes away at the Fox Theatre in Oakland. It would be sold out, with 2,800 concert goers eager to hear "Balanced" and whatever else the band would play that night. Her interview was scheduled for 4:00 p.m. with the concert starting at 7:00 p.m. A popular local act from the Bay area would take the stage and whip the crowd into a frenzy before Watermark took the stage. *Vibe* had requested and been given one hour of uninterrupted time with Watermark before the concert and twenty minutes after the concert. Watermark would not turn down an opportunity to get this kind of face time with one of the industry's leading music magazines.

Bentley pulled up in front of the Fox Theatre early, at 3:40 p.m., giving her a few minutes in the ladies room and to get familiar with the theatre and where she needed to meet the band. Giving her keys to the valet, she headed inside. Freshening up in the ladies room, Bentley began to feel a surprising sense of uneasiness come over her. She normally had a few butterflies before beginning an interview but never this sense of uneasiness, which was almost an impending feeling of dread. It must be the fact that she'd been unable to learn anything about Watermark's manager, Robert Best. Bentley always liked to be completely prepared for her interviews, her research into her subjects thorough, so surprises would be minimal, if at all. Going into this interview with Best without any background was getting to her, she had to admit.

Exiting the ladies room, she approached a security guard, introduced herself and asked directions to the backstage dressing rooms where Watermark were preparing.

"Someone as pretty as you, should not be walking alone back there. Not safe. Come on, I'll take you," smiled the security guard, reading Bentley's credentials, then extended his hand, "Hi, nice to meet you Ms. Paxton. You can call me Joey."

Her nerves calmed just a little.

"Thank you so much, that's very kind. I've never been here before so I'd likely get lost in the labyrinth," joked Bentley.

The security guard projected an air of confidence that only experience can bring. He'd likely seen it all in the years he'd been on the job.

"I work maybe thirty to forty concerts a year in this place, and the worst time is hours before the show when the roadies are busy putting the finishing touches on the stage setup, sound and lighting. It gets pretty hairy back there, lots of pressure on these guys. Wouldn't want to see you walk through that gauntlet all by yourself," winked the guard.

She followed Joey as they entered a long narrow corridor leading them backstage.

Arriving at the stage door where Watermark was getting ready, Joey rapped on the door. A few seconds later the door was opened by a well-groomed man who looked to be in his late thirties. The man glanced at Joey, then Bentley, broke into a wide smile and reached his hand out to Bentley. "You must be Bentley Paxton from *Vibe*. You are far more beautiful than your picture in the credits of *Vibe*. I am Robert Best, Manager of Watermark. Please come in, the guys are excited to meet you."

"Thank you, sir," stated Best, dismissing Joey.

"Looks like you've found your interview, Ms. Paxton. Good luck," said Joey as he turned and walked away towards the theatre lobby.

"Thank you, Joey for showing me the way down here,"

smiled Bentley.

Entering the room behind Best, Bentley found the band members of Watermark sitting on leather couches almost as if they'd been patiently waiting for her to walk through the door. Best made the introductions.

"Ms. Paxton, let me introduce Watermark. Say hello to Randy Sims, lead singer." Easing off the couch, Randy nodded his head towards Bentley, offered her his hand and said, "So nice to meet you, Ms. Paxton." Bentley replied, "Please, everyone, call me Bentley."After being introduced to the remaining four members of Watermark, Bentley smiled and said, "Okay, let's get to work, we have an hour and then I need to get out of here so you can get ready."

Turning her attention to the lead singer, she began.

"Randy, your voice has been compared to that of the legendary Steve Perry of Journey fame. The breadth of your range is amazing. What do you say about those comments?"

Not even making an attempt to reply to her question, looking at her unblinking, it was Best who replied. "Randy has one of those voices, Bentley, that can fill an arena with no help from amplification. It is not only powerful, but he can take it into every key. He is truly gifted."

No reply or additional comments from Randy. Weird, thought Bentley. Looking at the rest of the band, Bentley stated, "I understand all of you collaborate on the songwriting and lyrics for Watermark's music. Which one of you would like to talk more about that?"

Again it was Best who answered. "It is a creative process with each of the guys taking part. They are all very talented songwriters and could all be solo artists, but collectively they are writing some great music, some of which you will hear tonight. They are also writing music for other up-and-coming artists as well".

Noting the blank stares of the band members, she turned and asked Best, "Who are some of the other singers or bands they're writing for?"

With a smile Bentley found a little too smug, Best replied, "Unfortunately, for contractual reasons I am unable to comment on actual names, but suffice to say you would definitely know some of them. In fact some of the songs that are currently moving up the Billboard 100 charts have been written by Watermark."

The next forty-five minutes of the interview went by with Bentley asking questions of the guys, but being answered by Best. During the entire hour, the band did not say one word to her. Creepy, she thought. Obviously Best had complete control of what was going to be said about Watermark.

Closing her notebook and placing it back into her carry bag, she stood.

"Okay, I guess I'm done here. Thank you gentlemen for your time and your feedback. It was very informative," thinking this last comment, at least, might elicit a response from the guys. It did not. Just a slight smile and a nod of their heads as Bentley rose from her chair and turned to leave.

"Can I have a few words with you, Mr. Best, out in the hallway?" asked Bentley, looking at Best.

Saying goodbye to Watermark, she stepped outside the dressing room and into the hallway behind the theatre stage, which was still busy with stage hands scurrying around, shouting and barking commands. Joined a few seconds later by Best, she turned to him and asked, "Thank you for your time, Mr. Best. I must admit I found it somewhat strange that the band members didn't answer any of their questions. Didn't even make an attempt. Why is that? Why do you answer for them?"

That uneasiness and dread crept back into Bentley's stomach as she waited for Best to reply. "My contract with Watermark does not allow for individuals of Watermark to comment directly to reporters, or anyone for that matter, on the inner workings of the band. I am the only one contractually allowed to make those comments, Ms. Paxton. Now if we are done, I must get back in the room and ensure the guys are properly preparing for the show. Thank you, Ms. Paxton, once again." Handing her his business card, Best turned and entered the dressing room, closing the door behind him.

Just as the door was about to close, Bentley shouted, "Excuse me, Mr. Best. I have one more question for you if you don't mind."

Returning to the hallway, Best asked, slightly testy, "What else can I answer for you Ms. Paxton?"

"I was unable to find any background information on you or your history in this industry. I found that strange, considering that legally you must be registered with the IAMA as manager of Watermark. You were not even listed on their registry."

She looked at Best, waiting for him to respond, when she noticed the stagehands were testing the lighting. There were red lights, blue and orange lights bouncing off the walls around them. Suddenly Bentley witnessed Best's eyes flash bright red just for a split second, it was so quick she barely noticed it, but she was certain she'd seen it. Very creepy, she thought as a chill went shivering down her spine. *What is it with this guy?*

Then he spoke. "We are all living in extraordinary times right now, Ms. Paxton. The world is changing. Wait for it. We will meet again, Ms. Paxton, I am sure of it." With that he turned and disappeared into the dressing room, locking the door shut once inside.

The chill running down her spine had caused the hair on her arms to rise. Shaken at the strange words spoken by Best—and by those eyes—she turned to walk the hallway back up to the lobby and to her car. She would not stay for the concert or the after-concert interview with Watermark and Mr. Robert Best. She was done with this interview.

Bentley remembered what Best had said earlier. *The world is changing! Wait for it.* Best is definitely weird.

Chapter 10

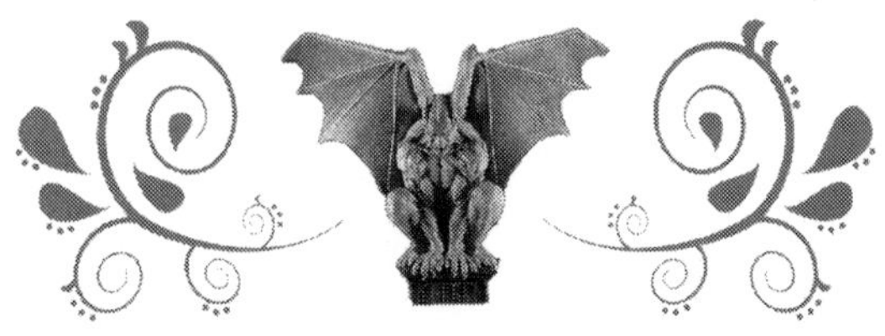

Visibly shaken from his encounter with the man on the plane, Thomas gathered himself together and made his way up the gangway from the plane into the terminal of Fiumicino Airport. Looking for a restroom, he found one just a few yards to the left as he exited the gangway into the terminal. Emptying his bladder into the urinal, he leaned his forehead into the wall and closed his eyes. Immediately Thomas could see the flash of the crimson red eyes of the stranger in his mind, causing him to open his eyes and straighten up, when he realized he had finished urinating for some time already. Zipping up his blue jeans, he turned to leave, noticing a lineup of people behind him waiting to use the restroom after a long flight, who were not impressed with Thomas's daydreaming.

He made his way to the baggage claim area in the massive Fiumicino Airport. He found himself searching the faces, amid the sea of people coming and going, trying to glimpse the man from the plane who confronted him. Was I dreaming that his eyes had actually turned a bright red, thought Thomas? He knew me and he knew why I was being summoned by the Vatican. He must have a beef with the Vatican and was privy somehow to the information that awaited Thomas. That is impossible, he thought. The Vatican is extremely secretive about its internal workings, and unless you have the proper security clearance and have been specifically invited by the Vatican, no one knows what goes on there. Why do they want me? I have not even conducted a mass on my own yet. This is crazy.

Seeing his luggage drop on the carousel, he made a move to reach down and pick it up before it passed him by and did another 360-degree rotation around the carousel again. There were just too many people in this airport to maneuver. As he bent down to snatch his bag amongst a pile of others dropping down the chute, it was suddenly grabbed by a hand that came out of nowhere. The hand with an expensive wristwatch pulled his bag away. Glancing up to see who had grabbed his bag by mistake, Thomas froze.

All of the passengers crowding around the carousel became a blur to Thomas. Looking into the fiery red eyes of the stranger from the plane who called himself Robert Best, he barely heard his voice.

"Father O'Sullivan, please let me be of help. I got your bag. If you don't move fast in this airport you won't see your bag again, it's likely to get snatched up by some weary passenger thinking it's theirs, and then what do you do?"

Struggling to maintain his composure, Thomas shot back at this stranger: "Who are you?! How do you know who I am and what I'm doing here?!"

Placing Thomas's bag in front of him, his eyes a normal pale blue, Best looked directly at him and said, "I hope you have a pleasant stay in Rome, Father. It is a beautiful city and hopefully your bosses will let you get out and enjoy the wonderful sites this country has to offer."

With that he turned and walked away, leaving Thomas frozen in place, staring after him, unable to move. Just as he was about to disappear into the sea of people, Best turned back towards Thomas, his eyes again glowing that deep crimson red, sending deep chills down Thomas spine. With a voice that sounded like pure evil, Best continued, "I am sorry to hear about Father O'Malley. He was a good man and I know you loved him. What a shame." Then just like that he was gone.

Shaking badly, Thomas thought he would be sick. Dropping

to one knee while hanging on to his suitcase he fought back the need to wretch and sucked in gasps of air, trying to make sense of what just happened. *Sorry to hear about Father O'Malley? What has happened to Father O'Malley, wondered Thomas, and how the hell would this Best know anything about Father O'Malley?* His mind suddenly was drawn to another voice calling out to him.

"Father O'Sullivan, are you all right? Father, are you okay?" Thomas looked up to see a young man not much older than he was, in clerical clothing, with a concerned look on his face.

Fighting the waves of nausea washing over him, taking a second to gather himself, he replied, "How did you know who I am?" while wondering to himself if everyone in this airport knew everything about him.

"I am from the Vatican and have been sent specifically to pick you up. I assume you would know that someone from the Vatican would be here to pick you up. I am Father Kevin Zorn," the young man said, extending his hand to Thomas.

Thomas looked up at the young man, thinking he was far too young to be a priest.

"You are American. You are also young like me. Is the Holy City injecting youth to liven up the place?" commented Thomas half-heartedly as he took Father Zorn's hand and lifted himself up.

"Yes I am. South Dakota, to be exact. You seem quite upset, Father O'Sullivan. Did you have a rough flight?"

Thomas reached down to slap the dust off the knees of his trousers.

"Not exactly, Father Zorn, but I wish that's all it was. Let's just say I have met some interesting people since my plane landed in Rome," muttered Thomas, not wanting to talk anymore about his recent experience. Best's comment about Father O'Malley was very weird indeed. He would call Father O'Malley when he got to wherever he was going with Father Zorn.

"If you have all your bags, Father O'Sullivan, we can head right out this exit, as the Vatican shuttle is waiting," Father Zorn stated, pointing to the nearest exit doors.

"Okay, sounds good Father, I have no idea why I'm here, but I'm looking forward to my visit. If it's okay with you may I just call you Kevin, and you call me Thomas?"

"Yes, we can do that," smiled Kevin, "But we must use our formal names when we are at the Vatican at all times. Vatican City is many centuries old, and its practice of tradition will never change, I'm afraid," he added..

Climbing into the back seat of the Vatican "shuttle," Thomas, who'd been expecting a bus, instead was surprised to discover it was a full stretch limo.

"Relax, Thomas, and enjoy the ride. It will take us about thirty minutes to get to the Vatican. Ask any question along the way and I will be glad to answer them. I have been assigned to the Vatican now for about three months, so I am quite acquainted with the city. I must admit you are the first Irish cleric I've met. The Irish accent is very pleasant and very popular in the United States."

"Thank you. I always think we sound like we are speaking gibberish. By the way, while we drive you will have to explain to me why the people of South Dakota would carve their President's faces into the side of a mountain. In Ireland we typically like to forget who our leaders were, not remember them so completely as to make mountains out of their images," laughed Thomas.

The next thirty minutes passed with Kevin explaining the sights of Rome, while the limo weaved in and out of traffic. Arriving at the Vatican security gates, Thomas produced his letter from the Vatican. After careful inspection the security guard handed the letter back through the window to Thomas, motioning the driver to continue. They drove on through the gates, eventually pulling up into a parking stall in a large parking lot. The Vatican was enormous, like a large university campus, thought Thomas. Anxious to find out what his destiny was here at the Vatican and his reason for being summoned, Thomas followed Kevin through a series of hallways. Eventually they stopped and entered an office marked "Administration." The

Administration office of the Vatican was huge, filled with smaller offices and a secretarial staff busy answering phones, moving about, using the photocopying machines among other things.

"Father Zorn, before we meet my superiors would you be so kind to find me a phone to use? I need to call Father O'Malley in Ireland. I made a promise to him that I would call him the second I landed in Rome to let him know that I am okay and I have arrived," asked Thomas.

"Certainly, Father O'Sullivan. Why don't you come and sit in Father Sescoloni's office and use his phone? He is attending to other matters and will not be in his office at all today."

Closing the door behind him, Thomas dialed the overseas operator and was connected to Father O'Malley's office at the rectory in his parish at Church of the Immaculate Conception & St. Patrick back home in Bandon, Ireland. The phone just rang through with no one picking up. That was unusual, he thought. There was always someone in the church during the early evening hours who would have picked up the phone. Thomas began to worry now about Father O'Malley and the words uttered by Robert Best, "*I am sorry to hear about Father O'Malley. He was a good man and I know you loved him. What a shame.*" Giving up on the phone for the time being, Thomas decided he would try again later, after his meeting with his superiors.

Coming out of Father Sescoloni's office, Thomas was troubled.

"Everything okay, Father O'Sullivan? You look upset once again. Is there anything I can do?" asked Father Zorn.

"No, nothing, Father Zorn, but thank you. I was unable to reach Father O'Malley so I'm just a little worried, that's all. I'll try later on after our meeting. His health is failing, so I just wanted to make sure he is okay."

Thomas's instructions in his letter stated he was to report immediately to Father Rudy Zacharias upon his arrival at the Palace of the Holy City in the Vatican, at the Congregation for the Doctrine of the Faith. This office, commonly referred to as CDF, is the oldest of the nine congregations of the Roman

Curia. The CDF is responsible, in a nutshell, for maintaining the integrity of Catholic doctrine.

Father Zorn notified one of the secretarial staff that Fathers Zorn and O'Sullivan were ready to see Father Zacharias. The two of them had a seat in the large waiting area, which was adorned with large portraits of the previous Popes who had sat at the head of the largest Church in the world. Front and center was the current Pope, Paul VI. Thomas immediately found himself drawn to the image of Paul VI. He was an incredible leader for the Church, thought Thomas, and his leadership and love for people was felt profoundly by all clergy throughout the world. In Ireland he was especially revered by the people, in a country that was in a state of perpetual ferment, and in conflict with its protestant neighbors to the north.

A middle-aged lady approached Thomas and Kevin from one of the many hallways that branched off from the main lobby where they were waiting, and asked them to follow her, as Father Zacharias was ready to see them. They followed her down a long hallway that held one office after another, with name plates adorning each door with the name of the priest and his title. They finally approached a door towards the end of the hall where the secretary stopped and knocked on the door. Not even waiting for a reply, she opened the door and announced to whoever was inside that Fathers Zorn and Father O'Sullivan were here.

The secretary stepped back into the hallway and motioned for them to enter.

They walked into a very spacious office, complete with a gigantic mahogany desk, and bookshelves lining the walls. A large portrait of Pope Paul VI dominated the wall directly behind Father Zacharias desk. Off to the left was a conference table and chairs for eight people. Four of those chairs were occupied with priests. A fifth priest whom Thomas assumed was Father Zacharias, standing behind a chair at the head of the table, approached them with his hand extended, a broad smile adorning his face.

"Father O'Sullivan, I am so glad to meet you. I am Father

Zacharias. Thank you for coming, please have a seat at the table. Thank you, Father Zorn, for taking good care of Father O'Sullivan," gestured Father Zacharias as he shook Thomas's hand.

"Father Zorn, you know everyone at the table, so Father O'Sullivan, let me introduce you to Father Giroux, Father Penterin and Father Walchuk. All of us here, including Father Zorn, make up the committee tasked by our Holiness with a very important project that the Vatican takes very seriously. Please sit down and we will discuss in detail why you have been summoned to Rome. May I get you anything to drink, Father? Some water, tea or coffee maybe?" asked Father Zacharias.

The feeling of dread had crept back into the pit of Thomas's stomach while he was listening to Father Zacharias introduce himself and the others in the room. The combination of not knowing what had happened to Father O'Malley and the news he had been summoned to Rome for an important project authorized by the Pope himself left him feeling more than a little unnerved.

"I am fine for now, thank you, Father. I must admit I am quite anxious as to why I was brought here. No sooner had I completed my training with Father O'Malley and taken my vows than I found myself on a plane to Rome," stated Thomas, noticing the change in expression in Father Zacharias face when Father O'Malley's name was mentioned.

"Is something the matter, Father?" asked Thomas, looking at Father Zacharias.

"It's Father O'Malley. I am sorry to have to tell you that he passed away in a tragic accident this morning. We just found out ourselves less than an hour ago. I am very sorry to have to tell you this, Father O'Sullivan. I know you were very close to him."

Thomas was stunned. It confirmed what Best at the airport had said to him. *How did Best know that?* Thomas was in shock.

He felt weak and knew he would be nauseous. He didn't even hear Father Zacharias speak.

"I think it would be best if we allowed Father O'Sullivan to take the rest of the day off to gather himself and recover from his trip. We will resume our discussions in the morning. Father Zorn, will you please escort Father O'Sullivan back to Administration for his room assignment. Before you do let's take a moment and say a prayer for Father O'Malley."

Chapter 11

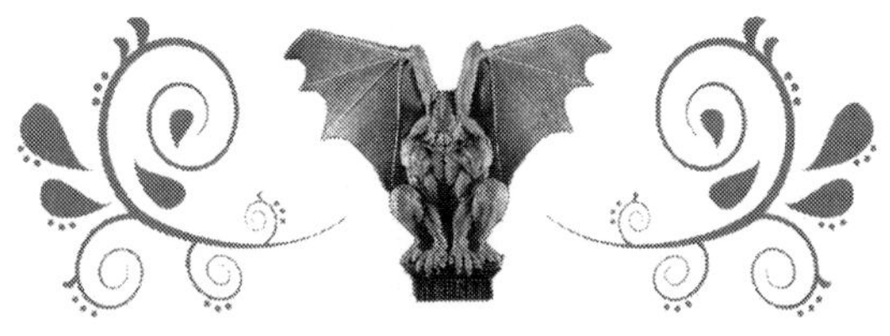

Thomas rested in his assigned room after awakening from a brief nap. He was still numb from the news of Father O'Malley. Earlier he had reached church staff back in Bandon, and they described a terrible accident that had occurred early in the morning after Father O'Malley had just brewed his morning tea as he did every morning, consulting his daily agenda book while sitting at the kitchen table. He had decided to go down to the church basement to retrieve something and had slipped and fallen down the stairs. His neck was broken and he was killed instantly. Sister Jennings heard the crash and rushed down to his quarters, where she discovered Father O'Malley lying awkwardly at the bottom of the stairs. His tea was still hot in the cup, sitting on the table as if waiting for his return.

Thomas's thoughts were put on hold as there was a knock on his room door. He opened his door to find Father Zorn standing in the hallway. "Father Zorn, good to see you again. Please come in and sit."

Placing his hand on Thomas's shoulder in a reassuring manner, Kevin replied, "Actually, I was just on my way down to the cafeteria to have some dinner. Have you eaten? Would you like to join me?"

The thought of food brightened Thomas's mood immensely.

"Sounds great, Kevin, I'm starved. Let me grab my sweater."

They had just sat down to a hearty meal of roast chicken and potatoes in the Vatican main cafeteria when Kevin commented, “Terrible news, Thomas, about Father O’Malley. It must have been quite a shock to hear that so soon after your arrival.”

Thomas was growing fond of Kevin and enjoyed having conversations with him. They had lots in common and it was comforting knowing he’d have a friend during his stay here.

“It certainly was a shock. I know he had been in failing health for some time, but to have him pass in such a freak accident is hard to fathom. I want to share something with you, Father, that happened to me just prior to you picking me up at the airport that I’m finding hard to understand.”

With that, Thomas proceeded to explain the strange events of Robert Best introducing himself on the plane and then corning him in the gangway and telling Thomas that he knew the reason for his visit to the Vatican. He explained the red crimson eyes to Kevin and how they chilled him to the core. When he told Kevin of Best approaching him again at the luggage carousel, and saying how sorry he was over the death of Father O’Malley, Father Zorn to turned white as a sheet.

“Thomas, are you sure you have never met this man before? For Best to know about Father O’Malley’s death is bizarre. Father O’Malley died at approx 7:30 a.m., literally while you and Best were still in the air. He would have to have received a phone call right when he landed.”

Thomas was losing his appetite as he pondered the strange set of events with Best. Leaning back in his cafeteria chair, he looked intently at Kevin as he added to what his companion had just said.

“You also have to consider that the timeline between when he was reported dead by the paramedics and our landing is so tight for Best to have received a call. This is downright spooky, Kevin,” Thomas stated out loud.

Pushing his half-filled plate away, Kevin leaned in closer to the table and lowered his voice as he spoke.

“We must speak to Father Zacharias about this Robert Best in the morning. The Vatican police can do some background checks on this guy. He threatened you, Thomas. There has to be a reason he's doing this and they will find out. If he is in Rome they will find him and question him."

Something inside Thomas was telling him that Best would not be found, that he would disappear like a ghost—a ghost whose purpose in confronting him Thomas still did not understand.

Later that evening Thomas prepared for bed, first by going through his ritual of deep prayer. He prayed to God for safekeeping of Father O'Malley as he now joined his Father in Heaven. Thomas also prayed to God for understanding and His love and protection for his encounters with Best. "Heavenly Father, Bless Thee O Lord, give me eyesight for I am blind about what has been happening. Give me the strength and the courage to see what is in front of me. I pray this in your holy name and your son Jesus Christ. Amen."

Thomas awoke the next morning at 5:30 a.m. feeling foggy from a restless stream of images of Best and those nasty red eyes that had robbed him of a good night's sleep. He had promised Kevin he would meet him at 7:00 a.m. in the cafeteria for breakfast before they were to meet with Father Zacharias at 8:00 a.m. Preparing his clerical wardrobe for the day, he reflected once again on the previous day's events. *Who was this Robert Best? How did he know me and my reason for coming to Rome and the Vatican? Could he somehow be connected to Father O'Malley's accident?*

Breakfast was relatively quiet, he and Kevin not saying much. After finishing breakfast they made their way back to meet Father Zacharias for 8:00 a.m. Entering the office of Father Zacharias, Thomas noticed the other priests from yesterday were already sitting at the conference table, waiting for him and Kevin. Father Zacharias instantly brightened the room with his infectious warmth and caring smile.

"Good morning, Father O'Sullivan and Father Zorn. I hope, Father O'Sullivan, under the circumstances, that you were able to get some rest last night?" asked Father Zacharias.

"Some, Father, but it was a restless night. Hopefully God's

grace and the copious amounts of coffee this morning with Father Zorn will get me through the day," smiled Thomas, shaking everyone's hands.

Motioning for everyone to come to the table, Father Zacharias began.

"We have lots to discuss, Father O'Sullivan, about why you were brought here in the first place, and I know you will have lots of questions for us afterwards, so let's get started, shall we?" Thomas noticed that today there was an overhead projector setup with a screen.

"Father O'Sullivan, what I am about to share with you is known only to a select few outside the offices of the Prefect of the Congregation for the Doctrine of the Faith. The people sitting at this table, including yourself, have been tasked with a project by the Holy Office, one that His Eminence is discreetly placing great importance on."

"Let me get right to the point. As you are well aware, Father O'Sullivan, of the Bible's views on the End of Times, including the its description of the return of our King Jesus Christ in the Rapture and his reign on Earth with his believers for a thousand years, I do not need to school you on the Bible's teachings on this, but I do want you to know what the Church's stances on these teachings are."

Thomas was dumbfounded. He was brought all the way to Rome away from his homeland and his Church to talk about the Bible's view on the End of Times? *Doesn't the Catholic Church have more pressing things to do than to worry about something they cannot control?*

Father Zacharias continued: "It is the belief of the Catholic Church and the belief of the top leaders of the Christian faith from around the world that the Rapture is nearly upon us. Likely in our generation, Father O'Sullivan, or the next generation at the latest."

Thomas interrupted Father Zacharias, raising some eyebrows among the others sitting around the table.

"Excuse my ignorance on this subject Father, but this is a

subject that is not new. It's in the Bible in black and white. We know it will happen. It is at the core of our belief, But having said that, is it something we need to be discussing here and now?"

Father Zacharias continued as if he had expected this type of reaction from Thomas.

"Very much, Father O'Sullivan. As I said, the Church, including His Eminence, believes the time is very near, and so we need to prepare. Let me show you a presentation that will help clarify why we believe the time might be imminent."

Father Zacharias nodded at Father Penterin to begin. Father Penterin stood and approached the overhead projector and turned it on. Father Zorn jumped up and switched off the room lights. With the room cloaked in darkness, the light from the projector was concentrated but intense, casting shadows throughout the room. Father Penterin stood in front of the projector, partially blocking the light, causing a halo effect around him. He put the first overhead slide on the projector. What appeared on the screen was a graphic picture portraying hundreds of decaying bodies in a pile in Istanbul, Turkey, as part of the 1918 worldwide flu pandemic that killed over fifty million people. The next slide showed a picture of thousands of people clamoring for food being distributed by the Soviet government in the Ukrainian famine of 1932 that killed over five million people. Another slide showed the great flood in China in 1931 that killed over 3.7 million people. More recent natural disasters included the devastating hurricanes that ravaged Bangladesh, killing close to half a million people, and the horrific drought the last four years in India that has killed over 1.5 million people. Father Penterin asked Father Zorn to turn on the lights and then he turned off the projector. Father Zacharias stood.

"Throughout the twentieth century the world has been rocked with natural disasters of tremendous magnitude. The Church believes that the size of these natural disasters and the sheer amount of lives taken during the century has been unprecedented in recorded history. The Church also believes that these are direct signs that God is increasingly unhappy with mankind and has unleashed an ever-increasing number of natural disasters as a warning that the upcoming Judgment Day is soon upon us as described in Revelations."

Father Zacharias continued, "Judgment Day is imminent. The signs are clear, Father O'Sullivan. The Church believes that God will not unleash Judgment Day until every man, woman and child on this earth has had the opportunity to be exposed to the teachings of Jesus Christ and to accept Jesus as their personal savior. Father Penterin, if you would," motioning to Father Penterin.

Father Zorn once again turned off the lights and Father Penterin turned the projector back on. The next slide was a graph. The graph depicted a timeline starting in 1900 at the bottom left to the present day, 1981, at the far right. On the left side of the graph, starting at the bottom and going straight up, was a line representing the world's population in millions. Along the bottom was the percentage of the population that had been exposed to the teachings of Jesus Christ and the opportunity to accept Jesus Christ as their personal savior.

Father Zacharias made his way around the table until he was standing opposite Thomas, looking at him directly as he spoke.

"You can see from this graph, Father, how far we and other Christian faiths have come in spreading Christianity around the world. The Church believes that during the next thirty to fifty years all peoples from all corners of the world will have been exposed to Jesus. It is at this time, the Church believes, that the Judgment Day will come and the Rapture will begin. Can we have the lights back on, please?"

Thomas could not help but think of the chilling words Best had spoken to him as they were departing the plane and walking up the gangway leading into the terminal. "I know why you are here in Rome and what your mission is at the Vatican. I also know that we will meet again someday," Best had stated. *Is Best really the Devil, who had appeared to warn Thomas?*

Deep in thought, he was brought back to reality when a kick

to his shin underneath the table from Father Zorn brought him back to attention.

"Father O'Sullivan, you seem somewhat distracted. Did you want to take a break?" asked Father Zacharias.

Father Zacharias was looking at him and talking, but Thomas could not hear him. All he could hear were the words spoken to him by Best in the gangway. Glancing over at Kevin, noticing the grimace on his face, he finally found his way out of the fog he was in. He looked at Father Zacharias. "I am sorry, Father; I was completely lost in thought. Did you say something to me?"

"Glad to have you back, Father. I said, why don't we take a short break for fifteen minutes and then we will resume our discussions."

Making his way to the restroom, Thomas was wondering what had happened to him during the last forty-eight hours. He had gone from completing his deacon internship with Father O'Malley, taking his vows and then being whisked off to the Vatican in Rome, only to be confronted by a very strange man, then learn upon landing that Father O'Malley had died tragically just after he had left for the airport. *What is happening to him?*

As he returned a few minutes later to Father Zacharias's office, he bumped into Father Zorn on his way in. Whispering so the others could not hear, Kevin said to him, "I know this has been a lot thrown at you, Thomas, in the last few days. It was for me, too, when I was summoned here for the same reasons you were. Your purpose for being here will be explained to you shortly. Hang in there, my friend. You will need to explain to Father Zacharias, and the rest of the committee, your encounter with Best."

Looking at Kevin incredulously, Thomas asked, "Do you think Best really is related to why I am here?"

"Yes, I do. There is no other explanation. Father Zacharias needs to be aware of this encounter. Let him finish explaining why you are here, and then you can tell him of your experience. Remember, Thomas, you are here for a reason. God is calling out to you."

Returning to the table, Father Zacharias welcomed everyone back and said a short prayer, asking God for His blessing for Father O'Malley and for the strength and courage for Father O'Sullivan to endure.

"Father O'Sullivan, do you have any questions for me or anyone else at this table before we continue?" asked Father Zacharias.

"I do, Father. But please continue. I will present my questions and any concerns after I have a complete understanding of what the Church is asking of me."

"Fair enough, Father. Let's continue with Father Penterin's presentation."

The lights dimmed again, and Father Penterin continued with the slides outlining more disasters, with Father Zacharias explaining how it related to the Church's beliefs about Judgment Day. The slides also articulated the Church's belief that the Antichrist was also busy during this time preparing for his reign on earth. They spoke of the Devil's failure in 400 A.D. to destroy mankind, as told in ancient church books, thwarted by the bravery and heroics of seven soldiers empowered by God's grace to defeat Satan once and for all. And that his failure then fuelled his ultimate return and victory now, as revealed in Revelations. Thomas found himself fascinated by the timeline of events that were captured on the slideshow and how the disasters seemed to be increasing in recent years, and how terrifyingly real was the staggering loss of human lives in these cataclysmic events. After about two hours of these discussions, Father Zacharias called for a break to eat some lunch.

They sat down at a table away from others in the cafeteria. Sensing that Kevin was being purposely quiet in order to invite questions, Thomas obliged.

"Kevin, why is it that you were brought here?"

Taking a moment to finish the mouthful of food he was working on, Kevin wiped his mouth with his napkin, and then looked at Thomas intently before speaking.

"I was summoned to the Vatican six months ago, Thomas. This is my third meeting with this committee. My first time here I had as many questions as you, maybe more. I found it strange that the Church would concern themselves with an event they could neither predict nor control. I soon came to realize how enormous Judgment Day could be for the people of this world, and the chaos that will exist. Leadership and direction amongst the faithful will be needed, Thomas. That is what this committee is all about. We need to prepare the Christian people of this world for what is coming. It may never happen in our lifetime, Thomas, nor for many more to come, but it will happen. The Church believes it will happen soon, and I believe that too."

They finished their lunch with more talk of the committee, and soon they returned to Father Zacharias's office. Thomas noticed everyone was in their seats and waiting. *Do they ever take a break*, he thought?

Father Giroux, who to this point had said very little, now spoke.

"Father O'Sullivan, the Church believes, as stated by Father Zacharias earlier, that the Judgment Day is near. His Eminence, Pope Paul VI, through the Prefect of the Congregation for the Doctrine of the Faith, has ordered that a task force be put together to study and prepare for the Judgment Day, Rapture and Tribulation as stated in the Gospel of Matthew and the Book of Revelations. With your cooperation, Father O'Sullivan, the people in this room now represent that task force. The task force has been given a name that will be known only by the people in this room, His Eminence and the Prefect. The name of the task force is "Paratus" which is Latin for "Preparation."

Thomas addressed Father Giroux directly. "Then let me ask the obvious question. Why have I been chosen? Surely there are hundreds, if not thousands, of clergy from around the world more experienced and qualified than myself?"

Father Zacharias answered, "Father Giroux and Father Walchuk were chosen because of their decades of combined research into and study of the Book of Revelations on behalf of the Church. I have been assigned to oversee the task force and to report back to the Prefect our progress and our theories. The task force chose Father Zorn and you, Father O'Sullivan, because of your educational background, your respective geographical locations, being the United States and Europe, in particular the U.K. Also important to this committee is your youth. This task force will be in existence for decades, so there will come a time when you will be handed the leadership of Paratus. There is no completion date to our work. We don't know what to expect, as you can well imagine, but preparation is our goal. Father Walchuk, if you please."

Thomas turned his attention to Father Walchuk.

"Father O'Sullivan, you will spend the next six months here at the Vatican with the rest of us as part of Paratus. We will study the Book of Revelations, break it down, and interpret as best we can its true message—if that is even possible—about mankind's End of Times. We will accept and adopt a common theory as to how it will take place and use that as a blueprint for the Church to prepare for the likely events that will accompany the Judgment Day. If these events occur during our generation, we will be the ones to lead and guide our people of faith from around the world as well as humanly possible. If our Lord feels it is not time then we will of course have prepared the next committee to take over Paratus. We will pass this blueprint, our knowledge and findings to our replacements and them to their replacements, if that is so," outlined Father Walchuk.

Father Zacharias continued, "In six months from now, with the work on Paratus completed, you will go back to Ireland to your Church and serve the Lord as you were so called to in the first place. I and/or my replacement will call Paratus back together here at the Vatican every six months, or as deemed necessary, to continue our study of this potential event. The Catholic Church will continue to convert as many people from around the world to Jesus Christ along with the other Christian faiths. Satan will be sadly disappointed, when after the Tribulation, there is no one left on this earth for his pleasure."

After wrapping up the discussion over the next few hours, questions and concerns from Thomas and the others were discussed and answered. Father Zacharias called the meeting to a close, telling everyone to report to the task force to begin their work, starting after the weekend mass services, on Monday morning in a special room that had been designated for Paratus.

Thomas glanced around the room, watching the weary clerics gather their notes and prepare to leave. He knew he must share the events of the encounter with Best with the committee.

Glancing at Father Zorn, he said, "Before we break away, Father Zacharias, I do need to share with everyone an encounter with a stranger I experienced while making my way here."

He spent the next thirty minutes explaining his encounter with Best on the plane and then again in the gangway. Hearing Best's chilling words to Thomas caused everyone in the room to look at each other with alarm, but when Thomas told them of the third encounter with Best at the baggage carousel, and his statement regarding Father O'Malley, Father Giroux gasped.

Father Zacharias turned to Thomas and said, "It could very well be this Best was an intuitive person in determining that you were a priest making his way to the Vatican for a special purpose. But his statement to you in the gangway and again at the luggage carousel points to something more. We are under attack by Satan, make no mistake, gentlemen. He is a liar and a deceiver. He is also very aware that Judgment Day is near, and will do whatever it takes to stop the flow of Christianity as this day nears. Prepare yourselves, my brothers, and pray often to Our Father for protection. We will need it."

Chapter 12

Lying beside his beautiful wife of four years, Dalton Lockwood was deciding whether or not to wake her for some early morning lovemaking. It was Saturday morning; maybe he'd better just let her sleep. *She is so damn gorgeous*, thought Dalton. He was incredibly fortunate to have Ann as his wife. She had been beautiful, rich, and one of the nicest people you could ever meet when Dalton asked her to dance at a trendy night club near her parents' mansion in Belgravia, in the heart of London. That was almost eight years ago. Time flies when you are crazily, madly in love as Dalton was with Ann.

Her family's money had meant nothing to Dalton when he asked her to marry him, as he also came from a wealthy family. Just not as wealthy as Ann's. Her family was part of London's super rich. Ann's father Sherman Oakley headed Oakley Steel, a family-run firm with plants all over Europe. In fact, Oakley Steel was the largest producer of steel in all of Europe. Sherman's grandfather, Theodore Oakley, or "Teddy," as he was known, started the firm and grew it into an empire during the first half of the twentieth century by satisfying the demand for steel generated by the two world wars. Sherman's father, Lexington "Lex" Oakley, when he took it over from Teddy, expanded the family business even further by building foundries in France and Spain along with smaller foundries throughout the United Kingdom, including Northern Ireland and Scotland.

It was Sherman who made the boldest moves. When worldwide demand for steel fell during the recessions in the 1980s and 1990s and prices for raw steel plummeted, Sherman expanded even more. He leveraged the entire empire and borrowed heavily from the European banks, expanding into previously impenetrable Russia, the Middle East and South Africa. He also bought 40 percent of the shares in America Steel of Pittsburgh, the third largest steel producer in the United States. Ann would not enter into the family business, opting to leave that to her four brothers. Instead Ann focused on her studies and overseeing the Oakley charitable foundations, and there were many.

Graduating with a Masters in Education from Oxford, Ann had intended to become a teacher but found working with the various large charities more rewarding. Pushing her father to give more to children's causes around the world, she established the Oakley Foundation and, together with her father, the British government, the City of London and the Royal Family, built the largest and most advanced Sick Children's Hospital in the world. Ann was extremely proud of her family's contribution and she worked countless hours pushing all levels of government to get it built. The Oakley contribution of one billion dollars was at the time the largest private charitable donation in history, a staggering amount that shocked the world. The hospital took over three years to build, but upon its completion in 1995, Londoners realized how ground-breaking it was and embraced the Oakley's as if they were the Royal Family. The state-of-the-art hospital would be able to treat some of the sickest children in the world.

As the public face of the Oakley Foundation, Ann was recognized and revered everywhere she went. She reminded the people of London of their beloved Princess Diana. Her kindness and patience with those of all classes endeared her to the everyday common people as no other person had been. Her marriage to Dalton, the heir to the Lockwood Furniture business, one of the largest manufactures of office furniture in all of Europe, was well received by the public and both families. They were insanely in love with each other and everyone knew it and embraced it.

It was 8:30 a.m., and Dalton decided to let Ann sleep, so he quietly slipped out of bed. As he made his way through their bedroom to the shower he heard Ann stir and then say, "Excuse me. Where do you think you're going? Get back here, you. It's Saturday morning and you decided to let me sleep. I would give up a week's sleep, baby, just to make love to you on a Saturday morning."

"Done!" beamed Dalton as he climbed back into bed.

After an intense hour of passionate lovemaking, Dalton, sweaty and exhausted and extremely satisfied, climbed out of bed and headed for the shower after giving Ann one last passionate kiss. She leaves nothing to chance in bed, giving herself to me in every way, Dalton thought, just as she does in the real world. A true giver in every sense of the word. Dalton loved her so much that he would do anything for her.

****

Sitting up in bed, resting against some big soft pillows, Ann also felt very satisfied. Saturday mornings, if they could swing it with their schedules, were very intense, with Dalton refusing to stop until she had climaxed multiple times. Listening to Dalton in the shower attempting to sing the Beatles classic "Come Together" made her laugh. She was the luckiest woman in the world. Dalton was an extremely handsome man, super sexy, and could have had any woman he wanted, but he'd chosen her. He loved her and she knew it, she felt it. That love for her and complete devotion and commitment made her feel so safe and secure, something her money could never give her. Getting out of bed to retrieve her housecoat, she slipped downstairs to put the coffee on before Dalton got out of the shower. She wanted Dalton to enjoy the aroma of fresh coffee being brewed wafting through their spacious flat. Making her way to the kitchen, she stopped dead in her tracks halfway down the stairs.

Staring up at her from the bottom of the stairs was a monster sent straight from the depths of Hell. Stumbling backwards onto the stairs, unable to scream, Ann reached out to grab the rail and steady herself as she woke up from her sleepwalking. Because that was all this was. She shut her eyes in disbelief. She had to be sleeping. Opening her eyes again, she was able to scream this time.

Moving up the stairs as if it was floating, this creature, half human and half bat, with eyes that burned a bright crimson red, had an oversized head with a mouth full of razor-sharp fangs that looked like they could rip her apart. It had wings that were wrapped around it as it ascended up the stairs towards her. Frozen with fear, she could not move as this monster came closer. She also realized that the entire home was cloaked in darkness, and it was freezing cold, as she could see the steam from her heavy breathing. The cold sweat forming on her face and chest was also cold. *What is going on!? Where did this thing come from and what is it doing here in her home!?*

The creature was almost upon her, and Ann, still frozen in fear and unable to move, closed her eyes with the knowledge that just a minute ago she was about to make a pot of coffee, and now she was going to be viciously ripped apart by some hideous creature from Hell. Dalton would come out from the shower and see his wife's body splattered all over the house. This beast, now just a few feet away from Ann, stopped, looked down at her with those burning red eyes and screamed, in a voice that only could have come from Hell. "Your seed ends now! Your lineage to the coward warrior Davit will end right here!"

Unable to comprehend what this monster was saying, she was able to move, finally, and began to push herself backwards, away from this beast and up the stairs, where she could make a run for her bedroom. She would alert Dalton and the two of them could figure out a way to escape this nightmare. Suddenly the creature stood up to its full height of at least ten feet, and spread its wings. The sound of its wings opening with such suddenness was like cloth being yanked violently from its bolt. A rush of cold air blew across her face, then chilled her to the bone as the sweat on her body absorbed it. The beast's hideous and ugly body was a mass of muscles, scales and large, protruding veins. To her utter horror she saw that this beast had a penis, fully erect, and the thoughts that entered Ann's frantic mind were incomprehensible. *This thing is going to rape her!* Tilting its head back on its deformed shoulders, its tongue rolling out of its mouth, licking its fangs, it began to scream again in a voice she did not recognize, "Nex of Davit est super mihi. ortus of meus sperma mos attero mankind forever!!" (The death of Davit is upon me! The birth of my seed will destroy mankind forever!)

The deafening roar as it screamed snapped Ann again out of her frozen state. She turned and with a newfound strength, began to run up the stairs and away from this nightmare. As she reached the top of the stairs she glimpsed Dalton walking out into the hallway from their bedroom, a towel around his waist, a look of shock on his face as he stared out at the horror show that had invaded his home. Suddenly Ann felt a white-hot, searing pain in the right side of her rib cage. She looked down to see the claws of this beast clamped down on her side. Pulling her back down the stairs towards it, the beast was now roaring like a pack of crazed lions. As it flipped her onto her back on the stairs, she now stared straight into the eyes of Lucifer himself, thought Ann, as she fought to get away from its grip. Positioning itself like an animal about to rut, the beast began to lean into her. The fear pulsating worse than the pain in her side, she struggled to maintain her sanity and remain conscious.

Suddenly she heard a loud bang. Then another loud bang and then several more loud bangs. Looking up, she saw that the beast had recoiled backwards against the railing, and was injured. Not sure what was happening, she then heard a loud voice. It was Dalton. He yelled down to her from the top of the stairs, "Ann get up, come upstairs now! Hurry!"

Turning towards him as she ran up the stairs, she could see Dalton brandishing the 9 mm semi-automatic pistol they kept in their closet. The gun boomed again as Dalton unloaded another volley at the creature as it tried to right itself and come after Ann. The shots made the creature tumble in a massive heap down the stairs. Reaching the top of the stairs, Ann threw herself into Dalton's arms. Trembling and crying, she sobbed, "Dalton I am so scared! Why is this thing after us?! What is it?!"

"I don't know, Ann, and we don't have time to think about it. We just need to get out of here, now! Follow me. We'll escape through our bedroom window, onto the roof and down onto the rear terrace. We can jump down to the ground to safety from there and away from this thing—whatever the hell it is."

Turning to run down the hallway, Dalton grabbed her hand and they began to make their way to the bedroom. As they were about to make the turn into the bedroom they heard a sound almost like a large schooner unfurling its sails to capture a breeze that had made its way across the water. Too late, they realized that it was the creature, with its massive wing span flapping up over the railing to cut them off just in front of the bedroom. Its eyes burning deep red and glowing with pure hatred and madness, its raging voice booming, it screamed, "Let her go now or you will die!! I will tear you to shreds! Let her go!"

"Go fuck yourself, Batman!" yelled Dalton as he maneuvered Ann into the bedroom, then raised his pistol towards the beast to fire. Falling onto her back in the bedroom, Ann was barely able to see, almost like a blur, the claw of the beast darting out from underneath its folded wings as it perched on the railing about four feet away from Dalton. Its claw grabbed Dalton around his neck and flung him hard about twenty feet through the air. She could hear the sound of breaking glass as Dalton was thrown into the large oval mirror at the end of the hallway.

Jumping to her feet, Ann raced out of the bedroom, turning left, away from the creature and back towards the stairs, hoping to escape out the front door. She caught a glimpse of Dalton's twisted, contorted and bleeding unconscious body at the end of the hall, covered in broken glass. Not allowing that sight to slow her down, she sprinted for the stairs. Reaching the top of the stairs a few seconds later, she felt the now-familiar white-hot pain of the beast's claw as it dug into her shoulder and pulled her back onto the hallway floor. The excruciating pain surged through her shoulder, and she felt her will to run ebbing away as she thought of Dalton. She opened her eyes as she lay on her back, to see the creature standing in front of her on its enormous hind legs. It opened its gigantic black wings, screaming the gibberish language again, "Complectere mirum qui dominum suum mundum et absterget Deus sordes ab Davit semper. Ecce domini tui magnitudinem" (Embrace the wonder of your Master who will wipe clean the filth of Davit from you forever! Behold your Master's greatness!)

The fear of what was about to happen to her as she watched this creature from Hell maneuver its member towards her, was too much for her to bear, and thankfully darkness came upon her, as she found herself slipping into unconsciousness. Abruptly she was punched hard across the face by the huge claw of the beast; she heard the bones snap in her jaw and cheekbone. Now barely able to remain conscious, she heard the beast scream hoarsely, "You will not close your eyes to your Master who is about to give you a life that will change this world forever! Your destiny begins now!" When the beast entered her the pain was unbearable, and the realization she was actually being raped by this monster took the breath out of her, she was so terrified. The pain was so intense that she knew she was going to pass out, and hoped it would happen quickly. The crimson red eyes of the beast bore down on her, willing her to remain awake. Sensing the beast was about to disgorge itself inside her, she braced for what was about to happen. Lifting its grotesque bulbous monster head to the ceiling, it let out a primal scream so evil-sounding, it could only have been the scream of the Devil himself. She felt its seed being pumped into her. It was like a flame thrower spewing out of control inside of her. Now she knew why this beast had entered their home. It was here to rape her, as she had been chosen. Why, she didn't know, but she was chosen, she was sure of it, and that scared her even more.

Suddenly the chest of the beast opened up, the tip of a large shard of mirror glass protruding through. As the beast fell backwards off of her, she saw her beloved Dalton covered in blood, teetering on weak legs after just slicing his hands wide open as he had shoved the glass into the beast. Tears now burned to the surface of her eyes as she lay unable to move. Falling to his knees, Dalton leaned down on top of her and the two of them sobbed. Speaking through his tears, Dalton cried, "I am so sorry, Ann. I am so very sorry I let it do this to you. I should have been able to stop it. I'm sorry. Forgive me."

"Dalton! Dalton!" screamed Ann, but it was too late. The beast had recovered and now had picked up Dalton once again by his neck, and lifted him into the air. "You will die not knowing that your pathetic wife will give birth to your Master's child! Your memory will be replaced before your head hits this ground!" bellowed the creature. Then the beast squeezed its claws around Dalton's neck with incredible speed, and as if the claws were garden shears, it snipped Dalton's head cleanly off its shoulders. Dalton's head fell with a thud only inches from Ann's face, briefly giving her a vision of his face frozen in a state of fear. She knew that image would forever be seared into her memory, and she was glad for that, because she knew she would kill this beast someday. If it took her the rest of her life, she would avenge what had happened to her and Dalton today.

Flinging the rest of Dalton casually against the wall, the creature looked back at Ann with those menacing red eyes and spoke with a normal and very human voice, "You now carry a baby that you will spend the rest of your life caring for. You will protect it. That is your destiny. Death will come to you and everyone you love and care for if you do not protect and love this baby. Your family, your friends, the family of your husband and his friends. Do you understand?"

Not waiting for an answer, the beast turned and pulled its wings close to its body once again and moved down the stairs towards the door. As she forced her head to turn towards the front door, Ann saw a naked man, devoid of the beast's features, open the door and turn back towards her with those burning red crimson eyes, and say, “Do not forget what I just told you. Protect the baby or else.” The beast/man then turned back and walked through the open door, leaving the sunshine to pour through the darkness.

Ann did not want to embrace the sunshine, only the darkness, and she closed her eyes to welcome it.

Chapter 13

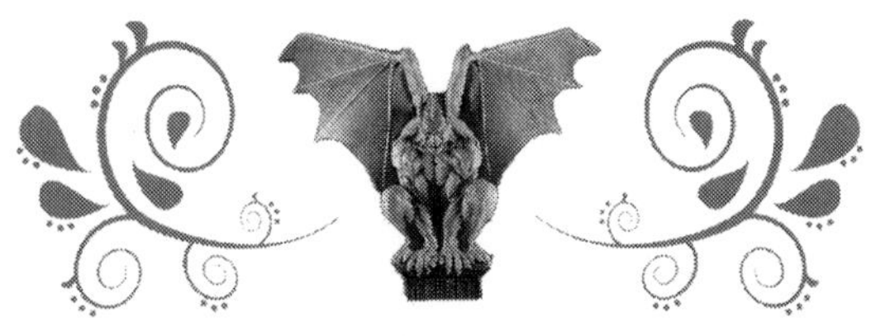

There are cowboys, and then there are guys who only dream of being a cowboy. There are wannabe cowboys, and then there is Bert Asker. If you were to look up "cowboy" in Webster's dictionary, you would see a picture of Bert Asker. He is the epitome of a genuine cowboy. He has the classic rugged good looks, a voice like Sam Elliot's, is a successful rancher and loves to live his life as a cowboy.

Bert Asker is a fourth-generation Asker farming the land his father, grandfather and great-grandfather farmed and ranched. Currently managing over 25,000 acres of ranchland forty miles northeast of Cheyenne, Wyoming, that included over 30,000 head of cattle, the fifty-nine-year-old Bert, aging but still tough as nails, loved every day the good Lord gave him to farm this land. With his son Brent ready to soon take over the business, Bert knew that ranching was in his family's blood like DNA.

Brent is as good a rancher as I am, thought Bert. He was very good, with great instincts, something you needed to have to make it in the cattle business. Competing with the feedlots was no walk in the park, and Brent understood what it took to raise good, healthy and fat Herefords. Having worked side by side with him almost every day since Brent had been around twelve years old, Bert loved his son dearly. They were father and son, but they were also best friends, with both of them committed to the ranch and their families. Ever since Brent's older brother

Byron had been killed on the way into town in the farm pickup by a drunk driver on his way home from drinking all night in the bars in Cheyenne, Bert was determined even if it killed him to hand the ranch to Brent intact, debt free and profitable. That was how his father had turned it over to him, and that was how he was going to do it with Brent. The banks had come close over the years to getting their piece of Asker Farms on more than one occasion when beef prices plummeted. Through some timely luck and sheer hard work, they'd made it through. The mad cow disease that threatened his herd and his livelihood had been the hardest thing to overcome. That had been sixteen years ago when Brent was just twelve years old.

Seeing Brent, just a scrawny little kid back then, work eighteen hours a day that summer, identifying and separating the healthy cattle from the sick ones, was an incredible revelation. With Bert spending most of his time in Cheyenne lobbying the Department of Agriculture not to take the drastic measure of destroying the entire herd to eliminate the threat of the disease, it was left to Brent and Byron to work the herd along with the hired ranch hands and employees. It was a nightmare that eventually cost Asker Farms 11,000 head of cattle, a loss that almost devastated the ranch. The State of Wyoming declared a state of emergency and successfully lobbied Washington for emergency funding to assist the ranchers to deal with the crisis. Without that aid Asker Farms would most certainly not have survived.

A year after the mad cow crisis, the Askers were dealt an even worse tragedy. After feeding her boys a wonderful and filling Sunday dinner after a relaxing day of church and the Twins game on TV, Betty-Ann, Bert's wife of twenty-two years, found a lump on her breast while bathing. The cancer was well advanced, having spread to the lymph nodes by the time it was discovered and within months had spread to her organs, including her brain. Betty-Ann passed away at the young age of forty-two, leaving a deeply saddened and devastated Bert a widower and single father of two teenage boys. Over the years, with the hours Bert spent working the ranch and looking after the needs of Byron and Brent, there had been no time in his life to start any new relationships even though there were many women in town who tried to win over his heart. The memory of Betty-Ann was enough to sustain Bert, and he focused all of his energies on the ranch and his boys.

When Byron was killed in the car accident seven years later, at the age of twenty-three, an even bigger piece of Bert died within him. He went after the drunk driver with a vengeance, pressing the police and the DA to press charges for vehicular manslaughter, charges that were rarely laid and even more rarely successfully prosecuted. He was relentless, and eventually charges were laid, but just before trial was to begin seven months later the perpetrator copped a plea and was sentenced to community service. Knowing the DA was not interested in looking bad in court and losing the case, Bert was furious over the plea bargain and physically confronted the District Attorney, resulting in assault charges being brought against him. It cost him a three-month prison term, leaving Brent, only nineteen years of age, to run the ranch on his own.

****

Brent, who had maintained honor roll marks all through high school, turned down multiple scholarship offers for football to concentrate on the ranch. When Brent gave up on his college football career, it hurt his dad more than anything, and Brent knew his dad felt personally responsible for him missing out on the opportunity to pursue his football career in college and the education that would have come along with it. His dad tried to convince Brent to let him sell the ranch so Brent could to go to college, but Brent would have none of it, showing the classic Asker stubbornness. He was proud to be the fifth generation of Asker to ranch the farm and he dedicated himself to turning things around on the farm. Through all of this, his high school sweetheart Lori Weston was right there at his side, supporting him with a degree of maturity which is rare among high school girls. Most girls would head off to the parties after the football games, but Lori instead would go to the ranch with Bert and Brent to finish the chores before the end of the night. She was Brent's best friend and his dad loved her like a daughter.

With Brent's encouragement Lori left for Colorado State University in nearby Fort Collins, accepting a scholarship in Communications. She would come home almost every weekend to be with him and work at the ranch. She turned down scholarships at bigger top ten colleges so she could be closer to home and the ranch. When he proposed to Lori in the summer before her final year of college, when both of them were barely twenty-two years old, she did not hesitate. They were madly in love, something they had both known since he asked her to the fall dance in grade nine for the first time. They talked about the fact that marrying Brent meant that she also married the ranch. There would be no moving to Denver to pursue her career, a big beautiful home in the suburbs. No, it would be life as the wife of a cowboy rancher. Brent was truly blessed, as Lori made it clear she would have had it no other way. She had only one condition for him, and it was important to her, so he agreed, though both of them knew it would be very difficult to adhere to. Lori insisted that for the next year while they were engaged, waiting to be married, they refrain from sex. Lori wanted the marriage to him to be perfect, and even though she had not saved her virginity for marriage she had never given herself to anyone else except Brent. It was her way of testing their commitment to each other, and being the cowboy that he was, Brent grumbled but agreed. Bert was ecstatic on the news of their engagement and insisted they get married on the ranch. They agreed, as did Lori's parents, who thought it was a great idea.

Brent and Lori celebrated her graduation from Colorado State University in the spring, then prepared for their July wedding at the ranch. Bert was like a nervous mother of the bride when it came to the wedding, offering advice or help on all the planning. It got to the point where Brent had to sit down with his dad and gently inform him that he needed to leave the planning of the wedding to Lori. Seeing the crushed look on his dad's face was secretly hilarious to Brent, but it melted Lori's heart knowing how much this wedding meant to Bert. They decided to continue to keep Bert involved, much to the chagrin of Lori's mother. The wedding was going to be huge, with friends and family who would total close to three hundred and fifty people, and the guest list seemed to grow by the day.

****

With the wedding only a month away, Bert asked Brent, after the evening chores were finished around nine in the evening, if he was up to a drive into town for a cold beer. Since Lori was still in the city with her Mom shopping for her wedding dress, Brent was all for a cold one after another long, hard and hot day.

"Can I grab a quick shower, Dad? I smell worse than the cowshit on my boots."

"No way. If you smell like cowshit then I must smell like cattleshit, so together maybe we can smell like Hugo Boss. Come on, let's just get going, both of us need a beer and a Bud on tap sounds like the perfect solution. Otherwise I'll settle for a Bud out of the fridge and that couch right there," laughed Bert, pointing to the living room.

Driving thirty-five miles or more to the outskirts of Cheyenne just so they could grab a beer at the tiny little beer shack "Little Kelly's" seemed appropriate. The beer was good and it was cold, plus they served a great plate of nachos, so that was all that mattered to Bert and Brent. The time on the drive into town went quickly, as their conversation was filled with talk of the wedding. Arriving at the bar, they ordered a beer and nachos and settled into the booth.

"Are you getting nervous yet, son? Your wedding is only a month away."

Grabbing a handful of the complimentary salted peanuts from a bowl on the table, Brent began shelling them and placed a few in his mouth.

"Hell, yeah, Dad, I'm nervous! I'm nervous only because I keep thinking Lori will change her mind about marrying me and take a good job in the city somewhere instead. This past year has not been easy, Dad. When Lori and I got engaged last summer one of her conditions was that we could not have any sex till after we were married. It was important to her that we do this—sort of like a test of our love, you know?"

Reaching for the peanut bowl himself, Bert realized how hungry he was as he looked at his son.

"No wonder you're so damn grumpy, son," chuckled Bert.

Brent leaned back into the cushion of the booth bench and flung the empty shells on the floor in frustration.

"Well, it has caused us some problems. We went from acting like rabbits to . . . nothing. I haven't handled it very well, and I've acted like an immature kid this past year. My anger issues have pushed her away at times, and if wasn't for Lori's insisting that we counsel with Pastor Simmons I'd have lost her, Dad. We have been meeting with Pastor Simmons for months now."

Fixing his son with a serious look, Bert tried to reassure him.

"You will not lose Lori. That will never happen, son. I have never in my life seen anyone as much in love as you two. It's wonderful to see, to be quite honest. I am so damn proud of you, son, opening up to me about this. You are an Asker, without a doubt. Your mother was the same way, Brent. She did not put up with my anger any more than Lori will with yours, I can tell you that. Women want to feel secure in a marriage, and if there are a lot of anger issues it makes them feel insecure. Your mother almost left me when I lost complete control when that asshole Ben Ledger tried to buy my land and herd during the mad cow disaster. Ledger knew I was desperate with the banks, and he tried to take it all away from me, lobbying the banks to sell my land to him. I was going to kill that son of a bitch. If it wasn't for her demanding I get it together and keep my cool, I'd be fighting against ledger and the banks on my own."

Brent was glad he had come for a beer with his dad. He just

had a way of putting things into perspective.

"You're right, Dad. I love her so much, and Pastor Simmons has been great. I feel pretty good that I have things under control. I just hope that Lori knows what she is in store for on our wedding night!" laughed Brent.

"Thanks for the warning, son. I think I'll get a room in town the night of your wedding," chuckled Bert.

Pushing his hat back on his head, Brent couldn't help but laugh at his Dad's comment.

"I think that would be a good idea, Dad," he winked.

"Just wish your mother and brother could have been here to be part of this." pondered Bert, looking off into the distance, feeling his eyes well up with tears.

Almost instinctively Brent leaned across the table and squeezed his dad's forearm.

"I know, Dad, I think the same thing sometimes. It sucks not to have them here, but you know what gets me through that, Dad?"

"What?"

"You, Dad. I just think of you and I know that I am so lucky to have the greatest dad ever. I mean that. You have been there for me in more ways than one, ever since I can remember. I love you, Dad," smiled Brent, fighting back tears himself.

Bert was silent, studying his son, searching for words to describe how he felt, but instead he found himself trying to stop the faucets that had become his eyes. Grabbing the napkin, Bert wiped his tears away, just beamed at his son and said, "I love you, son. Thank you for being there for me, too. Without you I don't know if I could have made it through the death of your mother and brother. Lori is a lot like your mother, son. Strong. Beautiful and smart. You are lucky, Brent, but so is she, because you are a great guy and she knows it and will cherish that. I can tell. Now enough of this girl talk, let's drink some beer. Cheers, son!" declared Bert, raising his glass to Brent.

After clicking glasses, the father and son, dog-tired from a hard day of branding new calves, polished off another four beers and two plates of nachos, then rose to leave. Excusing himself to visit the restroom before they headed off for home, Bert made his way to relieve himself. Feeling the effects of the Bud draft, Bert could only smile to himself. It had been a long time since he and Brent had taken a few moments alone with each other to kick back. They should do it more often, he thought.

Entering the dingy and filthy restroom, Bert noticed a guy wearing a Cardinals jersey with McGWIRE emblazoned on the back already occupying the urinal, so he headed for the only toilet stall beside the urinal. The sudden rush to pee made Bert fumble for his zipper, almost not making it. *Jeepers*, he thought to himself at the vision of walking out of the restroom with a big piss stain on the front of his pants. Well at least Brent would have had a good laugh at his expense.

"You have a fine son there, cowboy. Pretty decent daughter-in-law you're getting, too," stated the stranger from the other side of the toilet stall.

"Who the hell?!" a confused Bert said as he backed out of the stall to see who the hell this stranger was who obviously knew him.

As Bert was about to turn towards the urinal a seemingly invisible hand came out of nowhere, grabbing him by the throat and throwing him against the wall. The grip on his throat was vise-like and very powerful. He could not breathe. Then he realized, when he looked at the stranger, that he was pinned against the wall three feet off the floor by this maniac. Looking down into his face, Bert could not believe what he was seeing. The man's face was missing human qualities. It was huge, way longer than it should have been, and his mouth was full of large fangs dripping in saliva. His lips were purple, and then there were his eyes. His eyes were burning a bright red like the tail lights at night with the brake lights engaged. He felt he was about to pass out from lack of oxygen as he struggled uselessly against the iron grip of this man holding him up against the wall.

With a voice that could only have been summoned from the depths of hell, the man boomed: "Your daughter-in-law has been chosen! I have been waiting for her for a very long time, tracking her lineage for over seventeen hundred years! Her destiny will change this world forever! You and your son will both die!"

Suddenly the stranger dropped Bert to the floor, standing over him as he fought for air. As he stepped away and headed for the door, he glanced back at Bert. Now his face was completely human, except for the burning bright red eyes, and he told Bert in a quiet, measured, normal, human voice, "I will be back. Soon it will be time."

Then he opened the door and disappeared into the bar.

Regaining most of his air and standing on his feet, Bert was shaking and had no idea what just happened to him. He knew for sure that what had happened was real. It wasn't the four beers, and no one had dropped anything into his beer either. He also knew that Brent would not know about this. He would deal with this himself if that was possible. Bert didn't know if he would ever see the stranger again, but if he did, he would kick his ass.

Heading out into the bar to find Brent and head for home, Bert found himself doing something he had never done before in his life.

He prayed.

Chapter 14

For a few seconds all Grew and his father could do was stand there in stunned silence, staring at the horrible carnage before them. Somewhere in the periphery of his perception, Grew could still hear the soccer match on the television down the hall in the living room.

A monster towering approximately eight feet above the floor stood over a badly beaten Katherine. It was slimy black and grey in color, with legs and arms that were bulging with muscles stacked on top of muscles. Its hands were more claws than fingers, with large talons at the end of each claw. It had a set of grey, almost transparent wings on its back that were folded into its body. The creature's head was very large, with pointed ears. It was looking down at Katherine speaking in a language Grew did not understand. Katherine was bleeding from wounds on her face, chest, arms and legs as if she had been fighting off this beast. Her one eye was swollen shut and the other was staring at it, transfixed in utter fear.

Snapping Grew out of his trance was a scream so carnal, so guttural, that it scared him even more than what he was witnessing. He turned back towards the hallway, where the scream was coming from. Shamus, his father, armed with his shotgun, was screaming at the top of his lungs, running past Grew towards this monster. The beast also turned its ugly head towards his father when it heard the primal scream. Its eyes were fiery red, tinged with a split second of surprise, as if it hadn't thought there was anyone else in the house. The boom from the blast of the shotgun was deafening, sending a ferocious round of buckshot point-blank into the midsection of the creature. The blast sent the beast flying backwards into the wall. Shamus followed the first blast with another one, pumping the shotgun like a pro. Grew noticed his Dad had a look of complete madness on his face as he continued to pump rounds into this monster that had invaded their home.

Grew rushed to Katherine's side while his dad finished off the creature. Sobbing, Grew could not believe what was happening. In a matter of just a few seconds, this beast had brutally killed his mother, and had almost killed Katherine before he and his dad could get from the living room to the kitchen. This was madness. He lifted Katherine's battered head up and placed it on his lap, stroking her hair, assuring her that everything would be all right. Then he heard a laugh. It was a sound so evil that it sent a shudder down his back. After pumping all of its shells into the beast, Grew's dad was raising the shotgun over his head in a desperate attempt to try to kill this thing. *The beast is still alive after all of those shotgun blasts*, thought Grew. *What in God's name is this thing? Not anything close to human. It was laughing hysterically now.*

Lifting itself up from the wall with gaping wounds all over its body from at least six direct-hit blasts from a twelve-gauge shotgun, the beast straightened to its full height, towering in front of Grew's dad. The glow surrounding the beast in the dark, with steam jetting from its flared nostrils, made it look like some prehistoric creature not yet discovered for the history books. Its bright red eyes glowed menacingly down at Shamus. Suddenly, with such speed that Grew, six feet away, felt only the slight movement of air against his skin, the beast's claw shot out from under its folded wing and grabbed Shamus's throat, lifting him in the air till he was pinned against the ten-foot-high ceiling, Grew screamed, "Noooo!!", but it was too late. The beast clamped down even harder on his dad's throat, crushing it, squeezing the air and the life out of his dad. Finally, the huge powerful arm attached to the claw applied the final pressure and the beast tore Shamus's head completely off, his torso falling with a thud to the floor.

Setting Katherine's head gently down on the floor, Grew rose and launched himself at the beast, knowing it was certain death but the hatred for what this thing had just done to his family pushing him over the edge. Katherine, becoming more conscious, sat up and screamed at Grew, "Grew, no! Stop! It will kill you!" It didn't matter. Grew was dead before she finished her sentence. The beast saw him coming and thrust his other claw right through Grew's chest, impaling him. To Katherine's horror the beast then retracted its claw, and as Grew fell face first to the ground, the beast drove its claw into the back of his head, crushing Grew's skull. Still clutching Shamus's head in its other claw, it flung it aside and stood once again, moving towards Katherine.

****

Crying, with tears stinging her damaged and swollen eye, Katherine tried to move away from the beast, but she quickly bumped up against the kitchen wall. She had nowhere to go as there was another wall to her right and the toppled kitchen table blocking her path to the left. Looking up at the beast, Katherine shouted, "Why?! Who are you and why are doing this?! Why are you killing us?!"

There was no answer. She was presented instead with another sequence of bizarre images, as the beast began to transform in front of her. Its wings started to fold back and shrink and then disappear into its back. The huge arms grew smaller, their massive muscles shrinking. and its claws started to retract, as thin fingers formed that morphed into hands. She thought, *is this thing turning human?* Its hulking legs, with their massive, slimy, black and grey quad muscles studded with black protruding veins that seemed to stitch all of the muscles together, slowly wilted and began shrinking into normal human legs. The transformation continued, and as the beast's upper body/torso began to contract, the sound of bones and muscle shrinking and disappearing was grotesque. The large, hairless pectoral muscles covered in slime began to collapse into its chest cavity, as a normal, fit human chest appeared that was even partly covered with chest hair. Its head, outsized and covered in protruding black veins, also grew smaller, taking on human features, growing hair. Its mouth, just a few seconds earlier full of menacing sharp fangs, now appeared normal as the fangs were replaced by normal human teeth. The slime-covered black and grey skin began turning white. Katherine thought she was watching a special effects horror movie, but she knew this horror was no dream. It was real, and this thing that now appeared human had murdered her entire family.

The transformation now complete, this man/beast standing in front of her still retained one aspect of its monster image, its eyes. They were still burning crimson red.

Then Katherine saw it, and the sight of it made her tremble with such fear she thought she would vomit. This thing had a huge erection, and its eyes burned into Katherine as if telling her exactly what was going to happen to her. The whole reason for this carnage, death and destruction became clear, and it hit Katherine harder than if the beast had clobbered her over her head with one of its massive claws. She was going to be raped by this thing. That sick realization was too much for her, and she began to wretch, vomiting on the floor, then sobbing and crying so hard she thought her chest muscles would snap.

Through her sobs and tears she cried, "Why are you doing this?! Why did you have to kill my family?! Why!?"

Reaching down suddenly, the man/beast grabbed Katherine by the back of the hair and pulled her head back, leaned within inches of her face and spoke in a human voice, "You have been chosen because you are the seed and the direct descendant of my enemy Abgar! I am your God, the Prince of Darkness, your beloved God's feared enemy! I have waited a very long time for you. Over seventeen hundred years I have waited. My time has come for this world, and this time I will not fail. Where is your God now? Where was he when I was tearing your beloved Grew to pieces like he was a piece of garbage? Tell me that, Katherine McCloskey. Your God does not exist. He is a mirage, a fairy tale told to stupid people for centuries that is passed on to the next generation of stupid and naïve people and then again and again. For thousands of years, mankind has bought that bullshit. Soon the stupidity of mankind will be exposed and its true fate will be revealed!"

The creature pulled her head back again, then slugged her with his fist across her face so hard she felt as if she'd been hit with a sledgehammer. She could hear the bones in her nose snap as she fell back onto the floor, her head hitting the carpet with a thud. White shards of light flashed in and out of her mind from the numbing pain..

He stood up again, standing tall, the room getting dark and cold. His body was surrounded by a white glow and the steam from the cold air escaped from his mouth as he breathed. Katherine did not notice the cold. She braced for what was about to happen to her. Then he began to speak again, but it wasn't English. She recognized it as Latin. She had heard enough Latin spoken in church by the priests in all of the ceremonies she had witnessed over the years.

"Ecce Christus filius Dei semen inimicus Abgarus est ante me. Mea magnitudine erit restituo hoc impostor semen aeternum. Parate sum adventum. Mox reges saeculi." (Behold Christ, Son of God, the seed of my enemy Abgar is before me. My greatness will replace this imposter's seed forever. Prepare for I am coming. Soon I will rule this world.)

Suddenly he was on top of her, crushing her against the floor, mounting her with raw and brutal force. She struggled with all the strength she could muster, but it was useless. He had her completely pinned, his strength was incredible. Then he entered her, his erection filling her, violating every inch of the inside of her, the pain unbearable, suffocating. His pelvic thrusts cut into her like a knife, excruciating pain like nothing she had ever experienced. Katherine prayed for it to end so she could just die, she had completely lost her will to live any longer. His grunting sounded like that of a wild animal as his thrusts quickened. He was nearing climax. Not wanting to see its glowing red eyes, Katherine closed hers. Then he came inside her, his semen pumping into her, filling her with an evil she felt right down to her soul, wondering if he had taken that as well.

Climbing off her, he screamed down at her, his eyes burning. "Look at me, bitch! You should thank me! I just scrubbed your soul clean of that belief you called faith!"

He then turned and walked away. Katherine could hear him laughing hysterically as he did so. As the blackness crept into her mind, as she slipped into unconsciousness, she thought to herself, *is my nightmare over? Or is it just beginning?*

****

Father O'Sullivan, wrapping up budget discussions with the church deacons, rose out of his chair as an indication that they were done; otherwise, these people would drone on for hours. Suddenly the door to the meeting room burst open and a hysterical Margaret Kearney, the church administrative secretary, came running in, shaking, shouting, "Father! There has been some sort of accident at the McCloskey home, a terrible accident! The police called asking you to come to the hospital right away! They have taken her to St. Vincent's in Dublin by air ambulance! Katherine is badly hurt and she keeps crying out, asking for you! Please hurry, Father!"

Shocked by the sudden news about the McClosky's, Thomas reached for the back of his chair to steady himself.

"Where is Grew? Shamus and Patricia? Are they at the hospital as well?" asked Thomas.

"I am not sure, Father. The police did not say. They just asked for you to hurry," replied Margaret, shaking badly. Margaret was very close to the McClosky's, especially Patricia, as they often worked together in church fundraisers and got together in women's groups in the church. "Oh, my dear, Father, I hope that Katherine will be okay."

Thomas rushed from the church and sped to St. Vincent's University Hospital, driving his church-owned diesel Peugeot 307. The drive was not far, only twenty-five miles, but he would have to cut right through Dublin into the south part of the city in Dublin 4, taking the M1 motorway. Hopefully traffic would be at a minimum on this late Sunday afternoon. There were closer hospitals to Balbriggan than St. Vincent's, including the Beaumont, but none of these had air ambulance landing facilities for the helicopter. Katherine had to have been hurt very badly to be taken by air, thought Thomas. What possibly could have happened?

The sense of impending doom that Thomas felt this morning during mass when he'd seen Grew and Katherine now returned. Thomas could not explain this feeling, but he knew it was not good. It brought back the memory of the last time he had felt this way. Almost thirty years ago in Rome, at the airport, when he was confronted by the American, Robert Best. Best's evil red eyes and his words had cut into Thomas like a knife. His comments about Father O'Malley's death just hours after Thomas had said goodbye to Father O'Malley and before Thomas even knew about it. Best had been pure evil, and the memory of that encounter was as fresh in Thomas's mind as if it had just happened.

He manoeuvred through the traffic to make his way to the M1 motorway, which would take him right through Dublin to Dublin 4, where St. Vincent`s is right off the M1 on Elm Park. Traffic was slow but Thomas knew it would not be on the motorway. Just a few minutes later Thomas was on the M1, and as he expected, traffic was light and moving briskly. He gunned it, not caring if the police stopped him.

Arriving at St. Vincent`s precisely twenty-five minutes after he left St Colmcille's, Thomas quickly parked in the first available stall he found and rushed to get inside. He noticed an unusual number of police cars parked in front of the emergency entrance as he drove past. The gale force winds blowing through Thomas`s stomach would have bent a large tree as the dread continued to build. The distance from the outdoor parking lot to emergency was about a city block, and Thomas found himself in a full sprint. Even though he was fifty-eight years old, Thomas kept himself in excellent shape, jogging five miles a day, five days a week. It was a routine he'd begun soon after settling in at his first parish posting in the small town of Tullamore, County Offaly. In fact it had been recommended by the late Father Zacharias at the Vatican over thirty years ago when Thomas was chosen for a special task force that he keep himself in good shape as his energies would be tested frequently. Thomas felt the tentacles of dread working their way inside his stomach; indicating that his energy would indeed be tested and he would need all of his strength in the hours ahead.

Reaching the doors to emergency, Thomas was not even winded. That would not last long, as he was about to have the breath sucked right out of him. Hurrying inside, he saw a nurse busy writing on a clipboard in the middle of the emergency room and approached her. "Excuse me, Miss, can you please help me? I am looking for a patient who recently arrived in emergency. Her name is Katherine McCloskey." said Thomas, panic written all over his face.

"Yes, follow me, I will take you personally. She is in surgery at the moment but should be done in there and likely into recovery in another hour. You must be Father O'Sullivan. The detectives are waiting for you," stated the nurse as she led Thomas into the elevator.

"How is Katherine? Will she be okay?" asked Thomas.

"It is best you speak with the doctors treating her on the extent of her injuries, but I can tell you this. She has been horribly beaten and viciously raped. If she survives it will be a miracle. Your prayers will be needed Father."

Arriving as the elevator doors opened on the third floor where Katherine was in surgery, Thomas walked into a mob scene. What should have been a quiet and orderly hospital floor was in chaos. There were uniformed Garda everywhere, plainclothes detectives huddled together talking in hushed tones. Thomas could not help but notice the deeply strained looks on everyone. The nurse directed Thomas to a group of plainclothes men huddled near the nurses' station. "Detective Fitzpatrick, this is Father O'Sullivan," she said, then turned to rejoin the chaotic scene.

"Detective Fitzpatrick, please tell me what is going on. I have heard nothing about what has happened other than being asked to get down here as there has been an accident involving Katherine McCloskey. The nurse told me on the way up here that she has been raped?" an exasperated Thomas asked the detective.

"Let's go talk in one of these rooms, Father. Nurse, can we use this room for ten minutes please?" Fitzpatrick asked a nurse standing in the doorway of some sort of examination room.

"Ten minutes, detective. We will need that room soon enough, the number of bodies that are coming into emergency tonight," the distraught nurse declared.

The detective entered first and held the door open for Thomas and closed it behind him. "Please, Father, sit. For what I am about to tell you, I promise you will want to be sitting." Detective Fitzpatrick spent the next twenty minutes describing the scene at the McCloskey home, the ravaged and decapitated bodies of Patricia, Shamus and Grew. The staggering amount of blood found in the home.

"It was a slaughterhouse, Father. The McClosky's were butchered, and it is by the grace of God that somehow Katherine has survived, though she is not out of the woods yet. The doctors will tell us more in the next few minutes, as she will be out of surgery very soon," explained Fitzpatrick.

Shocked by the news of the gruesome deaths of the McCloskey family, Thomas closed his eyes in silent prayer, clutching his rosary beads tightly in his hands as he prayed. Detective Fitzpatrick waited patiently for Father O'Sullivan, knowing the news would have hit him hard as he was close to the McClosky's according to reports from some of the police at the scene who heard of Katherine's persistent requests to speak with Father O'Sullivan while she was being loaded into the ambulance. After a few moments Thomas opened his eyes, which were filled with tears, and spoke. "I was very close to the McCloskey family, Detective. I spent many a Sunday evening eating Patricia's wonderful stew. I cannot believe they are gone. Who could have done this, Detective, do you have any leads or theories?"

Walking towards the far wall, then stopping, Fitzpatrick turned back towards Thomas and replied, "Well, we believe it started out as an armed robbery by a home invasion gang. There has been an increase in home invasion robberies throughout the county in the last several months. At some point it turned bad, real bad. We found Shamus's Remington 870 twelve-gauge shotgun at the scene with five empty shells, consistent with the four in the magazine and one in the chamber. We believe Shamus fought back, shooting one or several of the perpetrators, and that this gang, enraged at the attack by Shamus, decided to violently slaughter everyone, decapitating them except for Katherine. They viciously raped her instead and beat her badly, leaving her for dead. There is a tremendous amount of blood and tissue on the scene that is being gathered by the crime lab for analysis that hopefully will give us a clue to the identity of whoever did this. Katherine has survived so far, Father, and we are waiting for clearance by the doctor to interview her."

Thomas stood abruptly, looking Fitzpatrick in the eye as he spoke. "You're not planning to hold vigil here tonight so you can pounce on her when her eyes open to question her. Are you out of your mind, Detective? With the trauma she has been through, she cannot be brought back to that nightmare so soon. For the love of God, Detective, she will need a couple of days' rest."

Detective Fitzpatrick held a hand in the air in defense while he spoke. "Father O'Sullivan, I understand how you feel, I really do, but right now I have a bunch of killers roaming the streets of

Balbriggan or another town close by, and they need to be caught as quickly as possible before they do this to someone else. Katherine is the only witness to this crime, and if she survives, I have to question her, Father."

Thomas knew the detective was right but he did not like it. "Fine, but along with the doctors, I will be in that room as well. She has been beaten and raped. Detective, she watched as her husband and his parents were brutally murdered!"

"I agree, Father. She needs you when she comes out of this. Can you tell me why she would have repeatedly asked for you when she was discovered?"

Exhaling deeply, still not quite believing what had happened, Thomas replied, "Katherine and the entire McCloskey family were very spiritual people, and after what Katherine has been through it would make sense that she would reach out to her family priest. Oh my God, Detective! Katherine's parents—Kenneth and Joanie—have they been notified?"

"Yes, they arrived shortly before you did. Hysterical, of course. They are in the waiting room just outside of surgery. You are welcome, Father, to join them there. I would think they will need your comfort, and you will be there when the surgeons emerge from surgery. Why don't I take you there now, Father?"

Thomas accompanied Detective Fitzpatrick to the surgical wing of the third floor, with its large waiting area for family and friends. While walking with the detective to meet with the Kearney's, Thomas asked Fitzpatrick for a few moments while he used the restroom. Stepping into the men's room, locking the door behind him, Thomas stood in front of the mirror, noticing that he was sweating profusely. Splashing cold water on his face, he knew there was an evil presence at work here tonight. The McClosky's had been targeted and he had no idea why. He knew he did not need to see any evidence or the crime scene to know this was not the work of some gang of ruthless home invasion robbers. Evil had visited Balbriggan tonight, he was sure of it. Not an evil gang of thugs but something entirely more evil, demonic perhaps. He clutched his cross pendant, bent to one knee and, while leaning on the sink, began to pray silently: "Heavenly Father, Creator of all that is good, Destroyer of all evil, give me the strength and the courage, the vision and the wisdom to see and defend against the evil that has come to Balbriggan. Place your son Jesus Christ's healing hands on Katherine and make her well, Lord. Heal her body and her spirit, Dear Lord. Give Kenneth and Joanie Kearney the strength to heal from this tragedy, Lord. I pray this in your name and in the name of your son, Jesus Christ, Amen."

Kissing his cross and tucking it back into the top of his coat, Thomas began to rise when suddenly the lights in the tiny closet-sized bathroom shut off, cloaking him in complete darkness. The bathroom began to shake violently, pitching Thomas hard against the wall, causing him to slip to the floor. He felt a sharp pain in his back from the blow against the wall. As he reached towards the sink to help pull himself up off the floor, the taps suddenly turned on, startling him. The room began to shake even more violently and the lights began to flicker on and off. Finding the sink, Thomas grabbed on, only to be scalded by the hot water. Falling back to the floor in shock from the sudden pain of the scalding water, Thomas felt he was in the middle of a large earthquake. *Something very evil is at work, he could feel it!?*

Then, as quickly as the violent shaking had started, it ended. Taking a second to gather himself, Thomas reached for the sink once again in the dark to pull himself up. He noticed the taps also had shut off. The lights came on, causing him to squint from the brightness. As he lifted his head to look at himself in the mirror he saw a dark shape move behind his reflection in the mirror, and it frightened him to his core. Thomas whipped around, but it was gone. Was it his imagination in all the chaos surrounding him in this dark and shaking room? No, he was not mistaken. He would never forget what he'd seen. Because he had seen it thirty years ago in the terminal at the airport in Rome. It wasn't the moving shape that frightened him so much; it was that this dark moving shape had *red, burning eyes!*

Knowing he had to get out of this room immediately,

Thomas reached for the doorknob, thinking it would be locked, trapping him inside; surprisingly, it was open. He pushed the door open and quickly exited. Seeing Detective Fitzpatrick leaning against the wall opposite the restroom with an impatient look on his face, Thomas asked him, "Did you feel that?"

"Feel what, Father?" A puzzled look on the detective's face. *Why is Father O' Sullivan sweating so badly?*

"The shaking, the whole floor was shaking, as if an earthquake had hit the hospital!" Thomas said, observing his surroundings in the hallway, noticing that everything looked untouched.

"Father, are you okay? There was no shaking in the hospital, what did you feel?" a concerned Fitzpatrick asked.

Shaking badly, Thomas gathered himself.

"Never mind, it's been a crazy evening, let's go see the Kearney's, Detective."

In the surgical area waiting room just a few minutes later, Kenneth and Joanie Kearney, upon seeing Thomas, jumped off the couch and rushed to him. Embracing both of them, Thomas comforted them with reassurances that Katherine would be okay. As Detective Fitzpatrick excused himself to return to his team in emergency, Thomas asked the Kearney's to sit so they could pray.

He prayed with the Kearney's for their daughter as well as for understanding of the tragic events that taken place at the McCloskey home. They prayed for the souls of Shamus, Patricia and Grew, and that the perpetrators would be found before anyone else was hurt and that justice would be brought to bear on them for their crimes.

Just then a nurse walked into the waiting room from the surgery and approached the Kearney's. "The doctors are done, and they will be out in the next few minutes to brief you on your daughter's condition. I can tell you she is heavily sedated right now and resting," explained the nurse. After answering a few more questions, she left them alone in their thoughts, silently waiting for the doctors to emerge. They didn't have to wait very long. Just a few minutes after the nurse left, the operating room doors opened and a surgeon walked out, taking off his mask as he approached.

"I am Dr. Kenney, your daughter's surgeon," he said, extending his hand to shake Kenneth's and Joanie's hands. Then, turning to shake Thomas's hand, he said, "You must be Father O'Sullivan, Katherine has been asking for you. Let me explain how she is doing. First, she has sustained extensive injuries, including severe head injuries. She has a broken left wrist that required surgery to place a pin, a separated left shoulder, a broken jaw and nose, and multiple lacerations to the left side of her body, most of them requiring stitches to close. She has internal bleeding, including a bruised kidney. She suffered a severe blow to her head that caused a serious concussion. She has swelling on her brain that we are monitoring very closely. Also—and excuse me because I know this is painful—the sexual assault was especially violent, leaving her with multiple cuts and bruising. I am very sorry to have to tell you all this bad news. But your daughter is a fighter."

The moan from Joanie was audible as she burst into tears, sobbing uncontrollably. Kenneth, stunned at the news of the severity of his daughter's injuries, tried to comfort his wife.

Dr. Kenney continued, "Your daughter is very lucky to be alive. She has a long road of recovery ahead of her physically, and with the loss of her husband and his family, her mental well-being will take as long, if not longer, to rebound. Father, may I speak with you in private for a moment, please?"

Crossing to the other side of the room, out of earshot of the Kearney's, Dr. Kenney spoke to Thomas in a hushed tone, "Father, her injuries are severe and there is a very good chance she won't survive the night. She has a chance of surviving these injuries, but it will not be easy. If the swelling surrounding her brain does not subside within the next few hours we will have to induce her into a coma. The Kearney's have enough to deal with right at this moment without hearing this. I was hoping you could break it to them once they have recovered somewhat."

The extent of Katherine's injuries was a shock to Thomas.

Looking at Dr. Kenney, he nodded. "Certainly, doctor, I will do that. If they have questions will you be nearby to answer those?"

"Yes. I myself, along with the rest of the surgical team, will be nearby to monitor her progress through the night. There is one more thing I need to tell you, Father, that I feel it is also best for you break to the Kearney's. Katherine is pregnant."

The news that Katherine was pregnant hit him like a punch in the stomach.

"What?? That is impossible. Katherine had a hysterectomy over five years ago!"

"Are you aware of Katherine receiving an egg donor? That would be the only possible way she could be carrying a child."

The gale force winds of dread returned and were blowing right through Thomas. He thought he would be sick.

"No, not at all. I am sure they would have discussed that with me if that was something they were considering doing. Katherine is busy at school, and that sort of procedure would not be covered by healthcare and they certainly did not have the money for it themselves. How far along is she, doctor?"

"She is ten weeks into the first trimester, Father. When Katherine awakes from surgery in the next few hours I will decide at that time whether she is strong enough for you— and only you—to see her, for just a few moments. She was adamant in her delirious state coming into emergency that she speaks with you. I will allow only you, no police and not her parents, not yet anyway. Understood, Father? I will check on her as soon as she is moved to ICU, and I will let you know then where she is at."

"Yes, thank you doctor, and God bless you."

Turning to leave, the doctor stopped and looked back at Thomas and said, "Pray for her, Father, she will need every prayer you can muster."

While Thomas was speaking with Dr. Kenney, a nurse had come out to see the Kearney's to inform them that Katherine was being moved to ICU on the second floor and that they could move down to the lounge area and wait there for the doctors to come and give them an update. Thomas helped Kenneth comfort

Joanie as they made their way to the second floor. Reaching the second floor and the waiting area outside the ICU they sat down, and Joanie, through her tears, asked Thomas, "Why did this happen to Katherine, Father? To the McClosky's?"

Dropping his head slightly, Thomas picked up Joanie's hand and held it while he spoke.

"This was a violent crime with tragic results. Katherine and the McClosky's were in the wrong place at the wrong time, Joanie. The perpetrators picked their house at random. There was nothing you or anyone else could have done to prevent this. It was an evil act by some evil people. I know this is a very difficult time for you both, but let's remember that Katherine is alive and we need to continue to pray for her recovery. You will need to be strong, for when she comes out of this she will need you. She has lost her husband and his family. The doctors can try to mend her body but she will need us to help heal her soul."

Just then Dr. Kenney entered the room. "Excuse me for interrupting, but Katherine is awake. She will not be for long, however. The swelling on her brain is increasing so we must put her into a comatose state to allow the swelling to subside. I am very sorry. She is asking for Father O'Sullivan. Normally I would not allow anyone. However, I feel I can give Father O'Sullivan a few minutes with her. I am sorry, Mr. and Mrs. Kearney that you will have to hold on before you see her. It will be too much for her if all three of you go in. If you have no objections, then, Father, we must hurry."

After giving the Kearney's hugs of reassurance, Thomas joined Dr. Kenney in the hallway. As they made their way down the hall to Katherine's room in the ICU, Dr. Kenney said, "Okay Father here we are. You have ten minutes with her, that's it. Her jaw is broken and will be wired shut once the swelling in her brain subsides. She can talk because she feels no pain with the heavy sedation. As you can well imagine I must warn you not to question her in a way that will get her upset. She must remain calm. Okay. Go ahead. Father. Remember, ten minutes."

Entering Katherine's room, Thomas found her awake and

relieved to see him. Thomas was startled to see her in such bad shape. Her head and the left side of her face were covered in bandages, revealing just the right side of her face and right eye. Her left arm was also heavily bandaged and suspended in a sling. Pulling the bedside chair close, he sat down beside her bed, resting his hand on Katherine's right hand, careful of the IV tubes. Giving her hand a slight squeeze he said, "Katherine I am so sorry. You have been through so much."

Leaning in close to Katherine, he heard her whisper, "The attack, Father. It killed Grew. Tore him to pieces. Slaughtered him and his parents, Father." Sensing that she was getting upset, Thomas cut in and reassured her, "Katherine, let's take this moment to pray. Dear God, help Katherine find comfort in your love for her. Although we don't always understand why things happen the way you plan, help Katherine to rest so she can heal herself both physically and for her losses. Your great wisdom will reveal Itself to her soon, when she is ready for that. Lord, Protect Grew, Shamus and Patricia as they enter your great kingdom. Lord, keep them safe. We pray in your name Lord and the name of your son Jesus Christ, Amen."

Seeing tears tumbling down Katherine's right cheek, Thomas said to her, "The Lord feels your pain, Katherine, let his unending love for you wash through you, and let his love comfort you Katherine. Now I want you to rest. Your parents are here outside this room, Katherine, waiting for you to get better so they can see you. They send their love, Katherine . . ." Thomas was interrupted by Katherine whispering to him.

"It was the devil, Father, it was Satan himself who did this. He killed everyone so he could rape me, Father. He was a monster, its eyes were bright red, and it was killing everyone. I thought it was going to rip me to pieces too, but then it changed into human form right before my eyes. He started speaking in Latin, then he raped me, Father. I am pregnant, aren't I, Father? I know I am because I can already feel something grow inside me. Oh, my God, please help me, Father . . ." Katherine was very upset now and Thomas needed to get her to calm down.

"Katherine, I believe you, but I need you to calm down. You are very sick and you must be still."

Getting out of his chair, Thomas stood and walked quickly to the door, opened it and, seeing a nurse nearby, called out to her to get Dr. Kenney quickly. Returning to Katherine, he once again put his hand on hers and spoke gently to her. "Katherine, everything will be okay. I will be here for you. I am not leaving. Do you understand? Calm down, everything will be okay, my dear, I promise." Seeing Dr. Kenney arrive, Thomas stepped away from the bed while the doctor administered another sedative to Katherine that would relax her and put her to sleep.

"Father, I have to ask you to leave now. She needs to get her rest. I will come and see you and the Kearney's in a few minutes to discuss her condition," said Dr. Kenney.

Exiting the room, Thomas was numb as he processed what Katherine had said about the attack. Was she delirious? What really happened in that house, he thought to himself. Thomas knew what Katherine had said was true. He'd felt its presence in the bathroom on the way up to surgery earlier. Satan was very busy now in our world, Thomas was sure of it. But why? Why had he targeted the McClosky's?

Thomas shuddered as he recounted Katherine's words, "*Its eyes were bright red.*"

Chapter 15

Bentley tried to cram in some much-needed study time before she had to get in her car and into the traffic on Interstate 880 from her University of Berkeley campus apartment and try to beat the late-afternoon congestion. Bentley Paxton was just a few weeks away from completing her Master's degree at the Berkeley School of Journalism, and those weeks couldn't go fast enough. The past two years since she'd moved to northern California from the east to attend Berkeley, had been a wild ride, to say the least. A busy concert schedule in the bay area had kept her busy covering the events for her employer, *Vibe* magazine, in addition to interviews with musicians in the area not in concert but passing through. One thing Bentley had learned early on in this business was that it was not difficult getting interviews with established musicians. Their egos would not allow them to say no, the opportunity to get their face and their name in *Vibe* to promote their latest album for free was too good to pass up.

Bentley had to finish her final paper by Monday morning for her degree; she was close to being done but would need all weekend to finish it. Today was Thursday, and she had to work tonight covering the Spice Girls concert at the San Jose Arena in San Jose. It was a fifty-mile trip one way, piece of cake as long as she was on the 880 before 3:00 p.m. Spice Girls, whom Bentley had interviewed once before for *Vibe* over a year ago, liked her and had eagerly accepted an interview request from Bentley's new employer, *Music Talks*. The interview would be conducted in their dressing room one hour before the concert while they would be finishing putting on what would surely be very sexy costumes for the show. It would be a fun interview for Bentley, as the Spice Girls, all of them, were nice, kind and very accommodating to interviewers. Bentley would watch the concert from the VIP section for the press and would attend the post-concert party. Normally Bentley avoided the parties, which she could do without. Everyone got too friendly backstage after a concert fuelled by booze and drugs, and there would always be someone trying to make a pass at her, so rather than create a scene Bentley would just avoid them. Plus the performers usually did not attend them anyway, just the stagehands, press, agents and managers rubbing shoulders. But her new bosses at *Music Talks* insisted that she attend them. Good exposure for the magazine, they said. Yeah, right.

Bentley could not complain—so what if she had to look glamorous for an hour or two amongst a bunch of drugged, drunk and horny rock stars—because working for the industry's premier publication was a dream job. The money was great; most of her interviews were professional and went off without a hitch. They were usually problem free because Bentley was prepared for each and every interview, so if curveballs were lobbed her way, her hard work in preparing would allow her to hit it out of the park anyway. That was why *Music Talks* had hired her. Sure, she was beautiful, she knew that, but you don't get to work for a major league publication like *Music Talks* because you are great looking. Bentley was smart and well educated, and that, with a tremendous work ethic plus those good looks, made for a lethal combination in this business.

As Bentley had declared to her school that print media would be her concentration during her two-year Masters program at Berkeley, she decided that for her final summation project, she would present a paper that explored why people gravitated to certain music genres. For example, why did someone become a bigger fan of country music as opposed to rock music? Was it just the environment they lived in or how they were raised in that environment that influenced their music tastes? If that were true, how could individual family members growing up in the same household, in the same environment, have completely different music tastes? Did some countries encourage a musical subculture, as with Italy being known for opera, the UK for rock, the US for country, Spain for salsa? Did the way an artist looked influence people to like that artist's music? Were individual people attracted to Christian music because of the message or the words, the melodies or the beat, even though a lot of Christian music sounded exactly like pop music?

As with her job, when Monday morning came and it was her time to present her paper, Bentley would be prepared and ready. That was just who she was. There was no need to panic because she had to cover a concert tonight and therefore lose a whole night of work on her project. She had until Sunday midnight to fax her paper to her professor, and it would be great, she knew it, and it would propel her career not only with *Music Talks* but beyond.

Bentley checked her watch and saw it was 1:45 p.m. She needed to get ready in order to be on the road by 3:00 p.m. Getting up from her desk in her one-bedroom apartment, she made her way to her bedroom to begin getting ready. Bentley couldn't help but remember the one interview in her career so far that had lobbed a curveball at her that she did not hit out of the park. The interview of the band Watermark, and its manager Robert Best, almost two years ago in San Francisco. It had not been lack of preparation on her part; she simply hadn't been able to find any information on Watermark's manager Best, and it cost her. The interview had been a cluster job, with Best playing Bentley like a puppet the whole interview. It was creepy and scary, that experience with Best, and she made a promise to herself that she would postpone or cancel an interview if she was unable to be properly prepared again.

Bentley decided she would wear her new brown leather pants

she'd bought last weekend. Not only were they really comfortable for an expected long night but they looked great. The pants were chocolate brown in color, with an even darker brown trim. She chose an off-white blouse that hung loose on her. Bentley, with her tall, five-foot-ten athletic figure, liked to wear boots but avoided heels as it pushed her height close to six feet, so she chose a flat-soled dark brown boot. She did not like to be taller than the stars she was interviewing, as most of them found it intimidating and it could affect the interview, so she was careful about wearing heels. To finish off her look she chose a three-quarter-length dark brown sheer sweater with a hood. Very chic, she thought, perfect for a concert.

Armed with her notes for her interview with the red hot Spice Girls, Bentley set off in her VW Beetle convertible. She loved her bug, and she often drove with the roof down, but not when she was going to work. After spending an hour on her hair with the straightener, she was not about to allow it to be ruined in ten seconds on the 880 to San Jose. It was almost three, she was on Interstate 880 and the traffic congestion had not yet settled in, so she was feeling good. She was happy, her career was fast tracking, and she was days away from finishing her education with a Masters degree. She had done it all on her own, keeping her independence intact, not having to rely on anyone else. She was grateful that her contract work with *Vibe*, and now as a well-paid journalist with *Music Talks*, had allowed her to obtain her education with no student loans or debt.

Her thoughts were interrupted by her cell phone ringtone. Checking the caller ID she saw it was her boss at *Music Talks*, Jonathon Green, Chief Editor. Answering the call, she said, "Bentley Paxton, *Music Talks* underpaid junior staff writer. How may I help you?"

"Very funny, Bentley. Sounds like you're driving, are you on your way to see the elegant diva Spice Girls?" asked Jonathon.

She loved to tease her boss and get under his skin, and this call would be no different.

"Change of plans, actually. I thought it would be in the best interests of *Music Talks* if I took in the Robert Downey Jr jam at the LA County lockup. It's important that our readers know that we are sensitive to artists who try to revive their careers in music, and that we support them."

"Great idea. And while you are doing that, ask Robert, how you can revive your career in the music business," laughed Jonathon.

"What's up, my furry friend?" asked Bentley.

"Hey, I shaved my beard off months ago. When are you going to stop saying that? Anyway, I'm sending you an email with interview details for a record label executive interview in two weeks down in LA"

"Oh yeah, and who would that be?" asked Bentley.

"Avery Johnson from Alive Records."

The red-hot successful Avery Johnson. Bentley was being handed a top interview. It was a clear sign the magazine had now elevated her into their top tier of journalists.

"I heard he has a real reputation in the industry. Should be interesting," replied Bentley.

"Guess that depends on what type of reputation you're referring to. Johnson is a heavy hitter and is the next big thing in the business. Anyway, in my email, along with the details for the interview I've included some questions that the magazine would like to get some answers on, okay?"

"So now you're dictating what my interview questions will be. See, I was right. I am the underpaid junior staff writer."

"I have a feeling if I don't offer up some kind of script for you, the Avery Johnson charm reputation I assume you were referring to will leave you speechless and unable to ask any question other than, 'Will you marry me?'", joked Jonathon.

Laughing at her boss's crack, she had a comeback ready to go.

"I'm saving that privilege for you, baby, don't you know that?"

"Okay, enough already. Have a great time with the sex goddesses tonight and get some good stuff on paper, will you?"

"Will do, my furry friend. Later," replied Bentley as she hit the END button, dropped her phone in her purse and concentrated on her driving, as her exit to the San Jose Arena was coming up soon.

Later that night, Bentley made her way home from a long night at the concert, where she and the Spice Girls had a blast in the interview, giving Bentley a great story. Jonathon would be very pleased. Tonight she would get a good sleep, and then, starting in the morning, it would be, as jocks like to say, 'balls to the wall', getting her summation project done. It was almost 1:00 a.m. by the time she pulled into the parking stall at her apartment. As she rested her head on her pillow and waited for sleep to take over, she thought of her upcoming interview with Avery Johnson in a few weeks. *Hmm . . . should be interesting indeed.*

The next ten days flew by like a blur for Bentley. Not only did she finish her paper for her Masters, but early unofficial feedback from her professor was very positive. She finished typing up the Spice Girls interview and faxed that story to Jonathon. He was ecstatic with the piece, thought it was well written and praised Bentley's ability to allow the group to feel comfortable enough to open up with her in such a personal way. Her interview with Avery Johnson from Alive Records was tomorrow. Bentley found herself feeling a little giddy today, and she didn't know whether it was because it had been such a big week for her that went so well or her upcoming interview with Johnson. Her research into the career of Johnson as a musician and then into producing and finally as a record label owner revealed a fast and meteoric rise that left some people in the industry more than a little jealous and intimidated by the hard-driving and ambitious Johnson. Kind of like herself, thought Bentley, as she'd rubbed some people the wrong way along the way, she was sure of it, as she worked hard to establish herself in this industry. There were no questions from her editor at *Music Talks* for the Johnson interview. Just another ploy by Jonathon to motivate her to pull off a great interview—as if she needed to be motivated.

Waking up at five the next morning to catch a flight to LA from Oakland International Airport that would have her landing in LAX thirty five minutes later, Bentley was more than a little groggy from a light sleep. She would make some of it up on the flight, she thought to herself. Choosing to wear a short black skirt along with a loose black blouse that revealed just a little cleavage, Bentley finished her hair and makeup, pulled on her knee-high black leather boots with the flat soles and made her way to the parking garage and her Beetle for the short twenty-minute drive to the airport. Traffic was light, as it was still early enough. Bentley found herself a little nervous over this interview. This surprised her because she normally was never nervous for an interview, simply because she was always so well prepared. She was definitely prepared for this interview with Johnson. His life was not cloaked in secrecy that was for sure. Weird, she thought, as she found herself checking her makeup in the rearview mirror, realizing it was still dark outside and she could only see headlights from the cars behind her.

Standing to board her 8:35 a.m. flight, Bentley could feel the stares of the male passengers waiting to board as they sipped their morning Starbucks. Get a life, thought Bentley. Most of the men travelling alone on this flight commuted to LA several times a week for business with their pregnant wives at home getting the other kids to and from school while their husbands sipped Starbucks, stared at other women and ate lunch in a fine Los Angeles eatery, then arrived back at home in early evening frustrated as they compared their wives to the beautiful LA women they'd been ogling all day. In a few minutes Bentley boarded, and soon they were in the air for the very short flight. The interview with Avery Johnson would be, of course, at his recording studio in West Hollywood, just minutes from LAX, at 10:30 a.m. The plan was to then go for lunch, after which Avery would drop Bentley off at the airport for her 2:00 pm flight back home. Upon arriving at LAX, Bentley hailed a cab for the forty-minute ride to Alive Records, which would put her there a few minutes early.

As the cab dropped her off at Alive Records on Santa Monica Boulevard at 10:15 a.m., Bentley noticed that the building, with its dark brick exterior and smoked-glass windows, could have passed for a dental office building, it was so nondescript. The only indication that it was a recording studio was a small stainless steel sign with the Alive Records logo at the entrance to the parking lot. What is a recording studio supposed to look like, anyway? It's not as if they need big splashy signage on Santa Monica Boulevard advertising their studio in the hope that some unknown artist will stop in unannounced and turn out to be the next big act in the music business. In reality, Bentley thought, there would likely be private parking around the back with a separate entrance to ensure privacy for the many stars in the music businesses that were Alive Records' clients. Walking into the front entrance and into the reception area, Bentley was taken aback for a brief second at the dynamic and very cool-looking feel to it. She even had to look up in order to see the beautiful woman behind the elevated reception desk who was beaming a huge smile back at her and said, "Good morning! My name is Jenn. Welcome to Alive Records. You must be Bentley Paxton from *Music Talks*!"

Instantly liking Jen with her warm and welcoming smile, Bentley replied, "I am, and thank you. Your office is beautiful. I'm here to see Avery Johnson for a 10:30 appointment."

Jenn was very beautiful, and for a split second Bentley wondered if she was Avery's girl, fighting a tinge of jealousy.

"Certainly. He's expecting you. I'll let him know you're here. Please make yourself comfortable. Can I get you anything? An espresso, coffee, tea, juice, whatever you like," smiled Jenn.

"A bottled water would be great, Jenn, thank you."

Taking a seat in the very plush leather chairs in the reception area, Bentley was impressed at Mr. Johnson's taste in decorating his studio. Very modern, with the raised reception desk slightly tilted towards the front entrance, and the décor, this was not at all like the nondescript exterior. Jenn reappeared from the back and invited Bentley to follow her, as Avery was ready to see her. As Jenn led her into Avery's office, he came around his desk to shake her hand and say, "Good morning, Bentley, so nice to finally meet you in person."

Taking his hand and feeling his warm and inviting touch, Bentley replied, "Actually, we have met, Mr. Johnson. Several years ago in Columbia, Missouri. I was covering the Splendid Seven concert for the local paper, the *Daily Tribune.* I interviewed you and your band, but my feeling is that not too much was remembered from that concert, if you know what I mean." Bentley was mildly surprised that he had forgotten their interview years ago, but he was young and so was she, plus the Splendid Seven gig had been one big crazy party after that concert. Even though Avery was not yet thirty, he looked accomplished and mature. He was well tanned, with dirty blond hair that was not long but not close-cropped either. His dress was professional, yet casual, black dress pants with a purple striped dress shirt unbuttoned at the collar with no tie. No rings, but a huge and no doubt very expensive stainless steel watch on his wrist. She caught a faint whiff of expensive cologne that was pleasant. It gave him a slight air of vulnerability, thought Bentley.

Avery's mouth opened wide in a big smile, revealing very white and straight teeth.

"My God, you are so right! I do remember now, how could have I forgotten? Well, maybe I do know how I could have forgotten, those were crazy days back then. Unfortunately the Splendid Seven did not last with me. I left them soon after that concert, as I remember. Just couldn't keep up with them boys. Don't mind recording for the rockers, but managing them I think I will pass on. You look great, Bentley, please have a seat over here on the couch and we can get started. If you don't mind I took the liberty to book reservations at the Boxwood Café for lunch over at the London West Hotel at noon. The food is great, it's typically quiet and it's close. I see you have some water. Can I get you anything else before we get started?"

Taking a seat on a couch opposite Avery, Bentley smiled back at him.

"I'm fine, Mr. Johnson, thank you. I must say I love your studio. Your taste in décor is very good."

"Thank you, but I give most of the credit to Jenn. She has a great eye for that sort of thing, 'cause I certainly do not—and please call me Avery," he said, smiling.

Shifting in her seat, taking the notepad out of her briefcase, she began.

"Okay, that sounds good, Avery, then let's get started. Tell me about yourself before you got into this business, even before you became a musician. Tell me about your childhood, your family and who were your early influences that drew you into the music business."

Leaning back into the couch, Bentley could tell Avery was comfortable talking about himself, a sign of confidence, not the cocky kind, more like self-assurance, as if he knew where he'd come from and where he was going.

Avery told Bentley about his comfortable upbringing, how hard his parents had worked and how much he'd loved and respected them both. Avery answered all of Bentley's questions with fervor and enthusiasm. His personality and charm were magnetic, and he was very likeable and believable. No wonder people flocked to him in this business. Bentley also knew that Avery Johnson could be cutthroat when he needed to be, and she wanted to hear more about that side of him. "Avery, you have a reputation in this business of being fair and honest with your clients both in producing and negotiating recording contracts. However, you also are known to have walked away from clients who are some of the biggest in the industry. Why is that?"

Leaning off the cushions and towards her, Avery replied, "That fairness and honesty you referred to? I expect exactly the same from my clients. I don't care what my clients do in their private lives, they could be the biggest screw-ups ever, but when they work with me, either directly or through their agents, I expect them to be fair, reasonable and honest in return."

"Forgive me for saying this," Avery said, "that does sound very noble, but, for example, one of your clients in particular, J 'Tick Tock' DBL J is battling drugs and alcohol and is constantly in trouble with the law. How can Tick Tock be honest and fair?"

"For one, I do not manage the career of Tick Tock. I only produce and record his albums. When he comes in to record he is a total professional. He is a very easy client to work with. I do not babysit these people. I know that this business chews up and spits out artists like Tick Tock every day, but at the end of the day, when it comes to his career, he does things right. His longevity is a testament to that fact. I expect my clients to behave professionally and be prepared to work their butts off when they come into my studio. What Tick Tock puts up his nose or how he behaves in public is not my problem. That is why I manage very few musicians nowadays. The spoils of this business ruin them, and it used to break my heart seeing them flush their careers down the toilet with drugs and everything else. So I choose to separate myself from that, otherwise I'd be a regular on the Dr. Phil Show."

Bentley continued her interview with Avery, asking him some more tough questions that he did not take the high road on. She was more and more impressed as the interview wound down. Avery Johnson was a straight shooter, very business-savvy and seemed to be genuinely caring for people, especially his clients, friends, family and the people who worked for him. Finally, at 11:45, Avery interrupted Bentley. "Let's finish up over lunch. Bentley, I'm famished."

"That sounds great. I just about have everything I need, Avery. May I use your ladies' room and take one minute to freshen up?" asked Bentley.

Avery rose from his couch and pointed her down the hallway.

"Certainly. There's a restroom just down the hall, first door to your left outside my office. Go ahead and I will meet you out front in reception."

Fifteen minutes later, Bentley and Avery were sitting

comfortably in a booth at the trendy Boxwood Café. Trendy, but not so trendy that it would attract celebrities and, with them, the paparazzi. Avery ordered a Heineken for himself and Bentley ordered a glass of white house wine. Avery suggested the spicy tuna tartare with pickled ginger and roasted pine nuts as an appetizer, which she thought sounded yummy. For her main dish she ordered the sautéed salmon with lentils and lettuce, while Avery ordered the risotto with caramelized sea scallops and mascarpone cheese.

They both took their time enjoying their food, without much conversation. There was something in the air between them. Bentley felt it and wondered if Avery felt it as well. He took the lead and turned the conversation back to business.

"So, do you have any more questions you'd like to ask?"

Bentley took a sip of her wine as she thought about his question. "No, I don't think so, I think I have it all. Wait a minute, I do have one more question for you. Why is a young, good-looking and successful guy like you, in a dream industry surrounded by beautiful women, still single?"

Leaning across the table towards Bentley, Avery said,. "I'll answer that if you answer my question first."

Bentley looked into his eyes as he spoke and felt herself blush slightly. "Oh yeah, and what question would that be?"

"Why is a young, good-looking and successful woman like you, in a dream industry surrounded by great-looking men, still single?"

She could feel herself been drawn towards his charm, just as her boss had warned her. She struggled to maintain her composure.

"Touché, Mr. Johnson. You forget—I'm the interviewer and you're the interviewee. I ask the questions remember?"

"I will answer your question, Bentley. Over dinner tonight. Change your flight to the morning. Alive Records will get you a room right here at the London West. I'll treat you to the best LA has to offer for dinner tonight. What do you say?"

Staring back into his dreamy eyes, Bentley fought back what

she was feeling.

"Thanks, Avery, for the offer. That's very tempting, but I do have to be back this afternoon. In addition to getting this interview typed up for my editor, I have to get ready for another interview and concert tomorrow night in San Francisco." In reality she easily could have stayed in LA overnight and still have more than enough time to prepare for tomorrow night's concert, but she was finding herself attracted to Avery, and staying longer would not be a good idea.

The disappointment was clear in his eyes.

"That's a shame, but maybe next time, okay? How does one get hold of you? The next time I'm up in your area I'll give you a call and maybe we can grab some dinner then."

It took all of her strength not to say the hell with it and just stay. There was an obvious attraction between them that she would have liked to explore further. Just not now, she thought.

"That would be lovely, Avery, I would enjoy that. Let me give you my card. My cell number is on the card."

Lunch finished up with both of them a little nervous, filling the time with conversations about some of the interviews Bentley had done over the previous few years since she'd been in northern California. She told Avery the story of the one interview that had got away on her with Watermark a few years ago. The strange behavior of the band members and their over-the-top manager, Robert Best. When Avery heard the name Best, his interest was immediately piqued, and he said, "What an amazing coincidence. He was the manager of Watermark? Funny that never came up in any of the background checks I had Jenn do on him. I also had a strange encounter with that dude here in LA. Bumped into him at a club not too far from here, or actually he bumped into me. Said he was an up-and-coming manager. The next thing I know he's in my reception at ten the next morning with his client Devon Devine and telling Jenn he has an appointment with me that we had scheduled the night before in the club. I did not make an appointment with this guy. He gave me the creeps, and then seeing his client Devon Devine, who literally never said one word the whole time they were in my office. Very strange."

After a few more minutes talking about Best, Bentley noticed the time was getting up there, and she needed to get to the airport to catch her flight home. Avery paid the bill and they got up to leave, heading to the valet parking, where the attendant brought up Avery's BMW. Driving to the airport, both of them were quiet, that almost awkward feeling that comes with the discovery of mutual attraction. Pulling up to departures for Delta, Avery put the car in park, got out and came around to open the door for Bentley. Reaching out to shake her hand goodbye, he said, "I enjoyed my time with you, Bentley. I'm hoping you'll be nice to me when the final edits come through for the article." Avery chuckled at his own kidding remark, then continued, "Have a pleasant flight home, and I hope to talk with you soon."

Bentley found herself reaching up and giving Avery a slight kiss on the cheek and a slight hug. She was finding it hard to say goodbye.

"I hope so, Avery. Thank you for lunch and your hospitality at your studio. Talk soon." With that, Bentley turned and headed into the terminal, wishing she had decided to stay instead of leaving.

Chapter 16

There are very few cities in the world that make the transition from winter to spring to summer like Montreal. There was a joyous and almost festive mood amongst the mostly French-speaking citizens of the city from March to May. The changes in the weather were obvious, and once spring came, it stayed. Unlike other Canadian cities, in the west, that were teased with spring weather and then got slammed with a spring snowstorm that sapped all the joy out of the change of seasons and led instead into complaints of another lousy spring. Not so in eastern Canada, and the beautiful international city of Montreal. The city wasted no time getting its streets scrubbed and cleaned from the ravages of another winter. After five months of sanding the slippery winter roads, the city street cleaners came out in full force. City workers power-washed the street signs, getting rid of all of the dried slush that splashes up from the tires of endless winter traffic. A litany of small pieces of garbage that litter the boulevards once the snow has melted away was swiftly gathered up by the city. In no time the city of Montreal looked brand new again, beautiful and full of grandeur, ready to welcome the flow of tourists that came every spring and summer.

Montreal, with over three and a half million citizens is the second oldest city in North America. It is also the second largest French-speaking city in the world, next to Paris. Its distinctive European influence is obvious to anyone visiting Montreal for the first time. The famous rue Sainte-Catherine, known for its shopping and dining, comes alive like no other street during the spring and summer months, when citizens and tourists alike stroll along its cobblestone sidewalks.

Born and raised in Montreal, Gerard Louveneau loved the city and embraced its rich cultural variety. A graduate of the Faculty of Law at prestigious McGill University, thirty-two-year old Gerard was a mover and a shaker in the law courts as a young, ambitious and skilled Quebec Crown Prosecutor. Gerard had emerged from the prosecutions office as a force to be reckoned with, as he'd been a pivotal force in the case against Montreal's notorious Hell's Angels gang. In a series of sweeping arrests of Montreal's Angels, along with many other organized crime figures, resulting from a two year investigation called 'Operation Put Down,' it had been Gerard's job in the Crown Prosecutor's office to liaise with the various enforcement agencies involved, which included the RCMP, Quebec Provincial Police (QPP), and Montreal and Quebec City police forces, to ensure that evidence gathered from all of the police agencies was organized and cataloged, and that all investigators' notes were uploaded into a central computer program. The end result was that the Crown was so well organized when the case finally made it to trial the bad guys didn't stand a chance. They went down like dominoes, and there was jubilation throughout the agencies involved, with lots of credit being passed around by the media. Gerard's relentless hard work behind the scenes was the glue that made it all stick, and the higher-ups quietly heralded his work as the critical component in the successful prosecutions that came out of 'Operation Put Down'.

While briefing the investigators assigned to the task force at the beginning of the two-year investigation on the importance of keeping timely and accurate notes, Gerard informed them that their attention to detail and diligence would pay off in spades when it came time to prosecute. Gerard told them that defense lawyers would go after investigators' notes for inaccuracies with a vengeance. He also walked them through the process of the new software program that they would use to fill out their reports on a daily basis after every shift if possible. Gerard told them that every investigator from every agency would be doing the same and that it would be his task to collate these notes in chronological order to present to a jury in any future trial.

The best thing that came out of that two-year frenzy for Gerard was that he met his future wife Francoise LaParriere, herself an accomplished young investigator for the QPP assigned to the task force. It was during one of these early briefings that Gerard took notice of this beautiful investigator assigned to the task force and took the bold step of asking her out for dinner. She accepted, and they began to date after that with more and more frequency, both of them falling madly in love. They made the decision that they would not run the risk, professionally or to the investigation, that might lead to a conflict of interest, so they each went to their respective bosses to inform them of their relationship. Their bosses decided that it would be in the best interests of the investigation that Francoise be reassigned. One of them stepping away from the investigation was the best thing that could have happened to their relationship. They spent more time together, and eight months after they'd first met Gerard asked Francoise to marry him. She accepted, and four months later they were married. As they were both Catholic, they tied the knot in a huge ceremony at the beautiful and venerable Marie-Reine-du-Monde Cathedral. Completed in 1894, Montreal's primary Roman Catholic cathedral was designed as a one-third-size replica of St. Peter's in Rome, down to a copy of Bernini's Baldacchino over the altar. Even at this scale the church is pretty grandiose in effect. Attending the wedding, in addition to both extended families, was a large contingent of police officers and personnel from the police community as well as from the Crown Attorney's office in Montreal. Both Gerard and Francois were well liked in the law enforcement community, so the wedding guest list swelled to the point that, had they not drawn a line and put a limit on the number of invited guests, there would have been no one left to patrol the streets of Montreal!

On all accounts the Louveneau's had it all. Fast-tracking careers, money, happiness, and they were truly in love with each other. Something was missing, however, in this relationship, and Francoise's female intuition was telling her something was wrong between her and Gerard. The ink had barely dried on their marriage certificate, and Francois already was feeling insecure. Her husband was extremely handsome and successful and seemed to be admired by beautiful women wherever they went out. These days women didn't care if a man was married; if they wanted him they'd just go for it. Gerard would frequently be invited to lecture recruits at the Montreal City Police Academy on the proper methodology on note taking while conducting day-to-day police work and investigations. Canadian police academies across the country were taking very seriously the importance of police officers taking thorough and accurate notes during the course of their jobs as a result of more and more cases being thrown out of court because of incomplete or inaccurate notes. Gerard, with the success he'd had in Operation Put Down in evidence gathering and the emphasis put on investigator's note taking, was seen as the poster boy for the importance of proper note taking and the techniques needed to be taught and instilled into the psyches of recruits.

Francoise could well imagine the pretty, young, nubile recruits all googly-eyed over the gorgeous star Crown Prosecutor famous for busting up the gangs and the mob. It was an insecurity that Francoise hated in herself. She knew she was a beautiful woman who had nothing to worry about, as her new husband loved her.

It was at one of these one-day lectures at the Academy where a young and beautiful young recruit named Tiffany Coutierre caught Gerard's eye with her obvious infatuation with the accomplished and well-known lawyer. During the lunch break these lectures, Gerard liked to sit out on a bench by the trees on the Academy grounds when the weather was nice, and on this late spring day it was bright and balmy. Finding an empty bench with his Styrofoam container of takeout from the Academy cafeteria, Gerard was interrupted by a visitor and was surprised to see it was the gorgeous blond recruit from his class.

"Excuse me, Mr. Louveneau. If you don't mind, may I join you out here to eat lunch? It is so beautiful outside I just had to get out of that school and take advantage of some fresh air."

Wow, she's a looker, thought Gerard. No harm in having some conversation with her. The recruits were often trying to ingratiate themselves with the instructors, thinking it would help fast track their own careers.

"Well, certainly. And you can call me Gerard. I am sorry but I do not know your name. I just show up and give my lecture, which I am sure all of you forget the minute it's over—along with my name!"

The beautiful Tiffany turned on the bench to face Gerard, her face breaking into a wide smile.

"Absolutely not, Gerard. Your talk on getting into good habits in taking notes is not only interesting but very informative. I am looking forward to this afternoon's talk on the force's investigative software program. We have to use it every day, so learning from you, the one who literally designed the program—it doesn't get any better, in my opinion. Oh, and my name is Tiffany Coutierre."

He finished the bite of his sandwich as he replied.

"Thank you, Tiffany, very flattering. I will be watching to see if you are still awake by the end of the day." After about a half-hour of small talk, Gerard checked his watch and said, "Well, listen Tiffany, we'd better get back, otherwise they will be sending out a search party to look for us. I am sure the recruits will be coming back from lunch full of anticipation for this afternoon's lesson."

They walked back to class together, Gerard enjoying Tiffany's obvious flirtatiousness. Holding the door open to the class for her, she made sure her ample breasts brushed against his arm as she passed by him on her way into the class.

As the afternoon's lesson wound down, Gerard handed out a twenty-five question multiple-choice test for the recruits to complete. Once it was completed, they could drop it off on his desk and head out for the day. After about forty minutes, the recruits began to finish up one at a time and drop off the test on his desk on their way out of class. When Tiffany walked by she dropped off hers, gave Gerard a wide smile and, as she placed the test on his desk, she brushed his hand. A slightly embarrassed Gerard looked up at her as she was about to turn and walk away, and as she did so she gave Gerard a wink that was soaked in sexual innuendo. Wow, that woman is something else, Gerard thought to himself. As the last recruit handed in his test, Gerard gathered them up and dropped them in his briefcase to take home, where he would correct them later and email the Academy administrator with the results, in addition to any comments he might have. Normally he would spend another hour after the tests were completed to correct them and then drop them off to the administrator on his way out, but he was in a hurry today as he was to meet up with some guys from the office to catch the Canadiens playoff game on the giant TV screens at the Peel Pub on St. Catherine Street. Francoise, if her shift ended on time, would join Gerard at the pub to catch the last period of the hockey game.

After Gerard had finished gathering up his stuff, he grabbed his briefcase and headed out the door. Waving goodbye to another instructor as he exited the front doors of the Academy, Gerard headed off to his government-issued Buick Park Avenue in the staff parking lot. As he rounded the corner of the building to the parking lot, he was startled to see the blond bombshell recruit Tiffany Coutierre standing beside his car. Approaching the car, a little embarrassed and uncomfortable, he asked her, "Did you forget something in the class, Tiffany?"

"Well, I am a little embarrassed, to be honest. I came to class today with another recruit and there must have been some confusion after class because when I went out to the parking lot after the test she had already left. I noticed your car was still here and was hoping you wouldn't mind dropping me off at the first subway station on your way home."

Damn, she is so gorgeous, thought Gerard, how could he not say yes to giving her a lift? "Sure, I am heading south to St. Catherine to catch the game at the Peel with some friends, so jump in. I can drop you off on the way."

Pulling out of the parking lot, Gerard caught a glimpse of Tiffany sitting beside him as they made small talk, noticing that she had unbuttoned the top button of her blouse, exposing a little cleavage. Gerard had a feeling he knew where this was going. Her beauty was intoxicating. He just needed to keep it together and get her to a train stop without doing something he would surely regret. Heading south on Boulevard René-Lévesque, it wasn't long before Gerard was passing a subway station. Neither of them said anything. They just kept making small talk, then Gerard said, "Tiffany you know what? Why don't I just drop you off at your place, I have some time yet before I am to meet the guys, so I don't mind giving you a ride home."

Brushing her hand against his, she replied, "It's okay, I can take the train. I don't want to put you out. With this traffic it will slow you down, but thank you."

Feeling her touch and the tone of her voice, Gerard was losing control of the situation and he knew it, but he couldn't stop himself. She had an amazing effect on him as he was sure she had on most men. "No seriously, it's okay, Tiffany. I don't mind. Just tell me where to go."

Thirty minutes later they were tearing each other's clothes off in the bedroom of her condo. Hot passion, combined with the knowledge that what he was doing was terribly wrong, seemed to fuel Gerard's desire even more. Tiffany was incredibly beautiful, as he explored every inch of her after carrying her to her bed. Their lovemaking was intense and seemed to last for hours. Finally Gerard released himself inside of her, nearly passing out from the intensity of the whole experience. With both of them awash in sweat, exhausted from their powerful, passionate lovemaking, they found themselves collapsing into each other's arms. Gerard was the first to speak. "I can't believe what just happened?!"

"I am not sure but I know that it was pretty damn good. Are you complaining, Professor?" smiled Tiffany as she snuggled her moist body close to Gerard's, her heavy breasts cushioning against his arm.

"Tiffany, I am married," he replied, pointing to the band on his finger. "I'm a fucking idiot?!"

Tiffany crawled back on top of him, looking him in the eyes, her amazing breasts inches from his face.

"Hey, don't beat yourself up. You are here right now because you wanted to be. The fact that you wanted to be here means there is something wrong in your marriage. Am I wrong?"

Forcing the thought of his wife and his marriage out of his mind, Gerard reached for Tiffany, kissing her hard, his tongue meeting hers inside her mouth. She propped herself up so her breasts fell directly onto his face, covering it as he caressed and kissed them. She straddled him, and they made fierce and passionate love once again, turning over with Gerard back on top of her, thrusting inside her. This time Tiffany came first, screaming out in pleasure, her body stiffening beneath Gerard's. He followed soon after with an explosive climax, collapsing on top of her, physically spent.

After a few hours of a deep sleep in each other's arms, Gerard sat bolt upright in bed, looked at his watch and said to Tiffany, "Holy shit! It's almost 9:30 p.m. My wife was to meet me at the Peel before the end of the game!" A panicked Gerard leaped out of the bed.

"I'm sorry, Tiffany, it's not your fault. But I never should have come here. I must be out of my mind. You are an incredibly beautiful woman. You don't need a married man complicating your life."

He noticed her watching him scramble to get his clothes on with a look that said she had seen this scene play out many times before.

"Let me be the judge of that, why don't you. See me again, Gerard. Don't make me wait till next month when you are out at the Academy again teaching another class," purred Tiffany as

Gerard finished dressing and headed for the door.

Kissing her on her forehead, Gerard opened the door, and before he turned to leave he said to her, "We will see, okay? No promises. Let me absorb what has happened here. Take care."

Rushing out to his car, Gerard heard his phone start to ring. Looking at the caller ID, he realized it was Francoise. Shit. Not sure what he was going to say, he answered it, "Hi, sweetheart, I was just going to call you."

"Where are you? I have been waiting here for over half an hour now. Nobody has heard from you and the game is just ending. Why haven't you answered your phone?"

He was in full lying mode now and he hated it.

"I went out with some other instructors at the college as a last-minute thing. I was only going to stay for one period max, then head over to the Peel, but next thing I know the game is almost over and I'm racing to you now. I should be there in ten minutes."

"Well, go for it, but I'm leaving and most of the guys have left, too. I'll just meet you at home. What did you think of the game and who won?"

Oh, shit, the score, thought Gerard, he'd never thought of that. "Honey, I have another call coming through, and it's the office so I'd better take it. I will see you back at the house in a few minutes. Love you, bye," Gerard said, clicking the phone's end button. Jeepers, he thought to himself, *what the hell am I doing?*

He listened to the post-game show on the radio on his way home, getting the full details of the game to make sure he wouldn't be caught flat-footed with Francoise, while he tried to sort out in his mind what he had done and where he would go from here. What just happened with Tiffany had come from so far out in left field Gerard could barely wrap his head around it all. He loved Francoise without a doubt, he knew that. He also knew that their sex life had never been great even when they were dating. It just seemed that they worked so much and their schedules were so different that when the opportunity arose to be intimate it was more choreographed than spontaneous. It was still good, but making love to Tiffany was at a whole new level, something he had never experienced before. Gerard knew he would hear from her again, and he needed to make a decision quickly on how to deal with this. Either to continue the affair or end it. Then decide whether to tell Francoise of his infidelity or write it off as an isolated incident that would never happen again.

Pulling up the driveway, he knew what he was going to do. He would tell Tiffany that it had been a great night but nothing more would ever come of it, that it had been a mistake. He would then tell Francoise and pray that she would forgive him and give him another chance. He needed to shower, and then holding his wife close in his arms was going to be the extent of things for tonight. Grabbing his briefcase, he went inside the house. Walking in through the door in the garage, then directly to his den, Gerard opened his briefcase and realized that he had the tests that he needed to correct and fax a results sheet to the Academy administrator. Damn, he thought. He would get up early in the morning, correct them, add his comments and fax the results sheet before 9:00 a.m. He had done it before even though it made the administrator pissed. Dropping the stack of tests back on his desk, causing them to fall half on the floor and the other half all to splay across his desk, he turned to head upstairs to the shower when he noticed one test paper had a bunch of doodling with some sort of red mark on it. He reached down to the floor and picked it up and saw that it was the test paper from Tiffany. She had written in bold letters on the front of the paper, 'To my sexy instructor. Call me, you won't regret it! Tiffany 519-566-1212. Underneath the note was a stamp of her red lipstick lips. Gerard instantly felt weak and aroused, again thinking of her. *Damn it, Gerard. Stop it! Get it together!*

"Are you okay, honey? You look like you've seen a ghost," smiled Francoise as she approached Gerard wearing her nightie underneath a very short and sexy satin housecoat.

"It's been a long day for the Professor, darling. A shower to wake up this weary body and you will wish you'd been sleeping when I arrived home," Gerard replied playfully as he discreetly shoved Tiffany's paper underneath a stack of others on his desk.

"Sounds good to me, I'll be waiting," she purred as she turned to head upstairs.

Standing by himself, shaking from what could have been if Francoise had seen the paper from Tiffany and the explaining he would have had to do, he turned to head upstairs when he saw a movement from either a large object or a shadow that startled him. Following the movement down the hall, he heard a bloodcurdling scream from upstairs.

It was Francoise! She screamed again, *and this time it chilled Gerard to the bone.*

Chapter 17

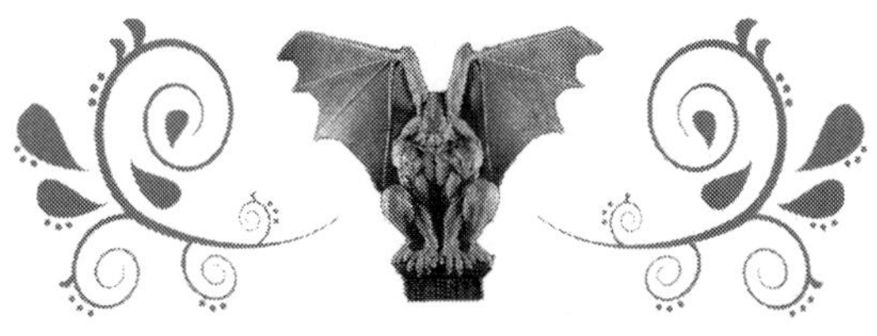

Driving home from Little Kelly's, Bert was quiet, lost in his thoughts about whatever the hell had just happened in the restroom with that stranger. His talk of tracking the lineage of Lori for over seventeen hundred years and that she had been chosen. His demonic look and strength frightened Bert, and that is not easy to scare this old cowboy, he thought. He was not scared for himself, he was too old for that, he was just scared for the threats this thing or man had made about Lori and Brent. Then he heard Brent say, "Dad are you okay? You're awfully quiet all of a sudden."

Pushing those thoughts out of his mind, he reminded himself that his son was beside him and they just had a great evening together sharing some heavy stuff.

"Just thinking about how wonderful it's going to be to have Lori join us at the ranch. It's been a while since there has been a womanly presence at home, huh, son?"

"You miss Mom, don't you Dad? Why not consider meeting someone? You need someone in your life. Find a nice lady for friendship and see where it goes."

As he looked over at his son while he drove, the truck's dashboard lights were all that illuminated the interior, but the glow was enough for Bert to see the serious look on his son's face.

"Yeah, I've often thought of maybe meeting someone, son, but you know with the ranch and everything I'm just too damn tired and don't seem to have the energy for it. The memories I carry of your mom sustain me, son, they really do."

"You sure loved Mom. You know, I hope I'll be so lucky and have as good a marriage with Lori as you did with Mom."

He reached over and squeezed Brent's forearm as he spoke.

"You will, son, Lori is a great girl. Why doesn't she live with us now rather than waiting till after the wedding?"

"Well she wants to wait till we're married before she moves in with us. It's only a month away anyway, plus her mother would disown her if she moved in now. Why would you ask that, Dad? That came out of left field."

A feeling of dread had crept into the pit of his stomach and he couldn't explain it. That weirdo from the bar was definitely getting to him.

"I just want her to be safe and sound leading up to the big day. Never mind, son, just a fussing old crow meddling in someone else's business."

"It's nice to know you care, Dad, it really is. Lori loves and appreciates everything about you and what you've done for us."

As Bert and Brent were nearing the ranch they drove the last few miles in silence. He was overcome with a feeling of dread and fear over the welfare of his son and his future wife after his strange encounter at the bar earlier. Was he so overtired, he thought, that maybe he was just imagining things? Whatever that had been in the restroom was not human, if indeed he was not imagining it. In a couple of days this will just be a weird memory, he thought.

They reached the entrance off the main road to Asker Farms, with its log posts on each side of the entrance road and an arched banner made of iron announcing 'ASKER FARMS' that spanned across the entrance road and about twenty feet in the air. On each side of the sign there was also a cowboy leaning against a post with one leg bent at the knee and his cowboy hat tilted downward, also cut out of steel. The grand entrance signage gave the farm a Ponderosa feel to it like the famous Bonanza television series.

****

"Whoa, Dad, stop! There's something in the middle of the lane, looks like one of the dogs!" shouted Brent. Bert slammed on the brakes, coming to a stop just in front of the motionless body of a dog. Jumping out of the truck and into the headlights of the pickup, Brent ran up and bent over the dead body of one the ranch's many farm dogs, Dixon. Using his boot to roll the dead dog over, Brent did a double take when he saw what had been done to it. Two steel railway spikes had been driven into each of its eyes through the back of its skull. Brent buckled over at the gruesome sight.

As Bert climbed out of the truck and approached the dead dog, Brent heard him say, "Oh sweet Jesus, what the hell?! Who the hell would have done this?!" Brent then watched his Dad walk back to the truck where he retrieved a twelve-gauge shotgun from the rack off the back window in the super cab Ford pickup truck. Walking back up to Brent, he said, "There is a sick son of a bitch around to have done this, and they could still be here. Drive the truck up to the house and call the sheriff to get up here. I'm gonna walk around and see what the hell is going on."

"Dad—no—wait for me. I'll grab the rifle in the house and we'll go together. It could be dangerous to go by yourself."

With a shout that startled him, Bert made it clear he was not about to negotiate.

"Do it, son! Now! Stay in the house till I return, do you hear me?"

"Jesus, Dad, I hear you. Be careful, okay?"

****

As Brent headed back to the truck, Bert walked three quarters of the way up the lane, then turned towards the main barn where he could see from the little bit of light coming from the moon that the barn doors were opened. They kept the horses in this barn, all nineteen of them. The horses were used primarily by the workers, as well as Brent and himself, plus of course Lori. Why the hell would have Mel forgotten to secure the barn doors? Mel was his only full-time ranch worker, whose last responsibility before he left for the day was to feed the horses and fill the water trough. He never leaves it open, thought Bert. Whoever killed Dixon might very well be in the barn. The yard light that was powerful enough to light up the property around the house and barn was out for some reason. Approaching the barn with his shotgun ready to blast any intruder, he could hear a sound coming from within, like labored breathing or wheezing. Walking cautiously through the darkened barn doors, Bert reached for the light switch to flick it on, but the switch was already on. Bert clicked it up and down a few times to no avail, the lights were not coming on. There was another set of light switches that turned on the halogen lamps that hung in a row down the middle of the barn tresses about twenty feet away. Keeping close to the wall as he made his way to the light switches, Bert could hear the labored breathing again. It sounded like it was coming from the first stall to the left, closest to the barn door where he had just come through. Someone was hurt and in a lot of pain. Bert called out, "Mel, are you okay? Mel, is that you"? Not hearing any response, Bert was able to reach out and turn the overhead barn lights on. The inside of the barn instantly filled with light, blinding Bert for a brief second. There was no sound whatsoever coming from any of the stalls. The whir of the overhead fans could be heard but that was it. Moving quickly across to the first stall where he'd heard the labored breathing a few minutes ago, he realized it was now very quiet.

He was not prepared for what he saw when he peered into the stall. Mel was lying on his back in a pile of hay in the corner of the stall, barely alive. Rushing into the stall, Bert knelt down and examined Mel, searching for his injuries, his mind frantically wondering what had happened.

"Jesus, Mel. What the hell happened?! Where are you hurt? Help is on the way!" Bert knew he had to get back to the house to tell Brent to call the paramedics. He heard a gurgling sound coming from Mel as if he was trying to speak. Leaning in close to Mel, he could barely hear him whisper through a clenched jaw, "The devil, boss, the devil."

Those words whispered by Mel chilled him to the bone. There was evil in this barn, he could feel it. He'd felt it earlier this evening, in the bathroom with the stranger and his burning red eyes.

Hearing Brent approaching the barn, Bert jumped up and raced out the doors. He stopped Brent before he was able to reach the barn and yelled, "Go back to the house, son, and call an ambulance to come out here! Hurry!"

With panic written all over his face, his son asked, "What's the matter, Dad, what's happened?!", looking past him to try to peer into the barn.

Barely able to control the fear in his voice, Bert commanded, "It's Mel, son, he's badly hurt, now go call in the ambulance," as he turned to head back into the barn.

He ran back into the barn, knowing Mel did not have long to live. It appeared his back was broken, as he couldn't move. He was covered in deep lacerations to his face and body. His clothing was ripped to shreds. Whoever had done this to him had to have been a very large and powerful man, as Mel was strong and tough as a bull. Leaning in close again so Mel could hear him, Bert told him, "Hang in there, buddy, everything is going to be okay, the ambulance will be here any minute."

Suddenly Mel's eyes opened wide and he tried to speak again, but nothing came out except muffled wheezing. His reaction made Bert look up and behind his shoulder to see what had startled Mel. Then he saw it, and it turned his blood to ice. The same stranger who had attacked him at the tavern was now standing in his barn ready to attack again. But he was no stranger. He was a monster standing over seven feet tall with the same hideous face filled with lethal-looking fangs dripping in anticipation of ripping him to pieces. The creature's long arms ballooned with massive muscles and were tipped with claws that could shred him apart like a rag doll. Seeing his shotgun leaning against the wall of the pen about ten feet away, Bert did not waste any time and lunged for the gun. Diving for the shotgun just as the monster took a swipe at him with those huge claws, barely missing him, he rolled over on his back and back onto his feet, lifted the shotgun up to his waist and, pumping a round into the chamber, aimed at the middle of this thing's chest and fired. The sound of the boom in the small space of the pen was deafening. The blast caught the creature squarely in the chest, sending him flying back hard against the wall. Bert did not hesitate, and pumped another round into the creature, causing a large chunk of its upper chest and shoulder to disappear in spatter against the wall. The thing was screaming like a badger with its leg caught in a steel trap. He pumped another round in the chamber and fired again, blasting most of the right side of its head off. Any human would have been instantly killed with the first blast, but this thing was still trying to stand up. Bert knew he only had one shell left in the chamber. He pumped one last time and sent the final volley of shotgun blast right into the middle of its face, obliterating it like a smashed watermelon.

Dropping the gun to the floor, Bert could hear the emergency sirens in the distance. Better send cleaners with mops and pails for that thing plastered all over the wall, he thought. Why hell had opened its gates in his barn he was too numb to even fathom as he turned to head up to the house.

Suddenly there was a powerful arm around his neck yanking him backwards. This can't be happening? *He'd killed this thing!* The powerful arm around his throat was cutting off all his air supply and he was rapidly choking. Reaching up and grabbing the arm to try to wrench it free, he could not budge it. Glimpsing the face of whoever was grabbing him from the corner of his eye, he could see that it was human. Its eyes were glowing that deep menacing red. This thing that he thought he had destroyed had transformed into a human again, as it had done previously. Backpedalling, trying to slam the creature against the wall of the pen, was useless; this thing was far more powerful than he was. He felt the tinge of darkness creep into the corner of his eyes as he desperately tried to suck air into his lungs, but the grip would not loosen. As the life began to ebb from him and the darkness crept in all around him he thought of Betty-Ann, how he knew he would soon be joining her, and those peaceful thoughts were the last he would ever have. The human form of the beast called Robert Best jerked Bert's head ferociously to the left, breaking his neck, killing him instantly, then dropping him to the ground in a heap. Falling onto his chest, Bert stared straight up, his head twisted a sickening one hundred and eighty degrees.

****

Dialing 911 back in the house, Brent heard the roaring boom from his dad's shotgun. Frantically telling the 911 operator the situation and to send an ambulance out to the ranch, Brent heard three more booming blasts from the shotgun. Panicking, he told the operator he did not know the extent of the injuries but that he had to go. Hanging up the phone, he grabbed the 9mm pistol from its case in the top shelf of his dad's bedroom closet and raced out the door to the barn. Not having heard anything since the last shotgun blast, he yelled out his dad's name, asking if he was alright as he headed for the barn doors. Hearing the sirens of what had to be the sheriff approaching, he bolted inside the well-lit barn, and immediately wished he hadn't. The pungent smell of gunpowder mixed with the normal smells of the barn was overpowering. Reaching the open door to the pen immediately to his left as he walked in the barn, he confronted an image that would be seared into his memory for as long as he lived. His dad laying in a crumpled heap on the pen floor, his head spun completely around now backwards, looking up at him, his swollen eyes reflecting the horror he must have seen before he was killed. Then he saw Mel, lying on his back dead, his lifeless eyes staring straight up at the ceiling.

Seeing what looked like a pile of blood and guts all over the wall of the pen where dad must have hit his assailant with the shotgun, Brent braced himself. He turned and walked cautiously further into the barn, holding his 9mm shoulder high.

Hearing the police cars pouring into the farmyard, he could see movement at the far end of the barn. Walking towards the movement, he yelled out, "Stop where you are, there is no escape! This place will be swarming with cops in seconds! I will shoot your fucking head off if you so much as move again!"

He moved towards the motion in the rear corner of the barn. Suddenly he heard a deep, throaty laugh that sent chills down his spine, followed by a voice that sounded like pure evil: "I am not done here. I will be back for you and Lori."

Then Brent saw the glow of the fiery red eyes coming from the direction of that awful voice in the corner of the barn about seventy-five feet away. *What could it be, some sort of animal or a cougar?!* He didn't care to find out, instead opting to unload his pistol at those eyes, firing off all thirteen rounds in succession as he moved towards the red eyes and the movement. As the last bullet exited the 9mm, kicking back the action on the pistol, he heard the evil laugh once again, and a motion that was so rapid it looked almost like a naked man. It moved like a blur out the back of the barn doors and into the night.

There was a commotion behind Brent, and he turned to see Sheriff Clarkson, followed by several deputies, entering the barn with weapons drawn. Dropping to his knees, Brent felt a rush of nausea and bent over, throwing up all over the floor, as he heard the Sheriff yell, "Jesus, Mary, Christ! Bert! Oh my God. Where the hell is the ambulance?!"

Brent could hear noises and commotion, everything going black as he passed out on the barn floor. He felt, faintly, hands gripping him from beneath, as if he was being lifted.

****

Coming to a few minutes later, Brent, for a brief second didn't realize where he was, until he heard a voice beside him that could not have been more welcome at this moment. Sitting up on the living room couch, he looked into the bloodshot and teary eyes of Lori, who reached down and wrapped her arms around him. He cradled her head in his neck as she said, "Oh, baby, I am so sorry. I just can't believe what has happened. I'm so thankful you're okay."

Lifting her head off of his shoulder, he looked into her eyes.

"When did you get here? How long was I out? My dad, Lori, he was killed so horribly. I just can't believe he's dead," said Brent, tears welling in his eyes.

Lori's warm tears spilled onto his hands as she spoke.

"I know, baby. I just found out two minutes ago when I got here. I arrived home from shopping with Mom when I was trying to reach you on your cell and you weren't answering so I got worried and drove out here. When I saw all the police cars and ambulances I don't think I was ever so scared in my life," Lori said out loud.

She was interrupted by a hand touching Brent's shoulder.

"Excuse me, Brent, I need to ask you a few questions if you are feeling better," said Sheriff Clarkson.

Brent bent down and gave Lori a deep kiss, her tears feeling wet against his skin. He then looked up at the sheriff.

"Yes, by all means, sheriff. Have you tracked this maniac down yet?"

The sheriff reached over to the footstool beside the coffee table and slid it toward him so he could sit in front of Brent and Lori.

"Just to bring you up to speed first. We have roadblocks set up on all roads leading out of the farm plus all entrances onto highways 85, 80 and 25 leading away from here. Before you blacked out in the barn, Brent, you mentioned one man as the intruder. Was there anyone else? We believe with the amount of carnage in that barn there would have had to been a number of people involved."

Panic and fear rose up inside Brent as he asked the sheriff, "Is there anyone else dead besides my Dad and Mel?"

The sheriff took off his cowboy hat, turning it over in his hands as he replied, "How many horses do you keep in the main barn, Brent?"

"We keep nineteen horses in that barn. We currently have two mares that are pregnant. Why are you asking me about the horses?"

Sheriff Clarkson paused for what seemed like an eternity before he spoke.

"There are twelve butchered horses dead in their stalls, Brent. The remaining seven must have escaped. The horses were slaughtered beyond belief. Throats were cut wide open, some had deep, long lacerations over their bodies, and then a few, Brent, had their heads cut right off. There are two of your dogs killed as well, a German shepherd on the shoulder of the lane coming in and a retriever in the barn. Both of them were impaled with railway spikes through their eyes. Very gruesome. I've never seen anything like this in my entire twenty-seven-year career, and I'm sorry to have to be so blunt in telling you the details."

Brent was stunned at the carnage described by Sheriff Clarkson. Lori broke out in full sobs, the loss of Bert, Mel and the animals too much for her. Cradling Lori, tightly Brent said,. "My dad and I discovered Dixon on the driveway when we got home from Cheyenne. Dad grabbed the shotgun from the truck and headed off to the barn, while he made me drive the truck to the house and call you. My God, who could have done this, sheriff? Who would have wanted to do this to us? My dad and I have no enemies, certainly none that would do something like this," hugging Lori close to him as he spoke.

Sheriff Clarkson placed his hat back on his head and rose from the stool as he spoke.

"Considering the nature of these crimes, Brent, we have called in the FBI out of Cheyenne. They should be here momentarily, so be prepared for a long night of questions as they do their thing. I'm going to step outside now and wait for them. You need anything, you just let one of my deputies know, okay? Once the Feds are done here, I suggest you spend the next few nights at Lori's parents' place, at least until the barn has been cleaned up."

The FBI arrived a few minutes later, bringing with them an army of agents and equipment. They went through the barn in meticulous detail, looking for evidence. Photos were taken for blood spatter patterns, tissue and blood were gathered, and everything was looked at in the barn and the surrounding property. All potential evidence was documented, bagged or photographed.. They questioned Brent for over an hour about any potential enemies his dad could have had who might somehow be connected to the murders, including the financial condition of the ranch, which might have caused Bert to turn to unsavory people for money to keep it afloat. Nonpayment might have resulted in his murder. All theories were discussed, and Brent made it clear that the ranch was not in debt and that ever since the financial bath the ranch had taken from Mad Cow Disease, his dad had dedicated himself completely to the recovery of the ranch and within several years had successfully turned things around, helped by the huge demand in Asia for North American beef driving prices sky high and pulling his Dad and many other ranchers out of the abyss.

It was almost morning. Finishing up with the police, Brent and Lori left the farm to head into the city to her place to try to somehow get some rest. Brent could not shake the macabre image of his father's head twisted completely around. He would never forget the horror of that memory. Lori insisted in driving Brent's truck, so he slid all the way over in the seat and snuggled close to her. Feeling the lump in the back of his pants, he reached back and pulled out his 9mm pistol and put it on the seat beside him. Opening up the glove box, he pulled out the box of 9mm hollow-point shells.

"I'm not taking any chances, Lori. Whoever did this could be looking for me still," Brent said as he reloaded the clip and then jammed it back in the grip of the semi-auto pistol, placing it in the glove box.

****

They drove past two roadblocks before they made it onto Interstate 25. Brent found himself nodding off as the exhaustion of the night began hitting him hard. Lori, with Brent's head pressed against her shoulder, drove on in silence, letting him get some rest. Lori was literally numb from the events of the night, unable to believe that Bert was gone. Poor Brent, she thought to herself, he has been through so much this past year. Enduring Lori's insistence on abstinence during their engagement and agreeing to the many counseling sessions with Pastor Simmons regarding his anger issues had taken its toll on their relationship—and now this. They needed Pastor Simmons now more than ever, and she decided she would call him as soon as they arrived at home so he could come over and help Brent come to grips with the events of the previous night.

It was almost five in the morning when they pulled into the driveway, and Lori could see the police car parked at the corner keeping an eye on the house just as Sheriff Clarkson promised. Her house was dark and quiet, with her parents sleeping blissfully unaware of the carnage that had taken place at the Asker Ranch. As she nudged Brent awake, he opened his eyes, commenting that he couldn't believe he'd slept all the way there.

****

Climbing out of the truck, Brent reached back into the glove box to retrieve the 9mm. Stuffing it into his back belt, he walked up the driveway with Lori and quietly opened the front door as to not disturb Lori's parents. They quickly realized that was the least they needed to worry about. The death and destruction at the Asker Ranch had made its way to Lori's house. Turning on the living room lights as they entered the house, Lori screamed hysterically. Brent was stunned at what he was seeing. Pulling the pistol from his back belt, he surveyed the scene. Lori's parents, who were deeply religious, had numerous crosses of various sizes adorning the walls of their home. Two of the larger ones had been driven through their foreheads and out the back of their skulls. Whoever had done this had propped them in a sitting position side by side on the living room couch. Lori was still screaming hysterically as Brent shouted at her to call 911.

Moving through the living room and then into the dining area before reaching the kitchen, he held the pistol out in front of him, gripping it with both hands. There was blood all over the kitchen, and it looked like this was where they'd been killed before being dragged into the living room. As he moved back towards the living room, Brent shouted, "You can't hide you motherfucker, I will find you!"

The voice of a man, calm and smooth, scared the wits out of Brent as he spun around towards its source.

"Who is hiding?" A completely naked Robert Best sat in a chair that had been empty just a few seconds ago, his unmistakable bright red eyes mocking Brent.

"What the hell?!", Brent yelled, knowing this was who he'd seen at the back of the barn just hours earlier. Raising his gun to fill this thing full of holes, he hesitated for a second, as he was drawn to the sight of Lori, lying on her back unconscious, on the floor in front of her parents' feet by the couch. In a motion that was just a blur in the corner of Brent's eye, the killer grabbed his wrist holding the gun and with incredible strength threw him flying across the room, slamming him into the wall. The gun went flying in the opposite direction.

The man was on Brent so fast he barely even saw him coming. Best grabbed him by the throat with powerful hands that lifted him off his feet and into the air. Looking down into those burning red eyes, Brent knew he was staring into the face of the devil. His face and body seemed to be changing from normal human features to something else; his face was now covered in grotesque scars; his mouth was full of long and sharp teeth. His body was huge with overdeveloped muscles, and the fetid stench of death permeated the air around him. His grip was so tight Brent could not breathe, and he felt he only had seconds before he would pass out. This beast then started to yell something at Brent that he did not understand, but it chilled his blood cold.

"Morieris tuum sicut inutiles Patris. It's Lori volo. Expectavi enim centuries dirigitur." (You will die just like your useless father. Its Lori I want. I have waited centuries for this moment.)

Suddenly Brent heard a loud bang followed by three more loud bangs. This beast recoiled backwards, releasing its grip on Brent's throat. Lori had somehow gotten up and found the pistol and was emptying it into this thing. As it fell back onto the floor from its wounds, Lori moved in closer and fired five more rounds into the creature. As it lay prone from the force of the bullets, instead of dying, it began to laugh. Its evil and guttural laugh boomed through the house, scaring Brent and Lori to the core. Reaching out to take the gun from Lori's hand, Brent moved and stood over top of the beast and emptied the remaining rounds into its head, killing it once and for all.

With the pistol spent, Brent slumped his shoulders and let his arms fall to his side, dropping the pistol to the floor. He looked over at Lori, who was moving towards him, ready to collapse into his arms. Suddenly out of the corner of his eye, he could see movement below him. He looked down to catch a glimpse of the burning red eyes of this beast as it moved with such speed that Brent had no time to react. Launching itself off the floor, it jumped onto Brent, clamping its jaw full of razor-sharp teeth onto his neck. He screamed in pain as he tried to pull free, but its strength was too powerful. *My God, this thing was trying to bite his head off!* Feeling a large chunk of flesh being torn from his neck, Brent struggled to maintain consciousness, the pain unbearable. He could feel and see his blood spurting everywhere. He knew he was about to die.

Feeling close to blacking out, with no strength left, he fell to his knees with this beast still on top of him. Expecting his head to be yanked off his shoulders, ending his life, he could see Lori leap on the back of this thing, trying to pull it off before it bit down on him again. The beast, unbelievably, *stepped off of him,* stood up with Lori still on its back, then flung her across the room where she smashed against a large mirror on the wall, sending the mirror and her to the floor in a thousand pieces of broken glass. This beast then turned and moved towards her. Brent was losing blood badly and could not stop his body as he fell face first onto the floor. The last thing he would see before everything went black was this thing choking the life out of Lori.

****

Seeing Brent fall forward with a large piece of his neck and shoulder gone, Lori knew he was now dead as well. In a few more minutes she would be dead too, as this beast was choking her to death with a grip that was not human. Lori knew she was staring into the burning red eyes of the devil, its evil so unspeakable, but yet so real, that she just wanted to die as quickly as possible. Unable to get any air into her lungs, she was choking to death, blackness creeping into the corners of her eyes, ready to take her. In a matter of a few hours Lori had lost everyone she ever loved, all murdered by this creature from hell, so she welcomed the death that was soon to come. Still choking the life out of her, the beast lifted Lori high in the air by her neck with incredible strength, screaming with a voice that was not English but Latin. She could not understand the words but she knew it was Latin.

"Magnum hoc hodie. Tu semen et Edil finaliter ferens ulciscar annorum centena dirigitur." (This is a great day. You are the seed of Edil and I will finally have my revenge after waiting hundreds of years for this moment.)

Seconds before Lori was about to pass out, this thing released its grip, causing her to fall hard to the floor. Gasping, she sucked bursts of air painfully through her bruised and damaged throat. Back from the brink of asphyxiation, she tried to lift herself off the floor. The beast would have no part of that and slugged her so hard across the face she felt her jaw snap. White-hot pain shot through her brain like searing fireworks. The beast's long and powerful arm shot out again, slugging her square in the middle of her face, smashing her nose and breaking numerous teeth. Bleeding profusely, struggling to keep from passing out from the intense pain, she cried out through her broken and bleeding mouth, "Why are you doing this?! What have we done?! Who are you?!"

Then, in a matter of mere seconds, she watched the beast transform itself.

Changing back now to human form, with the grotesque facial scars and razor teeth gone and the body's massive muscles reduced to those of a normal athletic man, Robert Best, with his evil red eyes still glowing, brightly replied to Lori's pleas, "You will give yourself willingly to me with no resistance or you will die. You were chosen for this over seventeen hundred years ago."

Her mind was spinning out of control from what this thing was saying. Through her destroyed and broken face, she cried out, "What are you saying, I don't understand! I was chosen over seventeen hundred years ago?! What are you talking about? I was chosen for what?"

"Be quiet! No more talk!" boomed Best. Turning to face the fallen and broken Lori, he exposed himself to her. The cold fear that Lori had felt during her attack did not come close to the sheer terror she now felt. She was about to be raped by this monster.

Chapter 18

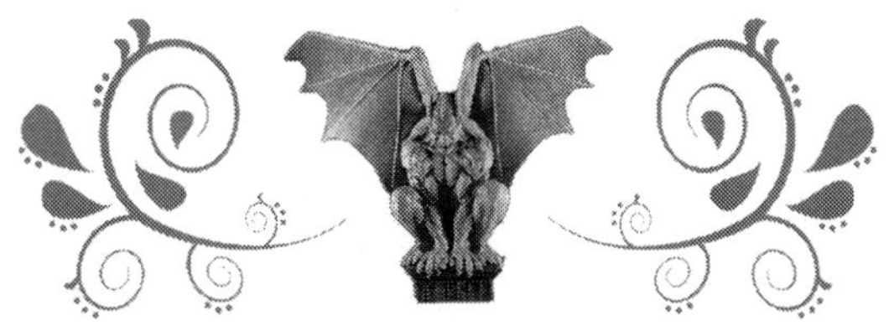

LAPD Homicide Detective Steven Benning was a veteran of dozens of murder investigations in the Los Angeles area over his twelve years of police work, including the last six in Homicide. However, nothing ever prepared Steven when the victim of the murder was a child. Getting the call this afternoon with his partner, Detective Samuel Showenstein, was a case of being in the wrong place at the wrong time. Already saddled with enough unsolved murder investigations on their case file, Showenstein and Benning were working the computers searching databases in the offices of the HSS (Homicide Special Section) section of Robbery-Homicide in police headquarters on 100 West First Street. This day most of the HSS detectives were either temporarily assigned to the high-profile murder investigation of District Attorney Hubert Ferney, on leave, on course or lucky enough to be out of the office when the call came in about the attack on six-year-old Graham Caruthers.

Captain Rodney Bitters barreled out of his glass-walled office overlooking the sea of detective's desks called the bullpen, mostly empty at the moment except for Benning and Showenstein, support staff and a few other detectives. Shouting at the top of his lungs he bellowed, "Benning! Showenstein! In my office. Now!"

Great, thought Steven, looking at Sam as they made their way to Captain Bitters' office, they were likely going to get dragged into the political quagmire surrounding the Ferney investigation. Pulling up a chair in front of the Captain, they listened as he gave them a case they wished the Captain would have given someone else. "We got a murder of a kid. Out in Arlington Heights. Lives in Norco, reported missing by the parents at seven this morning when they went to wake him for school. It's not gang-related, not a gang area, nor is it a sex assault. The kid has been butchered—very brutal—so get out there. Uniforms are on site preserving the scene."

Making their way to the crime scene, both detectives rode in silence as they knew this was not going to be easy. These types of crimes involved some of the sickest human beings on the planet and usually turned up a world of filth on the perpetrator that caused many detectives to transfer out of Homicide or Sexual Assault Divisions because of the severe nature of the investigations. The only bright side to these investigations was the successful arrest and prosecution of the accused. Knowing that your hard work was responsible for taking these freaks off the street made it all worth it at the end of the day.

Even with only six years in the division, Detective Benning was considered a veteran, but Detective Showenstein was still a rookie. At thirty-six, Showenstein was three years older than Benning but had only eleven years with the LAPD, including less than a year in Homicide. Transferring in from Property Crimes Division out of the West Los Angeles Division, he'd been investigating break-ins in the prestigious areas of Bel Air, Brentwood, Century City, to name a few, for the past seven years. After his first four years in traffic, Samuel, or "Sam", as he liked to be called, made a name for himself in investigating property crimes, with a penchant for detail and patience, resulting in a high success rate in solving difficult cases. The HSS Section went after Sam, recruiting him before another of the specialty divisions snapped him up.

Because he'd grown up in an Orthodox Jewish family, it had been assumed that Sam would follow as his chosen life path his two older brothers into theological studies of Judaism to eventually become a rabbi and serve his Jewish community. He had shocked his family and ostracized himself from them by entering UCLA at age eighteen, majoring in Criminology to pursue a career in police work. Graduating with a Masters degree in Criminology at the age of twenty-six, he immediately entered the police academy, where he graduated as the top student, and was earmarked by the department as one of those recruits who would be special.

Sam met his future wife Bethany, also Jewish, at UCLA and they were married upon graduation from school with all of Sam's brothers in attendance, but his father, who still refused to let go of Sam's perceived betrayal. Bethany graduated from medical school and went on to become a plastic surgeon with a thriving and successful business in Pasadena. School and careers delayed Sam and Bethany's plans for a family, but that had all changed three months ago when Bethany started missing periods, culminating in a positive pregnancy test. Both of them were elated, and at the age of thirty-six Sam would finally be a father. But the realization that he was soon to be a father made these types of crimes even more difficult for Sam to investigate.

****

Steven, on the other hand, had married his high school sweetheart Chelsea right out of high school, and other than poking a stick at some college courses, never graduated from college, instead applying for the police academy three times before finally being accepted. Once in the academy, Steven showed recruiters right away that he had the street smarts and instincts to be a great future investigator. It was just a matter of time before Steven left the patrol car for a suit and tie as a detective. Traffic Division lasted only six years before Robbery-Homicide came calling, looking to tap into Steven's street savvy and natural instincts as an investigator.

Chelsea's father Will owned a second-generation plumbing and heating business in the El Monte area of LA, where Chelsea had worked ever since high school. When her mother passed away when Chelsea was fifteen, Chelsea took over the office duties of the business, working as many hours as she could around her school commitments. Once she graduated, Chelsea decided to forego college and work fulltime for her dad's business, much to the delight of Will, who had come to rely on his daughter's skill at running the business. The Benning's had a great marriage; money was not plentiful, but they were comfortable.

****

Arriving at the crime scene near the intersection of Monroe Street and Dufferin Avenue in the Arlington Heights area of Riverside, the two detectives saw that uniforms had the entire area blocked off from Irving Street to Cleveland Avenue. The whole block was full of squad cars, ambulances, fire trucks, rescue trucks, CSI vehicles and the van of LA County Coroner Medical Examiner Eunice Epp, anxious for the detectives Showenstein and Benning to view the body so she could do her work. The body of six-year-old Graham Caruthers had been found in a wooded area just off Dufferin Avenue, dumped there by the perpetrator like a piece of garbage. It had been discovered by a retired army veteran walking the ditches collecting recyclable bottles and cans. Sam had the veteran repeat his story while Steven spoke with the uniform in charge, Sergeant Jeremy Jenkins. Other than draping a sheet over the body, they had kept the scene clean for investigators. All of the uniformed officers on scene were on edge whenever there was a child involved. As the detectives met briefly before viewing the body, Steven said to Sam, "Jenkins has everything locked up tight as per usual, I see. Kept everything on ice for our arrival. Epp is having a knipshit waiting for us, told Jenkins she will give us ten more minutes then she is taking the body away. I say let her take it; we can view the damage at the morgue. Heard it's horrific though, the kid was cut so bad it looked like he was stuffed into a paper shredder.

What did you get from the guy who discovered the body?"

Consulting his notepad, Sam replied, "Retired Vietnam vet who covers this area three to four times a week picking up bottles and cans. None of his screws are loose, all tight. The body reminded him of kids blown up in bombed villages over in 'Nam. Didn't see shit, though, no suspicious vehicles, nothing. CSI gathering evidence, including tire tracks, what is likely the dump vehicle, probably a van?"

Steven then went over what he'd learned from the uniform in charge.

"Okay, Jenkins' guys took statements from the property owner plus surrounding homes. There are not many, as they're all acreages out here with the homes set far back from the road. No one seen dick-all, there are vehicles running up and down these roads all night long. No one saw anything unusual."

Sam gave off a big sigh, wiping the sweat building on his forehead. This was going to be one of those cases, he thought as he looked at Steven.

"Well, we know the body was dumped. Caruthers lives in nearby Norco, maybe twenty minutes away."

With a grimace, Steven said, "Okay let's go notify the parents, take a statement, canvass the neighborhood for witnesses to the kid being taken and then head down to the morgue and see the body. Epp is an uncooperative bitch at the crime scene, much nicer on her turf, so let's get outta here."

After notifying Epp that they would view the body later that afternoon at the morgue, Steven asked Jenkins if he could spare a few bodies to help canvass the Caruthers' neighborhood. Joining Sam, they left the scene for the Caruthers home in Norco. Nobody liked notifying the next of kin, the worst part of the investigation without a doubt, and the stress is amped up a thousand-fold when it's a kid. It was the Carruthers kid without a doubt, but the parents would still have to identify the body. The mutilated condition of the body would make identification difficult and the horror for the parents much worse.

Arriving at the Caruthers home, Steven pulled the unmarked

car into the driveway. Looking at Sam, he said. "You want me to take this?"

Sam paused for a second before replying. They took turns on these notifications, and it was his turn. Because it was a kid, Steven was trying to take it off his shoulders, but Sam wouldn't have it.

"Thanks man, but I got it. Let's just get it done," he said as he grabbed his notebook and climbed out of the car.

Notifying the parents on the death of their son was brutal. The detectives had no choice but to describe the viciousness of the attack on their son, as the parents would have to identify the body later that day and downplaying it now would shock and horrify them unnecessarily when they viewed the body. Giving them space to grieve before they started in with some questions, Sam and Steven stepped into the Caruthers' kitchen to discuss the case. Steven had been trying to reach Chelsea for the past hour since he discovered she had not gone into work, but she was not answering the home phone or her cell. Nothing to worry about, thought Steven, but it still bothered him that she was not picking up.

Finishing up the questioning with the Caruthers about an hour later, Sam and Steven informed them they would get a call from the coroner's office notifying them when they would need to go in to identify their son. Then they left for the LA County morgue. Steven tried calling Chelsea once again, but as before, just got voicemail. Steven looked at Sam and said, "Sam, listen do you mind if I take you back to headquarters and you can grab a pool car? I need to check on some things and I'll catch up with you later on at the morgue or back at the office."

"Sure, no problem. Everything okay?"

"Yeah, just want to check on things at home. Chelsea never went into work today and I've been unable to reach her at the house or on her cell so just want to take a drive over to the house before I head to the morgue."

Twenty minutes later, Steven dropped Sam off at the headquarters pool car lot and headed for the house in Arcadia just a few minutes northeast of the city. Now getting really worried, as Chelsea has never done this before, Steven dialed Chelsea at the house one more time, letting it ring over and over while he made the short drive. On the eleventh ring, finally the click of the phone being picked up. Steven didn't give Chelsea a chance to speak, as in a panic he blurted, "Honey, where have you been, I've been trying to reach you all day! You had me worried sick. I am up to my eyeballs in shit here at work. We got a murdered kid, it's bad, really bad, so not hearing from you I was ready to pop."

"I enjoyed cutting that little Caruthers kid, Detective Benning. Those little bastards bleed so fast, though. When are you coming home, sweetie?" A voice that sounded impossibly evil and wicked spoke back to him from his home phone. The blow to Steven's stomach was so hard it knocked the breath right out of him.

"Who the fuck is this?! Where is my wife?! Put her on the phone right fucking now!" demanded a horrified Steven.

The guttural voice sounded like a hand-held voice box pressed against this guy's throat.

"You better hurry, Detective, it won't be much longer until you won't even be able to recognize her." The voice sounded like it was from a horror movie as it taunted Steven.

Steven was shaking so badly he could barely hold onto the phone as he shouted, "You better not touch a hair on her body, you sick motherfucker, or I'll blow your goddamned head off, you hear me?!"

"Looking forward to it, detective. Since you're only a few blocks away, I will see you soon."

Gunning the car the last few blocks, Steven threw the siren and the lights on in the unmarked car. What the hell was going on, Steven thought, his head swimming with terrible scenarios. What the hell was the Caruthers kid's killer doing in his house? Checking his Glock handgun, snapping off the safety, Steven pumped a round into the chamber. Making the turn onto his block, he speed-dialed Sam on his cell: "Sam, don't ask me how, but the killer of the Caruthers kid has Chelsea in my house. Get some cars down here now! I'm going in." Before Sam could respond, Steven snapped his phone shut, ending the call.

Rocketing up his driveway, he slammed the car into park and jumped out, approaching the front door of his house, his gun extended out in front of him ready to fill this sick fucker full of holes. Opening the front door and entering the house, he found it dark and quiet. Yelling out, "Chelsea, baby, where are you? Let her go and come out with your hands in the air, whoever the fuck you are!"

Not hearing any sounds, he made his way down the hallway, checking each room as he did so. Reaching the master bedroom, Steven aimed his gun in ahead of him as he peered inside. What he saw was beyond comprehension, something so unbelievable he was temporarily stunned.

Then he heard, "About time you got here, detective. Just in time. Chelsea has been very cooperative."

Steven felt nausea rush over him, his brain unable to decipher what he was seeing. A thing, or some creature with fiery red eyes, had mounted Chelsea and was raping her, its shape that of a very large man with grayish-black skin covering a huge body of muscles, a face covered in scars festering with open sores, and huge teeth, far too many to fit in his mouth, that were dripping saliva all over Chelsea. His wife was alive, but her eyes were blank, not even registering that Steven was in the room. She was covered in blood from wounds inflicted by this monster.

Taking aim, he fired. The loud barks from the Glock echoed in the bedroom as Steven blasted three rounds at this thing. Opening its mouth even wider, it laughed—the most hideous sound he could imagine. The shots hit this thing squarely in the chest, but it did not even flinch. Steven fired four more rounds into the monster, two of them hitting it in the head, causing it to make a guttural screaming sound—then once again, that hideous laugh.

"My seed entering your bitch wife will change this world! Your wife has been chosen! I have waited hundreds of years for this opportunity!" screamed the creature as its huge torso continued to crash down onto Chelsea.

"Nooo, stop it! Get off her!" cried Steven, bringing his Glock up and firing the rest of his clip, all ten rounds, into this thing. The blasts had enough force to buck this thing off of Chelsea, but incredibly, that was all it did. Climbing off the bed and standing up to its full height, it had to have been eight feet tall, towering over Steven. It was a sight he could only compare to something he might have seen in a comic book. Chelsea moaned but did not move.

"Satan ego. Sum Lucifer. Ego Antichristus. Ego hoc verum dominum universi. Incidam inimicus familia mea Babkin semine. Tempus meum huc omnes humanae patiantur." (I am Satan. I am Lucifer. I am the Antichrist. I am the true Master of this universe. I have cut the lineage of my enemy Babken with my seed. My time is here and all of mankind will suffer.)

Steven threw his gun to the ground and charged this monster in a frenzy fuelled by rage at what this thing had done to Chelsea. Reaching the beast, Steven dropped his shoulder to slam this thing to the ground. Instead Steven found a hand as big as a frying pan and as strong as an elephant wrapping a death grip around his throat, lifting him up in the air till his head hit the bedroom ceiling. Looking down into those evil red eyes, he knew he was going to die in the next few seconds. Looking over at Chelsea as the darkness began to take over, he saw his tortured wife, bloody and in a catatonic state, just staring up at the ceiling with blank eyes as if she were in a coma. What she must have just gone through before he arrived!

"Die, knowing your wife carries the child of Satan!" The beast's red eyes burned into his soul as he spoke. Reaching up with his other monstrous hand, he squeezed Steven's head and began to twist it. The last sound he heard as his neck was being broken and spun around by the beast was the wail of police sirens approaching the house.

****

The beast, now fully human and in the earthly form he called Robert Best, knew the first wave of his plan was now near completion. Standing naked in the living room of the Benning's home, he looked down at the barely conscious Chelsea, wondering, by the look of the state she was in, how much of this attack she would remember. Best thought about the other women he had attacked around the world, impregnating them with the seeds that will grow and become an integral part of his master plan to destroy all of mankind. If they only knew what was coming their way, he thought as he prepared to disappear from the Benning's home. He could hear the SWAT team lobbing stun grenades through the windows of the home. Humans are so pathetic, he laughed to himself. Why God cherishes them so much after everything they have done to this planet and themselves is still unclear to me to this day.

Mankind's days are numbered, thought Satan. *Soon they will find out that their faith in their absent God will cost them their lives and an eternity—not in a mythical blissful heaven but in a very real perpetual state of misery and sorrow.*

Chapter 19

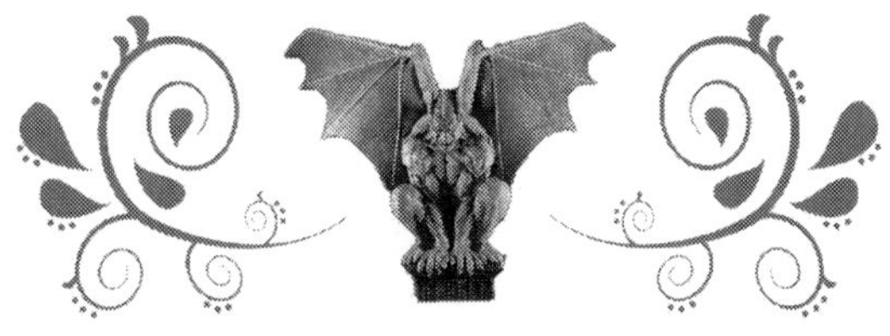

After receiving the panicked call from Steven, Sam took off north to Arcadia with his siren blaring and his lights blazing. He placed a call into dispatch telling them to get as many cars in the area over to Steven and Chelsea Benning and that Chelsea was being held hostage by the killer of six-year-old Graham Caruthers. *How could this possibly be happening,* thought Sam, *the Caruthers boy's killer was at Steven's?* How could that be? Knowing that Steven would rush the house with his gun out, ready to smoke this psychopath, Sam prayed that he hadn't got himself killed in a rush to rescue Chelsea.

Thankfully, traffic was relatively light as Sam rocketed east on Interstate 10, passing cars as if they were standing still. Making it to the exit for Rosemead Drive, Sam now had to navigate heavier traffic and lots of traffic lights. When he finally made it onto Huntington Drive, he could already see the flashing lights of multiple black-and-whites about a half-mile up the street. This is not good, thought Sam as he gunned it for the final few blocks. Coming to a screeching stop in front of the police tape going up across the road, Sam leapt out of the car and bolted for the Benning house half a block up the street. Reaching the house, he ran up to the group of uniforms congregating on the front step. Flashing his detective shield to the group, he said, "Detective Showenstein, Benning's partner. I need to get inside."

A tall powerful and muscular black officer stepped out to

meet Sam and said, "Detective, I'm the officer in charge, Sergeant Bill Rollings. I recommend you don't go in, sir. It's not pretty."

The front door suddenly burst open, and paramedics carrying a stretcher with Chelsea came down the stairs. IV bottles were already started as they rushed her to an ambulance on the curb in front of the house. Sam was horrified to see the unconscious, battered face of Chelsea as she was quickly rushed to the waiting ambulance. Turning and rushing inside the house, he saw it was empty of officers except for three uniforms protecting anyone from intruding on the crime scene. Sam flashed his badge, "Homicide. Where is Detective Benning?"

Sam heard Rollings' voice behind him, "Follow me, Detective, he's in the master bedroom." Taking Sam down the hall, the sergeant glanced back at Sam before they stepped into the bedroom with a look that said, "Prepare yourself".

Walking into Steven and Chelsea's bedroom was like walking into the Twilight Zone. There was an incredible amount of blood spatter and tissue on the walls. It looked like a war zone. The sight of Steven Benning lying on the floor in front of the bed with his head twisted completely around was so eerily frightening it took Sam a few seconds to realize he was looking at the gruesome murder of his partner. He fought the nausea dancing in his stomach, threatening to erupt. Gathering himself, he needed to begin the process of taking charge of the crime scene. Taking a deep breath, he looked at Rollings and asked, "Who was first on the scene?"

"Patrol Officers Meek and Bensen." Rollings nodded at the uniform standing guard at the bedroom doorway and said, "Go get Meeks and Bensen and bring them in here." Rollings looked back at Sam and asked, "Detective, are you okay? This was your partner."

Sam lifted his hand up as if to stop any more comments from Rollings and said, "I'm all right, Sergeant. There is one crazy motherfucking killer or killers out there, and the longer this sympathy party continues the farther away they are getting."

A minute later, Meek and Bensen arrived at the doorway to the bedroom. Sam and Rollings stepped out into the hallway with them. Sam asked, "Can you describe the scene when you arrived, and more importantly, did you find any sign of the killer?"

Meek spoke. "When we got the call from dispatch we were maybe ten minutes away, literally a few blocks away, finishing up a domestic disturbance in the area. We were on scene within five to ten minutes of receiving the call. When we arrived the house looked quiet. Bensen went around back and I went through the front. We searched the house, we did not see nor did we hear anyone in the home. We discovered Detective Benning, as you see, and a naked Chelsea Benning on the bed unconscious, badly beaten but alive. Other patrol cars began arriving, including the ambulance. A search of the property began, including the immediate area with no sign of anyone. That takes us to right now."

Sergeant Rollings took over. "Thank you, officers. You can help secure the area outside."

Sam re-entered the bedroom and was careful not to disturb anything, as CSI would arrive on scene soon. He began to take in the scene in the bedroom. He was determined to keep his emotions at bay at the thought of what had just happened to his partner so he could focus on the crime scene. He seen Steven's 9mm on the floor near the body. Counting all of the spent casings on the floor, it was pretty obvious that Steven unloaded on the perpetrator here in the bedroom. The number of the shots fired indicated Steven had likely been firing at more than one attacker. Bending down over Steven's body, Sam thought it must have taken superhuman strength to break Steven's neck and turn it all the way around. Steven's attacker had to be a very large and powerful man. Judging by the amount of blood on the bed, floor and walls, the attacker would need medical attention. He would check with all hospitals in the city and the state for anyone coming for treatment of gunshots, especially someone large in size. The spray of blood on the headboard and the surrounding wall behind it told Sam that Steven likely came into the bedroom with the attacker assaulting Chelsea on the bed. Standing at the foot of the bed, Steven had fired into the attacker, causing the blood spatter patterns. Walking over to the headboard and the wall, Sam got a good look at the chunks of tissue stuck to the wall. He could not determine if it was brain tissue or body tissue. CSI would take all of the samples in for testing.

Sam heard a commotion outside the bedroom. *Here comes the brass*, thought Sam. This was about to turn into a three-ring circus. Walking into the bedroom was Captain Bitters, accompanied by Assistant Police Commissioner Anthony Morgan. Seeing Steven's nearly decapitated body on the floor Bitters, blurted, "Aah, Jesus Christ! Un-fucking-believable!"

Morgan said, "Detective Showenstein, how are you doing? Are you okay? CSI will be here in a few minutes to clean this mess up. Quite a shootout, to say the least. What can you tell us about what you think happened here?"

They all gathered in the living room, where Sam brought them both up to speed on his theory about the scene as CSI arrived and took over the bedroom. "When I got the call from Steven, he said that the killer of the Caruthers kid had Chelsea and was in his house. Knowing Steven, he would have come in here with guns blazing. There were a lot of shots fired from Steven's gun. He either killed some of the attackers or has badly wounded more than one of them. Too many rounds and too much blood. I'll get notice out right away to all hospitals in the state to be on the lookout for gunshot victims coming into emergency, especially anyone who is a big man."

Captain Bitters said, "Good idea. Head back to the station and get started on that. You are going to carry the load on this investigation, Sam. Are you up for it? It will get political real fast, seeing the victim is one of our own. Anthony and I are on the way to the hospital now to check on the status of Chelsea. We have a meeting in two hours with Commissioner Rodriguez and I need you to be there. So let's get moving."

As Bitters and Morgan left, Sam turned to the CSI Officer in

Charge, Lieutenant Megan Stern, who had arrived while he was in the living room with Morgan and Bitters, and asked that CSI get the tissue and blood samples to the lab and that the lab give it top priority. Seeing Morgan at the scene, Stern knew where this was going. Steven's murder investigation would be given top priority all the way down the line. Steven was well liked in the department, so the emotional element would speed things along even more. Plus the fact the killer was potentially linked to the murder of a six-year-old boy would make the investigation even more political. Sam also spoke with Sergeant Rollings, instructing him to have some uniforms canvass the neighborhood for witnesses who might have seen the attackers arrive or leave the scene. Rollings replied that he would get four uniforms started right away.

Leaving the scene to head back to HQ, Sam placed a call to Bethany to let her know that all the reports that would soon be appearing on all the local network channels about a cop being murdered were about Steven.

"Oh my God, Sam, this is terrible. I feel so bad for Chelsea, how awful for her! How are you doing, sweetheart? Maybe you should be taking a few days off," a worried Bethany said.

He purposely did not give Bethany any details on the crime scene, including what had happened to Steven, plus he softened the brutal attack on Chelsea as it would only frighten her and make her more worried about him than she already was. "This was my partner and friend, Beth. I've been asked to lead the investigation and I have to do this. I promise I'll be careful. This case will be given the department's highest priority so I'll have lots of help around me."

"Okay, baby, I know, I understand. I will likely not see very much of you in the days ahead, so just keep that cell charged up so you can call me when you get a free minute or you need someone to talk to. Also let me know when the hospital is letting people in to see Chelsea. I would like to see her when she's better. I love you, Samuel Showenstein. Please be careful."

"I will, and I will call you soon. Love you tons."

Arriving at his desk twenty minutes after he left the Benning's, Sam spent the next few hours putting together his investigation package for both the Caruthers boy's and Steven's murders. Files were opened, beginning paperwork completed, and he opened a new file on the LAPD computer investigator's software, where he would transfer his notes and daily activities that would form the investigation package. No more hand writing reports, all computer written now and accessible twenty-four hours a day by anyone with authorization. Sam knew the Commissioner and the higher-ups in the department would be logging in regularly. A child and a homicide detective murdered by the same killer in a planned and vicious manner are extraordinary to say the least. Checking his watch, he realized he had five minutes to get up to the fifth floor to meet with Commissioner Rodriguez and his cronies. Oh, joy, he thought. Grabbing his umpteenth cup of black coffee, Sam headed up to the fifth floor where the Commissioner's secretary whisked him right into his office. The room was full and they were all sitting around the boardroom table waiting for him. He immediately noticed the Mayor and the Deputy Mayor were also in attendance. Yup, this is political. The heads of Robbery-Homicide, Missing Children, plus Captain Rollings and Assistant Commissioner Morgan were at the table. Commissioner Rodriguez spoke first: "Welcome, Detective Showenstein, thanks for coming up. Firstly, I will tell you that there was strong opposition from the people at this table to you leading this investigation. Your obvious connection to Detective Benning as your partner plus your lack of experience is a cause of concern. It was at the insistence of your Captain that you will run with this for now. He is thin on bodies and feels you're one of his best investigators regardless of your experience, plus he knows you're strong and will keep the emotional element under control and use it as a focusing mechanism and not a distraction. How do you feel about that, Detective?"

"I want this investigation. Steven was my partner and he was my friend. I am a professional and I will conduct myself accordingly. You can count on the fact I will be focused and clear on what lies ahead and what needs to be done. Even though the attacks on the Caruthers child and Steven are yet to be proven to be connected, I believe they are. The killer admitted as much to Steven before Steven arrived at his home, plus they were similar in their exceptionally violent and brutal nature."

It was Commissioner Rodriguez who spoke next. A highly respected and veteran policeman with over twenty-five years of patrol and detective work, he practically bled blue.

"I agree in your assessment. What is your plan for the next forty-eight hours, Detective?"

Sam addressed the Commissioner: "I have uniforms canvassing the neighborhoods of both crime scenes. CSI are on scene. Blood and tissue samples will be sent to the lab. Detective Benning fired all seventeen rounds from his Glock at close range. There will be severely injured gunshot victims needing treatment, so all hospitals in the state as well as Nevada are on the lookout for any gunshot victims and will report to local police when they arrive. There could very well be casualties amongst the attackers such that they may very well dump the bodies nearby. Any and all gunshot victims found will be matched for ballistics. After this meeting I am on the way to the morgue to see the body and the ME report on the injuries. I'm hoping that Chelsea will recover enough soon so that she can give me a statement. The doctors will call me the minute she awakens from her coma. She has severe brain swelling, so it could be a few days at the minimum. I could use some boots on the ground."

Now Captain Bitters spoke up: "I've pulled four suits off the DA Ferney investigation, and they're at your disposal, Sam. More will be coming in the next few days as I continue to shift things around. A command center is in the process of being set up in Robbery-Homicide, including a direct number that will be made public for anyone, anonymously or not, who has information to call in. Everything will be coordinated from there, Sam. You will brief your team tomorrow morning at 9:00 a.m."

The head of the Missing Children Section, Captain Howard

Lenert, said, "I am having a team going over all of our files for the past five years, looking for any missing children who have turned up dead by exceptionally violent means, for any possible connections to the Caruthers boy's murder."

"Very good, Howard. Get it to Captain Bitters and the command center as soon as you find anything. Gentlemen, let's wrap this up. Anyone have any further questions? Good, let's get busy," ordered Police Commissioner Rodriguez.

Thirty minutes later Sam was walking into the LA County Coroner's building on North Mission Road. He was greeted by the always-grumpy ME, Eunice Epp, "You're late, Detective, but then I guess my time is less important than yours, isn't it?"

Not in any mood for verbal jostling with Epp, he cut her off. "Listen that's my partner you have back there on a slab. Right now I don't care whose time is the most important. If it makes you happy, I am sorry I'm running late."

Looking at him intently, sensing she'd better not push it this time, Epp replied only with, "Follow me." Sam thought he saw her smile slightly as she turned away from him, thinking she'd won a small victory with his apology, even though it was a sarcastic one. No matter, to Epp it was just as good.

Following the portly Epp down the hallway towards the autopsy room, he couldn't help but compare her to the actress who played the woman who'd chased the spirits from the home in *Poltergeist*. Epp had arranged to have the Caruthers kid and Steven available for Sam. As she pulled back the sheet on Steven's gurney, Sam was presented with a gruesome sight, seeing Steven again, this time naked, chest facing down but his head completely twisted backwards so that it was staring straight up at him. "Jesus, that's awful," he said, taking a step back from the table.

Epp promptly replied, "You got that right. Never seen anything like it in eighteen years working in this place. The strength needed to have done this would have to be almost superhuman. To snap a person's neck is one thing, but to twist it all the way around is a whole another matter completely."

Seeing the destroyed body of Steven lying like a cold, discarded piece of meat in the sterile environment of the coroner's lab, with his wife fighting for her life in the hospital, struck Sam like a punch in the solar plexus. Fighting back the emotion of the situation, he struggled to regain his composure and focus on what Epp was describing.

"He was strangled before his neck was broken. If you notice the bruising on his neck, it too indicates the attacker was a very powerful man. The bruising pattern indicates an extraordinarily large hand. He would have had the ability to crush Detective Benning's throat, killing him instantly. If you ever catch this man, Detective, I suggest you shoot first and ask questions later."

Finishing up her initial assessment of Steven, Epp moved on to the Caruthers kid. "Now this was strange on my first go-round, examining Graham Caruthers. His body, as you can see, is covered in deep-cut slash wounds. The puzzling thing for me so far is I don't believe it was done with any type of weapon or knife. I believe it was done with some sort of prosthetic attached to the attacker's arms."

That was not the assessment he'd expected to hear. Something began to twist deep down inside the pit of his stomach.

"Why would you think that? The wounds look pretty consistent with a sharp knife or sword."

An air of excitement now entered Epp's voice. This was her wheelhouse. He listened intently.

"Firstly, I have studied the wounds under a microscope and there are no microscopic traces of metal usually left behind when a metal blade is used. The wounds would not be so thick if made with a knife or sword. Secondly, they resemble the wounds consistent with that of a claw, as if the kid was attacked by some sort of wild beast. Which explains why the cuts could be thicker, if done by a claw of an animal as opposed to a blade? Thirdly, while I was examining the wounds under a microscope I found traces of tissue in the wounds that are not from the child. The tissue belongs to whomever or whatever clawed this kid. I've sent samples of this tissue to the lab for testing."

"So you're saying Caruthers and Detective Benning were attacked by a werewolf?" he replied, in a semi-sarcastic tone.

"Until I get the results back from the lab, that is a strong possibility," Epp shot right back.

Shifting his weight onto his other leg, Sam paused slightly before he continued, as a way to diffuse the tension that was building between the two of them.

"Seriously, if this was an animal that attacked the Caruthers kid, the person who attacked the Benning's also knew about the Caruthers kid and admitted to that killing, so where does an animal come into play?"

"That's your job to find out, now, isn't it? Now this is where it does get interesting and ties the two murders together to the same attacker. Minute pieces of tissue were found on Benning's body that is consistent with the tissue samples taken from the Caruthers boy's wounds. The tissue on Benning likely was from debris splatter when the Detective was firing at the attacker from close range. I also sent these samples to the lab to be tested to confirm the match. I am willing to bet the farm these tissue samples from the kid and Benning are the same," Epp stated to Sam with a serious professional tone.

****

Leaving the Coroner's Office after Epp had finished explaining her theories, Sam was more confused than when he had arrived. The Caruthers kid's attacker could have been an animal. Could the large and powerful person who broke Steven's neck and spun his head around like it was a corkscrew have been the same attacker who attacked Caruthers? Sam would keep this theory to himself until the tests from the lab came back. *Son of a bitch*, he thought. What really happened at the Benning home? He wished Chelsea would wake up from her coma so she could shed some light on her attackers sooner rather than later.

He worked through the evening reading the reports filed by

the officers first on the Caruthers crime scene as well as at the Benning home. He unofficially declared the two murders carried out by the same attacker or attackers based upon the report by the Coroner's Office and the phone call by Steven's attacker admitting to the killing of the Caruthers kid. The lab report confirming the DNA match of the tissue samples from Caruthers and Benning would make the two murders officially connected. It was almost midnight when Sam rose from his desk to head home for the night, his back stiff from sitting on the edge of his seat typing reports for the previous five hours, when suddenly his cell phone buzzed in his holster. Bethany, he thought, wondering when he was coming home, but looking at the caller ID he saw it was Eunice Epp. Answering his cell, Sam said, "Jesus, are you still working? I thought I was the only crazy one still burning the midnight oil."

Her voice, even for this late hour, was elevated and agitated. She spoke in a burst, "Sam, I got a phone call from the lab! A good friend of mine pulled me a favor and went to work on the tissue samples, spending all night testing them, then confirming, then retesting, because she could not believe it."

He found himself gripping the phone so tightly he thought he would crush it.

"What did she find out, Eunice, for Christ's sake?"

Epp continued, her voice shaking.

"The DNA from blood and tissue samples of both the Caruthers boy's body and the dump site, as well the Benning home, is indeed from the same attacker. The DNA code, however, is not human, nor is it from any animal. *It is from an unknown source never seen or typed before!*"

He dropped the phone on his desk, not even watching it as it bounced off his desk and onto the floor. He didn't even hear Epp's voice, still crackling through the earpiece.

The twisting in the pit of his stomach now ratcheted the bile right up to his throat. He barely made it to his garbage can beside his desk before he vomited violently. Reaching down and picking up the phone, he heard the audible beeping of a disconnected call before he snapped it shut and placed it back in its holster. He cupped his face in his hands, thinking to himself, *what happened to Steven and the kid!? Who could have done this?!*

Sam grabbed his briefcase and headed for the exit out to the parking lot. As he burst through the exit door and into the night air, the sweat on his body was turning to ice, and it wasn't from the warm California air.

Chapter 20

The blood-curdling scream from his wife Francoise startled Gerard, causing him to bound up the stairs as fast as he could, wondering what had frightened his wife so much. Reaching the top of the stairs and turning towards the hallway, he could see Francoise standing in the doorway of their bedroom. He hollered at her, "Honey! What's the matter? What's going on?"

Suddenly Gerard heard three loud bangs. Gunshots. Then three more rapid-fire loud bangs. Oh, my God, someone was shooting Francoise!

Slowly backing up out of the bedroom with a look of complete terror on her face, clutching her service 9mm semi-automatic pistol at her side, Francoise had fired off six rounds at something, Gerard could see as he made it up the stairs and now ran the ten feet down the hallway to his wife. Putting his hands on her shoulders and turning her face towards him, Gerard thought she had seen a ghost. She was white as snow, and her eyes could not even meet Gerard's, as she turned immediately, staring back into the bedroom. Leaving his wife in the hallway, Gerard stepped into the bedroom to see what had his wife frozen with fear. *Oh, sweet Jesus,* thought Gerard, *looking at a scene playing out in his bedroom that was straight from hell.*

A creature not quite human, more beast than man, was charging across the room towards Gerard. This thing had to have been seven to eight feet tall, with huge, overgrown muscles covering its slimy gray-and-black-skinned body. Its head was massive, bald, grayish-black like its body, but with grotesque open wounds all over its face where it had taken bullet rounds from Francoise. Its mouth was gnashing as it charged, revealing hideous long, razor-like teeth that looked like they could chew a two-by-four piece of lumber like a granola bar. It was on him in a flash, slamming him against the wall with such force it knocked the wind out of his lungs. Falling to the floor, he gasped for air, scared out of his mind, looking up at this thing and wondering what the hell was going on in his house. What was this thing and where did it come from?

The creature looked as if it was temporarily distracted by something in the hallway, allowing Gerard to crawl away from it and get back on his feet. Making his way over to the bedroom closet as fast as he could while keeping a close eye on this creature, he frantically searched Francoise's inventory of police-related stuff, hoping to find another weapon of some sort. The beast, seeing him move across the room, charged again, letting out a roar that would have made a lion sound like a kitten. Desperate to find something, Gerard clutched what looked like Francoise's taser gun. As the creature bore down on Gerard, he whipped out the taser, and at the last second he fired. The two wired probes found their mark, hitting this thing in the chest and pumping 50,000 volts of electricity into it. The creature, temporarily stunned for a split second, ripped the probes from its body, looked down at him with menacing eyes burning a bright red, and laughed, a guttural gurgling shriek that ran fear right through his soul. Bullets couldn't stop this thing; he was foolish thinking that an electrical blast would stop it. Suddenly, with incredible speed that he barely glimpsed, it reached down and wrapped its massive claws around his throat and squeezed, then lifted him in the air. Looking around the room for an opportunity to escape, if he could only get free of this vise-like grip around his neck, he could see Francoise, recovered from the paralyzing fear that had stricken her earlier, moving slowly through the room, clutching her pistol in a double-handed grip, moving up behind the beast. Screaming at the beast, she commanded,. "Let him go or I swear to God, this time I will kill you!"

Turning its head to look at Francoise as she spoke, the beast squeezed even harder on his neck, almost crushing his windpipe. He desperately struggled to get air into his lungs; he knew he only had seconds before he would lose consciousness. Blackness was already creeping into the corners of his eyes. The creature whipped its grotesque head towards him, grunted, then threw him across the room with such force into the wall that the white-hot pain shot through his body like fireworks. Struggling to maintain consciousness, Gerard saw the beast turn towards Francoise. She did not hesitate, and began firing shots into the head and chest of this thing, any one of which would have killed a human instantly—but this was no human. The beast fell backwards as Francois moved forward, firing the remaining shots in the gun. She quickly and expertly released the spent clip from her 9mm and replaced it in a split second, slamming another magazine into the grip of the gun. Reloading another round in the chamber, she began firing again, concentrating on the chest and head of the beast. Her assault was working, as it fell onto its back, wounded, no longer able to defend itself. Firing the remaining rounds in the clip, Francoise had killed it, finally. He could see her visibly shaking from the sheer terror of what she had just done. Looking down at the creature, she finally let her arms drop to her sides, the pistol falling from her hands and landing with a thud on the floor; she turned to Gerard, tears streaming down her face as she stepped away from the creature and moved towards him.

He tried to rise, but the pain brought him right back down to his knees. He looked up to see something that was impossible. *The beast is moving! How can this thing be alive after being shot at least twenty times in the head and chest?!* He opened his mouth to warn Francoise, but everything seemed to move in slow motion. Francoise, seeing the panic in his face, started to turn back towards the creature. As she did so, she was confronted by the full size of the beast towering over her, its upper body mangled from the gunshot wounds. The beast let out a roar and swatted its huge clawed hand against Francoise's face, knocking her flying against the bedroom dresser cabinet. She smashed into it, breaking it, with drawers tumbling down around her and on top of her as she lay in a heap on the floor. Gerard now knew that they were going to die. This creature from hell had been shot point blank over twenty times in the upper body and was not even phased. His throat aching and on fire, he shouted at the creature, "Who are you?! Why are you doing this to us?!"

Ignoring him, the beast reached down and picked up Francoise roughly off the floor and threw her onto the bed. Desperate to do something to stop it, Gerard picked up a piece of splintered wood from the smashed nightstand and charged the beast. Launching himself into the air, he flew across the bed, slamming into this thing, catching it somewhat by surprise. Knocking the seven-foot creature to the floor, he did not waste any time and drove the wooden stake into the side of its neck, causing the beast to scream in agony as it bucked him off. Covered in the beast's blood from the strike to its neck, he yelled at Francoise to run. He could see that she was too badly hurt to get off of the bed, her face bleeding badly from the blow from the beast. Gathering Francoise in his arms he lifted her up and headed for the door to gain as much distance from this creature from hell as he possibly could. He could hear sirens in the distance, thank God. Someone had heard the gunshots and called it in; with all the chaos around him he never had a chance to call 911 himself.

As he carried Francoise out of the bedroom and into the hallway, he felt the grip of the beast's massive claw clamping down on his shoulder, yanking him backwards, breaking his shoulder in the process, shooting white-hot pain through his shoulder and neck. Releasing his grip on Francoise as he fell backwards onto the floor, his shoulder now a mangled mess, he looked up into the glowing red eyes of this monster, who was preparing to finish him off for good. Gerard could see Francoise struggling to stand, but as he tried to move the beast slammed his huge foot down on his broken shoulder, sending bolts of unbearable pain throughout his body. The beast reached down and grabbed him by the broken shoulder and flung him, as if he was a rag doll, down the stairs, where he tumbled end over end, crashing into the wall at the bottom. Darkness took him this time and he knew the darkness was death.

****

The beast now focused on Francoise as she began to run towards the stairway after Gerard, screaming at the top of her lungs. As she was about to descend the stairs, the beast, with blurring speed, moved to block her passage. Before she could turn to run the opposite direction, the beast snapped his claw like hand out and wrapped it around her neck and, while squeezing, lifted her straight up in the air. She looked into the eyes of the creature, seeing the globes of red fire, and knew this thing had risen from the depths of hell. What it was doing here now, killing her and Gerard, she had no idea. Death would be upon her soon, and she found herself, as she stared into the red eyes, welcoming death. Just kill her now, she commanded those eyes. Instead, the beast loosened his grip ever so slightly, allowing a miniscule amount of air to enter her lungs. He then carried her into the bedroom, throwing her hard against the bed. Stepping back from the bed, the beast stretched its massive arms to its sides, almost reaching both walls in their bedroom. Suddenly the room became very dark and very cold. What the hell was happening now, she thought? Hearing the wail of police sirens getting louder in the distance, she knew help was on its way, but she also knew it would be too late, as she would be dead within the next few seconds. A white glow surrounded this creature now, illuminating him in the darkness of the bedroom. Then, suddenly, it began to transform itself in front of her eyes, leaving her frozen and unable to move, transfixed at what she was seeing.

With the sound of a thousand snakes writhing around, the

beast's body began to morph. The massive arms and muscles were shrinking, its head growing smaller and its tree-trunk legs shrinking. The oily grey and black skin was getting paler, turning white in color like that of a human. The skull continued to shrink, and the baldness was being replaced with black hair, the mouthful of razor teeth were also being replaced by a normal set of a man's teeth. Within a few seconds of her being thrown on the bed, this beast was now completely transformed into a normal man. His nakedness completely exposed now to her, the man began to speak in a language Francoise did not understand but believed to be Latin.

"Meus sperma mos iam terminus progenies of meus denique hostilis Gamar. The primoris phase of meus vinco intentio subvertio mankind est universa." (My seed will now end the lineage of my final enemy Gamar. The first phase of my master plan to destroy mankind is complete.)

Shivering in the cold, her breath issuing in visible puffs of mist, Francoise, her nose and jaw broken and her neck swollen from being choked, was paralyzed with fear. The realization of what was about to happen, why this thing was here in the first place, was now clear to her. She had been chosen by this thing and it was about to rape her. The police were so close, only a few minutes away.

****

Gerard, lying in a crumpled heap against the wall at the bottom of the stairs, tried to get up but was unable to. His shoulder broken, he now believed his hip was broken as well. He looked up at the bedroom and could see the white glow emanating from the darkness. Francoise, his bride of just over a year, whose love Gerard had so stupidly risked earlier that day with his tryst with Tiffany, was being killed up in that bedroom, of that he was sure. The police he could hear coming up the block towards the house would be too late to help her. He had failed her, unable to protect her. He prayed that his injuries were fatal and that he would soon die, as he didn't want to live anymore. Soon he felt the darkness come again for him; he would succumb to it, let it take him, he was ready for it, the pain and guilt too much for him.

****

The beast, now completely transformed into the man known as Robert Best, saw the fear in Francoise's eyes and cherished it. Fear was a wonderful thing for him. He fed on people's fears, they made him stronger. His massive manhood now fully erect, he mounted a quiet Francoise, who offered no struggle, too fearful and resigned to resist. Entering her, Best inhaled her fear, sucking it deep into him, letting her fear empower him. Pumping her like a wild beast, Best was close to filling her with his seed, seed that would soon grow into his child. This child, along with the ones already growing in the other six women, would execute his plan to destroy this world once and for all, forever. The toxic mixture of that knowledge and the fear emanating from Francoise was too much for Best, and he unloaded inside of her. Good. He was done. Beautifully done, laughed Best, as he climbed off of her, triumphant in his work. He heard the police burst through the front door, there had to be dozens of them, chuckled Best. Always too late, he thought, but then again that is how he planned it because he had the power. He was in control. Humans were merely the pawns he needed for his master plan to be complete. Soon he would have the full power to end their existence once and for all. The mighty God, the all-knowing Supreme Being and his army of protective Angels will wish they'd finished him off seventeen hundred years ago, laughed Best as he stood up off the bed. The return of the King, the great son Jesus, made Best laugh so hard he thought he would crack a rib. He will return, alright, but his return will be to a scorched fiery earth devoid of any life whatsoever.

****

Montreal police SWAT team members burst through the front door of the Louveneau home after being dispatched when it was known that multiple gunshots had been fired inside. Thinking that the Louveneau's were being attacked by gang members bent on revenge for the role Gerard had played in bringing down the outlaw motorcycle gang organizations, they came in ready to do battle. Seeing Gerard unconscious at the bottom of the stairs, the SWAT team slowly and carefully stepped over him and continued up the stairs. Reaching the top of the stairs they split into two groups, with one group heading to the right down the hall, and the other heading to the left, where they saw a white glow emanating from an upstairs bedroom. They stormed towards the bedroom with their M16s ready to fire, when they were stunned to hear loud laughter coming from inside the bedroom. They poured into the bedroom, shouting for everyone to get down on the ground, when they quickly realized there was no one in the bedroom except for a woman unconscious, badly beaten and naked. Using hand signals to communicate, they spread out through the bedroom and the rest of the house but there was no sign of any attackers.

As the SWAT leader was signaling his commands he couldn't help but think, *who the hell was that laughing?!*

Chapter 21

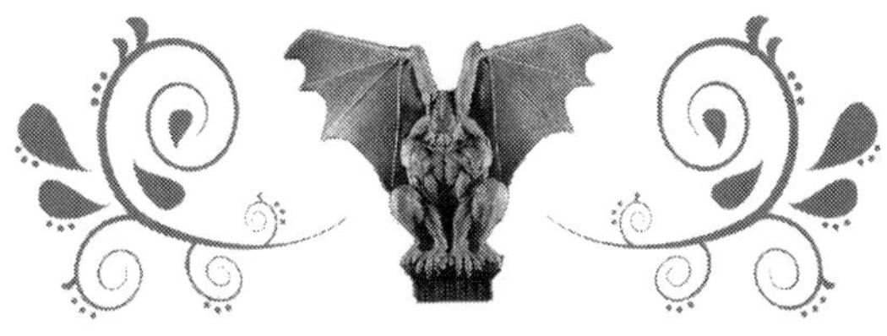

Brent Asker was ready to go home to the farm after spending three weeks in the hospital recovering from the devastating injuries he'd suffered from the vicious attack by the monster that had invaded the Asker Farm and then Lori's parents home. Large portions of his shoulder muscle had been torn off, as well as tissue from the lower side of his neck. No major arteries were cut in his neck, but the loss of tissue and muscle would require multiple skin graft surgeries to repair the damage. His doctors had told him that he would lose about fifty percent mobility in his shoulder, rendering it almost useless. With grafting of tissue and muscle into the shoulder over time, he might regain the ability to lift his arm above his shoulder, but it was unlikely, and even if he were able to, he would have almost no strength in it. The size of the wound made him highly susceptible to infection, so a steady diet of antibiotics in the coming weeks would be necessary. Getting out of the hospital and back to the farm and being with Lori was all he wanted right now. The events of the attack were now burned into his memory bank forever. The same could not be said for Lori. After making almost a full recovery from a broken jaw and broken nose plus numerous lacerations, Lori, thankfully, has no memory of the attack.

He had lost his father Bert, murdered by a monster that also took the lives of Lori's parents. He'd had many days and nights to think about the attacks. Knowing that the creature had raped

Lori made him physically sick. The investigators listened to Brent's account of the attacks, but he knew they didn't believe him; they thought he was still very traumatized by the attacks. The attacks and murders were so bizarre in nature and so extremely violent that the police were working on the assumption that a gang of ruthless and violent thugs were behind it. Yet they couldn't explain why nothing had been stolen from either Lori's home or the farm. What would motivate thugs to attack and kill in such a way if they were not there to rob the place? Why slaughter all of the animals? Targeting Asker Farms to conduct a random, brutal, and violent attack did not make sense, especially when they also attacked and killed Lori's parents at their home. None of the roadblocks set up ever produced any suspects. Brent demanded the investigators test the blood and tissue samples from the scene for answers and was told that had been done and they were waiting for the results; it was standard protocol to test crime scene blood and tissue for potential matches in the FBI DNA database. Lori's inability to confirm his story made things even more frustrating. The investigators were putting a lot of stock in the gang theory even though they had zero evidence or leads to support it. All Brent could hope for was some sort of answers to come out of the forensic tests. But he knew nothing would come up in the tests. How could you map a DNA sample from something that is not from this world? The investigators dismissed his accounts, and behind closed doors probably thought he was nuts. Who wouldn't? It was so terrifyingly and frighteningly bizarre that even he had a difficult time believing that they'd been attacked by a beast from hell.

He was to be released from the hospital first thing in the morning, once his doctor made one last check on his bandages and wounds later this afternoon. Lori would be by before dinner for her daily visit, then back again in the morning to pick him up. Lori was managing things at the farm like the real trooper that she was. She was very familiar with most of the farm operations, the chores and responsibilities that needed to be done on a regular basis. She was also receiving lots of help from neighboring ranchers pitching in.

Glancing at the clock seeing the time was now 3:00 p.m., he decided he'd better take a nap while waiting for the doctor and before Lori arrived. Just as he was getting comfortable, he heard a voice enter the room.

"Won't be long and you'll be back branding a hundred head of cattle a day again," smiled Sheriff Clarkson, entering the room with another man in a suit.

Surprised to see the sheriff, he hoped they had some positive news on the lab tests.

"Pretty sure that won't happen anytime soon, Sheriff," chuckled Brent.

Stepping in close to the side of his bed, the Sheriff turned his attention to the man in the suit who accompanied him.

"Brent, this is Agent Cole Robertson from the FBI. As you already know, they have been actively working this case from the very beginning. We wanted to talk with you for a few minutes before your discharge if you're up to it."

No lab results. More theories.

"My story stays the same, Sheriff. I know what I saw regardless of how strange it sounds to the authorities."

Agent Robertson now stepped closer to Brent's hospital bed and said, "As you can appreciate, Brent, it is quite a story. However, we did receive the lab results back on the DNA from the blood and tissue collected at the crime scene at both the ranch and Lori's home. In addition to you, you're Dad, Lori plus her parents, and your ranch employee Melvin Gonzales there was no other DNA found at the scene! We cannot explain this, Brent, as we know there were multiple shots fired from your father's shotgun as well as the 9mm pistol fired at the Weston home. The lack of DNA from the attackers at both scenes is very strange and something we have no answers for at this moment."

He felt like launching himself out of the bed to attack Robertson, but the pain that resonated through his shoulder quickly dispelled that idea.

"You're telling me there was no DNA gathered at the scene

from that demonic creature? There was blood everywhere from that thing, I saw it with my own eyes hit the walls when I shot the damn thing multiple times. You guys refuse to believe me, don't you? Son of a bitch, this is insane!"

This time Sheriff Clarkson jumped back in. "I understand your frustrations, Brent, everyone does. What Agent Robertson is trying to say is there were copious amounts of blood and tissue gathered at the scene, however we were unable to identify the DNA."

Brent was stunned but not surprised. Looking at them both, he asked, "Were you able to determine if the blood and tissue samples were human?"

Agent Robertson hesitated, then looked at Sheriff Clarkson briefly before turning his attention to Brent. "No. We have determined that the samples were not human. In fact we have been unable so far to type the DNA to anything, animal or human."

So finally they believed what he'd been trying to tell them since the night of the attacks. They were not attacked by a gang of thugs. Satan himself had attacked them and raped Lori. Forensics wouldn't tell them anything.

Agent Robertson sensed what Brent was thinking and continued. "Until we can find some evidence we have very little to go on, Brent. There is a good chance that whoever or whatever did this will strike again. Then, if we're lucky we can get to them before they make another clean break. It is a long shot, we know, and it means someone else potentially getting hurt, but it's all we have. I'm sorry, Brent, that we can't do more, we're all sorry."

After the Sheriff and Agent Robertson left, Brent tried to nap, but he was too wound up to sleep. He could not shake the feeling that the creature had not randomly attacked them, but that they'd been chosen. But why? If only Lori could remember the attack, as awful as that would be, it could very well prove to be the turning point in the investigation. Even if the investigators did believe Brent, what could they do? They had no evidence, especially no DNA. If they'd only seen what I had, he thought.

He knew the devil existed, it was talked about in the Bible every Sunday. Why would it manifest itself in such a brutal and vicious way—and to them? What could they possibly do? They were dealing with a force of this world so evil and horrible, only God Himself could help them. He could think of only one thing they could do…Pray.

Brent woke suddenly from the gentle touch of the attending nurse informing him the doctor would be in soon to see him. Looking at the clock, he saw it was 7:30 p.m. *What the hell,* he thought? He'd been out for almost four hours? Looking at the nurse, he asked, "Was Lori here? She's my fiancée; she is usually here around six."

"She was here a little before six but you seemed to be resting so peacefully that she decided she would see you in the morning. She sends her love and has some great news to share with you in the morning when she sees you."

Damn, he wished she'd woken him up. He needed her close tonight for some reason. Maybe it was the visit by the Sheriff and the FBI, but he needed to get out of this place. His thoughts were abruptly interrupted by his surgeon, Dr. Tinsley, as he entered the room. The doctor's usual politeness was coming through, but he was all business most of the time, and tonight was no exception.

"So my tough-as-nails cowboy patient, how are we doing tonight? Let's take a look at those wounds and see if we can get you out of this place. You probably have come to love it so much I wouldn't blame you if you asked for more time here to continue to heal. What do you think?"

He looked at the doctor as he pulled on rubber gloves, picked up a pair of surgical scissors from a tray on the counter beside his bed and began to cut through the bandages on his shoulder.

"If you were to wheel me out to the taxi stand out front right this minute, it would not be fast enough, doctor. I appreciate everything you've done to put me back together, but hey, come on, doctor, it's been, what, a month? Time to go. Let someone else sicker than I am take over this concrete-hard Sealy Posturepedic."

The doctor took a serious tone as he gently pulled back the bandages.

"Don't be fooled, Brent, you are sick, very sick, in fact. The threat of infection is still very much a factor. Your wounds have come a long way, though, they're looking better every day. I will get you back here in three months for some further skin grafting to continue to build up the lost tissue in the affected areas. You are a long way from being out of the woods Mr. Asker, but now it's just a waiting game, waiting for the wounds to heal. As long as you follow the program and get plenty of rest, everything should be fine, and if not you'll be back in Club Med. That sound okay to you?"

Brent winced as Dr. Tinsley continued to probe along his wounds.

"You have my word, doctor. Cowboys never lie, and they always do as they're told. Surprised you never heard of that legend."

"Nope, sorry, missed that John Wayne movie, Brent. You are free to go in the morning after the nurses have given you breakfast and your medication. Is Lori picking you up in the morning? I will need to see those wounds again in two weeks, so will want you back here then, okay? Any problems, you get back here pronto. You'll be fitted with a special sling after breakfast that will make things easier for you, along with a pile of bandages for Lori to play nurse with every night as she changes the dressing. No lifting whatsoever with this arm. I don't care how well you think you feel. You are on strict doctor's orders to rest, Brent. A nurse will stop by the ranch every three or four days to have a look. Other than that, I will see you in a few weeks."

The next morning after he had his breakfast the nurse arrived to change his bandages and rig up the sling that would keep his arm immobilized, allowing the wounds to heal. Looking at his wounds as the nurse worked away, he realized he was now used to seeing the physical damage, was no longer shocked. The scars were horrendous, and he would carry them as a constant reminder of the damage the monster inflicted on himself and his family, even though he was the only one who really knew what happened. Lori's memory loss was a good thing, he kept reminding himself, but there are times when he felt alone in this tragedy, and if Lori were to remember what happened then it would validate his story, but that was just selfish thinking. Being strong emotionally right now was important for Lori and him as they tried to recover from this. Lori's grief was based upon the knowledge that violent and viscous strangers randomly chose their homes to attack them and commit murder. They had decided to postpone their wedding in the hope that once he was physically healed they would elope. Neither of them was interested in a big wedding. All of their loved ones were dead, they just had each other now. They talked of eloping to Las Vegas and then taking some time lying on a beach somewhere to give their souls the time to recover. That was all about to change with the news that Lori carried with her as she entered the room to take him home.

Lori came into the room, and he immediately could see a difference in her. Gone was the dark cloud that had surrounded her. Today she was vibrant, cheery and energized. It was as if this windowless hospital room all of a sudden had rays of sunshine pouring through its walls.

"Good morning, sweetheart! Sorry I missed you last night, but you were sleeping like a baby, and I didn't have the heart to wake you," said a beaming Lori as she bent down and planted a big wet one on his lips.

He looked at her, unable to contain how he felt. He loved her so much.

"God, I missed you. Next time, you wake me, you hear? You look fantastic today. What's up with you?"

She placed her hands on his cheeks as she spoke. They were cool to the touch and smelt so fresh.

"Well, be thankful there will be no next time in this place, thank goodness for that. How about I take you back to the ranch and fix you up a real breakfast of the greasiest bacon, eggs and hash browns you ever tasted? What do you say, cowboy?" a giggling Lori teased as she kissed Brent again on the forehead.

"First you have to tell me the name of that happy sandwich you ate on the way over here, because that's what I want for breakfast."

He loved it as she laughed while gently pulling his good arm, encouraging him to get up.

"No sandwich, sweetheart, just some excellent news that both of us I think needed for once. Let's get you dressed and I'll tell you all about it in the truck on the drive home," replied Lori, her voice resonating with excitement.

Twenty minutes later, with Brent's personal belongings in a bag sitting on his lap, Lori was pushing him in a wheelchair out to the parking lot and into the truck. Buckling him up made it a little uncomfortable with the arm in the sling, but he wasn't about to complain. With Lori's excitement, he wanted to make sure he had his seatbelt on in case she rear-ended somebody, she was so giddy.

As Lori made her way out of the hospital parking lot and into the traffic, he couldn't stand it anymore. "Okay, honey, what's going on? Tell me, for crying out loud!"

She looked over at him and smiled.

"Open the glove box," she told him.

Opening the glove box, all he could find in addition to the truck registration was a few maps and a small blue and white plastic box. "There is nothing in here Lori, what am I supposed to find?"

"The box, Brent, jeepers you didn't even look at it!" laughed Lori.

Pulling the plastic box out of the glove compartment, it took Brent a few seconds to register what it was he was staring at, and then it hit him. The blow to his solar plexus from the realization that he was holding a home pregnancy test kit could not have hurt him more than if it had been a sledgehammer.

Turning to Lori with a horrified look on his face he was

speechless. Trying to come up with something to say to her, he just stammered and mumbled while holding the box in his hand, "What does this mean?"

"Honey, I'm pregnant. I have been throwing up in the mornings for days so I finally took the test. It was confirmed by my family doctor this morning before I came to pick you up. I am so thrilled, Brent, I hope and pray you are, too," Lori said as she glanced over at Brent and then back to the road.

The only thing Brent could think of as he searched for words was that his wife was carrying the child of the demon that had attacked them and raped Lori. This was not Brent's child. They had not made love since their engagement almost a year ago.

Obviously Lori, with the head trauma she'd suffered not only has no memory of the attack but she also had forgotten other important details of their lives, too. His good hand now shaking badly, Brent dropped the box onto the floor by his feet. Looking at Lori, all he could say was, "I love you."

"I love you to Brent. I know this is a lot for you to think about just getting out of the hospital, but it will be fine, sweetheart. Our baby will be beautiful, and if it's a boy, guaranteed he will be born with cowboy boots on," beamed Lori as she reached over with her hand, rubbing Brent's leg as she spoke.

The rest of the drive back to the ranch Brent just nodded most of the time as Lori rambled on and on about the baby, their future together and if it was a boy they should name him Bert to honor his father. It was surreal for him listening to her and her complete obliviousness to the true nature of the child she was carrying. *This is insanity,* he thought. As they pulled up to the ranch and Lori jumped out to help him out of the truck, he already knew what he had to do.

This baby cannot be allowed to live!

Chapter 22

The sound of his wife Bethany's soft breathing as she slept peacefully beside him was the only sound Sam could hear in the darkness of their bedroom. He tried to absorb what Medical Examiner Eunice Epp had revealed to him earlier that evening while he was working late at the office. The blood and tissue samples gathered at the Carruthers crime scene and the Benning home were from the same attacker. This was not startling news, as he'd already been expecting that based upon what Steven had told him on the phone. What was startling, however, was that the DNA was not human nor of any known animal. Then what the hell was it?

Unable to sleep, he got out of bed carefully as Bethany stirred but did not wake, then quietly slipped downstairs. Looking at the time on the stove in the kitchen as he poured himself a glass of water, he gave out a big sigh, knowing this was going to be a long day indeed.

Making his way upstairs to get ready for work, he decided to shower in the main bathroom instead of his master bath. It would be better if he could get out of the house without waking Bethany. If she knew he hadn't slept, then had left for the office at 4:00 a.m. it would only make her more worried about him than she already was. Finishing up his shower, he tiptoed into his bedroom to gather some clothes, his badge and gun, in almost complete darkness except for some moonlight peeking its way through the blinds, when he heard Bethany whisper, "Don't tell me you are going to the office now? It's four in the morning, honey"

Busted.

"Beth, go back to sleep, dear, I'm okay. Couldn't sleep very well and I have a few things I want to track down on the computer before the office fills up with bodies," he whispered back as he bent down to kiss his wife on the forehead, then whispered into her ear, "Remember, honey, lots of rest is good for both of you."

His wife smiled back at him, her white teeth luminous in the darkness of the bedroom. Rolling over into the middle of the bed and fluffing her pillow, she said, "I love you, Sam. Be safe, and come home early for once."

Arriving at the office twenty minutes later, Sam made a beeline for the row of coffee machines on the second floor of Headquarters, one floor below Robbery-Homicide. Settling in front of his computer at his desk, he went to work opening up the COPLINK database, giving access to police intelligence on suspects from across the US. He also worked the standard NCIC database that police agencies had been using for years. What Sam hoped to dig up was a long shot—that maybe there had been other similar murders that involved unknown DNA samples in addition to particularly vicious attacks where the female victim was sexually assaulted. After a few hours he called it quits, as the office started to fill up and he was not having much luck. Just a few cases that were also pretty violent, but there was no sexual assault, so he made a note to do some more searching in a few weeks in case the perpetrator struck again.

It was almost nine, so he decided to leave before Bitters arrived and pinned him down for updates on the case, to head over to the coroner's office and see Epp. Hopefully she'd have further theories as to the lab results on the attacker's DNA. When he arrived at the coroner's office on Mission Road, Epp was expecting him. "I figured to be seeing you camped outside my door when I arrived at six this morning. Come on, let's go to my office. I want to keep this private for as long as I can," she said.

Back in her office, Eunice closed the door behind Sam, directing him to a chair in front of her desk. She looked like shit, he observed, had obviously slept very little and didn't bother covering it up with makeup. Her hair was finger-combed, and he bet she was working on her second pot of coffee already. Looking at him, she said, "I'm going to go down the hall and fill my cup, you want some?"

"No thanks, Eunice, already reached my one cup a day limit."

"Jesus, one cup a day, what the hell is that? Why drink any at all? You're probably some fitness nut, tree hugging kind of guy, aren't you Detective?" Epp chastised him as she left the room to fill up her cup.

Returning a minute later, she sat down at her desk, and seeing the look on his face, said, "I know what you're thinking, Showenstein. You're probably thinking that the dozens of stiffs laying on the slabs down the hall probably look a helluva lot better than I do right now. Well you're right, but I don't give a shit. I am up to my eyeballs in bodies, we are severely short staffed, I have pathologists quitting everyday because they can't handle the workload. It's getting critical around here; we have more and more bodies being dumped here every day. It's a goddamn war zone out there. My examiners and pathologists are heading to the smaller communities to get away from this rat race. I should be spending my time lobbying the city for more staff, but instead I spend my time conducting autopsies. Do you like it when I vent, Sam? I betcha Homicide is a walk in the park. All you dicks sittin around, waiting for a shooting, so you can get off your asses and do something. Anyways, enough of that, we need to discuss the Benning case." Epp smirked in frustration as she looked for the file folder containing the paperwork for Benning and the Caruthers's kid.

"Did you ever stop to consider that the bodies being dumped at your doorstep that you're complaining about are mostly homicides that a dick like me has to get off his fat ass to investigate?"

Epp looked up from her paperwork to stare at him for a brief second before she sarcastically continued. "Good point, Detective, never thought to look at it that way. The blood work that's not of Steven and Chelsea or the Carruthers kid is devoid of any DNA material. That is impossible, Detective, and quite frankly unless the Benning's were slaughtered by an alien whose blood is different than what is found in humans, we have ourselves a clusterfuck mystery that I don't wish on any detective."

Exasperated, Sam sat back in his chair and just shook his head. "How can that be, Eunice? I mean, I thought there were some blood types for which DNA does not exist."

Leaving her stylish reading glasses on but resting on the tip of her nose, Epp continued.

"In fact, red blood cells do not have DNA because they have no nucleus. It's elsewhere that the DNA is found, the white blood cells and plasma. When you see red blood, it's much more than red blood cells that you see."

He was confused and frustrated, and it showed when he spoke.

"Are you saying, Eunice, that the blood found on the bodies of Graham Carruthers and the Benning's, plus the blood and tissue samples in the Benning bedroom, is neither from a human nor from any animal?"

"That is exactly what I am saying," Epp replied.

"What the hell am I supposed to do with this? What the hell am I going to say to the Police Chief and the Mayor that the Carruthers kid and the Benning's were murdered by, what did you say earlier, an alien? Jesus, I need a different job."

"Good luck with that, Detective. If anything new develops here I'll let you know."

Rising up from his chair to leave, Sam felt as if he had worked twelve hours already.

"Thanks, Eunice, for getting me the lab results so quickly.

Now I wish you'd have taken your time. I'm going to run by the hospital and check on Chelsea to see if there are any changes in her condition. Speaking with her would certainly help clear up a lot in this case."

Leaving the County Coroner's office, he didn't know what to do with Epp's report. Maybe he should just bury it for now until more leads were developed. If he took this to Bitters now, shit would hit the fan by the bucket load. The suits upstairs want results fast for the killing of a kid and a LAPD detective. They're going to want to know if there were any DNA matches on any known perpetrators from the attacker's blood. Telling them there were no matches would be telling the truth, but the fact that the DNA was not human or animal would give the mayor a coronary. Pressure was building, as the press was all over this story. They wanted progress, even though it had only been a day.

Deep down, Sam already knew where this case was going. Nowhere. Whoever killed the kid and his partner would never be found. The sheer brutality of the attack and the non-DNA were spooky, to say the least, and certainly a homicide investigation by the LAPD would not uncover any clues as to the identity of this killer.

Arriving at Methodist Hospital just minutes away from the Benning home on West Huntington Drive in Arcadia, he made his way to the intensive care unit housing Chelsea. Showing his police badge to the nurses' station, he inquired as to the status of Chelsea Benning and if any of her doctors were available to speak with him. An attractive younger nurse with a name tag that read Sylvia W., RN, informed him that Dr. Creamer was on shift at the moment and she would have him paged. She did say it would likely take a while before the doctor made his way down, so if he wanted to go get a coffee down in the cafeteria he had lots of time.

"Can you let Dr. Creamer know that the lead investigator on the homicide of Steven Benning and the assault on Chelsea is here to see him? Might put some bounce in those steps," winked Sam at the nurse.

"I'll see what I can do," smiled the nurse.

"Thank you, and I'll just take a seat over here till the doctor arrives. Already met and exceeded my coffee quota for the day," Sam stated as he found an empty seat in front of the nurses' station.

Approximately ten minutes later, a younger doctor approached Sam, extending his hand. "I am Dr. Creamer. I understand you are investigating the assault on Chelsea Benning?"

Sam put the *Reader's Digest* magazine down on the table and rose to shake Dr. Creamer's hand.

"Thank you for seeing me, doctor. I'm Detective Sam Showenstein from Homicide, investigating the attacks on the Benning's. Steven Benning was my partner. From a personal concern, has there been any improvement in Chelsea's condition? In regards to the investigation, when would I be able to speak with her about the events from the other night?"

"Firstly, I can tell you Chelsea is awake but heavily sedated. She received violent blows to her face, resulting in a fractured cheekbone, nose and eye socket, or orbital bone. She has multiple contusions all over her body. Lastly, she was sexually assaulted. Damage to her vaginal tissue was significant. The attacker was brutally violent, Detective, and literally beat the hell out of Chelsea. Why he did not kill her and let her live, I guess is your job to figure out. Now, I will allow you to speak with her, but only for a few minutes, Detective, and please try not to get her upset. Also, before you go in to see her there is one important thing you need to know. She is pregnant."

Chelsea was pregnant? The news shocked him. Steven would have been so thrilled, but now he will never know. Chelsea is carrying the baby of her murdered husband. Tragic—and Sam vowed he would get this son of a bitch if he had to climb onto a spaceship to find him. Looking at the doctor, he asked, "Does she know?"

"Yes, it was one of the first questions she asked when she became conscious," replied Dr. Creamer.

Sam gathered himself and took in a large breath.

"Okay, can I see her now?"

He followed Dr. Creamer into the room and was not prepared for what he was saw. Chelsea was battered so badly he didn't even recognize her. IV tubes ran out of both arms, her face and head were heavily bandaged. The portion of her face exposed was bruised and badly swollen. She has been brutalized, he thought, and whoever was responsible, he would find him and kill him. His heart went out to her, she looked so helpless lying on that bed knowing what had happened to her and about the murder of Steven. Seeing Sam enter the room, Chelsea began to cry, soft sobs with tears beginning to fill her eyes and spill over.

Dr. Creamer approached her, consoled her, instructing her not to get upset. He looked back at Sam before he left the room and said, "Remember, don't get her upset. You have twenty minutes."

Sam came close and put his hand on hers, attempting to reassure her that everything would be alright. "I am so sorry, Chelsea, for what happened to you and Steven. I am sorry I was not there with Steven, I should have been," a choked-up Sam whispered to Chelsea.

Speaking through a broken jaw too swollen to wire shut, bandages covering most of her face, she replied, in a voice so quiet Sam had to lean close to her just to hear, "It's not your fault, Sam. There is nothing you could have done. You would have been dead along with Steven. Please hand me my water, Sam."

As he held the glass of water close to her face and directed the straw into her mouth, she continued in a voice barely audible, "I was raped by a monster. Steven was killed by this thing, Sam. It was straight from hell. It was awful." Chelsea began to sob again.

He returned the glass of water to the nightstand and gently picked up her hand once again.

"Chelsea, you are getting upset and that's not good for you, please let's continue this conversation when you're stronger. You need to rest," Sam instructed her, worried that she was getting too worked up with grief.

Straining to look directly into Sam's eyes, she spoke not in a whisper this time but in a louder tone that surprised Sam, "Sam, listen to me! We were attacked by a demon, the devil himself! Steven shot it multiple times, a dozen or more shots, and it never flinched. It had the eyes of the devil, Sam. They glowed like pools of molten lava. It spoke in Latin. Then it raped me, Sam. I could feel its demon seed inside me immediately growing in my belly. I am pregnant with this devil's child! Dear God, please help me!" Tears were now streaming down her cheeks. Suddenly she began to gag and fight for air, as if unable to breathe. Her monitor began to make funny noises. Horrified, Sam rushed to the doorway and yelled for a nurse.

A nurse came running into the room, followed soon after by Dr. Creamer. After he barked out orders and administered a sedative to Chelsea, she eventually calmed down. "Detective, we must ask you to leave this room now. She is sedated and will be out for several hours. She cannot get upset like this. We were lucky this time. She has serious brain trauma, swelling, that requires rest. I never should have let you in so soon. From now on, and until I give the okay, she is not to have any further visitors, Detective. Is that clear?"

Numb, Sam just nodded his head and backed out of the room.

Walking down the hallway outside of Chelsea's room, he found a water fountain in the hallway, and instead of drinking he splashed the cold water on his face, not caring if half of it was landing on his shirt. That look in Chelsea's eyes—she was scared beyond comprehension when she described the attack. The devil, a demon, speaking in Latin? She felt the baby inside her grow immediately when it raped her?

The sense of dread he felt was overwhelming, the fear for Chelsea for what she must be going through was indescribable.

He leaned against the wall outside Chelsea's room, closed his eyes, and whispered a prayer in Hebrew, asking for God's protection to keep Chelsea safe, and to guide and give him strength in the days ahead.

Chapter 23

Alive Records was exactly that—'Alive'—this late in the day on a Wednesday. The place was a zoo, with the Grammy Awards on Sunday and all of the music industry VIPs in town right now. Avery's schedule was booked through Thursday, Friday and Saturday in advance of the awards show. Meetings with agents, clients and lawyers filled all day Thursday and Friday. Thursday night each year, he never committed to any one specific event, instead choosing to keep it open. Some years he was just too exhausted to attend, other years he let the evenings activities pay itself out. Friday night he would be attending the MusicCares Benefit at the Convention Center for its twenty-first year annual MusicCares benefit concert.

This year Barbara Streisand was being honored, so the place would have a diversified crowd for sure. Saturday evening was the Clive Davis Pre-Grammy Gala at the Beverly Hilton. Sony executive Clive Davis had hosted the Grammys' most coveted invite since 1976; the sit-down dinner for twelve hundred invited guests had had featured performances by Rod Stewart and Whitney Houston in the past and was attended by major business players such as Universal's Records James Rencor and Warner Music's Skylor Cohen. Confirmed to attend this year was music industry heavyweights David Geffen, Jeffrey Katzenberg, Grammy nominees Allison Kraus, R. Kelly and the legendary Bob Dylan. It was a must attend event and Avery would be there.

Accompanying him for all of the Grammy parties and dinners was of course Jennifer, his always reliable assistant who doubled as his token beautiful date. She didn't mind—part of the job she would laugh—plus it gave her a great seat for the hottest ticket of the year, next to the Academy Awards. He'd even thought of asking Bentley Paxton to accompany him, but she was already attending with the entourage from *Music Talks* magazine, so all he could hope for there was maybe getting a chance to bump into her at an after-Grammy bash. He purposely left that venue open and did not make a commitment to any particular party, so as to be able to end up at the same one as Bentley. Thinking about bumping into Bentley made his heart skip a beat, and he hoped he didn't qualify as a stalker, because he kind of felt like one, he laughed to himself.

Alive Records would be well represented at the Grammys this year with the success of the J 'Tick Tock' DBL J multi-platinum selling Rap album *Beware Out There* nominated for four Grammys in the Rap Category, including Best Rap Solo Performance, Best Rap Song, Best Rap Album, Record of the Year and Song of the Year. Avery was up for a Grammy as Producer on the Album of the Year and Best Rap Album for his production credits on *Beware Out There*. He and Tick Tock were up against the new rap artist Devon Devine and his producer Robert Best in the Best Rap Album and Best Rap Song categories, plus Devine was nominated in the Best New Artist category. The success of Devine and Best in the industry after Avery had rejected them in his office was a surprise, to say the least. Weirder things have happened in this industry, he thought, but the likelihood of those two being successful was a long shot.

Avery's attention was directed to his office door, as Jenn did her usual one rap on the door, then walked in with an announcement. "I have Thursday and Friday's schedule to go over with you if you have time now."

Damn, his day was crazy, but this was something he couldn't avoid.

"Sure, let's get this over with. Do you mind grabbing me a Coke first? Thanks, Jenn."

A few minutes later they sat down at the conference table in his office and went over the schedule. His calendar was full all day Thursday and Friday, meeting with the managers and agents of new artists he had recruited to produce and sign to Alive Records. The success of Alive Records over these past few years afforded him the luxury of new artists coming to him looking to sign with a major label and gain access to his highly regarded production team and state of the art recording studio. Most of the appointments lasted no more than an hour to two hours, though with some of the more complicated deals he had Jenn slot more time that included a lunch to continue discussions. Escaping at the end of the day was key, in order to get ready for the evening festivities. Jenn was a master at keeping everyone on schedule. Soon they had the schedule firmed up and they called it a day so the two of them could escape for a few hours to get ready for the night. He would pick up Jenn with the company limo around 6:15 p.m. as they decided to hit the Mick Fleetwood-Stevie Nicks benefit concert at the Music Box which began at seven sharp. Fortunately, living and working in West Hollywood allowed him close access to all of the venues for the weekend events.

The next several days went by like a blur. He and Jenn were working so hard that when it came to the evening events they were so exhausted it was difficult to just relax and enjoy the entertainment.

They got through it, and with great success, as they were able to get new clients signed, recording studio times scheduled and tentative release dates for each album's first single to the media outlets. Jenn would get all of the contracts to Alive Records lawyers for finalization next week when things returned to normal around the office. Come Sunday, though, the excitement of the year's biggest night in the music industry was palpable. Tick Tock's album should be a shoo-in for his nominated categories, giving Avery the credit he deserved for a masterful job on the album as producer. Winning the Grammy would be an exclamation mark on a lot of hard work and a little luck. Make no mistake, everyone wanted to win, and he was no exception.

Arriving at the Shrine Auditorium on West Jeffersen in Los Angeles for the big show in the limo with the Alive Records logo prominently displayed on the rear side windows, Avery and Jenn climbed out into a flood of photographers, fans and media. In the Vera Wang dress that he had ordered for her, Jenn looked like a movie star not the executive assistant of a music producer. Stopping for an interview with *Rolling Stone* magazine on the way into the venue, he caught a glimpse of Bentley Paxton walking through the VIP doors accompanying the editor of *Music Talks*. The breath literally got sucked out from him at the sight of Bentley. She was stunning, and would clearly stand out among all of the beautiful women packed into this place tonight. Finishing up with *Rolling Stone*, he and Jenn continued through the VIP tunnel at the Shrine and were on their way to their assigned seating when Jenn announced, "Ms. Paxton was looking quite ravishing, wouldn't you say, Mr. Johnson?", her tongue firmly planted in her cheek.

"Quiet, Ms. Steinart, or you will be banished to the cheap seats," smiled Avery, and added, "By the way, you look pretty darn ravishing yourself. You make me look good."

Clutching his arm as they made their way to their seats, passing and acknowledging celebrities as they did so, Jenn smiled up at him and said, "Well, thank you, Avery. You just bought yourself some brownie points that will go straight into the brownie jar, 'cause last time I looked it was completely empty."

When they reached their assigned seats, Avery was pleasantly surprised to find himself in the second row center stage, right behind Sir Paul McCartney. He took the time to say hello to Paul and other celebrities nearby, but the schmoozing soon came to a halt as the PA system came on advising everyone to find their seats as the show would be starting in ten minutes. There was a flurry of activity as stage hands and producers made last-minute adjustments to the stage and sound checks were being done along with settings for the multitude of computer generated lights. It would be one hell of a show, broadcast live with over forty million people tuning in. This year the live performances were sure to be great with Aretha Franklin, Bob Dylan. Stevie Wonder and Fiona Apple to name a few, plus Tick Tock, so that should be a real treat, he chuckled to himself. I'm sure Tick will ingratiate himself quite well with the rest of the stars backstage.

Looking for Bentley's seating assignment; he finally spotted her about fifteen rows back, to the left of the stage. Certainly a long way from the VIP section but still good seats nonetheless. There was not a bad seat in the place, with organizers sectioning off large portions of the auditorium seating to accommodate the massive stage setup.

Seeing Bentley sitting and chatting with the people from her magazine as well as others around her with such ease and grace made him marvel. A woman with such beauty and talent who handled herself with such dignity was rare, and he found himself wishing he was sitting in row fifteen.

The night went by very quickly, with Tick Tock's performance through the roof, and the night was made complete by Tick Tock winning for Best Rap Album and Avery picking up the Grammy for the album's producer. After the show ended, he and Jenn proceeded to the VIP section backstage for the photo sessions with the press for all the winners. They were congratulated by just about everyone they met, so it felt like they were walking through a gauntlet as they made their way backstage. Reaching the area designated for the photos, Avery heard a voice he knew at some point he would hear but was hoping he wouldn't.

"Congratulations, Avery, on your Grammy. You must be very pleased at how things turned out for Tick Tock. It was a great album."

The false praise spewing from Robert Best's mouth grated on Avery's nerves. He turned to face Best and accept his handshake, which was, as he remembered, vise-grip tight.

"I should be congratulating you for Devon's success. Taking

the Grammy from Tick Tock for Best Song was robbery. I should be demanding a recount. You've come a long way since you sat in my office uninvited, Mr. Best," Avery replied. The smug look on Best's face served as an instant reminder of how much he disliked this guy.

"Maybe you should have taken the opportunity to work with Devon. You had a shot at him, but it's your loss, Mr. Johnson," Best threw back at Avery.

"How about we just say it's been a gain for both of us. You seem to have done a good job producing the album. Now if you don't mind, Mr. Best, I believe I'm being paged for a silly photo op on this trophy they gave me tonight. Hang in there, Mr. Best, and maybe next year you might get one, too," and with that, Avery, with his arm around Jenn's waist, guided her forward and past Best, who glared at him as he did.

Looking over at Avery as they threaded their way to the photo area, Jenn said, "If I'm not mistaken, you don't like that guy very much. I thought your mantra was to treat all of your colleagues in this industry with respect, as if they were your friends. 'No enemies in this business, Jenn,' I remember you telling me."

"That guy is a prick. There's something very strange about him that I can't quite put my finger on yet. Guys like him don't last in this business anyway, Jenn. He'll be out of this business before you know it. Count on it," an annoyed Avery replied.

Forty-five minutes later they had finished up all of the photo ops with the press and swapped congratulatory comments with some of the other winners, when Avery declared to Jenn, "I promised Bentley Paxton during the photo sessions that I would give her magazine an exclusive interview, so I will do that now in the next few minutes before we head off to the wrap party. Do you mind?"

Jenn gave his arm a squeeze. "Actually I am about as exhausted as you could possibly imagine, Avery, so I'm going to take a pass on the party tonight. I have had enough, really I have, and tomorrow, as you know, is a very busy day. You have fun with Ms. Paxton at whatever party you decide to go to."

"Are you sure? Well, okay then, Jenn. Thanks for putting up with me during what we can both say has been our hell week, the week that makes the navy seal training first week seem like a walk in the park, wouldn't you agree?" laughed Avery, giving Jenn a big hug. "I'll call Danny and have him meet you out front with the limo. Tell him to go home for the night after he drops you off. I'll find a cab later." Avery waved to Jenn as she turned to go.

"Remember, Avery, tomorrow is a very busy day," Jenn warned her boss before she took off.

Making his way back into the press area, it wasn't hard for him to find Bentley. With all of the beautifully dressed woman at this event, Bentley could still stand out. Catching her eye, he blushed as she came over with a smile that could light up even the massive Shrine Auditorium. Touching Avery's elbow, she said, "We're all done here now, so if you're ready I'll take twenty minutes of your time if that's okay with you."

"Perfectly fine with me, Bentley." *More than you know*, thought Avery.

Following her to one of the breakaway rooms that the press had access to for such occasions, Avery couldn't help notice how extremely well Bentley filled out her dress. Man, she was beautiful. They entered a room no bigger than twelve feet by maybe ten feet with a round table, six chairs, and a small fridge on a table in the corner, with a side table stocked with finger foods. Bentley closed the door behind, locking it, and then said, "Don't be alarmed that I locked the door. It shows 'occupied' to anyone else trying to use the room. Just like the outhouses at an outdoor concert," laughed Bentley. "Can I get you anything to drink or eat, Avery, before we get started?"

"I will have a glass of red wine as long as you join me."

"I think I can handle that."

Pouring them each a glass of Merlot, Bentley told Avery, "Remember when I told you about that creepy Robert Best before he became successful, when I interviewed him when he was managing Watermark? Well, I bumped into him here in the press area, I think *Rolling Stone* was interviewing him, and the guy had the nerve to ask me to an after-Grammy party. After telling him that it was a work night for me, that us writers didn't have the luxury of relaxing tonight, he said to tell my boss that I was able to secure an interview with him tonight after I was done with the scheduled interviews. He said we could do the interview back at his suite at the Millennium Biltmore."

"What an asshole. What did you tell him?"

"I told him that *Music Talks* doesn't interview flash in the pan music producers who got lucky once. I told him that maybe the magazine would consider an interview after he proved he could stick in the business." She smiled as she handed him the glass of wine.

Accepting the wine, he rose from his chair to pull Bentley's chair out so she could sit down. "Wow, that would have bruised his oversized ego, I bet," laughed Avery.

Accepting his gesture of pulling out her chair, she said, "He told me that soon he will be managing and producing the biggest band ever, bigger than the Beatles. Can you believe that? *Music Talks* will have to wait months if at all to get an interview with this band. I said it sounded impressive, I asked him who they were, and he said it's a band still in the works but to stay tuned."

"What an arrogant ass. I hope I never see that creep again. Next time he shoots his mouth off in front of me, I might make the headlines with TMZ, but for all the wrong reasons," said Avery.

Picking up her glass of wine, she gestured to click glasses with his and said, "Well, enough about him, Avery let's talk about your Grammy and the success you and Tick Tock have had with *Beware Out There*."

Staring into her eyes over the next thirty minutes, Avery was swooning and had no idea what he was saying to her when she asked him questions. Her effect on him was crazy, but Avery knew one thing: he loved it.

Chapter 24

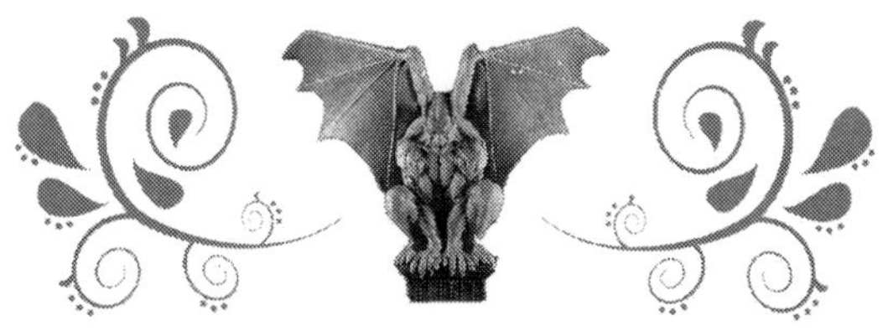

Gerard Louveneau, with multiple fractures, including his right shoulder and right hip, lay helplessly in his hospital bed at the Montreal General. His left ankle was also broken and surgery was required to insert pins. The wounds on his face had required over one hundred stitches. He was a mess, and he was facing months of recovery, including a month in this hospital according to his doctors. The horror of the attack on him and Francoise was vivid in his memory, in every detail. They had been in the hospital less than a week and he had yet to have a police officer or investigator visit his room to interview him on the events. They must have got enough information from Francoise to keep them busy. At one point he asked the attending nurses if the police had inquired about speaking with him, and they said they had not. Very strange, Gerard thought, and he wondered if he should make some inquires as to why, but maybe they felt he was too busted up and traumatized to grant an interview at this point. He was still unable to see Francoise yet, because he was incapacitated and she was still unable to leave her room. Fortunately, according to the nurses this morning, they were going to be able to bring her up to his room this afternoon.

****

Francoise, who was on a different floor in the hospital, had received terrible blows to her face, breaking her jaw and nose, with multiple cuts resulting in stitches scattered all over her face. Both her face and Gerard's looked like patchwork. Most of her facial scars would fade away, but one in particular might require plastic surgery in the future to hide the scarring. The scarring in Francoise's soul might never heal, she knew. The horrific and vicious sexual assault by that monster would be forever seared into her memory. Knowing that Gerard had survived his injuries and was recovering a few floors below her brought her comfort. She needed to see him and had been told by her doctors that she would be allowed out of the room this afternoon to see her husband and would likely be discharged tomorrow from the hospital. Thank God for that, she thought. She had so many flowers crowding her room she would have to rent a U-Haul to get them home. She'd had a flood of visitors from the department a few days after her admittance, once some of her facial swelling subsided. The well-wishers all expressed shock at the extent of her injuries and the brutality of the attack on her and Gerard. Most of them said investigators were working around the clock to find the thugs that did this to her and her husband. Francoise did not engage them and tell them what had really attacked them. This was neither the time nor the place. The first two days in the hospital she'd given the police investigators a detailed account of the attack, including the frightening description of the beast that had almost killed them both and had raped her. Her description of the beast was met with utter shock that led her questioners at one point to take a break and leave the room for a period. Francoise, an experienced police officer, knew why they'd left the room. They did not believe her, and they needed the time alone to discuss the validity of her story and, she was sure, her mental state. She'd expected this reaction but was hoping, once the investigators had listened to Gerard's side of the story, that between the two of them, one an experienced police officer and the other a valued and respected Crown Prosecutor, they would create a pretty convincing story regardless of how bizarre it sounded.

Her thoughts were interrupted by the entrance of her doctor, whose demeanor today seemed somewhat different. Dr. Berthiume was not his usual jovial self. His mood was definitely somber, and this scared her, as she thought of Gerard right away. He said, "Francoise, you are pregnant. When I looked at your file this morning, there it was."

Had it been possible, her jaw would have fallen to the floor.

"Did you just say PREGNANT?! How could that be? I was not expecting to hear this, doctor. I must tell Gerard! Why the worried look, Dr Berthiume? I would think this is good news considering all that has happened to Gerard and me."

Dr. Berthiume looked at her intently, dropping his head slightly before he spoke.

"Francoise your gestation period—or an easier way of putting it, you became pregnant within the last eight days. I know what this represents, Francoise, that it puts it in line with your attacker. If you want I can have DNA tests done and compare them with Gerard's DNA to confirm one way or another."

The severity and shock of this news hit Francoise like a thunderclap. There would be no need for a DNA test, she thought. She knew she was pregnant with the child of the devil and her world was about to turn upside down. Unable to control herself, Francoise vomited all over the side of the bed and onto the floor. Looking up at the doctor, she cried out, "Dr. Berthiume, I cannot carry this baby! You must abort it, please! I was raped by a monster! I cannot give birth to this baby! Oh my God! Doctor, please!"

Dr. Berthiume called out for nurses as he tried to settle Francoise down.

"Francoise, please calm down. Listen to me. An abortion is certainly an option. Talk with Gerard and if that is what you want then it will be done," he explained.

As a nurse prepared a mild sedative to help calm her down, Francoise once again begged Dr. Berthiume to move forward with the abortion immediately, now screaming at him, "Please, doctor, please! Get this baby out of me now! I feel its evil presence inside me. Now, doctor, please. Abort this baby now!"

Looking back at the nurse, Dr. Berthiume ordered her to administer a more powerful sedative, as Francoise was becoming agitated to the point of hysteria. Within minutes the drugs had made their way into Francoise's bloodstream, instantly calming her down until she became very drowsy then slipped into a deep sleep. Looking at the nurse, Dr. Berthiume said, "She will be out of it for several hours, but when she comes around have me paged. I want her wheeled down to her husband's room when she awakens, but page me first."

****

Leaving the room, Dr. Berthiume went to see Gerard before he finished his rounds with his patients. He needed to prepare him for the news of his wife's pregnancy. The shock to Gerard, and his reaction to the knowledge that his wife was pregnant with the child of the man who had sexually assaulted her, could send Francoise into a complete panic attack. Reaching the nursing station for intensive care, he asked who the doctor on duty was for Gerard Louveneau. The nurse replied that it was Dr. Emily Bouchiere and that she was actually in seeing Mr. Louveneau right at that moment. Excusing himself, Dr. Berthiume entered Gerard's room and asked Dr. Bouchiere if she had a few minutes out in the hall to talk about a patient. In the hallway he explained the situation to Dr. Bouchiere and asked if Gerard was ready for his wife to visit the room and reveal her condition.

"Jesus, what a tough situation for these two people to deal with on top of their injuries. His wife is obviously very traumatized by the news of the pregnancy, but for her to be claiming she was assaulted by a demonic monster in that context is very disturbing. I am all done with Mr. Louveneau, so now would be a good time to discuss this with him. I cannot stay but I will introduce you to him," explained Dr. Bouchiere.

A few minutes later Dr. Berthiume was all alone in the room

with Gerard, and pulled up a chair close to the bed and said, "Gerard, I am the attending physician for your wife Francoise, and I have made arrangements for her to come down here to see you within the next few hours. Before we bring her down I want to bring you up to speed on her condition."

Worry crossed over Gerard's face as the doctor spoke.

"Is there something wrong, doctor? I thought she was doing well, even being discharged soon."

Dr. Berthiume, sitting on a stool with his hands cupped together on his lap, fixed Gerard with a concerned look. When he spoke he lifted his hands to animate while he talked.

"Physically she is doing fine, Gerard. Her facial wounds are healing well and her jaw did not have to be wired shut, so she is healing nicely. I shared something with her today, Gerard, that I will share with you as well, that sent her into a frenzy. She needed to be sedated to calm her down. This will come to a shock to you, but you need to know so that when we bring Francoise down to see you, you are prepared."

A feeling of impending doom crept into the pit of Gerard's stomach.

"Dr. Berthiume, what the hell is going on? Please tell me. After what we have been through, nothing can shock us," Gerard said matter-of-factly.

"Your wife is pregnant," said Dr. Berthiume.

"What are you saying, doctor?! My wife is pregnant? Oh, my God, did the attack hurt the baby? Is that what you are trying to tell me, doctor?"

Dr. Berthiume paused before he spoke, knowing the news would devastate Gerard.

"Your wife was impregnated eight days ago, Gerard. She could very well be pregnant with the child of your attacker."

Gerard thought he would be sick. That fucking monster's baby is in my wife! He was stunned, fighting the nausea building in his gut.

"No, no, no! Oh Jesus, please tell me you're wrong, doctor! This can't be true. This cannot be happening," pleaded Gerard, in a state of shock.

"I am afraid it is true, Gerard. Your wife was hysterical, screaming that she is carrying the child of the devil. Gerard, she needs you to be strong for her now," Dr Berthiume explained.

Gerard looked up at Dr. Berthiume with a face that reflected pure horror.

"She is right, doctor. She is carrying the child of the devil. She was raped by the devil himself. I was there, don't you see? The most hideous monstrous beast you could imagine transformed itself into a human man before our eyes so he could rape her. That was his plan all along, to impregnate Francoise in order for her to spawn his devil child. Oh, Jesus, please help us!" Gerard began to sob, his mind unable to process this news.

"Gerard, please, that is impossible. Both of you were traumatized from this attack. As I said, Gerard, you must be strong for her."

Gerard's mind was racing, trying to decipher what the doctor had told him, and he was about to blow a gasket.

"Fuck you, doctor. Don't patronize me. We know what we saw! Please, I need to see her. Bring her down here now. I want to see her. She needs me. She must be going out of her mind."

Dr. Berthiume rested his hand on the railing, and then replied to Gerard's commands with an authoritative and calming voice. "I will leave now, Gerard, to make the arrangements to have her brought down here, if you promise me you will be calm and not get her worked up or frightened. Can you do that for me?"

Exhaling a big breath, Gerard fell back onto the pillow as he replied, "I can, doctor, just please go get her. Thank you."

Alone after the doctor left, he was horrified at the prospect of his wife pregnant with a child from that monster. Francoise must be frightened to death, he thought. He felt they were reliving the attack all over again. He knew one thing for sure. They could not allow this baby to be born. Never. Evil was growing inside of Francoise, and he would talk to Francoise about an abortion immediately so this nightmare could end once and for all.

Thirty minutes or so passed while he was deep in thought, when he heard noise from out in the hallway and it sounded like Francoise. Finally they were bringing her to him. The curtain surrounding his bed was pulled back and there she was. Wheeled into the room by Dr. Berthiume, she leapt out of her chair and, bursting into tears, came to him on his undamaged left side, hugging him, crying as she did so. Trying to console his wife by stroking her hair and whispering into her ear that everything would be okay, he heard Dr. Berthiume say, "I will leave you two alone now, Gerard. A nurse will be back in an hour or so to bring her back to her room."

Lifting her head off his shoulder, she looked him in the eyes and said, "I'm pregnant Gerard from that thing!"

He saw the pain in her eyes and it broke his heart.

"I know. Dr. Berthiume came to see me this afternoon to tell me that you were pregnant. I am so sorry, Francoise," he said, stroking his wife's tear-stained cheek.

She drew her face back slightly so she could look directly into his eyes while she spoke.

"I will not carry this baby, Gerard. I want it out of me now. I can feel the evil inside of me. I am not leaving this hospital until I have an abortion," she said, shaking with emotion.

"I know. I agree, Francoise. We will talk to Dr. Berthiume together today to get this taken care of," said Gerard, reaching for his wife with his good arm, pulling her close as she sobbed.

Suddenly he could hear footsteps enter the room, and then a voice that nearly gave him a heart attack. "Hello, darling, I see your bitch wife is doing better. Maybe she can scoot over and make room for both of your sweethearts. What do you say, my love?" The beautiful Tiffany Coutierre announced herself, standing at the end of the bed, dressed in a tight blouse and short skirt, looking like a scorned lover.

Looking at Tiffany and then at Gerard, Francoise tried to speak but was so shocked words would not come. Finally she managed to say, "Who are you? Gerard, what is going on? Who the hell is she?" A frantic and near hysterical Francoise glanced back and forth between Tiffany and Gerard.

"I am the best piece of ass your husband has had since college, sweetheart. Maybe you should pay more attention to what your husband needs, honey. He made love to me like he was a virgin," said Tiffany as she sneered at a horrified Francoise.

An hysterical Francoise fought off Gerard's grip, instead pushing down on his injured shoulder, causing him to scream out in pain.

"Oh my God, Gerard what is going on?! You motherfucking asshole. How could you! How could you!" Francoise was screaming now.

The white-hot pain shot through his shoulder as he cried out to her, "Francoise, I can explain! Please calm down. Tiffany, get the fuck out of here, you crazy bitch!"

Using her sexuality like a weapon, Tiffany shot right back at Gerard.

"Oh, honey, I will get the fuck out of here all right, but not quite yet. I am enjoying this. Tell your wife how you have been fucking me regularly since our first time at the academy," Tiffany jeered, clearly enjoying this.

Frantic, Gerard desperately tried to calm Francoise and shut Tiffany up.

"Francoise, she is lying. She seduced me after a class. It was a one-time thing, Francoise, I swear. She is a lunatic, look at her!" Gerard cried out to Francoise, unable to fathom how their nightmare could get any worse.

Screaming at the top of her lungs, Francoise launched herself at Tiffany, grabbing her hair as they struggled, crashing into the monitoring machines that were attached to Gerard's IV tubes, pulling them out of Gerard. Screaming in pain, he yelled out to the nurses. He needed to stop Tiffany before Francoise killed her, because the way she was pummeling her it looked like she wouldn't stop till Tiffany was dead. Then he heard Tiffany begin to laugh. It was not a laugh from a deranged woman bent on ruining the marriage of her lover. It was the laugh of the demon again. It was the same laugh that had come from that demonic monster that attacked them in their home! Where were the nurses? Why wasn't anyone rushing into this room, with all this noise?

Tiffany threw Francoise hard against the cabinet that was on the wall at the foot of Gerard's bed. Francoise fell to the floor in obvious pain. Gerard screamed at Tiffany to stop, when she looked at him with demonic fiery red eyes and said, "Why, don't you want to be with me Gerard, baby?" Tiffany cackled, then, tilting her head back, laughed a demonic roar that chilled him to the bone. Knowing that the monstrous beast was back, he desperately tried to climb off the bed to get out into the hallway for help when the beast tackled him back onto the bed. Clamping down on his ravaged shoulder, it punched him so hard on top of the shoulder where the flesh had been torn away, it sent shockwaves of unbearable pain pulsating throughout his body. He struggled not to pass out and, looking into the eyes of the beast, screamed, "What do you want with us?! Leave us alone. Kill me, but leave her alone!"

Tiffany's voice hoarse with evil, her tongue thrashing outside of her mouth, screamed, "Oh, I plan to, that is exactly what I am going to do!" Tiffany's eyes burned bright red, her face turned demonic, devoid of her beauty, as she screamed at him. Grabbing his bandaged right arm, she bent it hard backwards, snapping the elbow. Screaming in pain, Gerard knew he would soon die and desperately reached for anything on the bedside table with his good arm that he could stab Tiffany with. Suddenly he could see Francoise in the corner of his eye approaching the bed with the power cord from the monitoring machine in her hands, ready to strangle Tiffany.

Tiffany sensed Francoise approaching as well, because she spun around, catching Francoise square in the chest with a blow that sent her flying backwards against the wall with a sickening thud. She then came back at Gerard, driving her knee into his shoulder causing shards of white light to burst through his brain. Clutching his throat with her hand, she began to squeeze the life out of him. As his life slipped away the beast looked down at him with the demonic glowing red eyes and said, "You will die knowing your bitch wife will give birth to my child. I have waited seventeen hundred years for this moment. All of mankind is doomed to die!"

The last thing Gerard saw in this world before his throat was torn away from his neck by Satan himself was the look of horror in his wife's eyes as she struggled to get up from the floor beside his bed.

****

Meanwhile, out in the hallway, Dr. Berthiume was walking towards Gerard Louveneau's room to discuss with him and Francoise their wish to abort the fetus and then to bring her back to her room. He would make the arrangements for her to be discharged in the morning. Just before he was about to enter he heard a blood-curdling scream from within that sounded like Francoise. Bursting into the room, he knew Hell had a paid a visit. Twenty-one years as a highly trained and educated doctor did not prepare him for what he was seeing.

Gerard Louveneau's throat was completely gone. Blood was everywhere. His bandaged right arm was broken at the elbow and was bent in a fashion that almost looked inside out. Francoise was sitting on her dead husband's bed covered in his blood, rocking back and forth, mumbling gibberish that did not make any sense.

Francoise Louveneau had murdered her husband!

Chapter 25

It was a beautiful spring day in London with a crystal-clear blue sky and the sun's rays warming the city to a balmy sixty-five degrees Fahrenheit. Londoners were in a cheery mood; it's amazing what beautiful weather can do to people's moods. The hustle and bustle of one of the world's largest cities was about to host the Global Summit for Women, a huge event for the advancement of women's causes around the world. Originally, Ann was scheduled to be the spokesperson for the event that attracted some of the most powerful women in the world including politicians, businesswomen and civil rights leaders, but as a result of the attacks she withdrew from the summit.

Ann had much more pressing matters on her hands. It has been five months since the brutal attack on her and Dalton that had viciously taken his life and left Ann almost dead. Her recollection of what happened and her recounting of those events to Scotland Yard had fallen on deaf ears and the investigation was going nowhere. Simply put, the investigators did not believe her. They believed that she and Dalton had been attacked by a gang of thugs bent on looting the Lockwood's of some of their riches. They believed that Dalton had resisted their attacks and was brutally murdered as a result. The gang further attacked Ann and sexually assaulted her, and it was eventually discovered that she was carrying the baby of the rapist. Hospital psychologists treating her recommended to her doctors that she consider an abortion, that giving birth to this child would result in long-term emotional and psychological damage to her. Ann would have none of it. She was determined to give birth to this child, knowing full well in her heart that it was the child of the devil.

In reality she had no choice. The beast had made it frightfully clear that if she did not nurture the baby inside her and protect her pregnancy then he would be back, and this time he wouldn't just kill her husband. He would kill her family and all of Dalton's family, just as a beginning. Looking down at her swollen belly, she shuddered at the prospect of that thing returning and bringing death with it. She would give birth to this child no matter what. It was still part of her, and by way of some sick rationalization it was also her baby and so she wanted to protect it as only a mother would protect her child.

There was one thing that she could do and that was to continue to press Scotland Yard detectives to consider her story, no matter how crazy it seemed, to step up their investigation of the attacks, and to base it on the theory of a demonic beast. What she expected investigators to do, even if they believed her and found evidence that a demonic creature had killed Dalton and raped her, she had no idea. She just wanted someone to believe her, not think she was crazy. They thought she had gone mad from the events of the attack and from witnessing her husband's brutal murder.

The loss of Dalton, and in such a brutal way, was very difficult for Ann to recover from. What made things even worse was the fact that neither her own family nor Dalton's family believed a word she said about what had happened to him and to her during the attacks. This was like being attacked all over again. She had even gone to see her priest for spiritual answers to what had happened, and even the Church patronized her, encouraging her to seek professional help from a specialized psychologist who dealt in this sort of thing. Ann was sick of it and continued to press the authorities seeking results of blood and tissue samples from the scene of the attacks in the house. She was sure that DNA testing would show authorities that what they were dealing with was not human.

She would go it alone if she had to. To hell with her family if they did not believe her. When they began to distance themselves from her as if it was her fault, she decided she would have nothing more to do with her parents or her four brothers. The Oakley's were all about business, and this whole mess shone an unfavorable light on the family, so they chose to withdraw from Ann. She'd never been close to her brothers or their families anyway, so their actions did not surprise her. The lack of support and communication from her mother hurt her, however. She had at least thought her mother would show her some level of support—but nothing. Some initial visits to the hospital, but nothing since.

Dalton's family was marginally more supportive with frequent visits to the hospital during her recovery, but as soon as the stories started coming out to the family from the investigators, they thought the terrible injuries Ann had suffered were behind her outlandish recollections of the attack, and they too pulled away. The injuries, combined with the loss of her husband, had sent Ann over the edge, they thought.

It's okay, she thought, she did not need them, she would get the authorities to investigate if it took her a lifetime. She knew the key was the blood and tissue samples, and today she was going to the offices of the Metropolitan Police, Homicide and Serious Crime Command of the New Scotland Yard building on Broadway.

****

Lead Detective Jeremy Cookston had grudgingly agreed to be present this morning when Ann came to visit. He knew the grind; it would be the same as the last time she showed up. She demanded answers, requesting up-to-the-minute updates, reasons for delays, etc., all as a way to make the department accountable in her eyes for a lack of results in any arrests. Her story of her and Dalton being attacked by a demonic monster that transformed from a huge ten-foot beast to a man who then sexually assaulted Ann smacked of a very traumatized woman. Such a woman, bent on seeing some results, was a thorn in the investigators' side.

Detective Cookston was, however, very disturbed by the evidence gathered at the scene. The fact that Forensics was unable to type the DNA was mystifying to him and made it difficult to identify the attackers. The sheer brutality of the attack showed an elevated level of violence. This was a crime that could only have been perpetrated by someone very disturbed, who would certainly have a history with the police and should have been easily identified with blood and tissue samples gathered at the scene. Not being able to type the DNA was extremely unusual, and it was the opinion of the lab that the DNA was more likely animal based and not human, which was impossible. As a result, the investigation had stalled with no tangible direction to follow. No one had showed up in any hospitals in the country for treatment for serious gunshot injuries in the days following the attack, no witnesses had come forward who might have seen the perpetrators fleeing the scene. The neighborhoods had been combed for anyone who might have seen anything unusual that night near the Lockwood's' home.

Ann Lockwood showed up on time for the ten o'clock appointment, as Cookston knew she would. He directed her into an interview room, where Ann got right down to business.

"So tell me you have made some progress with the lab results," said Ann.

Travelling the same road with Ann on this was frustrating, but Cookston tried to remain professional.

"Nothing new to report, Ann. I am sorry. As I have told you many times, Forensics was unable to type the DNA, which I admit is very unusual. As a result, we were unable to search for matches in the DNA database that would have given us a match, and then of course a name. There were no gunshot wounds or seriously injured victims who entered an emergency ward of a hospital the day of the attacks or the days following. We checked out every gunshot victim that came to a hospital during that time, and nothing. There are no witnesses who saw anyone enter or leave from your residence during the time before, during, or after the attacks."

She erupted in frustration just as she always did.

"Jesus, Detective, how could such a brutal murder occur with a crime scene covered in the attacker's blood, no witnesses, nothing, and the police have nothing to go on?! Maybe you should now shift your focus to what really happened and the reason there is no DNA match. Have you checked with Interpol? Maybe a similar crime has occurred elsewhere in the world that would help the investigation."

"I understand what you're saying, Ann, and the frustration you must be feeling over this investigation. We have checked with Interpol, and there is no case on file that has any similarities to your case, so that is a dead end. I'm sorry to have wasted your time once again, Ann. I could have told you the same thing over the phone. We are doing everything we possibly can. We are as frustrated over this case as you are, trust me. Let us call you if we come up with anything new, okay?"

****

Leaving the police station a few minutes later, Ann was convinced that the police had already filed this case in the unsolved drawer, never to be seen or heard from again. Soon the police would no longer agree to sit down with her or even communicate with her, convinced that she was a lunatic. The recent death of Princess Diana was all anyone in this country cared about, including the police. Her death had plunged the country into a temporary fit of depression. England struggled with the loss. Ann considered herself a personal friend of the Princess and her death, though deeply shocking and sad, did not distract her from her own loss.

As she guided her Range Rover through the streets of London, she was overcome with a sense of loss, causing her to tear up. Pulling the SUV to the side of the road, she leaned into the steering wheel and sobbed. She cried knowing she had lost the love of her life, her husband Dalton, and would never see him again. Her own family had snubbed her, the police thought she was crazy, and she was soon to give birth to the child of a monster not even fathered by her dead husband. She was alone in this. Maybe she should consider ending this pregnancy. Take her life and that of the unborn child. Drive her SUV right off the London Bridge and into the Thames River. The memory of the dire warnings from the monster to protect this child haunted her. At the same time, how could she possibly give birth knowing what she knew about this baby?

She pulled into the garage a few minutes later, turned off the truck and sat quietly to ponder what she would do next. In order to abort the baby she would have to get it done privately by paying a doctor a huge sum of money not only to perform the procedure but to keep it quiet. Ann would not risk news leaking that she had aborted a fetus twenty weeks grown. She had worked far too hard for the charitable foundations to expose them to the type of scandal the tabloids would whip up about her if the news got out that she had aborted her murdered husband's baby. She would kill the unborn baby, it was the only way. She just needed to think about the best way to do it. She wasn't scared by the prospect. Not at all. But if she did give birth, what would she be giving birth to? That was what scared her.

Entering her home, she realized she was fed up with the police and her family's treatment of her. She had made up her mind. She would have an abortion to cleanse her body of this demon child, walk away from London to another country and start her life over again. The beast, or whatever it was, would never know and would never find her. She certainly had enough money not to have to work for the rest of her life, allowing her to hide from the threat of the beast in another country. That was exactly what she would do. Maybe move to Canada or Australia.

Dropping her purse and keys on the hallway table as she closed the door, she heard a voice call out from down the hallway that made her heart stop. It was impossible. The fear hit her so hard she struggled to keep from fainting. The few steps down the hallway to her living room felt like miles. As she stepped into the archway of her living room and stared at the man sitting on her couch, her body began to shake.

"Good afternoon, Ann. Making some plans, are you?" Robert Best spoke from her living room couch, where he was casually sitting dressed in a finely tailored suit, his sinister fiery red eyes blazing up at her. The shock of seeing her attacker, the devil himself, the murderer of her husband, sitting in her home, and realizing that he knew every thought that was in her mind, scared Ann so profoundly that the air escaped her lungs and she collapsed to the floor, fainting.

Coming to a few minutes later, she struggled to open her eyes. Images were fuzzy and grainy as her vision cleared. The horror came back to her in a flash when her eyesight allowed her to see who was sitting less than ten feet away from her. This was a nightmare she was in; it had to be, she thought. Blinking her eyes in the hope the nightmare would disappear, she knew that it really was him and he was back. She struggled to get up from the floor. Terrified, she screamed, "I don't understand, who are you?! What are you doing here? Leave me alone!" She backpedaled away from him, trying to get as much distance from him as she could, then scrambled to her feet and turned and ran down the marble tile hallway towards the garage door entrance. She needed to get to her vehicle and away from this place. This was madness. Why was he back? Grabbing the handle of the door leading into her garage, she didn't know if he would reach out with one of its claws and rip her head off as she tried to escape. Reaching the door to the Range Rover, Ann yanked it open and jumped into the driver's seat, reaching for the keys in the ignition to start the truck and make her escape—when she realized that she had taken the keys out. *Did I leave them in the kitchen as I came through the house*, she thought. Her hand shaking, she reached for the door handle to open her door and return to the house when she heard, "Are you looking for these?" She jumped in shock and looked over in the passenger seat to see the glow of the red eyes and the maniac smiling face mocking back at her with a set of keys dangling in his hand.

Screaming in terror, Ann kicked her door open wide and jumped out to head back into the house, locking the door behind her as she entered. Turning to run into the kitchen where she would call the police, she almost bumped straight into the man version of the monster that had attacked her five months earlier.

"Why are you in such a hurry?!" Best yelled into Ann's face as he clamped his steeled fist around her throat and picked her up as if she was weightless. Choking the life out of her, he maneuvered her back into the living room, then tossed her hard onto the sofa. Bouncing off the sofa and onto the floor, Ann desperately tried to get air into her lungs. It felt as if her throat had been crushed by the powerful vise-grip of his hand. Coughing and hacking, she looked up at him, glancing around for something she could use against him to protect herself. He looked as if he would kill her for sure this time. His red eyes glowed like two bonfires burning. Then he spoke, or rather he screamed, in a voice so evil it chilled Ann to the marrow of her bones. A voice that was frighteningly familiar. That was because she had heard it once before, five months earlier, before he raped her. "You think you can kill this baby that is inside you?! I told you I would kill not only you but everyone in your family and your dead husband's family! Did I not tell you that?!"

Ann gripped the granite candleholder that was on the nightstand beside her and threw it as hard as she could at the beast. Not waiting to see if she had hit her mark, she stood up in a flash and ran in the opposite direction, towards her front door. Passing through the expansive dining room to get to the front door entrance, she suddenly found her passageway blocked by the beast. Turning the other way, she was stunned to almost run into him again, blocking the entranceway she just passed through. She was trapped, with no escape. She cried out, "I will not give birth to your child! I will kill this baby if I have to jump off a bridge!"

Best, seething with rage slammed Ann into the dining room

wall so hard that pictures clattered to the floor around her. The impact of her head hitting the wall sent shards of white light pulsating through her brain. When he spoke it was with a voice that was now human and calm. “Maybe you didn’t notice your mother as you came into the home. She had come by to pay you a visit. She felt so guilty over her and your father’s treatment of you since our first encounter. You should really go and say hello.”

“What! Where? What have you done!” cried Ann as she sprinted out past him into the hallway and back into the living room. What she saw next made her knees buckle, forcing her onto the floor. Her mother, sitting prim and proper in her usual expensive pantsuit on the couch opposite from the one Ann had been tossed onto earlier, had her severed head sitting on her lap with her folded hands resting on top of her head. The glassed-over death eyes of her mother looked up at her as if to say that she was sorry for everything, for not believing her story after the attack. The tears ran down Ann’s cheeks, burning her eyes as they did. This monster had murdered her mother. *Please God, help me please*, she prayed as she fell forward onto the floor, burying her face into her crossed arms and crying, sobbing uncontrollably. *What was happening to her? Why was this happening?*

As if reading her mind, the beast bellowed, “This is happening, you stupid bitch, because you were thinking of aborting this child you are carrying! What did I tell you? Your mother is the first. Your father is next if you ever allow that thought to enter your brain again. I will know and I will be here the second that happens, with the severed head of your father in my arms. Do I make myself clear?!”

Her eyes awash in tears, her throat burning from vomiting, she looked up at the hellish burning red eyes and whispered, “Yes.”

Then the darkness came mercifully.

Chapter 26

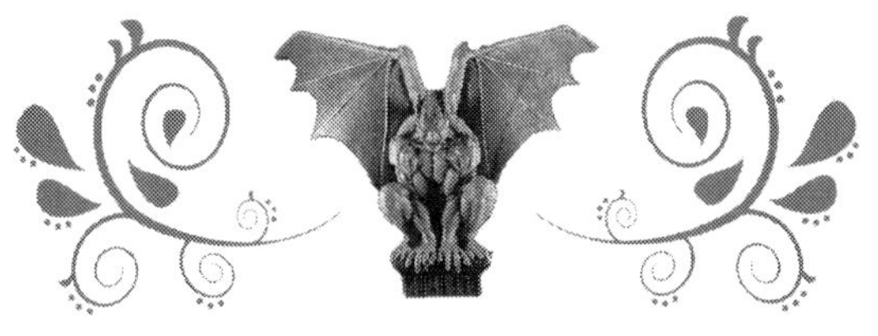

Five months had passed since the day Brent had found out the devastating news that Lori was pregnant, and every time he saw Lori's swollen belly he shuddered at the knowledge of what was growing inside of her. Lori was still in complete denial as to the true nature of her pregnancy, as if her mind had built a barrier between what had really happened and what she wanted to believe had happened. She believes her parents, and Brent's father Bert, were killed, but not murdered. The injuries Brent himself had suffered she did not discuss; in fact they never talked about any of it. Brent had not pushed Lori into discussing what happened at the ranch or at her parents' home only because she seemed so happy, and after what she'd been through and what she had seen he didn't have the heart to confront her with any of it.

As Lori's expected due date approached, Brent knew that they would have to talk this through. In fact he was not going to wait any longer. Lori would have this pregnancy terminated and he would do everything in his power to make sure that happened. Today he was meeting with their local pastor, Pastor Byron Simmons of the Beacon Hill Baptist Church in Cheyenne. Pastor Simmons had been counseling them for months about their relationship and was well aware that they had abstained from sexual intercourse during the past year. Brent needed his guidance on what lay before him. Lori did not know that he would be meeting with Pastor Simmons, and he planned to keep it quiet so he could hear what the pastor had to say about their situation before he went any further.

Brent's injuries were healing slowly but steadily. His shoulder would still require many more surgeries, mostly skin graft transplants to replace tissue that had been torn away by the beast. The deformity of his neck and shoulder area was significant and would certainly draw lots of stares if he were to stroll bare-chested down a sandy beach. Even though the mobility and strength in his left shoulder and arm were greatly diminished, he was determined to get as much of his strength back as he could. The thought of not being able to break a sweat working the farm frightened him and spurred him in his rehab.

The investigation by the Sherriff's Department and the FBI had gone nowhere, with no suspect arrests, nor any viable or promising leads. The police were mystified at the inability of the lab to map any of the DNA gathered at the scenes of the attacks. Brent knew better, being certain they would not find any. The reality of this nightmare was that they were dealing with the arch-enemy of God himself, so there was no chance their investigation would turn up any clues.

Lori was truly a godsend when it came to running the ranch while he recuperated. She knew exactly what to do and quickly hired a new lead ranch hand to take over from Mel, who had been viscously murdered along with his dad. Lori managed all of the insurance claims for the slaughter of the horses and was able to purchase and acquire new quarter horses to replace the ones they'd lost. Thanks to her, the ranch was back running at full capacity within weeks of the murders. Her complete amnesia about the day of the murders was either from the blows to the head she'd suffered or her way of emotionally dealing with the pain by blocking the memories completely from her mind. The doctors advised him not to push Lori to try to recollect the events at the ranch and her parent's home. Her memory of those fateful events would come back to her at some point in the future or maybe not at all.

He finished getting dressed, struggling as usual to get his injured shoulder and arm into the sleeve of his button-down long-sleeve western shirt, a staple since his injuries. No more T-shirts, at least in the near future, as they were impossible to get over his head. Pastor Simmons had agreed to meet him at ten this morning at his office in the church. Grabbing the pickup keys off the kitchen counter, Brent thought he should leave a note for Lori. She was out grocery shopping and he wanted to be gone before she got back. He left her a note saying he needed to do some errands in the city, that he would be back in the afternoon sometime, and she could call his cell if she needed anything. Letting the screen door slam behind him after he locked the front door, he climbed into the truck with some difficulty. He took a moment to reflect on the ranch and how much things had changed there. Gone were his dad, his mom, and his brother. The lead ranch hand, Mel, someone who had been part of his family for over twenty years, was gone. All dead. They never locked the doors to the home. Now he locked the door. The attacks by the beast had changed everything.

Using his good arm, the right one, to steer the truck while he made the twenty-minute drive into town, he wondered how the pastor would react to what he was going to tell him about the attack by the demonic beast on he and Lori's families, the subsequent rape by the beast and the child that Lori now carried. After about twenty minutes of driving with very little traffic he arrived at the Beacon Hill Baptist Church. The church itself was referred to as the Steel Church because it was built like a steel Quonset hut. Cheyenne being a farming community, the Beacon Hill Baptist Church certainly reflected that reality. The metal-clad building was drab and looked more like a farm equipment service and repair building than a church. He parked the Dodge Ram Quad cab truck with the Cummins diesel engine that his dad insisted on for every one of the ranch trucks they bought. The truck had dual wheels in the back, making it wider than most pickups, so finding a spot in the parking lot of the church was a challenge. It was busy today, he observed, for a Monday morning. This church was always such a gathering place, it seemed. Pastor Simmons and the church worked tirelessly for this community, so they were likely working on some sort of fundraising project.

Walking through the front glass doors, Brent noticed the place looked unusually quiet considering all of the cars. The interior of the church, in stark contrast to the industrial look of the outside, were finished in a deep mahogany for the trim and doors. Fine handcrafted and hand carved sconces and rosettes were to be seen everywhere on the wood trim. The floors of the lobby and throughout the church were lined with thick, plush and beautiful carpet. The windows were large and arced. The stage where the pastor's pulpit stood was grand, with many hand carved wood pieces, the stage ceiling lined with the latest in sound-dampening tile, providing rich acoustics for the choir. The centerpiece was the cross suspended from the ceiling directly above the pulpit. It was a thing of complete beauty. It had to have been eight feet in length and at least five feet at its widest point. The cross was cut in a v-groove design and contained multiple colors of different species of wood inlay throughout. Some very talented woodworkers and wood craftsman had put a lot of their time into this church to make it so beautiful.

The front lobby was empty and quiet. He headed to his right and walked down the hallway towards Pastor Simmons's office. Walking past the office of the church administrator, he noticed it too was empty. Now he wondered if the pastor was even in today and if he'd maybe forgotten about this appointment. He arrived at the doorway of the pastor, and sure enough he was not in his office. *What the heck, this is unusual*, he thought. He would go and check the auditorium; maybe he was there with a group of parishioners. He returned to the quiet and empty lobby and opened the doors to the auditorium. As he did so, he was greeted by approximately one hundred people all coming together at once in a big roar of a cheer when he entered the room. They were holding signs and placards promoting his return and how much he was missed. It was such a total shock and surprise! He certainly was not expecting something like this. It was like a huge surprise birthday party. People he had known for years from the church were there greeting him, welcoming him back, offering their condolences on his and Lori's losses. Then, sure enough, Lori emerged from the crowd, smiling from ear to ear, now running towards Brent and embracing him and whispering in his ear how much she loved him and how the people here wanted to welcome him back to the church and to the community after knowing how much he had gone through. Then Pastor Simmons stepped forward and shook his hand and gave him a hug. The pastor then stepped back and the crowd quieted down as he began to speak.

"Brent and Lori, on behalf of myself and the wonderful people of Beacon Hill Baptist Church, we welcome you both back and God bless your recovery. As a church, our hearts go out to you both and we wanted to take this time to let you know that we care about you both and we are so happy to hear about the upcoming birth of your child."

"Wow this was quite a surprise, I must say. To think I thought Lori was shopping," winked Brent at Lori. Then he addressed the crowd. "On a serious note Lori and I feel blessed that we have all of this support from you and from Pastor Simmons. This church has been so good to us and our families over the years. We have some scars but they will heal. We both think of our families every day, and even though it's hard to think they are gone and never coming back we look forward and with God's blessing Lori will give birth to a healthy baby." Brent wrapped his arm around Lori, pulling her close, and for a brief moment actually believed that Lori would give birth to a healthy and normal baby.

After about twenty minutes of accepting condolences and messages of congratulations from all of the church members, Lori turned to Pastor Simmons and said, "I know you to want to meet and talk, so I will let you both be. Before I go, would you mind blessing my unborn child, Pastor Simmons?"

"Certainly, Lori, I would love to do that," declared Pastor

Simmons. Placing his hands on Lori's swollen belly, he began to pray for the unborn child growing inside of Lori and asked that God keep it safe and healthy and to keep Lori healthy so that she could give birth to a new life in God's eyes. As he was praying, Brent noticed him stiffen and open his eyes briefly, as if the baby had suddenly jumped inside and he'd felt it. Lori was just standing there smiling with her eyes closed, soaking in the prayer. Pastor Simmons abruptly stopped in the middle of the prayer, removing his hands from Lori's stomach. Apologizing to Lori, he looked at Brent with concern, then turned and walked away. Lori, confused by Pastor Simmons actions, turned to Brent, who walked up and embraced her and, with a smirk on his face, said, "I think the Pastor had to go to the restroom really bad and couldn't hold it any longer, what do you think?".

Lori seemed to brighten just a bit at Brent's playful comment.

"That was really weird. Oh well, I feel so lucky and blessed, Brent. I love you so much," she said, looking up into Brent's eyes, causing him to melt. She was so darn beautiful, and her pregnancy was making her look even more beautiful. She was radiant. "I'm going to leave you two alone now. Try and pick a date when I won't have to worry if my water's going to break during the ceremony," she said with a huge smile as she kissed his cheek and then turned and left the church. *She believes I'm here to see Pastor Simmons about setting a wedding date*, thought Brent. He wished he was here for that reason. He couldn't think of marriage until they dealt with the devil's child that was growing inside her. It was consuming him, he knew it, but he also knew that he needed to do something about it. What that would be he didn't know, but he was hoping that Pastor Simmons would.

****

Pastor Simmons stood over the sink in the men's restroom after having splashed cold water on his face several times. The overwhelming sense of doom and dread that had overcome him when he had placed his hands on Lori's stomach was something that he never experienced before in his life of ministry. It had truly shaken him, and he was not sure how to explain it. The tragedies she and Brent had experienced in their lives recently were overwhelming. It seemed as if there had been a curse placed upon them. He'd felt something very evil and sinister when he prayed with Lori, placing his hands on her. Reaching down to splash more water on his face, he needed to gather himself, as he still needed to meet with Brent. No doubt Brent wanted to book some dates for a wedding before their child was born. Exiting the bathroom, he headed for his office and found Brent waiting in the lobby. Motioning for Brent to follow him he walked down the hallway to his office, where he held the door open for Brent and asked him to have a seat in one of the armchairs in front of his desk. Brent knew the routine well, as he had spent a fair amount of time over the past year with the pastor, sometimes just the two of them and other times with Lori as well. They were a young couple madly in love trying to navigate their way to a good Christian beginning to their marriage, something that was not easy to do, especially as they'd had a sexual relationship prior to their pledge of abstinence for a period of one year before they were to be married. The road was bumpy, but they had survived it, and it had been a good test for the both of them.

Waiting for Pastor Simmons to get to his chair and sit down, Brent began.

"Thank you, Pastor Simmons, for that reception today that was unexpected to say the least. It feels good to know that so many people care about us."

Pastor Simmons clasped his hands together in front of him, placing them on the desk as he replied.

"The tragedy and losses you and Lori have suffered are beyond belief and the hearts of the people of this community and this church go out to you both. They feel these losses, too Brent, there are very good friends of your father and of Lori's parents that are grieving right now over their deaths, so it has been hard for everyone. I cannot imagine how you two are feeling. So tell me, Brent, how are you two coping over these months since the attacks?"

"It has been hard, Pastor, especially in the beginning when I was immobilized in the hospital and had nothing but time to think about things. My release from the hospital and returning to the ranch has been a godsend. Its home, you know, and even though there will always be the memory of the murders and all of the horses at that ranch, it was a welcoming feeling getting back there," explained Brent.

Pastor Simmons' look grew more concerned.

"How is Lori doing? I see she is very happy in spite of her losses. The upcoming marriage and the birth of your child is lifting her above the pain and getting her through it, from what I can see. How is she really doing, Brent?"

Sliding forward in his chair, he knew would have to tell Pastor Simmons the truth somehow, but how could he possibly tell their pastor they'd been attacked by Satan himself?

"Considering what has happened to her personally and the loss of her parents, she's doing amazingly well. She has been remarkable. She took charge at the ranch when I was in the hospital; she's got the entire operation back on track and running smoothly. She is incredible," Brent explained.

Sensing some trepidation in Brent's voice, Pastor Simmons asked him, "You feel something is not quite right with her, Brent? I get a sense there is something you are not telling me."

Now was the time, Brent thought, when he should reveal the truth about the attacks to Pastor Simmons. That was why he'd come here. But after the warm reception by the pastor and the congregation, he felt it was an inappropriate time to talk about such things.

He felt very uneasy and uncomfortable at the thought of revealing such a bizarre story to the pastor. Nevertheless, he needed the pastor's help, his spiritual guidance and counsel over this, so he opened his mouth and let the words flow: "Pastor Simmons, I did not request this meeting with you to discuss a wedding date. There is something I need to tell you about what really happened at the ranch and at Lori's home."

For the next two hours Brent told the pastor every detail of the attacks, the monster that attacked them, and its transformation from beast to man who then raped Lori. Everything. He left nothing out. Pastor Simmons sat there in stunned silence, occasionally stopping Brent for clarification or to ask a question.

When he was finished, they prayed, and then Pastor Simmons said to Brent, "Do you understand what you are saying, Brent? You are saying that Lori is pregnant with the child of the devil. That is quite a statement, Brent. I want to tell you that I believe you, I do. I know that you and Lori have been abstinent over this past year, so that baby is not yours. Do you think at all that maybe the trauma of your ordeal has caused you to over think this attack and maybe relate the madman that did this to being the same as the devil. What could really be going on, Brent, is that Lori is pregnant with the child of the rapist, and that is what you both need to come to grips with and either accept this baby under those circumstances or choose other alternatives."

Brent looked the pastor directly in the eyes when he spoke.

"I am not over thinking this, Pastor Simmons. The memory of the attacks at the ranch and then at Lori's parents' home will forever be seared into my brain. I will never forget a single detail of what happened. That baby cannot be allowed to live, you must understand. Lori was chosen, I believe, because her bloodlines lead back to some ancient ancestor who is Satan's sworn enemy. I believe, Pastor, that this attack has been in the works for hundreds of years." Brent recounted again the ranting by the beast turned man prior to its raping Lori, speaking in partial Latin and English, but understandable enough that Brent could decipher why he had chosen Lori.

Clearly disturbed by Brent's story, Pastor Simmons replied, "Brent, when I said I believed you, I meant it. Leave this with me for a few days while I do some research and consult with some colleagues. I will get back to you before the end of the week and we will discuss this further. I agree with you that Lori should not be told about any of our discussions. Everything is going to be okay, Brent. Lori will be fine and she will want to know if you have some available dates for a wedding at the church, so give her these for now."

Pastor Simmons scratched some dates on a piece of paper after consulting his day planner, gave the paper to him and said, "Talk to Lori and pick a date from these available ones. The wedding is important to you both, but especially for her mental state, so work that out and let me know when we meet at the end of the week."

****

As they shook hands and said their goodbyes, Pastor Simmons reached over and gave Brent a hug, a reassuring embrace to let him know once again that everything was going to be okay. After Brent had left the church, Pastor Bryan Simmons sat down in his office chair, bowed his head and prayed harder than he had ever prayed in his life. Not only did he believe Brent's story of the attack, he felt it. He had felt it when he laid his hands on Lori's stomach. He felt the evil presence of the devil growing inside of her and it scared him to the very marrow of his bones.

Chapter 27

Sitting back in the recliner with her legs extended, she was resigned to the fact she would have to leave soon for the hospital. Marie Jimenez was living with her sister Sophia, Sophia's husband Hector, and their three children in a two-bedroom cramped apartment in Caracas, where she'd been ever since she was well enough to leave the hospital from the attack in Maracaibo almost nine months ago. Her sister's apartment was in a poor section of Caracas, surrounded by crime, but Marie felt safe here. Hector worked tirelessly in his job at the sugar refinery to feed his family. Gone was her beloved husband Rafael, the horrible memory of his brutal murder seared forever in her mind, refusing to fade into the part of the brain where faint memories are stored. Looking down at her nearly bursting belly, Marie had thought she would come to loathe the baby that had grown inside her, due to be born any day now. Instead she had come to feel quite the opposite. She refused to give the beast that had attacked her any thought whatsoever, successfully blocking it from her mind, and just focused on this child. It was her child, her blood, and this baby would need a mother to look after it. The baby was also a reminder of Rafael and their life together, and his legacy and his memory would live on through the birth of this baby, Marie promised herself.

Marie's deep thoughts were suddenly interrupted by the voice of her sister.

"Hey, earth to Marie, earth to Marie! Where you at, honey? 'Cause you are not in this apartment right now," laughed Sophia.

"Just thinking of Rafael and how much I miss him. How badly he wanted a son, a son that he could teach to be a major leaguer. He used to dream about it when we would sit on the front porch just holding each other, talking about the future," replied Marie.

Sophia sat on the arm of worn recliner and placed a reassuring arm around her sister.

"Oh, honey, I know this must be so hard for you, living in this hot little shack with all of us. I am so sorry I couldn't have done more for you. You watching my kids all these months has been such a blessing for me while I worked. Getting back to your home in Maracaibo, as painful as that will be for you, with all of those memories, and without Rafael, will be the best thing for you. You will have a new start for you and the baby, and I think, as your big sister, that it will be just great." Sophia leaned into her sister and gave her a great big hug.

Squeezing her sister's arm as she hugged her, Marie looked up at her sister and said, "Sophia, come on, without you and Hector I would not have survived that ordeal. You guys helped breathe new life into me. Your little babies are a gift from heaven. I love you so much, Sophia, and I am so thankful for you and Hector."

Fortunately, Marie had been able to keep their home in Maracaibo as Rafael had a moderate life insurance package through his factory job at the sugar processing plant Central Cumanacoa. The company had been wonderful to her since the tragic death of her husband. Not only had they processed the paperwork for Rafael's insurance policy in a timely fashion, they'd sent a team of factory workers to their home for two weeks to make all the repairs from the damage caused during the attack. They repainted the entire home so that when she felt well enough to return both physically and emotionally, hopefully the memories of that terrible day would have been scrubbed away along with the old paint. Sophia and Hector came to Maracaibo to be with her during her recuperation in the hospital. They helped with the funeral arrangements for Rafael, helped get her affairs in order, then took her back to Caracas to get away. Their only knowledge of what had happened during the attack was that some crazed killers had attacked them, bent on robbery and murder, brutally decapitating Rafael. Marie did not share of the details of the beast with her sister, nor did she reveal that she had been raped by it. Marie planned to return to Maracaibo and her home once the baby was born.

She asked her sister for her hand to help her off of the recliner so she could get busy helping with the kids when she felt a sensation in her abdomen and then the sudden release of fluid, soiling herself completely. Her water had broken. It was time.

As she lay on her bed after her water had broken, the contractions began slowly at first but soon became more and more frequent. This baby was not going to come slowly, thought Marie, it was in a hurry. Sensing that it was time to go to the hospital, Marie arose and got dressed. Sophia mobilized the children into her neighbor's apartment next door, left a message for Hector at his work and helped Marie into the family Volkswagen van for the short trip to the hospital. The contractions were long and very painful on the way to the hospital, with Marie screaming loudly as Sophia drove as fast as she could in the traffic. Sweating profusely, she yelled at Sophia, "You must hurry, sister! Or I will be giving birth right in your van. Please hurry!"

A few minutes later, Sophia navigated her way to emergency at the Centro Medico Docente La Trinidad, jumping out and opening Marie's door. Helping her out of the van, she turned and saw a wheelchair twenty feet away at the entrance to emergency. Sophia grabbed the chair and then wheeled a crying Marie into the hospital. Met by a nurse as they came in, Sophia informed them that her sister was in labor. The nurse did not hesitate and wheeled her down a hall and into a room with Sophia in pursuit. Summoning another nurse to page Dr. Triijo, the on-call obstetrician, the nurse prepared the room and Marie for the birth of the baby. As other nurses arrived, the room became a flurry of activity. Holding her sister's hand, Sophia reassured her that everything was going to be fine. Dr. Triijo then entered the room and spoke with the head nurse, getting a quick update.

Turning to Sophia and then to Marie, he quickly introduced himself, then while examining Marie, he said, "Yup, you are ready to go, my dear. I need you to push real hard, Marie, okay? You are going to feel some pressure and pain, but I need you to push with everything you have." The nurses were right there beside the doctor, anticipating his every move, as they likely did this multiple times every day.

Marie felt her insides begin to get very warm. The more she pushed, the more her stomach felt even warmer, to the point it was becoming very hot, and she said to the doctor between pushes, through clenched teeth, "Doctor, my stomach is feeling extremely hot, like it's on fire, Oh, God, it hurts so much!"

Dr. Triijo reassured Marie through her pain.

"It's okay, Marie, your body temperature will naturally rise during the pushing and contracting. The temperature you are feeling inside of your abdomen is again very natural, Marie. Just keep pushing, we are getting very close."

As she pushed with everything she had, the heat being created inside of Marie was like an inferno. She needed to get this baby out of her now before she ignited on fire. Feeling the baby move, she thought she heard the doctor say something, she could see looks of astonishment on the faces of the nurses, but she could not hear anything. *What is going on?* She realized Sophia was still holding onto her hand, but her sister's face was so blurry she could not make out what she was saying. *Something is very wrong*! She then saw some sort of red glow or light pierce the blurriness surrounding her, and it was emanating from below her, engulfing the doctor and the nurses who were leaning in close to him with a brilliant red light. *What is happening?*

All of a sudden everything around her became crystal clear and she could hear sounds again. The sound she heard was the crying of a baby. *Her baby.* Dr. Triijo stood and handed the baby, with its umbilical cord already cut, to a nearby nurse who swathed it in towels and placed it on Marie's chest. The nurse, who was sweating profusely, a look of wonder in her eyes, leaned in close to her and whispered in her ear congratulations that she was the mother of a healthy baby boy. The baby was beautiful and was resting peacefully on Marie's chest, its eyes squinting from the bright light in the room. A pleasant cooing sound was emanating from the baby that sounded almost musical. Looking up at Sophia, Marie said, "Can you hear him Sophia? Isn't that the most beautiful sound you ever heard? He is beautiful! His name will be Juan Rafael Jimenez!"

Meanwhile, Dr. Triijo, standing at the end of the bed, watching Marie with her baby, could not believe what he, the nurses, and Marie's sister Sophia had just witnessed. As Marie was pushing and the baby's head began to appear, a brilliant red light shone out from within her, covering him and the nurses with the intense glow. He could not even see what he was doing, so he just moved his hands around the base of the baby's head, and with Marie still pushing, he was able to feel the baby coming through, whereupon he lifted it up and away from the light and handed it to a nurse. As he pulled the placenta sac through as well, the light disappeared. Looking around at the other nurses, he saw that everyone was stunned at what they had just witnessed. Sophia was crying and praying that it was a sign from God, that this baby was a miracle sent to Marie. While wrapping the baby, the nurse brought to everyone's attention the unusual birthmark on the baby boy's inner right thigh. It looked like three half-notes together, almost like three backward number sixes. Very strange.

****

Knowing she was minutes away from giving birth to the baby she hoped had been fathered by her beloved husband James,, who had been cruelly and horrifically taken from her by a monster nine months earlier, Nancy Campbell clutched tightly the Red Sox jersey that James had always worn when they watched a game together. She clung to the hope that it would be James's baby that she was giving birth to as she lay on her hospital bed at Rhode Island Hospital in Providence, surrounded by the nurses and doctors, but her heart knew that it was not. The memory of her attack was seared into her brain, and the rant of the beast as it raped her that she had been chosen sounded as if she had heard it just a few minutes ago. Nancy knew that she would be giving birth to the child of a devil today, but she didn't care. Her life meant nothing to her anymore, and the only reason she hadn't taken her own life was that she was too scared and frightened that the beast would follow up on its threats to kill her family and James's family if she did not take care of the baby and raise it.

Despite her mother holding her hand, reassuring her that everything would be okay, Nancy knew better. Everything would not be okay. She had never told the police or anyone else about the true nature of the attack. Stating only that they'd been attacked by a gang of ruthless thugs bent on robbing them, she did not even tell anyone that she had been raped. She did not have the heart to tell James's family that the baby she carried was not their son's. The fear of the unknown hung over this pregnancy; what would the baby actually be when it was born? Would it be a monster just like the beast that attacked her? Would the beast come to claim the child and then kill her? She was frightened to death and she was all alone in her fear.

Nancy's contractions now were picking up steam, just minutes apart, and the attending nurse knew that the time was near and left the room to page the attending obstetrician. The contractions were now coming fast and furious, and Nancy, sweating profusely, was alarmed at the overwhelming heat sensation from her abdomen. It felt like an internal furnace turned up all the way to high. Her mother, sensing that her daughter was under a lot of stress and pain, dabbed a cold facecloth on Nancy's forehead trying to give her some comfort, reassuring her that everything would be fine. Dr. Bensen, the on-call obstetrician, entered Nancy's room, introduced himself to Nancy and her mother, then proceeded to look at her chart. He told Nancy that he would just examine her to see where the baby was at and how many centimeters she was dilated. Donning surgical gloves, he examined her and instantly felt the heat radiating from inside her. This was extremely unusual, and he asked Nancy how she was feeling. She replied that she was burning up. Telling Nancy that she could begin pushing, he determined that it would be best to get this baby on its way out. Dr. Bensen instructed the attending nurses to prepare for the birth of Nancy's child.

Pushing for everything she had, Nancy did not have to push very long, as the baby was on its way out. The pain was unbearable, and it took every bit of her strength to keep from passing out. Hearing the doctor give orders to the nurses, she realized he was preparing for complications. What could be wrong, she thought? Was the baby some hideous-looking monster that had them all in shock? Nancy could not tell, as her eyes were watering and stinging so badly from the pain-induced tears and the sweat dripping into her eyes. She could no longer hear voices, just muffled sounds. The pain in her abdomen suddenly stopped and the muffled sounds started to clear, and she could see looks of stunned wonder on the faces of everyone, including her mother. Her entire upper body drenched in sweat, Nancy looked down at the doctor and nurses, waiting for some kind of indication that everything was okay.

After a few minutes had passed that seemed like an hour, she caught a glimpse of the baby being placed in a waiting nurse's outstretched arms, wrapped in surgical towels. She looked over at her mom for reassurance, but her mother seemed to be in a frozen state, her eyes glued to the activities of the nurses and doctor. Not yet having heard the cries of her newborn baby, Nancy felt a growing sense of doom inside her. What was going on? Why was nobody speaking to her, telling her what was happening? In a panicked voice, she called out, "Dr. Benson is everything okay? The baby has not cried. Mother, what is going on?!"

Snapping out of her trance, Nancy's mother turned to her and said, "Everything is okay, sweetie, the doctor is just cutting away the placenta and the baby will be in your arms in just a minute." The look of concern on her mother's face did not comfort Nancy very much.

Finally, after what seemed an eternity, Dr. Bensen and the nurses cleaned the baby, wrapped it in a towel and gently placed it on an exhausted Nancy's chest. Still there were no cries or sound coming from the tightly wrapped baby, and she looked at it and was about to say something when Dr. Bensen, sitting on the side of the bed beside Nancy, said, "Congratulations, Nancy, you are the proud mother of a beautiful baby girl. Your body temperature had skyrocketed during labor, causing us a lot of concern, but as soon as the baby was born it immediately dropped back to normal. So both mother and daughter are extremely healthy."

"Then why has she not cried"…."

Just then there was a sound that began to fill the room. It seemed as if music was being piped into the room through the PA system, until Nancy cried out, "Can you hear that?! It's the baby! Listen to her, oh my God, that is so beautiful!"

The baby girl, tightly wrapped in towels with her little face exposed, was making a cooing sound that rang like the voice of an angel, its melodious euphony filling the room.

Nancy and her mother were awestruck, staring at the baby with amazement. Other nurses came into the room from the hallway, drawn by the beautiful sound. Everyone just stood and listened, including Dr. Bensen. He was speechless. Nancy began to cry, taking this as a sign from God that somehow He had intervened on her behalf and saved this beautiful child from its demonic conception.

Her soul filled with hope and joy, and the tears came in torrents, relief washing through her like a tidal wave. Nancy's mother, also crying, hugged her, whispering in her ear how blessed she was. It was a miracle, Nancy felt.

Leaning up in her bed, she lifted the baby from her chest and held her close, listening for a few more seconds before the baby began to cry. Even her soft cries sounded beautiful, thought Nancy. Nancy said a silent prayer to herself thanking God for saving her child. Oh, James, if only you were here to see and hear this, she thought. Looking up at all of the smiling faces in the room, she declared, "I will call my daughter Brittany Jamie Campbell!"

As she'd been tucked tightly in the towel, baby Brittany's unusual birthmark had not yet been discovered by the nurses before they wrapped her. It was on her upper right thigh and looked like three backward sixes, like musical notes.

Chapter 28

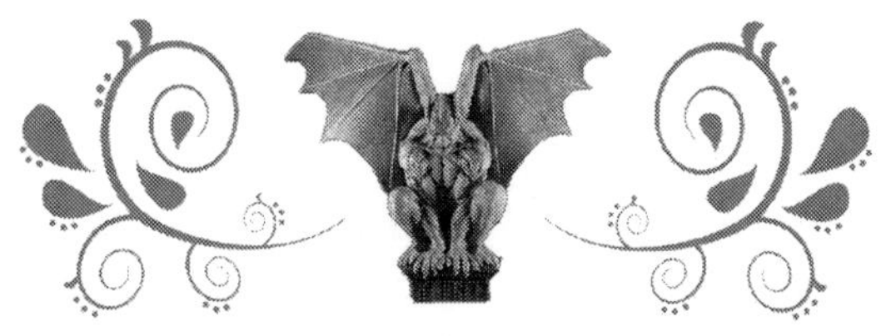

The weather in Dublin all week had been cool but pleasant, as the sun was out, and that naturally lifts the spirit of the Irish. With temperatures hovering in the mid-fifties, it was all middle-of-the-week hustle and bustle in the city. For Detective Rory Fitzpatrick of the Garda Siochana in Dublin, Major Crimes Division, it was just another day. Rory's caseload was out of control. He had already complained to his boss that continuing to dump more cases on his desk would severely weaken his ability to investigate these crimes. His protests were met with indignation; the government cutbacks had hit the Garda, Ireland's national police, harder than most departments. The Irish government, crippled by the harsh reality of a European Union financial bailout of their economy, was in survival mode. Emergency services, which included the Garda, Fire, and Ambulance, among many others, were operating at critically low levels.

The murder of the McClosky family in Balbriggan nine months earlier had been given top priority by the Department for weeks afterward, but when it became clear that the evidence was turning up no suspects, detectives were pulled from the investigation. The case became cold and was parked until new evidence turned up, meaning that only a witness coming forward to police would kick start the investigation again. The shocking and brutal nature of the murders dominated the press for weeks but soon began to die down as the investigation went nowhere. Even the people of Balbriggan, who had feverishly criticized the police for the lack of results in the investigation, turned silent as the months clicked by. Rory, as the lead investigator on the McClosky murders at the time, was under tremendous pressure from upper management to make an arrest in the case, so when he was reassigned he took it personally. Failing Katherine McClosky was a very hard thing for him to get over, and he never did.

The murder of the McClosky family was one of those crimes that left a permanent scar on your soul as an investigator, a scar that would only go away with an arrest. It was for this reason that Rory and other detectives involved with the case kept the investigation alive by working the case on their own time. Taking time that should have been spent with their own families, he and the others worked it, going over the evidence again and again, looking for things they might have overlooked. He hoped that someday someone would come forward with information on the perpetrators; it was just a matter of time. When that time came he and his men would pounce like a lion on its prey.

Rory and Father O'Sullivan had kept in touch throughout the investigation and even later, when it became cold. He often consulted with Father O'Sullivan over a cup of tea about his frustration at not being able to move the investigation forward. The priest's words always seemed to find a way to massage his soul, and they became good friends. He was also able to get updates on the mental state of Katherine, who, understandably, was still struggling to come to grips with what had happened. Living with her parents after the attack, she rarely left the house, according to Father O'Sullivan, despite having largely recovered from her injuries. Her emotional state was still very fragile, and it was hoped that the birth of her and Grew's child would lift her out of her emotional prison. Father O'Sullivan visited Katherine almost every day, hoping his spiritual guidance would move her, inch by inch, towards recovery. Rory was the only investigator whom Father O'Sullivan had told that Katherine truly believed she'd been raped and attacked, and her husband and his parents murdered, by Satan himself. With Father O'Sullivan's encouragement, Katherine had agreed to speak with Rory about what she believed had really happened the night of the attacks. Over time Katherine grew to trust him. Her story raised the hair on the back of his neck, and when he asked Father O'Sullivan when they were alone what he thought of her account of the events that night and if he believed her, the priest said, "I have known Katherine her entire life, since she was born. Her parents, the Kearney's, were in my parish for many years before that. I am a priest, Detective, so if you are asking if I believe in the devil, my answer is yes, I do. If you are also asking if I believe Katherine's story of that night my answer is also yes. There is an evil presence at work here, Detective, make no mistake. I am at a loss as to why this evil has chosen Katherine, but I feel it will reveal its intentions in due time."

Rory stared at Father O'Sullivan in disbelief.

"So you also believe her claims that it was Satan who raped her and that she is carrying his child?"

He watched as Father O'Sullivan's face furrowed into a solemn look of concern.

"If that is what Katherine believes in her heart then I believe her, Detective. It is not my place to judge her but to help heal her soul with the love of God. Only His Mercy and Grace can do that. As to what has happened to her and what she has seen, who are we to question or to judge her?"

Deep in thought, recollecting these memories, Rory was pulled from the abyss by the sound of his cell phone. Flipping open the phone, knowing it would be his wife wondering if he would be home for dinner, he was surprised to see it was Father O'Sullivan. Hitting the send button, he said, "Father, good to hear from you, I was just thinking of you."

This was not a social call. Father O'Sullivan was deeply troubled.

"Detective, I just got word from the Kearney's. Katherine has gone into labor. She has been rushed to St. Vincent's, as she is bleeding badly. Meet me there, Rory," said Thomas, and hung up abruptly.

****

Driving his Peugeot 307 through the afternoon traffic to St. Vincent's, Thomas silently prayed for Katherine. The poor girl had been through so much, and now she was fighting for her life all over again. Finally, on the M1 highway, traffic was well spread out and Thomas pushed the Peugeot more than he should have as he moved the car in and out of traffic towards Dublin 4 and the exit to St. Vincent's. Making his way into the public parking garage attached to the south wing of the hospital, Thomas scrambled out of the car and, as he'd just done to his underpowered car, Thomas pushed his almost sixty-year-old body to the max as he sprinted through the garage and into the hospital. Not sure where he should be going once he entered the hospital, whether to Emergency or Admissions, he ran up to a nearby nurses' desk and, breathing heavily, asked the nurse where he had to go to reach Katherine McClosky's room. After a few agonizing minutes of the nurse searching, she said that Katherine was in ICU at the moment and no visitors were allowed, so he would have to wait in the visitors' lounge on the third floor. Not wanting to waste any more time arguing with the nurse, Thomas made his way to the nearest elevators just around the corner from the nurses' station. As Thomas punched the button to take him up to the third floor, a doctor jumped into the elevator as the doors were about to close. As he entered he reached for the third floor button, but seeing it already pressed, he settled back against the wall and waited for the doors to close and the elevator to move. When Thomas looked over at the doctor, he thought he recognized him, he looked very familiar. The doctor, sensing that Thomas was staring at him, spoke up, "Excuse me, Father, do we know each other?"

Somewhere in the pit of his stomach, Thomas could feel it begin to churn.

"Yes, you look very familiar, but I am having a hard time remembering why. It could very well have been when I was here several months ago. My apologies for staring, doctor. A bad habit of a tired old priest."

Continuing the conversation, the doctor replied, "What brings you to St. Vincent's today, Father? The family of some poor dying soul requested last rites, perhaps?"

"I hope not, young man. I hope not," Thomas replied.

"She's dying, O'Sullivan. You're too fucking late, Father, as usual. It's okay, though. I will make sure she lives long enough for you to give your pathetic speech to the dying. Won't do her any good, anyway, Father. Her soul is going straight to hell," hissed the doctor.

The words just spoken by the doctor opened the memory of the incident at the Rome airport over thirty years earlier with the American businessman Robert Best, causing Thomas to gasp out loud, "It's you! How can that be?!"

The elevator seemed to be climbing endlessly, and then it became pitch black inside. Unable to see anything, Thomas backed up against the opposite wall from the doctor. Feeling his way along the wall using his hands, Thomas searched for the elevator buttons to try to get the door to open so he could get away from this maniac. Out of the blackness, Thomas heard the voice of pure evil speak: "What's the matter, Father? Don't tell me the great, well-respected Father O'Sullivan is scared of the boogeyman!"

Desperately trying to find a way out of the elevator, Thomas shouted into the darkness, "What do you want?! Why are you here?!"

With not a sound of any movement, Best was suddenly inches away from Thomas's face, his evil eyes glowing that familiar crimson red. "Why do you think I'm here, Father? You know why I am here. You have always known. We are both here for Katherine, aren't we," spat Best.

Clutching his cross that hung down the front of his clerical clothing, tucked below the buttoned blazer jacket he wore,

Thomas spoke the Lord's Prayer out loud: "Our Father who art in heaven, hallowed be thy name. . . ."

"Give it a rest, Father, save your breath. You might need it," seethed a demonic Best, his red eyes glowing menacingly. Without warning, Thomas was violently thrown to the other side of the elevator, slamming hard against the wall, causing him to fall to the floor, pain shooting through his back.

"In the name of the Father, our Mighty God in heaven and his beloved son, Jesus Christ, I command you, evil spirit, to leave. Go back to the depths of darkness from where you came!" Thomas bellowed towards the red eyes glowing back at him through the blackness.

Through the darkness a white glow began to appear surrounding Best, illuminating him as he spoke in a voice so evil that cold chills flowed down Thomas's spine. "Katherine has been chosen, Father. There is nothing you can do for her now. She will die, it is her destiny, but her child will live. Protect this child or the Legions of Hell will return to you and destroy everyone close to you, including your congregation, Detective Fitzpatrick and his family. Everyone, Father, will die. Your pathetic Church will not help you, Father, your beloved God cannot stop me, and He is powerless to stop what has been done and will be done. Do you understand me, Father?"

"Who are you that speaks this evil? You are the one who is nothing. Reveal yourself or be gone!" commanded Thomas, holding his cross straight out in front of him towards Best.

With a roar that reverberated off the steel-lined walls of the cramped elevator, Best screamed, "How dare you challenge me, worthless Priest! I could kill you as easily as swatting a mosquito! Remember what I did to the McClosky family, Father, before you speak again!"

Rising to his feet, reaching out in the dark to the rail along the wall for support, Thomas stood in front of Best in a defiant stance and declared, "I am just an old man, Best, or whatever name you are, so kill me if you will, just know it is the Power and the Glory of the Lord My God who will crush you like a gnat under His Mighty shoe!"

Another deafening roar followed, and Best, with speed that Thomas did not see, wrapped his hand around Thomas's throat, squeezing till there was no air able to get into his lungs, and hissed at Thomas, his evil red eyes blazing, "You are a fool, old man. The world is coming to an end, Father, you should know that. The Vatican recruited you to study God's Judgment Day and his wrath on mankind. How is that going, by the way?" Best laughed at Thomas. Unable to breathe and the pain threatening to make him lose consciousness, Thomas was suddenly released from Best's grip and dropped to the floor, gasping. Best then said to Thomas in Latin, "Obviam ibimus denuo quod Pater O'Sullivan certus sum. Facite vobis dico an plures arescentibus" ("We will meet again, Father O'Sullivan, of that I am certain. Do as I say to you or many people will die.")

Chapter 29

Coming to his senses, rubbing his throat, Thomas looked up and realized Best was gone and he was all alone in the elevator. Grabbing onto the rail, he lifted himself up, his throat and neck tender and sore. He needed to get to Katherine. He pressed the third floor button, and the elevator immediately began to rise. He had no idea how long he'd been in the elevator with Best, but it seemed like an eternity.

As a Catholic Priest, Thomas realized that knowledge and acceptance of an evil entity called the Devil, or Satan, or whatever name one used, came with the territory, and his teachers in the seminary spent a lot of time teaching new recruits all about the Antichrist and Hell. For a police officer, the chance encounter where he would ever have to shoot his service gun or even have to draw it in the line of duty is extremely rare. Most police officers never draw their weapons once in their entire career. The same with a priest. It is extremely rare that a priest would have an encounter first hand with someone or something claiming to be the devil or the supernatural. Thomas, however, had no doubt that he has met Satan, not just today but thirty years ago in Rome as well.

He stared into the mirror finish of the interior of the elevator walls, and he was startled at how beaten he looked. He could see red welts and swelling on his throat. Smoothing his hair and straightening his clerical collar with some discomfort, he turned when he heard the chime of arrival at the third floor. Exiting the elevator and turning down the hall, he made his way to the third floor nurses' station, where he requested the whereabouts of Katherine McClosky. Then he heard Detective Fitzpatrick call his name. Turning around, he saw the detective approaching, a look of concern written on his face. "Father, am I glad to see you. Katherine has been calling for you over and over again," he said.

"How is she doing, Rory?" Thomas asked as he followed the detective down the hall towards Katherine's room in ICU.

"Not very good, Father, from what I can tell. She is fighting for her life; the loss of blood has been dramatic. The doctors will fill you in," Rory said, somberly.

On reaching the ICU, Fitzpatrick, who had gotten here a lot sooner than Thomas and was well briefed on Katherine's condition, introduced Thomas to the doctors and nurses gathering in the hallway.

One of the doctors stepped forwards and shook hands with Thomas. "Thank you for coming, Father; I am Dr. Carrigan, Katherine's physician. Let me get right to the point on her condition, Father. She has lost an awful lot of blood. We are currently giving her a transfusion, but the damage has been extensive. For some reason we are dealing with what I call the 'Three delays'. One, Katherine delayed in calling emergency services when she knew she was in trouble. The second delay occurred when medical services were unable to get to her in a timely fashion, as Katherine had locked or barricaded herself in her room. And finally, by the time the paramedics were able to get to her the internal bleeding was so severe the only option was to get her to the hospital. The route to the hospital was plagued with hazards, dangerously slowing their arrival here at the hospital. The baby was moving inside of her in a dangerous fashion, causing the internal bleeding. Father, I believe Katherine was deliberately sabotaging this birth so that it would result in the baby's death and potentially hers."

Dr. Carrigan's description of Katherine's condition shocked Thomas and he struggled to maintain composure.

"I understand, Dr. Carrigan. May I see her?" asked Thomas with some urgency in his voice.

Glancing over at Detective Fitzpatrick before he spoke, Dr. Carrigan continued.

"Yes, you can, Father—but only you. May I ask you if you know why she would do this to herself and her baby?"

Thomas needed to see Katherine, and he was not in the mood to discuss Katherine's mental condition while she lay in her bed, possibly dying.

"Doctor, this young woman has seen the brutal slaughter and murder of her husband and his family in front of her very eyes. Her mental condition the last nine months has been severely tested, as you could well imagine. Please, Doctor, bring me to her."

"My apologies, Father. You are right, let's get you to Katherine. Please follow me."

Following Dr. Carrigan down the hall with Rory at his side, Thomas spotted Kenneth and Joanie Kearney, Katherine's parents, standing at the entry doors to Katherine's ICU room talking anxiously to doctors. When they saw Thomas coming. Joanie, sobbing uncontrollably, rushed towards him, hugging him, asking him for answers. Clutching him tightly, Joanie told him she was frightened about what was happening to her daughter. Thomas tried to reassure her that Katherine was a fighter and would fight now for her life and the life of her child. He then signaled Kenneth to come and take Joanie. Easing himself away from her grip, he told them both that he was going to see Katherine now and that he would pray for her well-being. He turned and followed Dr. Carrigan into Katherine's ICU room. He asked Rory to stay with the Kearney's and told them he would be back as soon as he could.

Quickly walking into Katherine's room, he was confronted with organized chaos. Nurses were busy reattaching fresh intravenous bags, monitoring her vitals, all scurrying about tending to the sophisticated equipment involved with Katherine's emergency. Thomas sat down beside Katherine on the bed, reaching for her hand. Her eyes suddenly opened at the touch of his hand, revealing pain and misery that broke Thomas's heart. She spoke in labored breaths, "Father O'Sullivan, I am so sorry. Please help me. This baby cannot be born, Father. It must die with me here today. Please tell the doctors to stop treating me . . . please."

He looked into her lost eyes as he spoke, covering her hand with both of his.

"Katherine, you are very sick and the doctors are trying to save your life and that of your baby. God loves you, Katherine, and he will fight for you. Your life means everything to him, please understand that."

Suddenly Katherine sat bolt upright in her bed as if she had no pain, then fixed him with a look of pure hatred and screamed, "You're not listening to me, Father! You have not listened to me ever since I was attacked! I was raped by the devil himself, don't you get it?! I am unable to conceive Father, you know that, but yet I am pregnant! It's because it was from him, Father! Satan raped me, please why can't you understand?!" Katherine sobbed, falling back down onto her pillows.

At that precise moment, and without a shadow of a doubt, he believed her. She was terrified and there was nothing he could do but pray.

Then her monitor started to sound a high-pitched warning. Nurses were arriving beside Thomas, asking him to step away from the bed. Looking down at Katherine, he could see her eyes roll back in her head as she began convulsing. His eyes welling up in tears, he stepped back from the bed and prayed out loud for Katherine, "Heavenly Father, Master of the universe, Father of Christ Jesus, your Son, save Katherine from the evilness that is killing her. May your mighty hands cleanse her soul from the wickedness that has invaded her! I pray this in the name of your Son, Jesus Christ, Father."

He was horrified as he watched Katherine's body shake uncontrollably on the bed. She was dying. Everything seemed in slow motion in his mind, as doctors converged on Katherine, trying to save her life.

"We're losing her. I have no pulse. I need the paddles now!" yelled Dr. Carrigan to the nurses. Seconds later, nurses pushed the defibrillator machine to the side of the bed, where Dr. Carrigan grabbed the paddles and yelled "Clear!" Giving Katherine an electric shock to try to resuscitate her heart, Dr. Carrigan yelled "Clear" again. Once again, Katherine's chest rose off the bed, but the monitor continued to flatline. Then, through a haze, Thomas thought he heard another doctor call out, "The baby, Dr. Carrigan! Save the baby!"

Checking the monitor one last time, a dejected-looking Dr. Carrigan yelled out, "She is gone! We must do a caesarean section to save the baby."

The room became a blur to Thomas after that. He barely perceived the flurry of activity before him as he moved back towards the wall in stunned silence. Looking back behind him through the viewing windows he could see a familiar-looking doctor observing through the glass. He *was* familiar—because it was Best! Shocked at seeing the beast himself, standing there watching his work of death finishing itself, Thomas snapped. Turning and rushing through the swinging doors out to the viewing room, he could see the glowing red eyes of Best burning bright with the glow of victory and satisfaction in them. Best did not notice Thomas rushing towards him until it was too late. Thomas tackled Best, sending the two of them crashing to the floor. Ending up on top of Best, Thomas looked down at Satan himself and, engulfed in a fury of hate he had never experienced in his life before, began to pummel Best in the face and head like a crazed animal. Blood spewing from his mouth and nose from Thomas's blows, Best looked up at Thomas and began to laugh. His evil laugh reverberated through the hallway. Thomas continued to hammer away with his fists till the red lanterns in his skull went dark. Screaming at Best, he yelled, "How dare you take her life, you pathetic piece of garbage! Why did she have to die? You will get your child, you maniac!"

His face destroyed by the multiple blows that had rained

down on him from Thomas's fists, Best replied with a calm and even voice through broken and bloody teeth, "You're right, old man. Listen!"

The sound of angels could be heard over all of the shouts coming from Katherine's room. It was such a beautiful sound that Thomas instinctively climbed off Best to peer through the viewing glass and into the operating room. He was moved to the very core of his soul. He knew that God had indeed intervened and maybe had not been able to save Katherine but had saved the baby. The soft cries of a newborn child, being held up in the air by the nurses as Dr. Carrigan cut the umbilical cord, was like a dozen angels singing in a choir. The shouts in the room were silenced as if everyone in it were stunned, unable to speak as they listened to the beautiful sound emanating from this baby. It was as if everyone in the room knew that they were witness to a miracle. The life of the mother gone, her still body lying on the bed, the baby squirming in the nurse's hand—it was an incredible sight. Looking back at Best for his reaction to the miracle of God, Thomas saw that he was gone. Then, through the beautiful sounds filling the room, Thomas heard a nurse cry out.

"It's a girl! Look at her birthmark! Can you believe it!? It is three musical notes. It is a miracle!"

Before Thomas could react, the nurses wrapped the baby girl in towels, cleaned her off and then rushed her into another room where they would begin hooking her up to machines to monitor her vitals. Gathering himself, he could barely believe what had just transpired. In a fit of pure outrage, Thomas had almost killed Best, but the beast just laughed at Thomas through the blows. His blood still wet on his hands and the front of his clothing, Thomas could barely keep from shaking from the miraculous intervention by the Glorious God in Heaven he had just witnessed. Best, realizing his defeat at the hands of God, had disappeared like a scared rabbit as God's mighty power revealed itself. A voice interrupted him from his thoughts.

"Excuse me, Father. You must see this. The birthmark on

the baby. I have never seen anything like it," Dr. Carrigan called out to Thomas from the doorway leading into another surgical room.

Looking back at the lifeless body of Katherine as the nurses began to cover her in sheets, Thomas silently prayed for her. "Thank you, beloved and gracious God, for giving Katherine the strength to deliver your miracle. Welcome Katherine into your Kingdom Lord, she well deserves your love." Motioning to Dr. Carrigan, he said, "Yes, I'm coming."

He followed Dr. Carrigan into the next room. It too was now a flurry of activity as doctors and nurses were busy in the care of Katherine's miracle baby girl. Taking Thomas close to the tiny crib where the baby was still singing away so incredibly beautifully, Dr. Carrigan reached down and pulled the towel away from underneath the baby's inner right thigh, exposing a mark that, when he saw it, sent a bolt of lightning through Thomas's body that shook him to his very core. He began to tilt backwards on his feet, struggling to keep from falling. Sensing Thomas's shock, Dr. Carrigan asked, "Father, what is it? What is the matter? The baby singing, this birthmark, is it not a sign that this baby is a miracle of God?"

Staring at the birthmark, the gravity of the real truth hit Thomas like a wrecking ball at a construction site. This baby was no miracle. Certainly no miracle from God. The baby was indeed the child of Satan, just as Katherine had tried to tell him. The birthmark was three musical notes like three backward sixes. The mark of the beast!

Meanwhile, in the hallway outside the ICU, Kenneth and Joanie Kearney, still unaware as to what had just transpired inside

Katherine's room, found themselves looking wonderingly at each other and Detective Fitzpatrick, as to why a doctor covered in blood was walking down the hallway laughing.

Chapter 30

Man's perception of Heaven and Hell as interpreted in their Holy Books and retold or written over the course of time has been a source of great amusement to the legend mankind calls Satan, Beast, Antichrist, Lucifer, Abaddon, Prince of Darkness, Beezlebub, or now even Robert Best. I have no name. I am nameless. I am many names. I do like it, though, when I am referred to by humans as the Prince of Darkness; it sounds regal. God's soldiers, His angels just called me the Dark One whenever they did battle. Spiritual battle with mankind is an ongoing, day-to-day ritual in my world, something that keeps me busy every minute of every day. In the last century, the movie industry growing by leaps and bounds and with man's technology developing at warp speed have provided scintillating and comic amusement for me. I enjoy man's movies more than anyone. I could care less man's idea of what heaven would be like for them when they died, but Hollywood's movies about their version of Hell are great fun and I enjoy them immensely. My world is not a fiery pit of burning flame where humans go to sweat and toil for an eternity in physical form. It is far worse. Like a pearl hidden in an oyster, the soul of man is the treasure. It is their spirit that I want. The pain and suffering of a tortured soul crying for salvation that will never come is the fuel that heats my furnace. The soul of man imprisoned in Hell is a beautiful thing, for I will kill and torture their locked souls over and over, every day, for an eternity.

The reality is that the world always has been ruled by Good and Evil. Mankind, since its inception, was always doomed for extinction just like the dinosaurs that walked before them. The problem is that the Holy Creator was always so enamored with man, loving them so much he created his son in their image. God is just a spirit in this world, like the Dark One. We are a mist, a wind blowing through the valleys, a sound ricocheting off a solid surface, a mirage, an apparition appearing human. Make no mistake: God or me, the Dark One, are not human, never will be, never want to be. I hate humans as much as God loves them. My spirit blows through their chests only because I am searching for the ones who also hate God. They are the ones that are ready to come to my Kingdom right now. They are the easy ones. I take them out by the hundreds every single day around the world. I do it by insinuating my dark and evil spirit amongst mankind, stoking hatred, jealousy, violence, lying, degradation, murder, and adultery, to name a few things that wreak havoc on society and mankind throughout the world. Softening up their souls for the Dark One and turning them away from the light of the mighty God is what I do. He is responsible for all that is good and I am responsible for all that is evil. Don't you think I am winning? Look at our world now, it is teetering on self-destruction. Men are killing each other and the planet. God is losing this battle, and my ultimate plan will finish Him for good.

We are a presence, with a viewing glass at our disposal that can peer into every square inch of the world, into every human soul. Both God and I see and hear everything. We are almost the same. The difference is that He wants to love and I want to destroy. To love is to be weak, and it is that weakness that will bring Him to my feet, where I will show no mercy and I will destroy Him once and for all. God knows where my presence is at all times just as I know where his presence is at all times. It is spiritual warfare that has raged for an eternity. The ultimate goal that is most dear to Him is the survival of mankind, and for me it is the complete destruction of man. His obsession with their salvation and my obsession with their destruction are what give our world meaning. It is a chess match that has been raging ever since God felt that I was not a 'team player' in his Angel stable and so cast me out, sealing the fate of his beloved mankind. God's race to expose his love to every soul on earth and mine to stop him has kept us in spiritual warfare throughout eternity. I think I am winning, considering it has been over two thousand years and there are still people in this world who have never been exposed to God and his earthly body, Jesus Christ.

It has been a very, very long time since I have spent this much time on earth in human form, maybe hundreds of years. Not since my defeat over seventeen hundred years ago in 400 AD have I needed to spend this much time 'above ground,' so to speak. Using a human body to walk among man is something I do not enjoy. I hate it, in fact. The human body of man was created by my enemy, and to walk in the shoes of His creation is most difficult. Injecting his seed into these seven women was only possible for me because it was central to my plan and ended the lineage I hate.

Killing human beings, animals, creatures of the sea, the environment, and so on, is easy, and I do it every single day. Converting the souls of man from any faith to the slavery of Hell is the challenge, and where I meet spiritual resistance from God and his soldiers all of the time. He wins a few souls and loses a few souls. Converting most of the human race in one fell swoop into my spiritual prison requires a plan so evil, so diabolical, that God will be unable to react in time. The sheer number of souls lost all at once will neutralize God's abilities to use His mighty power to stop me.

I came so very close to ending the origins of Christianity, crippling the power of God back in 400 AD, and this time around I will not fail. God inches closer and closer to unleashing His Armageddon on earth as He has written in their books, but He will be too late. I will have unleashed my ultimate plan before then, leaving him precious few souls with which to begin his new Kingdom on earth. Knowing the depth of mankind's betrayal of

Him will most certainly satisfy my appetite for revenge for my defeat so many years ago.

To destroy mankind is to own their soul, something that I will do when I unleash my ultimate plan over the next seventeen years. I have waited for just the right time, and that time is now, starting with the births of the seven babies I created with the attacks on the seven descendants of the sons of King Tiridates. I have been tracking their lineage over these many centuries waiting for the right opportunity. The irony in the birth of these children and their role in my plan to destroy mankind is beyond brilliant. Now, with the unbelievable popularity and power of the internet, television and wireless, reaching tens of millions of the world's youth has been made possible with technology, and I plan to use it as one of my tools. Oh, how I love technology!

The only hiccup so far in the plan is my discovery of the unbelievable relationship between Father Thomas O'Sullivan and the McCloskey family. When I realized the Vatican had chosen O'Sullivan for their task force to study, monitor and then prepare the Church for God's Judgment Day, I knew God had made a bold move in our chess match of life. I will allow Father O'Sullivan to keep Katherine McCloskey's baby safe until the time is right. Then I will dispose of O'Sullivan just like I did Katherine. He is a tough old bird, that O'Sullivan, and a good soldier of God, which will make it even more fun when I kill him. The Catholic Church, to my amazement, has survived over all this time, including the scandals involving child abuse by its clergy, something I put into motion hundreds of years ago.

Men are weak and easy to manipulate, including priests. The Catholic priest is the most disciplined human soldier of God, and my biggest adversary on earth. A priest's training and commitment to God's word is unparalleled, so when I can weed out the weak ones and infect their souls with lust for children, the collateral damage done to the Church is spectacular. Recently the Church has moved swiftly to weed out the weak ones themselves, which means I need to look for other avenues of attack. Just another day at the office for the Dark One.

The Vatican, by putting together a task force to monitor world events like wars and conflicts, environmental disasters, disease, and so on for signs of God's coming wrath, has showed a strength of leadership unmatched in the Christian world. Most of what they would study are events I myself put in motion against man and this earth. Their ability to differentiate my work from that of God's fury will determine the Church's readiness to prepare their people spiritually for the Armageddon that is coming their way.

My human alter ego, Robert Best, will lay the foundation in the music industry to carry out my plan. He will do it by targeting the youth of the world—it all starts with them. Once I have their souls and their minds everyone else will follow. It is that simple. Man is easy to manipulate. They even do it to themselves all the time. Like the tobacco companies who project a public image of health and support of anti-smoking campaigns but behind the scenes are feverishly working to lure the youth into starting smoking. Losing long-time smokers out the front door is great for their image, but luring the young teenagers through the backdoor to become lifelong customers is the real evil. I love it, and I am a big supporter of the tobacco industry. Music, though, is the real key to the souls of the young.

Utilizing the universal language of music, my plan of putting together a superstar band of musicians unlike anything the world has ever experienced, a band so phenomenally popular with the youth, a sort of Backstreet Boys times ten in popularity, will isolate the young around the world for me to then suck the souls of their families, friends, and relatives. I will create such a following for each band member on their own in different parts of the world that when I put them together in a supergroup it will bring the world to its knees.

Governments will take notice of the radical social changes taking place in front of their eyes as more and more of their populations became rabid fans and followers of the band. As the internet grows like I know it will with companies working feverishly to devise ways to use the internet to reach out to the youth of the world in so many ways. Oh, yes, I have it all planned and in motion. The seven births are taking place right now and soon the world will get their first taste of the enormity of the talent of these young musical prodigies.

When I am done and the pieces are in place it will be too late for God to stop me. I will scorch this earth with my wrath, filling my cauldron of misery with the souls of men. The world will not become a Kingdom for His son Jesus Christ to rule but rather a prison of despair that will last an eternity. Oh, the anticipation is almost too much for me to bear, but I, the Dark One, have waited over seventeen hundred years, so I can wait another seventeen years and enjoy the fun along the way. I will continue to blacken the hearts and souls of innocent people around the world in the meantime to keep me fulfilled while I wait for my musical geniuses to grow.

Chapter 31

The sensational murder of Crown Prosecutor Gerard Louveneau at the hands of his police officer wife Francoise nine months earlier was back in the news again with the upcoming birth of his child. Locked away in the Douglas Mental Health University Institute in Montreal, Francoise had been in and out of a catatonic coma ever since the attack and murder of her husband, when she had been discovered by Dr. Berthiume in Gerard's hospital room, covered in his blood.

Francoise had suffered through a complete mental breakdown after what she had done to Gerard, a breakdown that was, in the opinion of investigators, the culmination of the stress of a woman pushed to the edge by the vicious attack on her and her husband eight months earlier. That attack, police believed, was a result of Gerard and Francoise having been involved with outlaw motorcycle gang activities, taking bribes to steer investigations and prosecutions against gang members facing charges. They never found conclusive evidence of this, as the gangs certainly were not talking and it would likely stay buried until Francoise made a recovery, which wasn't likely, considering her condition. What they did discover, however, was an informant who had tipped off authorities as to Gerard's illegal activities. The informant was a female police cadet who claimed to have had an affair with Gerard that started while he was at the cadet college teaching a course in proper police techniques and protocol in taking notes and recording information during an investigation. Police looked into the possibility of Francoise having murdered Gerard over the affair, but ruled that out, as the attack was far too violent for Francoise to have committed and would have required far more strength than Francoise was capable of on her own. Unofficially, police believed it was a contract killing by the biker gangs and set up to look like a murder by a jilted wife. As they had no evidence to prove it until someone came forward with new information, the police officially left it as a murder committed by Francoise, which could very well have been the case anyway. The media had a field day, with the murder case dominating the headlines in Montreal.

Doctors had recently moved her back to Sainte-Justine Hospital to begin the C-section birth of her child. The courts had decided to give temporary custody of the baby to Gerard's sister Julia and her husband, Jean Paledeau, until Francoise recovered enough to stand trial for her husband's murder. The Paledeau's could file adoption papers upon the outcome of the trial. If Francoise did not recover from her present condition the Paledeau's could petition the courts to grant them the adoption order at that time.

Arriving in Francoise's room, Dr. Berthiume checked her charts and conferred with the attending nurses. He instructed the nurses that they could begin preparing Francoise for surgery within the hour, as he did not want to wait any longer. Everything looked good with the baby, so they no longer needed to wait. Looking down at Francoise, unconscious in a coma, he thought to himself, this poor woman has been through so much, with the severe beating she took from her attack and then her violent episode resulting in her killing her husband. He felt partially responsible, as he'd been caring for Francoise at the time and he had not taken her rants about being raped by the devil and carrying the devil's child seriously. The woman was obviously suffering from a serious mental disorder, and he had only focused on her physical injuries. He should have ordered psychological testing before he left her alone with her husband.

How was he to know she would go crazy and rip out his throat? Something inside was telling him to take precautions on this delivery. Was he scared he was going to deliver the devil's child? He knew that was insanity, but he couldn't subdue the ache that was gnawing away at the pit of his stomach. Maybe he would make his way to his locker and chew on some Tums. Pulling his thoughts away from her, he decided he just wanted to get this birth over with and get her transferred back to the Douglas Institute.

Turning to leave the room, he almost bumped into another physician standing at the end of the bed. Excusing himself, he continued past him, but then he stopped and turned back towards the doctor standing in the room, as there was something odd about him. He also noticed all of the nurses were gone; there was nobody in the room but himself and this strange doctor. Why weren't the nurses busy preparing Francoise for transfer up to surgery? The doctor continued to stand at the foot of the bed and stare at Francoise. Speaking into the doctor's back, Dr. Berthiume spoke. "Excuse me, Doctor. May I ask why you are here? Do you have any business with the patient that I need to be aware of?"

The doctor turned to face him, staring at him with eyes that burned a crimson red, startling him. Then he suddenly said, "You will deliver this baby in precisely seven minutes. Do you understand?"

The ache in Dr. Berthiume's stomach began to twist.

"Who the hell do you think you are, coming into this room?! This is my patient. Who are you, anyway? Let me see some identification or I will call security," he demanded.

"Silence, you fool! Deliver this baby in precisely seven minutes or I will rip out your throat as I did her husband's," hissed Robert Best as his burning red eyes burrowed into Dr. Berthiume's. Striding past Dr. Berthiume and out into the hallway, Best could hear the doctor call out for security, just before all anarchy broke out.

Shaking from this encounter, not understanding what was

happening, Dr. Berthiume called out for security as he watched the stranger disappear down the hallway, when suddenly he heard a blood-curdling scream from behind him. Whipping around, he saw Francoise fully awake, screaming at the top of her lungs with her back arched off the bed. Running around the bed, he reached down and grabbed Francoise's wrist and felt her pulse. Her heart was racing. He had to calm her down, and fast. Suddenly, Francoise lifted her head off the pillow and with eyes as wild as a pack of dogs and her face just inches from his, she screamed, "I told you to abort this fucking baby, Doctor, didn't I?! You do it now, before it's too late, do you hear me? He wants it born! He has been watching me! Do it. Do it now!"

Falling back onto the bed, Francoise began to convulse. Then she started to thrash wildly, her arms and legs flailing all around, toppling her IV stand to the floor. It was total chaos in the room. Nurses were pouring in now, in complete shock, as the room was in shambles with various objects being flung about. Francoise was out of control, screaming fragmented sentences about the devil's baby having to die, to kill her and the baby.

Something inside him was telling him he needed to move quickly, as he only had minutes to spare to deliver this baby right away, as he'd been told. He barked out commands to the nurses to prepare to move her to surgery immediately. He quickly gave Francoise a powerful sedative injection to calm her down. The nurses then wheeled her out of the room and up to surgery. Following them down the hallway and around the corner to the elevators, Dr. Berthiume made a decision. He did not have the time to take the elevator up to surgery. He needed to do it right here and right now. Shouting out to the nurses guiding Francoise's gurney, he commanded them to wheel her into the closest recovery room as they were going to do surgery right now. The nurses protested they were not set up in there for surgery. Telling them to do it anyway, he commanded another nurse to call up to surgery to have them bring down the monitors and surgical tools as he was starting right now.

Rushing into the room normally used for recovery, they

quickly turned it into a surgical room. Scrubbing up for the surgery amidst the chaos, with Francoise beginning to thrash once again, demanding that the baby die, the head nurse, Suzanne Agnew, asked, "Dr. Berthiume, what the hell is going on? This patient is going to do damage to this baby. We have to get her up to surgery, we cannot do this here! What are you doing? She will die!"

"I must save the baby. We have no more time left. The level of stress on the fetus is too much, and it will kill it. We do the surgery now. Let's move!" In reality, the nurse was right. They did have time to move her up to surgery, but he was being compelled by a power he could not explain, but only feel, to deliver this baby within the next ninety seconds; if he didn't, something terrible was going to happen here. He could not explain it, he just needed to act. As the nurses worked furiously at his commands, they prepped Francoise's stomach for surgery. Taking his scalpel, he cut into her stomach and uterus, glancing at the clock with seconds to spare. Reaching into her stomach cavity, he pulled the baby out with the nurse holding the placenta sac. Cutting the umbilical cord away, he handed the silent but very much alive baby girl to another nurse so he could turn his attention to Francoise. The monitor showed her heart rate was very low, and that was not good. He would have to move quickly to try and save Francoise's life. Instructing the nurses on what to do next, he quickly closed the surgical wound.

What happened next was beyond anyone's comprehension. Francoise, still under an anesthetic, suddenly awakened while he was completing the stitches on her stomach. Looking at Dr. Berthiume as if he was the devil, she went berserk, screaming at him that he had let the devil's child live. Just as he was calling out for a heavy dose of Haldol to try to get Francoise under control, she used her foot to kick him squarely in the jaw, sending him flying backwards from the blow. Two nurses jumped on the table to try to restrain her. He watched in horror as Francoise had got hold of his scalpel, still on the surgical tray, and drove it into the neck of the head nurse, Suzanne. Blood spurted and gushed everywhere. Getting back on his feet, Dr. Berthiume began to prepare the Haldol himself, as the room was in complete chaos and the nurses were fleeing as Francoise jumped down from the table with the scalpel in her hand. She was looking for the baby. Grabbing the needle, he rushed Francoise to inject her and end this madness, but he was a split second too late. She was going to get to the baby before he got to her. The nurse who was wrapping the baby on the adjacent table had fled, abandoning it. The baby was unbelievably quiet and was just staring at everyone and all of the surrounding chaos around her, oblivious to the scalpel that was about to be driven into it by her mother gone mad. As she raised the scalpel above her head, about to drive it down into the baby, Dr. Berthiume heard a very loud bang echo in the room and then two more loud bang-bang sounds. The scalpel had flown out of Francoise's hands from the impact of the bullets ripping into her upper chest. Francoise was thrown straight back into the wall, dead before she even hit the floor. The security guard, his gun and posture still in firing mode, seemed to be in total shock at what he had just done. What he had just done, thought Dr. Berthiume, was save the life of that precious baby, who continued to squirm around on top of the table, oblivious to the chaos surrounding it, a content newborn waiting for its first taste of food from its mother.

Nurses, doctors and more security officers began to file in, when a sound began to fill the room. The sound literally stopped everyone in their tracks, grabbing their attention amidst the carnage. Everyone then turned towards the baby, almost forgotten in all the craziness and violence that had taken over the room. The baby was not crying, nor was it thrashing about, but it was singing. The baby, only minutes old, was lying on the table on her side looking at everyone with bright and attentive eyes and was singing with a sound that could only be described as angelic. It was so beautiful, so unexpected, that everyone had forgotten about the events that just earlier terrified them so much and stood transfixed at this newborn baby issuing a sound that filled the room with a beautiful melody that an orchestra could never approach. Then suddenly a nurse broke the trance with the words, "This is a miracle child! A messenger from God! Listen to this baby. Have you ever heard anything like this in your life?"

Then another nurse called out as she approached the baby, "Look at the baby's birthmark! Look, everyone!"

As they were all drawn in closer to the baby to catch a glimpse of the birthmark, the mother of this miracle baby shot dead just a few feet away, a nurse dead with her neck torn open just another few feet away, the smell of gunfire still permeating the room, Dr. Berthiume saw the birthmark. A very unusual birthmark indeed, but it seemed appropriate. Three musical notes, almost like a tattoo, just inside her right thigh.

As the beautiful singing continued from the baby, even as the nurses began to wrap it in a warm towel, Dr. Berthiume then noticed that strange doctor who had threatened him earlier. He was standing in the room with everyone else, but he stood just behind them all, alone but staring. He was staring at him with eyes that burned a deep bright red. Glancing back at the baby as the nurses carried it from the room, and then back at the strange doctor, a very strange and bizarre thought came to Dr. Berthiume's mind.

Maybe those musical notes on the miracle baby are not that at all. Maybe they are backwards sixes. The mark of the beast!

Chapter 32

Never in his twenty-seven years of pastoral work had Bryon ever encountered anything quite like the situation he found himself in with Brent and Lori. Placing his hands on Lori's stomach yesterday to bless their unborn child, he had been immediately overcome by a sense of dread and doom like nothing he had ever experienced. That episode, combined with the revelations from Brent regarding the nature of the attack, had left Bryon unnerved and shaken. Having received his theological training at the Southwestern Baptist Theological Seminary in Fort Worth in 1984, Bryon was well versed in church doctrine dealing with the supernatural, devil worship, demonic possession, and so forth, but he had never expected it to hit close to home like this. Bryon fundamentally and personally, never mind the doctrine of his church would not condone or support an abortion. God created life; it was not up to man to take that life. In Brent and Lori's situation, they chose, or Lori chose, early in the pregnancy not to abort. Now they were just a few days away, or even hours perhaps, from giving birth to a child with potentially demonic connections, a child that the mother wanted and the father did not. This was an extremely difficult situation, and Byron knew he was going to have to take action. Picking up the phone, he dialed a pastor friend of his from another county about two hours east of Cheyenne. Pastor Jim Sigardson was a close friend as well as a colleague, as the two of them had been in seminary together, remaining close through the years. He trusted Jim with anything, and vice versa. They had leaned on each other for advice over the years when dealing with difficult issues with church members. In one case in particular, Jim had a church deacon investigated for child pornography after he had discovered graphic images on the church office computer one morning. Someone had been on the computer the night before viewing the images and had somehow forgotten to close out the web browser.. When he called Bryon for advice before he called the police, Bryon suggested he do some detective work on his own to try to identify the perpetrator before all hell broke loose when the police got involved. Sometimes these things could get so out of control the collateral damage could bring down the church entirely.

That is what Jim did. He set up surveillance cameras throughout the office to capture who came in and who came out, as well as one camera directly focused on the computer screen. The cameras were accessible to Jim by logging into his secure website that the security company had set up for him at his home. So for three straight weeks, Jim stayed in his home office at night glued to his computer, watching what was happening or not happening in the church office. Then, sure enough, it happened. Around 1:00 a.m. on a Monday morning, just after a busy day of services and then a meeting Sunday evening in the church office with elders and deacons regarding the expansion of the church's offices, he entered the website. To Jim's complete shock, it was not only the church's worship pastor but one of his closest friends. Their wives were also best friends, and they had spent many nights having dinner and sharing wonderful evenings together as couples over the years. Jim watched in horror as Pastor Ed Birtle logged onto the computer using a login code that was the same for everyone and immediately began bringing up websites depicting children in sexually graphic images. Jim immediately called police to his home, where he replayed the surveillance video from the very beginning of Birtle's entry into the church office. It was almost 2:00 a.m., after Ed had been on the computer for almost an hour, when police officers rushed to the church to arrest him red-handed. It was a very difficult time for Jim, dealing with the aftermath of seeing his friend arrested and then convicted, his marriage ruined and the church scrutinized by investigators. It took the church years to completely shake that incident from its past. Now Pastor Bryon Simmons was about to lay an even bigger doozy on his friend with the hope that his sound advice and leadership would help guide him.

After saying a prayer asking God for strength and wisdom to help guide him, he picked up the phone and called his friend.

"Jim, it's Bryon Simmons. How are you?"

To hear Jim's familiar voice instantly brought a sense of calm to his tingling nerves.

"I'm doing well, Bryon, it's great to hear from you. How are things at the steel cathedral?"

Normally they would shoot the breeze about everything, including the state of their golf games and their wives, but not today. To enter into small talk before he was about to drop this bombshell seemed completely inappropriate.

"Jim, I don't mean to be rude, but I need to cut to the chase. I need to meet with you to discuss a problem I'm having with some church members. Would you be free to come out here tonight? It's important, Jim."

"Certainly I can, Bryon. You sound really upset, Bryon, and that worries me. Can you give me some insight?"

He knew he must have sounded stressed and short to Jim, but he couldn't help it. He *was* stressed.

"No, I'd rather not discuss this over the phone. How soon can you get here?"

There was a slight pause on the phone before Jim replied, and when he did he now sounded stressed and short himself.

"I'll leave right now, Bryon, and should be there by three o'clock."

"Thank you, Jim. I appreciate this. I'll see you soon."

****

Hanging up the phone, Jim sat at his office desk for a few minutes, a bit stunned from the phone call from Bryon. This was very unlike him. Byron was in some sort of trouble, he could sense it. Bryon Simmons was one of the finest men he had ever known. For him to ask Jim to come out to see him immediately over church members was serious indeed. Picking up the phone, he called his wife to let her know he would not be home for dinner.

"Hi, sweetheart. Listen, I have to take off to Cheyenne to meet with Bryon Simmons. Something bad is happening in his church and he needs to talk with me, so I told him I would be right out. It's going to be a late night, honey, so save me some leftovers, okay?"

His wife's voice instinctively reflected her concern.

"Oh, my gosh, Jim. Is everything okay with him? Do you want me to call Lynn?"

"No, it's an issue with some church members that he needs some advice on. Nothing serious. Lynn might not know anything about it, as Bryon might just be keeping it within the walls of the church for now."

"You know you'll be missing your son's playoff game."

Darn it, that wasn't good. Little Tommy would be disappointed in his dad.

"Ah, shucks, that's right. Well, I have to go honey. Bryon would not ask this of me if he really didn't need to see me. Give my best to Tommy and tell him to focus on defense, okay? And to win so I can be there for the next game. Thanks, Julia. I have to run now. I'll see you later tonight. Bye."

"Drive safe, my love, and give my best to Bryon. Call me when you're on your way home and I'll warm up some dinner for you."

"Will do. Love you."

Grabbing the keys to his church-supplied Jeep Cherokee, Jim headed out the door and began the two-hour ride to Cheyenne.

****

Meanwhile, in Cheyenne, at Asker Farms, Brent Asker joined Lori in the main barn, where she was overseeing the workers tending to the horses in their newly renovated barn.

"Lori, what are you doing out here? You have to come back inside. You're about to give birth and you're working the horses! The guys are fully capable of running things and don't need you or me out here right now, so come on inside, please. I fixed us some lunch, so don't disappoint me."

Her signature smile beamed.

"Alright, if you insist. And it's only because you made lunch. Tell me you made your tomato soup with pasta noodles?"

Lori was so darn beautiful it took his breath away sometimes. Today was one of those times.

"It's your lucky day, my dear, that is exactly what I made, along with a veggie wrap for you and me."

"Wow, I am loving this. I can't wait until I come into the house and you've put a fresh diaper on our baby, dinner is on the table and you're wearing nothing but your cowboy boots," cooed Lori with a grin from ear to ear.

"Careful what you wish for, Lori. Cooking a little food and changing the occasional diaper for daily sex is a small price to pay," winked Brent.

Leaning up to give him a smooch on the cheek, she replied, "We'll negotiate on that one, sweetheart. I'll be right in, just give me another minute, okay? Just making sure that Felix was able to get the drainage system in the barn working properly again."

Making his way back to the house, Brent was amazed at Lori's energy. She never seemed to take a break. She worked tirelessly on the ranch, looked after his injuries, changing the dressing bandages on his ravaged shoulder at least once a day, all the time walking around nine months pregnant. Soon the baby would be born, and he was dreading every minute leading up to it. He did not know how to stop it and was terrified at what Lori was about to give birth to. He thought for sure her memories of the attack would return, but they never did. Or maybe they did, he thought, and she had found some way to suppress those memories somewhere in her mind, knowing they were so terrifying painful. He was going to try to get her to open up about the attack over lunch. He had to try to get her to remember, no matter how painful that would be. The alternative was unacceptable. The baby could not be born. He would not be responsible for allowing the devil's own child to be born on this earth. Never. If it came down to it he would murder the baby right there in the delivery room. He had to, he had no choice. It would destroy his relationship with Lori, he knew that, but he was prepared to do what needed to be done. If only Lori would remember, she too would realize what needed to be done.

Walking in the front door, Lori called out, "Smells good, honey! I'm starving and I'm sure the baby is, too!"

Sitting down to eat, Brent looked at Lori, trying to get a read on her as to whether there was any indication of trepidation or fear on the birth of this child, and all he saw was overwhelming joy. She was radiant, beautiful and overjoyed with excitement. She truly didn't have any idea what had happened to her. He would probe her anyway. "Honey, how are you feeling? Any nervousness or feeling scared at all about having the baby?"

She looked down at her bowl of soup before responding, blowing on a spoonful before she lifted her head to look at him.

"Yeah, sure I am, but it's just a nervous feeling. It's not like I've done this before, you know. I think you're more nervous than anyone. Don't be so worried, Brent, everything is going to be just fine. Soon you're going to be the proud dad of a baby girl or boy. You want a little cowboy, don't you, honey? I think I've shown you over these last several months that a cowgirl is every bit of a cowboy as well. Don't you think so?"

"You know what, Lori? All I know is if it's a boy or a girl it will be very much like its mother, making it the most beautiful and perfect baby possible," said Brent to Lori, seeing her melt at his words, almost as if she had not been sure if Brent wanted this baby, but now was assured. If she only knew, he thought, how much he did *not* want this baby and the lengths he was about to go to in order to ensure it did not survive.

The look of love in Lori's eyes made him feel incredibly guilty about the thoughts dancing around inside his head.

"I love you so much, Brent Asker. When this baby is born the three of us are getting away from this place for a while. Somewhere beautiful. Can we do that?" asked Lori.

She was still cradling the spoonful of soup in her hand. He reached over and took the spoon from her and placed it back in the bowl. He then cradled her hand in his and held it firmly while he spoke.

"Yes, we can. Thanks to all of your hard work, getting the new staff, barn and horses working smoothly, while I sat here and watched TV. You are an amazing woman, Lori Weston. Wherever we decide to go together, we go first as Brent and Lori Asker."

Getting up off her chair, feeling the effects of her work in the barn and being so pregnant, she went over to Brent and sat on his lap and wrapped her arms around him, being careful not to put any pressure on his damaged shoulder, and said to him, "I just told you I loved you, mister, and you never told me you loved me back."

"I love you, Lori. More than you will ever know."

Chapter 33

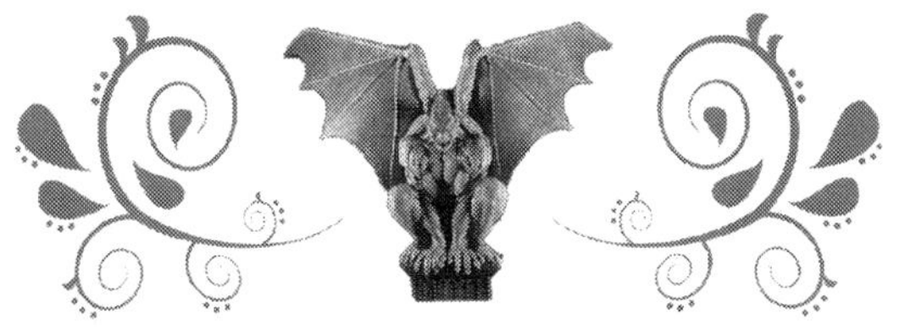

Pastor Bryon Simmons, knowing Jim Sigardson would arrive within a few hours, kept himself busy in his office conducting research on cases similar to that of the Askers, searching internet search engines and other websites trying to help him gain some perspective on what he was up against.

Brent Asker had made it clear to him that this baby could not live, and Brent was afraid that he would do something drastic when the baby was born. Bryon had to do something but he didn't know what he should do. Hopefully Jim would have some sound advice. Bryon was reluctant to involve the Church hierarchy at this stage until after he met with Jim. He wanted to involve as few people as possible for now. Looking at his watch, he saw that he had time to call up the Askers and pay them a visit at the ranch before Jim's arrival. Bryon wanted to meet with them again to see if Brent has softened his stance at all and if Lori was still oblivious as to her condition. Mostly, though, he wanted to see if placing his hands on Lori's stomach would elicit the same response or reaction within him. He needed to be sure. He called Brent at home, but it was Lori who answered. "Good afternoon, Pastor Simmons, how are you?"

The tone of Lori's voice resonated with excitement and joy. Under normal circumstances that would be perfectly normal behavior for anyone about to give birth. Lori's pregnancy was not normal.

"I'm fine, Lori, thank you for asking, but more importantly, how are you feeling? Almost that time, isn't it?" Bryon replied.

"It is, Pastor, and I'm so excited I can't wait. Brent and I were just discussing a 'cowboy' or 'cowgirl' scenario. It was so funny because he knows that if it's a girl that we'll be truly blessed 'cause she'll turn out to be tougher than old Bert ever was!" said Lori, her voice crackling with excitement.

"I am so happy for you both. Speaking of Brent, is he around? Can I speak with him for a minute?"

"He is Pastor we were just finishing up lunch. I will hand the phone over. Take care and we will talk soon."

He was about to tell her that he would be seeing her soon but was unable to, as she handed the phone to Brent before he could say anything more. Then he heard Brent's voice, saying, "Hi, Pastor, what's up?"

"Brent, further to what we were speaking about in my office the other day—and I know you can't say very much with Lori right there beside you—but I was hoping to come out there and sit with Lori once again. I want to see if placing my hands on her belly again will create the same reaction in me that it did the other day in church. Would that be okay?"

He could detect a hint of relief in Brent's voice when he replied, "That should be fine if I can keep her away from the barn. Getting her to take a break for lunch was a chore. See you soon, Pastor."

Pulling up in front of the Askers' modest home twenty-five minutes later, Bryon had that uneasy feeling overcome him once again. The overwhelming feeling of doom and misery spread through his body like a fast-moving virus. It was such an ominous feeling that he found himself hesitating for a brief second before he knocked on the door. As he was about to push the doorbell, the front door swung open, and Lori, smiling from ear to ear, welcomed him inside with a big hug. Her joyful welcome of his arrival was in stark contrast to Brent, who was sitting at the kitchen table with a blank look on his face. "Great to see you again, Pastor. Please, come sit down. Can we get you some iced tea or Coke? How about tea or coffee?" Brent asked.

Bryon looked at Lori, who was standing in front of the fridge waiting for his reply. "A glass of water would be great, Lori, thank you. Thanks for taking the time to see me. I won't keep you long, because I have to get back to the office. I just wanted to see you both one last time before the big day, as I know you are very close. How are you feeling, Lori? I bet you're anxious to get this over with, my dear," said Bryon as Lori joined him and Brent at the table, searching her eyes for any indication of fear or doubt. But he saw none, just a glow of anticipation.

"I feel great, Pastor, I really do. I've had my final checkups with my doctor and everything looks good with the baby, it's just a matter of waiting now. Hopefully not too much longer—maybe even today!" winked Lori, glancing at Brent, who looked glum and gave her a forced smile.

"Brent, how are you doing? How is your shoulder holding up? You know that you need to get that shoulder healed up pretty soon so you can hold your baby. It will go from a few pounds to a hundred pounds before you know it." Bryon teased Brent, but he didn't look like he was in much of a cheerful mood.

"Doing good, Pastor, the shoulder is coming along well. I should be able to slow down the dressing changes to maybe one a day or every few days, as the wound is healing fast now."

"That's great news, Brent. Let's join hands and pray, shall we?" Joining hands, Bryon began, "Heavenly Father, thank you for watching over Brent and Lori as they are about to enter parenthood. Thank you, Lord, for healing Brent's wounds and for ensuring Lori's baby is safe, born in your name, and that the birth will be a wondrous time for them. I ask, Lord, that you deliver a healthy and happy baby for them and that you welcome this new baby into your Kingdom. I pray this in your name, Lord, and in the name of your son Jesus Christ, Amen."

"Do you mind saying a prayer directly to our child, Pastor Simmons?" asked Lori, not waiting for an answer, taking his hands and placing them directly on her exposed belly.

Instantly feeling the dread overtake his insides when his hands were placed on her belly, Bryon closed his eyes to pray. As he was about to speak, an image came into his mind that scared him to his core. It was so real he thought it was actually happening, and maybe it was. A hideous beast with fiery red eyes was coming towards him from a black tunnel. He felt himself wanting to turn and run from this image, but he couldn't move; all he could do was stand there frozen in this nightmare as the beast came closer and closer, raising one of its massive arms with its claw-like talons. The face of this beast was encased in a mask of pure evil, hatred and death. The eyes were like two burning embers in a fire as it thrust its face directly in front of his. Spit was dripping from its gigantic teeth, its black tongue rolling around the inside of its mouth. Then it spoke to him. "You are nothing but a pathetic piece of garbage! You call yourself a Pastor? You don't believe, do you? You never have. You entered the seminary to appease your worthless parents, and you stayed because you were afraid and weak. You were afraid of what your father would think if you quit and left. You are a liar, Simmons! Your whole life is a lie. Stay away from Lori or you will die!" Then the beast clamped his claw around his throat and squeezed. Bryon no longer knew if he was dreaming or if this was real; all he knew was that he was dying. His windpipe was being crushed and the lack of air to his brain was causing him to black out.

Suddenly, out of his blackness, he heard voices. They were faint and in the distance somewhere, but they seemed to be getting louder. Then he recognized the shouts of Lori and Brent. "Pastor Simmons, Pastor Simmons! Wake up! Oh, my God, Brent! What's happening to him!? Brent, do something! I'm calling 911!"

Then Bryon was slowly able to open his eyes and see blurry images of Brent and Lori standing over him, shouting. He realized he was choking, which must have been why Lori was shouting that she was calling for an ambulance. He rolled onto his side to gasp for air. After a minute of wretching, he was finally able to get a steady stream of air into his lungs. With

Brent and Lori's help he got up off of the floor and onto a chair. He told them to cancel the ambulance, that he would be okay.

"Are you sure? What the heck happened to you, Pastor? You scared us out of our minds. One second you were praying for our baby and the next you were on the floor choking," said a frantic Lori, staring at him.

Glancing at Brent to make sure he had called 911 back again to cancel the ambulance, he said to Lori, "I'm fine, Lori, really I am. I'm sorry to have frightened you like that. I experienced a type of seizure that I get from time to time, but it's nothing to worry about. Listen, I must be getting back to the church. I have a meeting that I'll be late for if I don't get going now." Rising from his chair, checking his knees to make sure he was stable enough to walk, he bent down and gave Lori a hug and said, "You get some rest from here on out, do you hear me? No more chores till this baby is born and you've recovered. You take care, and I'll come and see that wonderful new baby in the hospital as soon as I get word."

He left out the front door, still badly shaken from his nightmarish experience. Brent followed him out to his car, opening the driver's door for him. He turned and looked Brent straight in the eye, and his words chilled Brent to the bone.

"Brent, what I just experienced in your kitchen was no seizure. The second I closed my eyes to pray for your unborn child, the demon instantly took control of my mind and with very vivid and powerful detail he described some very private events in my life that no one else knows. I know that sounds crazy, Brent, as it could have been easily described as a bad dream, but trust me when I say this. The threat against Lori and her unborn baby, I believe, is real. We may not be able to stop its birth, but we certainly will stop its existence in time. Have faith, Brent, the Lord God will prevail and strike down this threat. Now I must go. You call me if anything develops with Lori."

Rushing to get back to the church as he did not want to be late for his meeting with Jim Sigardson, Bryon was shaking like a leaf from his experience at the Askers. He was hoping that Jim could help him decide what to do, but Bryon knew he would need to contact the Baptist Church headquarters in Valley Forge. The danger was real; Bryon could feel it in every fiber in his body. He knew he did not have much time, as Lori would give birth any day now.

A few minutes later he was pulling into the parking lot of his church when he saw the church secretary, Mrs. Thorpe, standing in the parking lot in a complete panic.

"Pastor Simmons, please hurry there is an urgent call for you from the State Police! There has been a car accident involving Pastor Sigardson. I put them on hold, as I saw you drive into the lot as I was taking the call. Oh, my God, Pastor, I'm so worried."

"Calm down, Betty, I'll take it from here. Do something for me, please. I need the telephone number for church headquarters in Valley Forge. Please bring it to me in my office as soon as you can," instructed Bryon. This was terrible news, and Bryon ran into the church to his office to take the call.

"Pastor Simmons here. Who am I speaking with?"

"Pastor Simmons, my name is Trooper Jack Scanton of the Wyoming State Police. I'm afraid there has been a terrible accident. Pastor Sigardson, it appears, lost control of his car and left the road, tumbling down an embankment, where his car ignited in flames with him still trapped inside. It is our belief that he was dead upon impact at the bottom of the cliff. I am sorry to have to tell you this. His wife has been notified, and it is through her that we found out he was coming to meet with you this afternoon."

Bryon thought he was going to faint when he heard the news from the trooper. He could feel the nausea coming on and he knew he would be sick. "Excuse me for one second, Officer," he told the trooper on the phone. Turning to his wastebasket, he emptied his stomach into it. Wiping his mouth on his sleeve, he picked up the phone and with a weak voice said, "I cannot believe it. What happened, Officer? Where did it happen?"

Scanton replied, "The accident occurred just outside of Pine Bluffs on State Highway 80 just forty miles east of Cheyenne.

The accident investigators on the scene say it looks like a blown tire forced the vehicle to veer sharply to the right and exit the highway."

"Thank you, officer. I would appreciate if there are any further developments that you would please contact me. I am a close friend of Pastor Sigardson, and his wife is a very good friend of ours. I will call Julia now to see if I can offer any comfort to her."

Hanging up, Bryon knew he had two more important calls he needed to make immediately after he called his wife. One was to Jim's wife Julia and the other to the Baptist head office. Calling his wife Lynn would be hard, but he had no time to drive home and tell her in person. Things were developing too quickly and he needed to move just as quickly. He could not accept that a car accident had claimed Jim's life just a few hours ago. Evil forces knew he was coming to meet Bryon to discuss a strategy regarding Lori & Brent's baby, and he had been killed because of it. Sounded crazy, but he knew one thing for sure. *There are terrible evil forces at work in Cheyenne, and with God's help it will end here.*

He spent the next agonizing hour on the phone speaking with Jim's wife Julia, her agony and despair at the tragic loss of her husband tearing at Bryon's heart like nothing ever before. The shock of his wife Lynn's reaction to the news of the accident was displayed with tears and sobs. After getting control of her emotions, she made immediate plans to go spend a few days with Julia and the kids. The call to Baptist Headquarters in Valley Forge was frustrating to the point where Bryon struggled not to simply hang up the phone.

"Let me get this straight, Bryon. You believe that a pregnant, unmarried woman in your congregation is possessed by the devil. Her child is that of Satan himself. Her boyfriend was brutally attacked by this devil that tore a large chunk of his shoulder off, and he barely survived the attack. You reached out to a colleague, Pastor Sigardson, who was tragically killed in a car accident on the way to meet with you. When you place your hands on the belly of this pregnant girl you have an instant reaction that something horribly evil is inside her. Now, to top it all off, you are claiming you were attacked by Satan when you closed your eyes to pray for the unborn child, leaving you gasping for air. That is quite a story, Pastor Simmons," said a skeptical Assistant to the General Secretary Lillian Genoway.

"I understand how you must feel. I have been a devoted and caring pastor for almost thirty years and I have never encountered anything remotely like this. I have also never felt so strongly about something in my years as a pastor. This young couple is in serious trouble and I am asking for your help. You must have someone in your network that has had some experience in dealing with these matters." replied an exasperated Bryon.

"The General Secretary will return in the morning. I will discuss this with him first thing in the morning, Pastor Simmons. Expect a call from our office tomorrow morning," replied Genoway.

He knew this call was a waste of time as it was obvious AGS Genoway wanted no part of his mess, opting instead to hand it off to her boss. He would wait for the call from the General Secretary tomorrow.

"Thank you, Mrs. Genoway, for your time. I will wait to hear from the General Secretary in the morning," answered Bryon.

Suddenly Bryon felt his cell phone vibrate in his front pocket, and after a few panicked seconds of fumbling, trying to fish it out of his pocket before he lost the call, he saw the caller ID of Brent Asker. Hitting the answer button on his church-issued prehistoric Motorola flip phone, Bryon screamed a little too loudly, thinking if he yelled loudly enough somehow that would prevent the call from dropping. What he did hear at the other end of the phone froze him in his tracks and turned his blood to ice. It was him, the Anti-Christ, on the line, on Brent's cell phone. His voice sounded like death, if that was possible.

"Rounding up the cavalry are you, Minister? Have fun with that. Your Church only knows how to squeeze money from your people, not cast out demons, fool!" It laughed a sound so horrible and monstrous he felt the marrow in his bones begin to freeze.

His mouth turned to dust as he tried to speak. His fear was palpable.

"Who are you? Some mind control freak who can invade people's thoughts to try to scare them? Well, guess what, Kreskin, it isn't working, okay? So take your Vegas sideshow and go haunt some murderers or rapists in some faraway prison and leave the Askers alone!" commanded Bryon.

"Silence, fool! The fun is about to begin. I would suggest you make your way down to the hospital. You wouldn't want to miss the birth of my son, now, would you?" answered the Beast with a guttural voice that could only come from Hell itself.

About to respond, Bryon heard the line go dead, and then suddenly it was vibrating again. It was Brent's number calling again. Answering the phone with an anger coming from a place he had never known existed, he screamed into the phone, "You bastard! I will personally wrap my hands around your throat and choke whatever kind of life flows through your dark soul!"

"Pastor Simmons, its Brent! What is going on? Why are you screaming?"

Exhaling an energy built up inside him that would have blown a brick building down, he quickly gathered himself. "Sorry, Brent, I should have checked the number before I answered, it's been crazy since I left your home. How is everything with Lori?"

"That's why I was calling. Her water broke and we are on the way to the hospital in a few minutes. Lori is just putting together a few things to take with her. She thinks she has all night. I am scared, Pastor, I really am. I'm afraid of what will be born and what it's going to do to Lori and me. I am even more afraid of what I might do."

"Hang in there, Brent. I'm on my way to the hospital and I'll meet you there. This is in God's hands now, Brent. He will not fail us. He will fight this demon just as He always has. His love and grace for you and Lori and your unborn child has not changed. Trust in the Lord now, Brent. I know it's hard, with what you have been through and experienced. I believe there is an evil force at work here, but we have to put our faith in our Lord God and his forsaken Son, Jesus Christ. They will not fail us, Brent. Take Lori now, because she needs your strength more than ever, Brent. Do you hear me?"

"I choose to believe God will intercede, Pastor. I really have no choice. Let's hope He doesn't let us down. Thank you for everything, Pastor Simmons. You have believed in us from the very beginning, and your support has meant so much to me. I will see you soon and with God's blessing it will be a happy event," replied Brent solemnly.

****

Hanging up with Pastor Simmons, Brent turned to head into the bedroom to see where Lori was. Turning the corner into their bedroom, Brent gasped as he saw Lori lying on the bedroom floor unconscious. "Lori, wake up! Wake up! What happened?" he said, more to himself than anything, as Lori was out cold. He gently rolled her onto her back and that is when he noticed the blood. Lots of it. She was bleeding badly from the pregnancy. Panic set in. Frantic, Brent carefully picked her up, knowing he did not have the time to call an ambulance and wait for it to arrive. He needed to take her right now or she would die. His injured shoulder screamed in pain, and with a strength he'd thought he would never experience again, Brent was able to load her into the truck, snapping the seat buckle gently over her lap, then climbed into the truck, fired up the engine and stepped on the gas, kicking up a hail of stone and dust as he sped out the long driveway, making his way onto Interstate 25 and the twenty-minute drive to the Cheyenne Regional Medical Center. His shoulder still screaming in pain, he pushed the speedometer to the floor as he glanced down at Lori, who was not moving. Reaching over with his right hand while maintaining control of the wheel, he checked her pulse on her throat and relief spread over him as the pulse was strong.

Seeing the Interstate 80 East ramp on the way into Cheyenne, Brent began making his way from the middle lanes to the right lane to take the exit. Traffic was relatively light, so he was able to get over quickly and take the ramp. Slowing down to merge onto the Interstate, he glanced out his window to see if there were any cars coming eastbound. Seeing no cars whatsoever, he gunned the accelerator as he began to rocket down Interstate 80. Suddenly, somewhere in his peripheral vision, he caught a glimpse of a truck approaching him, but he couldn't see it. As he returned to focusing on the road ahead, it happened. Out of nowhere a truck came barreling down from what must have been southbound Interstate 25 merging onto westbound Interstate 80 but instead went straight through the one-way only lanes opposite his exit ramp and was headed right for Brent's driver's door. What the hell is this guy doing, thought Brent to himself. Instinctively speeding up to try to avoid impact, Brent knew in that instant that he was going to be creamed and die and likely Lori too. In a split second before the other pickup slammed full force and at full speed into his driver's door, he was able to catch a glimpse of the driver's face. Thinking he would see the frightened face of an out-of-control driver, he instead saw the face of death. The glowing red eyes of the beast, a maniacal smile spreading across its face, stared straight into Brent as if to remind him he was on his way to hell.

Knowing he was a second away from dying, he placed his hand on Lori's head and whispered he loved her, thought of his parents and his brother whom he barely got to know, and then he closed his eyes. The impact killed him instantly sent his truck flying into the ditch flipping over at least eight times. Brent was catapulted from the truck, landing approx 150 feet away from the truck.

Witnesses would later say that the truck that hit the Askers looked as if it was on a suicide mission, targeting their truck intentionally. Upon impact the out-of-control truck would explode like a fire bomb, spewing flames and wreckage all over the scene. What witnesses would never know is that police would never find the body of the driver or anyone else from the vehicle.

****

Arriving at the main entrance of the Cheyenne Regional Medical Center, Pastor Bryon Simmons approached the information desk and identified himself. Bryon informed the clerk that he was there to see the Askers, who would have arrived shortly before he had, and that he was there at their request, as they had asked him, as their pastor, to be present during the birth of their child. Searching his computer screen, the clerk stated that there was no one in the system yet named the Askers so it was likely that they had not arrived yet. She informed Bryon that he could wait in the waiting area and check in a few minutes back at the desk to see if they had arrived. Thanking the clerk, he turned around, concerned. They should have arrived long before he did. Did they get held up? Maybe they went to another hospital? They would not have done that, as this was the closest to them by far and Lori's doctor was here. Bryon silently prayed for their safety.

He looked around for the signs to guide him up to the maternity ward. He was not going to waste any more time. He would be right there when Brent and Lori arrived. Following the signs, Bryon took the elevator up to the third floor to maternity. Walking out of the elevator, he approached the nurses' station and inquired if the Askers had arrived. Looking at Bryon, the nurse asked who he was as there was no one in maternity with that surname. Bryon identified himself as the Askers' church pastor, and explained that they had asked him to be there when the baby is born. As Bryon was saying this, a nurse came rushing out of the glass-walled room behind the nurses' station and briskly advised the nurses talking with Bryon to prepare for a badly injured expectant mother in full labor.

Hearing these words, Bryon took a few steps away from the desk and gasped. His vision blurred as dark shadows raced through his brain. He was losing control and thought he might black out. He knew this monster had gotten to the Askers just like his friend Jim Sigardson. Clearing his head somewhat, trying to regain control of himself, he rushed up to the nurse who had broken the news to the nurses' desk and was now commanding the nursing staff in their preparations.

"Excuse me. I have a question I need to ask you, please?" Bryon asked the nurse.

"I'm sorry, sir, I am a little busy. I have a seriously injured accident victim about to enter my ward. Be patient and we will get to you," she replied.

Reading her name tag, he said, a little more forcefully, "I understand, Trish, but I am a pastor asked to meet a young couple by the name of Brent and Lori Asker who had gone into labor and were making their way to the hospital. It is very important if you can confirm for me the extent of their injuries so I can prepare for comforting this young couple."

Looking into his eyes with hesitation, the nurse said to Bryon, "There has been an automobile accident. The Askers were hit on the Interstate by another driver. Mr. Asker did not survive. Lori is alive—barely. Hopefully long enough to save the baby. I am sorry but I must get back to work." Staggered by this news, Bryon watched the ensuing chaos as nurses and attendants rushed equipment from one room to another, shouts emanating from the nurse named Trish. Then, with a clear focus, Bryon knew what he had to do. He could not allow this baby to be born. The second he saw Lori being wheeled into the surgical room being set up down the hall, he would rush her and kill the baby in her belly before it could ever see the light of day. Feeling his left breast pocket to check that he had his cross, he could feel the lump. He would use the steel cross with a pointed bottom as a dagger to stab the unborn child to death.

Suddenly he heard a commotion behind him. Whirling around, he witnessed chaos in full bloom. Medics from the medivac helicopter emerged from the opening doors of the elevator and were pushing a stretcher, holding onto IV bottles, followed closely by doctors shouting instructions to the waiting nurses.

Bryon could see the motionless body of Lori Asker lying, covered in blood, on the stretcher. Reaching into his coat pocket, he prayed to God for His forgiveness for what he was about to do. He pulled out his cross, thinking of his wife Lynn and his two young daughters. His daughters would grow up only knowing their jailed minister father was a crazed lunatic; he rushed the mob scene coming towards him.

Raising his hand, holding the cross high above his head, now just a few seconds away from reaching Lori and plunging his holy weapon into her belly, killing the demon seed, he could glimpse movement out of the corner of his left eye. It was a security guard. He was raising a weapon and shouting. Bryon could not hear him because he too was shouting. Screaming at the medics to get out of his way, he shoved hard to the floor a doctor who stepped in front of him to try to block his path to Lori. He must have seemed a raving madman to these people, but he didn't care, he just needed to stop them from delivering this baby. He knew he would likely have time for only one strike with his dagger into Lori, so he chose the middle of her stomach, where it swelled the highest, and brought down the steel-pointed cross as hard as he could.

Out of the corner of his eye he saw a flash coming from the hands of that security guard. Just before his hand was about to plunge into Lori's belly he felt a massive punch in the side of his neck that knocked him flying away from the stretcher and against the wall with such force the steel cross flew from his hand. A split second later he realized that it wasn't a punch. The flash he'd seen was from the gun of the security guard. The blood spewing all over the front of him and on the floor was from the gaping hole in his neck. He could see, but did not feel, all of the pairs of rubber-gloved hands that were pressing against the side of his neck, hands of the doctors bending over him with terrified looks on their faces.

As the life began to ebb from him, darkness filling his eyes, the remaining specks of light slipping away, Pastor Bryon Simmons of the Beacon Hill Baptist Church in Cheyenne,

Wyoming died with the knowledge that the last thing he saw was the fiery red eyes and the mocking grin of the security guard.

Chapter 34

Detective Jeremy Cookston of the Metropolitan Police, Homicide and Serious Crime Command, in London, England, sat staring at the boxes and boxes of evidence and reports concerning the murder and brutal assault of Dalton and Ann Lockwood. As lead detective of the case, he had been assigned to gather it all together in an orderly fashion for transport down to the records room in the sub-basement of the headquarters of Scotland Yard. Someday the case might be reopened in the newly formed Cold Case Section, but it would be years before that happened. A strange case, to say the least, he thought to himself. Lots of blood evidence, even eyewitness accounts from the victim herself, Ann Lockwood, but very few leads.

For the first five months, Jeremy had been met with a constant barrage of requests and inquiries from Ms. Lockwood as to the status of the case. Frustrated with police at the lack of arrests in her case, she continued to push the department to investigate the murder of her husband and the assault on her. Then suddenly it stopped. The brutal murder and beheading of Ann's mother in her home seemed to have taken the strength from her completely. She stopped calling constantly, and in fact eventually stopped calling altogether. No more inquiries—nothing. It was as if she had disappeared. Once, a few months earlier, Jeremy had called Ann to let her know that there was nothing new in the case. She acknowledged his call, thanked him for his diligence, and that was it. Very strange indeed, thought Jeremy as he bundled the boxes together in one big stack which he proceeded to wrap with packing tape. Building maintenance would transport the package down to records, where in all likelihood it would never see the light of day again. Jeremy thought he should contact Ann and inform her of the department's decision to mothball the case. He owed her that much. Looking through his contact database on the police investigation software program, he located Ann's number and dialed it. It was answered immediately.

"Good morning, Detective Cookston. Nice to see one of Scotland Yard's finest starting his day bright and early. What gives me the pleasure today?" asked Ann, with not a hint of sarcasm in her voice.

"I hate caller ID, by the way. Sorry to disturb you so early, Ann, but I just wanted to bring you up to speed on the investigation or a lack of," Jeremy stated.

"Oh, really. Do you have any new leads you are working on?"

Thinking this question would have, or even should have, smacked of sarcasm, it surprised him that her tone seemed genuine or even encouraging. "The news is not good, I'm afraid, Ann. The department has decided to close the investigation for good. I am off the case completely, and the only way this case will ever get investigated again is if new evidence emerges. I am sorry, Ann."

"I understand, Detective Cookston. You have done your very best, and for that I am very appreciative."

"The investigation of your mother's murder is still ongoing, Ann, by the same detectives you have spoken with. The department, as you know, considers the murder investigation of your husband Dalton and the assault on you completely unrelated to the murder of your mother."

"Very well, detective. Is that all? I don't mean to be rude, but I must be going. I am expecting a baby any second now, you know," joked Ann.

"My gosh, Ann, I completely forgot. How very rude of me. You must be getting close by now?"

"I wasn't kidding, Detective. I am leaving within the hour for the hospital, as the doctors are going to induce the labor. It's time, Detective. So thank you for calling me for the update, but I must be going."

"If I may, Ann, without sounding intrusive, is your family supporting you? Are they going to be there for you when you have this baby?"

"To answer your question, Detective, the answer is no. They never have through this whole experience, and since my mother's murder I have not heard from my father once."

The sudden change in Ann's tone was not lost on Jeremy. She was bitter. Maybe not so much any-more at the police department, but certainly lacking any support from her family had left her feeling isolated and alone. His heart went out to her.

"That is terrible. How could they be like that? Is there anything that my wife and I can do to help you through this? Anything at all?" asked Jeremy

"No, but thank you for asking, Detective. I have my full-time assistant who takes good care of my needs and is a very good friend as well. I have more money than I could ever spend, so I will manage quite well. Thanks again, Detective."

"Okay, well then, all the best with your baby, and I hope that all goes well, as I am sure it will."

Hanging up the phone with the detective, Ann rose from the couch to see Karen, her long-time assistant/maid/chauffer/nutritionist, to name just a few of her jobs—but most importantly, her best friend—standing with a look of complete impatience on her face.

"Ann, we have to leave, like, now! You are scheduled to give birth in forty-five minutes, girl. I have your suitcase packed and ready to go."

"Karen, they are breaking my water in an hour. It will be hours or maybe even a day before I actually deliver the baby. You need to start using the Digibox to record L.A. Doctors so you'll know these things," teased Ann.

"Yeah, right, like those American TV doctors actually know anything about medicine. Actors that look like male strippers cast as doctors. Only in Hollywood, Ann," shot Karen right back.

"Okay, you win, I'm going. Come on then, let's go, otherwise I'll be waiting on you, and you know what happens when I wait on you, don't you?"

"What? I get a raise?"

"Shut up, you. Let's go," laughed Ann.

After helping her into the Mercedes SUV, Ann buckled herself in as Karen guided the luxury truck into the light mid-morning London traffic towards the Portland Hospital for Women and Children, an expensive private maternity hospital. The drive was about thirty minutes, so they had time to talk, and Karen wanted to know how Ann was feeling—not physically, but emotionally. Her father had tried to hire a live-in 'assistant' right after the attacks on her and Dalton. It was obvious to Ann that her family wanted to hire someone to look after her so they wouldn't have to. She wasn't looking to be 'taken care of.' They thought she needed psychiatric care after her physical wounds healed, but they were wrong. All Ann needed was her family's love and support, but she got neither.

****

Karen felt terrible that she had not been there to protect Ann, but she knew there was nothing she could have done. Ann changed that day; she seemed to have lost her will to fight. She stopped hounding the police on the investigation of Dalton's murder; she even stopped her beloved charity work, something that was her life and that she cherished so much. Ann dropped completely out of the public eye as her pregnancy grew, and she relied on Karen more and more. She even gave her full access to her bank accounts and authorized her lawyers to give Karen power of attorney in all of her personal affairs. She could sign off on virtually anything regarding Ann's finances and personal affairs. It was an authority that she took very seriously and took great care with. She loved Ann as if she were her own sister, and she knew Ann felt the same. They were certainly not lovers as the media portrayed them, and even Ann's family thought they were a couple. They would raise this child together, as Ann had asked her to and she had graciously agreed. Ann was an incredible person, a person who wanted nothing from anyone but wanted to give everything to everyone.

****

Ann had informed her father that she would hire her own assistant, and she contacted a few agencies for a full-time live-in assistant. She had already interviewed seven women when Karen walked into her home. The bond was instant and Ann hired her on the spot. They very quickly became friends, and Ann trusted her right from the start. Watching Karen make her way to the Portland, Ann was amazed at how fortunate she was to have someone like her in her life. She trusted Karen completely. She and Karen had become very close, and Karen had been at her side ever since she'd hired her. Ever since, except for that one horrible day when Ann insisted she take the day off to go shopping. It was the day that her mother was brutally murdered in her home by the beast.

She had not yet told Karen the details of the attacks, or whose baby she was carrying. She was deathly afraid that if Karen knew the truth her life would be in danger. This baby would be born, with Karen's help she would raise it, and when the time was right Ann would do what she knew all along she had to do. This child would die, and she did not care if it cost her own life in the process, but she would not risk putting any more of her or Dalton's family's lives at risk from the terrible curse brought upon her for reasons she would never understand. She did not have a plan yet, but she would soon enough, and then she would strike.

Pulling into the massive complex making up the Portland

Hospital for Woman and Children, Ann felt a sudden and sharp pain in her stomach, causing her to lean over and place her hand on the dash to steady herself.

"Ann, what's the matter? Are you okay? Talk to me!" blurted Karen in a panic tone as she pulled over to the curb just before the parkade.

The pain was becoming more and more intense. These were worse than contractions. The baby was on the move and it was angry. Ann could feel it. It was as if it had felt her thoughts about killing it and had woken up and now it wanted out. "I don't think I'll need to be induced, Karen. It's on its way. Please hurry, the pain is awful!" cried Ann.

Ann gripped the door handle, in part to deal with the sharp pain shooting through her abdomen, but also to keep from flopping onto Karen's lap as Karen maneuvered the truck off the curb and sped towards the emergency entrance around the corner from the parkade. Arriving the wrong way in a one-way lane, Karen slammed on the brakes, causing Ann to pitch forward against her seat belt. Calling out in pain, she yelled, "Jesus! Karen, take it easy!"

Ripping open the door, Karen looked back at her like a panicked mother taking her daughter to emergency.

"Shit, Ann, I'm sorry. Stay there, I'm getting you a wheelchair."

****

Piling out of the truck, Karen noticed a empty wheelchair beside a bench in front of the emergency doors. Running over to grab it, she heard someone yell, "Hey, lady! You can't park like that! Move that truck the hell out of there. You're parked the wrong direction, so you'll have to back it out." A security guard waved his arms, approaching her.

"Save it, wannabe policeman! There is a lady in that truck who is seconds away from giving birth, so if you want to play Dr. Gynecologist and deliver a baby in front of these people and on this road then let's get some hot towels and get started. Otherwise you can help me get her into this chair and into that hospital!"

"Yes, ma'am! Tell me what I need to do," a suddenly cooperative security guard asked.

****

Struggling to stay conscious, Ann was in incredible pain. The baby was pushing hard and she knew it was just a few more minutes before this baby would be born. Lifting her hands up from below her belly, she gasped when she saw them covered in blood. Then her passenger door was yanked open and there was Karen standing there with a security guard beside her gripping a wheelchair.

"Oh, my God, Ann, you're bleeding. We got to get you in there now!" She could feel Karen's hand underneath, and then suddenly she was scooped up and placed in the wheelchair as if she weighed only an ounce. Karen's strength shocked Ann. Through her pain she managed a small smile as she heard Karen rip into the security guard to get moving.

With Karen wheeling her chair towards the automatic opening doors, Ann thought they would crash into them before they opened but at the last second before impact they opened into the chaos of an emergency room. The security guard being screamed at by Karen hustled her past everyone else and down a hallway, where nurses emerged from nowhere and took over from the security guard, pushing Ann into another room full of nurses and doctors prepped and ready, it seemed, for Ann. How could that be, she thought. With rubber-gloved hands coming at her from all directions, she was lifted onto the bed, where a pair of hands with scissors began to cut her maternity pants off while others were cutting her blouse off as well. The room was spinning out of control and Ann thought she was about to faint. Dropping her head to her left, where she could faintly hear Karen still barking out commands, it seemed, she tried to focus through the haze and the incoming darkness clouding her mind. Before her eyes closed completely she saw an image that frightened her like never before, except for one other time. When she was attacked by the beast! She could see Karen staring at her through the maze of nurses and doctors and the flurry of activity. *Her eyes! They are burning bright red!*

Her eyes were closing, and that final image of Karen was too much for her even though she knew she was just dreaming and had already been out cold when she thought she had seen Karen and her demonic eyes burning red. Ann fainted just as the doctor was lifting the crying baby boy into the waiting arms of the nurses.

Out cold, Ann had also missed the gasps of utter amazement from the staff huddled around the infant boy as the cries turned into beautiful melodic sounds that completely silenced everyone else in the room. Everyone was entranced listening to a sound so completely and incredibly beautiful that words could not describe it. The doctor and nurses, their faces still covered in masks, looked at each other, their eyes peering above their masks, reflecting the wonder they were experiencing. The sound of angels singing mixed with the soft cooing of a newborn baby. Then the silence was broken when the nurse holding the baby boy shouted, "Look at this! Look! His birthmark. Have you ever seen anything like this?"

"They look like musical notes!" cried another nurse, clearly overwhelmed by the whole miraculous event taking place in front of them. They gathered around the cooing newborn to witness the mark just inside the right thigh.

Then, just like that, they broke from their stupor and got

busy prepping the baby to take into the nursing room and into an incubator while doctors tended to Ann.

****

Robert Best leaned into the wall in the far corner of the hospital room, completely unnoticed, disguised as Ann's assistant Karen. With his eyes burning scarlet red, he couldn't help but think he had cut it really close with this one. Almost lost this baby, which would have been disastrous. So far, so very good, he thought as he watched them wheel Ann out of the room and into a nearby recovery room. She would be fine, he knew, in a few days. The shock of these events and the sheer miraculous beauty of her baby would lock her in as the caring mother he needed her to be for the next several years.

Chapter 35

Cardinal Kevin Zorn grew up in Rapid City, South Dakota, obtained his Masters degree in Theology at the University of North Dakota and graduated from the Cardinal Muench Seminary School in Fargo. He entered the priesthood at the ripe age of twenty-seven. Never in his wildest dreams had he ever thought he would end up assigned full-time to the Vatican in Rome, but his elevation to the position of Cardinal in charge of the Special Office for Spiritual Longevity, or SOSL, of the Roman curia as it came to be known and pronounced (sossil, like fossil) was no surprise to anyone else, as he has been a part of the office since its beginnings almost thirty-two years earlier.

Over the decades, since its inception, SOSL had evolved, to say the least. Originally the task force was named 'Paratus,' which meant 'preparation' in Latin, and was put together to track world catastrophes to see if there was a pattern developing that could be linked to the Biblical end times as described in the Book of Revelations. The Vatican, following the word of the Bible, wanted to make sure that as an institution they were prepared for this eventuality and that the billions of Catholics around the world would be spiritually prepared for these events if they were ever to occur.

Paratus was originally headed by Father Zacharias, who unfortunately passed away suddenly just eighteen months after the first meeting. The next most senior cleric, Father Giroux, took on the leadership of the committee, with a replacement chosen from London, a Father David Beckstead, taking the place of Father Giroux. Father Beckstead would eventually pass over the leadership of Paratus to Kevin, as time commitments elsewhere dictated that he step aside. Father Beckstead would remain on the committee as a very valuable member. Also on the original committee were Father Penterin and Father Walchuk, both of whom had passed away over the years and been replaced. The final original member was, of course, Father O'Sullivan of Ireland, whom Kevin had grown quite close to. Together they had chartered the protocol for the Church to follow if there were to ever come a time when God revealed his plan for mankind, with a devastating Judgment Day and an eventual new Kingdom on Earth led by his blessed Son, Jesus Christ.

Kevin would welcome the committee of five priests set to begin arriving at the Vatican in the morning for a busy three-day conference. The recent proliferation of violent government crackdowns on protesters in Middle Eastern countries, led by the evil Saddam Hussein of Iraq and the outbreaks in Lebanon with the Hezbollah was a key sign prophesied in the Book of Revelations. The level of unrest in the Middle East was at an all-time high, the financial markets in the US and around the world were in chaos, and the emergence of China, India and Brazil as economic superpowers had the Vatican concerned. The Pope, through the Roman Curia, had requested an updated report on the Vatican's preparedness for the Biblical doomsday that others in the Vatican believed was soon to come; Kevin had called the committee together just eighteen months after their last conference.

Father O'Sullivan, at Kevin's urging was arriving today on a direct flight from Dublin at approximately 5:00 p.m., when Kevin would pick him up personally. Kevin wanted time to meet alone with this trusted and loyal friend and very wise priest before the other members arrived to get his take on the current conditions around the world. When he had spoken with him on the phone last week to see if he would come a day earlier than the rest, Thomas was quite reluctant to do so, citing personal matters requiring his attention. It was only a few days ago that Kevin had received a call from Thomas informing him that he had changed his flight and would be able to join him a day earlier after all, as there were pressing matters that he needed to speak with Kevin about as well. That caught Kevin a little off guard, but he chose not to press Thomas on the subject over the phone, getting a sense from him that it would be better left till they met.

Kevin kept busy the rest of the day before he needed to take off for the Leonardo da Vinci Airport later in the afternoon. Keeping his assistant busy putting together the material packages that he had prepared for the conference, Kevin felt that he was as ready as he could be. Once the conference ended, he would have to prepare a detailed and lengthy report for the Prefect that would be used by the Church as its protocol for implementing plans to prepare its Catholic parishioners around the globe for the return of the King, Jesus Christ. Pretty heady stuff, he thought, but then again it involved a subject that was essentially subjective. Only the Vatican would put resources into preparing for this unlikely event, but then again when you were head of an institution with 6.5 billion members you had to be prepared for all eventualities. No one was more prepared when it came to its own affairs than the Vatican and the Catholic Church. If anything had ever come close to challenging that assertion, it was the scandals involving sex-starved pedophile priests that had ravaged the Church around the world. The reputation of the Church had been severely damaged and the cost of settling the lawsuits was staggering. Pope John Paul ll vowed to stamp out the flames of this ever-burning scandal against his beloved Church if he had to stamp them out with his own feet.

The packets that Kevin had put together meticulously and chronologically covered all of the world's natural disasters, the severity of the damage, the economic impact, the political fallout, and any patterns that were developing, including the where, why and when that would identify global regions that seemed to be affected most.

The information in the packets included the recent riots that seemed to be plaguing the Middle East, as well as detailed breakdowns of the governments and the control they exerted on their respective societies. The social and economic impacts of these uprisings could trigger a domino effect on surrounding countries and regions around the world.

The key to the conference would be for all of them to break it down, look for underlying patterns that were emerging, including the social and economic impact of the aid required to save the starving nations in Africa and other impoverished countries around the. With the exception of Father O'Sullivan and himself, the other four members of SOSL held economic degrees, including Father Beckstead, who was a PhD in Economics and also held a Doctorate in Political Science. Father Beckstead had published several books on the subject of the economic and political impact of natural disasters on societies.

Another disturbing trend gathering momentum around the world was a dramatic increase in demonic happenings, which included demon possessions, unexplained supernatural events, a global increase in devil worship and black magic, and a tenfold increase in the number of the Catholic Church's official exorcisms. Murder and mayhem were on the rise around the world, an alarming trend that could be an indicator of mankind's shift away from mainstream Christianity and embrace of alternative religions or outright movement away from any sort of religion. Satan had certainly made inroads around the world, thought Kevin. What was he up to?

Before leaving for the airport, Kevin took some time for prayer. He instructed his assistant not to allow him to be disturbed. Kevin stood in front of his office windows in the Palace of the Governorate of Vatican City State, on the second floor with a beautiful view of the exquisitely manicured lawns of the Vatican's government offices. Through his prayers he asked God for the wisdom he needed to lead this group of men committed to Him and the job they had been tasked with. He asked God for clarity, for that ability to see what He wanted him to see. After a few more minutes of prayer, Kevin opened his eyes, checked his watch and realized that he needed to leave to pick-up Father O'Sullivan.

His assistant had a car and a driver ready to take Kevin to the airport. On the thirty-five-kilometer drive over to the Fiumicino, he reflected back on his relationship with Thomas over the years and how much he had come to rely on his judgment and advice in regard to SOSL. His friend's background in psychology had given him great insight into the human psyche, why people do certain things and react differently in various situations and how religion, culture and politics play a role in people's reactions. Thomas had published many articles over the years on these subjects, earning him great praise amongst his peers. His leadership and wisdom as a teaching and healing priest had earned him high praise here in Rome. Kevin knew that Thomas was seriously being considered for a position at the Roman Curia, but he also knew his friend would resist such an appointment, as his heart was amongst the people, his Church in Balbriggan, his Ireland that he loved and cherished so much.

The shock and horror almost a year ago of the vicious and brutal killing of an entire family in his parish, leaving behind a pregnant widow, had devastated Thomas. Kevin had personally visited Thomas in Ireland after the tragedy, helping him and his church recover. Having a Cardinal from the Vatican come to their small church outside of Dublin seemed to the lift the spirits of the folk of that small town who had been affected so greatly by those terrible murders. The healing of the spirits of Balbriggan seemed also to lift Thomas's spirits, and he forged on, leading his church with more fervor than ever before. That visit and show of support by Kevin seemed to bond the two of them like brothers, as now they both knew they could rely on each other. Thomas was troubled about this trip, Kevin could tell. Nothing had been said directly when they spoke on the phone, but he sensed that a feeling of dread and gloom was enveloping Thomas, and he hoped, with God's help, to lift the burden weighing his friend down.

Arriving at the airport, the driver pulled the large black sedan with its tinted black windows and distinctive Vatican City State license plate into a special parking area in Arrivals reserved for the fleet of Vatican vehicles that were constantly coming to and going from the Fiumicino, or the Leonardo da Vinci Airport as it was now called. Kevin preferred to call it by its original name, easier to pronounce, and he was also not a big fan of da Vinci. As a Cardinal he would never say so publicly, but he felt there was a lot more that was not known about the great Da Vinci than was known, and it was not flattering. His reputation as a great artist, inventor, theorist and scientist would be greatly tarnished if the general public knew the real truth behind the legend. Not his problem to worry about, he reminded himself.

He preferred that his driver wade into the sea of people jammed into the airport to retrieve Thomas, as the sight of a Vatican Cardinal always drew a crowd of curious tourists, and attention was something that Kevin wanted to avoid. Even wearing his non-formal red vestment with the ever-present scarlet zucchetto on his head, Kevin would have still drawn a crowd of onlookers.

Almost twenty minutes would pass before Thomas emerged from the automatic doors exiting the terminal. With the driver carrying his bag and opening the car door for Thomas, he crawled into the back seat, greeting a smiling Kevin with a warm hug.

"So great to see you again, Thomas. How was your flight?" asked Kevin.

One of the few people Kevin allowed to address him by his first name, but only in private, was Thomas, who replied, "Uneventful and boring. No turbulence, very smooth flight. Just the way I like it, allows me to sleep like a baby, but unfortunately, sleep is not something I get much of anymore, Kevin," replied Thomas in his thick Irish brogue.

Clearly, Thomas was troubled, and Kevin quickly dispelled pleasantries and asked, "My friend, tell me what is the matter. You are not well. Your heart is heavy, why is that?"

When Thomas did not immediately answer his question, he sensed his need for privacy and said, "Let's wait and talk when we arrive back at the Curia, shall we?"

The ride back was quicker than the ride to the airport, as traffic was much lighter. They exchanged small pleasantries to fill the gaps of silence as they drove through the early evening traffic. Soon they arrived at the Vatican, and they walked in silence as they made their way up to Kevin's office. His assistant was waiting for them, and after welcoming Thomas, he placed a tray of tea and biscuits on the conference table for them and then left.

Kevin poured them each a cup of tea, and then placed the teapot back on the tray. Looking up into Thomas's eyes, before he spoke he could see that Thomas was deeply concerned. He had never seen him like this before.

"Are you hungry, Thomas? I can have a plate of hot roast beef and potatoes, your favorite, brought up. It's on the menu in the cafeteria so it will only take a minute."

Kevin noticed for the first time deep creases on Thomas's forehead. The creases furrowed when he spoke.

"No thanks, Kevin. We must talk. There is much I need to share with you."

"What is bothering you, my friend? How is that poor McCloskey girl? She is to have her baby soon, is she not?"

Thomas returned his cup back to its saucer, paused longer than he normally would have, and continued.

"That is what I need to talk to you about. There are many things I have not told you, but it's important that you know everything."

"Certainly, Thomas. Please speak freely, my friend."

"How long have we known each other, Kevin?" asked Thomas.

"Almost thirty-two years, Thomas. Why would you ask that?"

"Do you remember our very first encounter? You picked me up at the airport, here in Rome, before our very first SOSL conference."

"I most certainly do, Thomas. We were both so young at the time," reflected Kevin.

"Do you remember my strange encounter with Robert Best, the American businessman when I was deplaning, as well as by the luggage carousel?"

"I do, Thomas, that was very spooky indeed. What makes you bring that up after all these years?"

Kevin observed Thomas as he sat straight back in his seat, took in a deep breath and looked directly back at him with a stare that reflected not only the troubled look he had noticed since Thomas arrived, but something more. Fear.

"Robert Best is the devil, Kevin. He is Satan himself and he is on this earth in human form because he has a plan for mankind. I know that plan is for our total destruction, Kevin."

"That is quite a statement, Thomas. I believe you when you tell me Robert Best is demonic. What makes you think he is Satan disguised as an American businessman out to destroy mankind?" asked Kevin.

So for the next two hours Thomas told Kevin of his encounters with Best, from those so many years ago in Rome, the recent attacks on the McClosky's and Katherine McCloskey's claim that they were attacked by Satan himself and her brutal rape by the beast, to Thomas's strange experience in the hospital bathroom when he went to see Katherine when she was first brought in to the hospital right after the attacks. Then to the more recent encounter with Best once again in the elevator at the hospital on the way to see Katherine, who was about to give birth to what she claimed was the child of the devil. It was the telling of the birth of the McCloskey baby and its strange birthmark that convinced Kevin for certain that Satan indeed was planning something and that it involved Thomas and Katherine somehow. They both agreed on that, but neither of them could understand why.

"I believe my involvement with SOSL is part of this, Kevin. Best made direct reference to it during that first encounter when he said he knew why I had been summoned to the Vatican. I just don't understand how that ties into the attack on Katherine McCloskey."

"What will you do next with Katherine and the baby? They must be protected," said Kevin.

Thomas's next statement shocked Kevin.

"Katherine did not survive the birth of her baby, Kevin. I believe Best made sure she did not survive. He was there in the room when Katherine was giving birth, masquerading as one of the doctors".

"Good heavens! That must have been awful for you to witness, Thomas!"

"When I saw poor Katherine losing her fight to survive and then Best standing in the corner with a smirk on his face, I lost it, Kevin. I rushed him right in the room and attacked him. I was pounding him, blood all over my hands, and he just stared at me and laughed. Then the most incredible sound you could ever imagine erupted in the room. It was like a chorus of angels sent from the heavens. It was Katherine's baby girl singing right after birth. Instead of the sound of a baby's cries it was the sound of angels singing! I was completely stunned and gravitated to the sound, forgetting about Best completely. The whole hospital room was stunned into silence. Then one of the nurses broke the silence and cried out that the baby had an unusual birthmark. I turned to see the reaction of Best, but he had disappeared."

"This is incredible, Thomas!" exclaimed Kevin. "What was the birthmark?"

"I was shaking with exuberance at the intervention of God's will, Kevin. How He had saved this baby from Satan himself. Cast Best out of the hospital and saved the baby from him. However, I was shown the birthmark, and that all changed," explained Thomas.

"What did you see, Thomas?"

"The nurse had cried out that the birthmark was three musical notes—a sign from God—and it made such perfect sense with the beautiful sound emanating from the baby. When I saw the birthmark I knew we had been fooled. It was no mark of three musical notes, like some miracle, but instead it was the Mark of the Beast, Kevin. Three sixes, like 666, only backwards!"

The inside of Kevin's mouth went dry, and he struggled to get the moisture back on his tongue so he could ask Thomas.

"Where is the baby now, Thomas?"

"She is in the care of the hospital staff at this moment. I am thinking of placing the baby in the care of the Church at St. Brigid's Orphanage in Dublin for now."

"Good, Thomas, do that. Caring for this baby until we know more about what we are dealing with is the right thing to do. Are there any family of Grew's or Katherine's who would oppose the adoption by the Church?"

"Only Katherine's parents and they are obviously grieving for the loss of their daughter but are understanding of the baby being placed in the care of the Church."

"Okay, let me know if there are any problems, Thomas. Otherwise we will use some influence from Rome to make this happen. We must keep this baby in our care, where she can be watched at all times. Do you know what name the baby will be called?"

"Katherine's parents asked that she be called Chloe, so that is her name. It was the name given to Katherine's older sister who died at birth. I will keep you informed, Kevin, and if you will allow it I would prefer to skip this conference and get back to Dublin at once. There is a lot for me to do."

"Certainly, Thomas, I understand. A full report of our conference will be sent to you for your perusal and feedback. These events in Dublin lend credence to the Church's theory that the Judgment Day will indeed happen in this generation. Do you agree?"

"Satan's attack on Katherine and his interest in me certainly make for an unusual connection that mystifies me. Hopefully prayer will clear the mist soon enough."

Rising from his chair, Kevin embraced Thomas, then kept his left hand on his shoulder, squeezing it as a gesture of support.

"Thomas, you are a very wise and exceptional teacher of

God's will. His truth will prevail and reveal itself. Embrace prayer as never before, Thomas. God will speak to you and He will use you. Now go, my friend, and God bless. Please keep me informed."

Chapter 36

Detective Sam Showenstein glanced at his watch, noticing that if he didn't get away from the office in the next five minutes he would be late picking up his deceased partner's wife Chelsea Benning at her home, and he did not want that to happen. Chelsea, nine months pregnant and about to give birth at any minute, would likely tear a strip off of Sam for being late. Sam had insisted that he drive Chelsea to the hospital today, as her doctors had decided that if she had not gone into labor by now they would induce her.

Chelsea Benning was a fighter, as she'd showed in spades while fighting for her life after the brutal attack and rape that had left her clinging to life and had killed her husband Steven, Sam's partner in the LAPD. Assigned as the lead investigator of the attacks plus the murder of Carruthers boy, Sam had hit a brick wall in the investigation. Despite a ton of blood and tissue samples from the attacker, the crime lab was unable to find a DNA match. Without it the investigation had stalled, as there were no other leads whatsoever. No witnesses at the crime scenes, either at the home of the Benning's or the area where the body of Graham Carruthers was discovered. No motive for the attacks. Robbery was ruled out in the Benning attack as nothing was missing from the home. The only lead was the eyewitness account by Chelsea, who admitted to Sam in the hospital right after the attack that it was a demonic beast who had attacked and raped her and killed Steven. It was an incredibly bizarre account, but Chelsea stuck to that story throughout her recovery and hounded Sam relentlessly to follow this theory.

As the investigation slowed to a crawl from a lack of leads, Chelsea's almost daily phone calls demanding updates on the investigation suddenly stopped, as if it suddenly didn't matter to her anymore. Sam found this very strange indeed, until he realized that Chelsea had refocused her energies on the pregnancy and the well-being of her baby growing inside her. It seemed she had accepted her fate and her grief over the loss of Steven and instead looked forward to the birth of her baby. She never again mentioned the bizarre details of being attacked by a demonic beast. It was as if it had never happened. In a way that was a good thing; it meant she was ready to move on from the attacks and focus on her and Steven's baby.

Sam and his wife Bethany had given birth to a healthy baby boy nearly three months ago whom they named Sebastian. It normally would have been such a joyous occasion, but their joy was tempered somewhat by the tragic loss of their friend Steven, and Chelsea being pregnant and widowed. Chelsea and Bethany rarely ever got together anymore, especially since the birth of Sebastian. Bethany figured Chelsea was not yet ready to see her and Sam together with their baby, so she did not want to push it. They would wait till Chelsea had her baby and was ready to move forward with their friendship once again.

Through it all, however, Chelsea had never lost her edgy personality. Though they never spoke about the attacks or the demonic beast anymore, she was still as feisty as ever when it came to being on time, laughed Sam to himself as he gunned it down the freeway towards Arcadia and the Benning home. Sam and Bethany stopped in on Chelsea at home frequently since the attacks, but Bethany had eventually stopped coming, as her pregnancy made Chelsea uncomfortable. Sam would stop in for a coffee from time to time when he was in the area or would pick Chelsea up when she needed to get to an appointment. When Chelsea was still focused on the investigation she would grill Sam as if he was the perpetrator. Now she just grilled him about tardiness, his dress and his messy squad car. She is a rock of a woman, thought Sam, with all she has been through these past nine months and now having to give birth to her murdered husband's baby alone. It was the hope of Sam and Bethany that this child would bring peace and comfort to her life, new meaning for her that she would embrace.

Pulling into the driveway of the modest Benning home ten minutes late, Sam saw her bags sitting on the front step, which meant she was pissed. It was a sign that he was late. She had to set the bags on the step in order to make up for lost time, even though it likely only saved about thirty seconds. He was out of the car and approaching the steps when the front door swung open and Chelsea emerged, looking radiant and beautiful for a woman about to give birth.

"You're late, Showenstein, as usual. Even though I expect you to be late it still pisses me off. How does Bethany put up with it, huh? I'd kick your ass to the curb if you were my husband," deadpanned Chelsea, rolling her eyes at Sam while he heaved her heavy suitcases off the step.

"Holy shit, Chelsea, you carried these onto the step? Are you crazy? They must be fifty pounds each! You're less than two hours away from giving birth and you're pretending you're working in a warehouse stacking fifty-pound bags! Jeepers, girl!" scolded Sam.

"Save the speech, little brother. I had my neighbor Russ across the street come over and help me carry them out. Knowing you, I figured I was likely looking at taking a cab," winked Chelsea. "Come here, you, give me a damn hug. Thank you, Sam, for doing this, for taking me to the hospital. You and Beth have been such true friends I can't thank you enough," a teary-eyed Chelsea cried into Sam's shoulder.

Gently shifting Chelsea off his shoulder to face him, Sam looked her in the eyes and said, "We love you, Chelsea, very much. You are our best friend, and we will always be here for you no matter what. Do you understand me? You've been to hell and back, Chelsea, and it's too much for you, do you know what I mean? Lean on us; let us help you through this and your new baby, okay?"

Using her free hand, she wiped the tears that had run down her cheeks and threatened to smudge her mascara.

"I will, Sam, I promise. I'm sorry I wasn't there for Beth during the birth of Sebastian, you know. I feel bad that I haven't spent more time with her."

"Forget it, Chelsea. Beth knows that you needed space to deal with all that's happened. She loves you and can't wait to cruise the malls with you, sipping a latte and pushing your strollers!"

Her radiance returned as she beamed her beautiful smile.

"You tell her I'm on for that! Now we'd better get moving, Detective, otherwise I'll make you explain to my doctor why we're late and you think I'm cranky! You ain't seen anything yet," laughed Chelsea as she took Sam's helping hand into his unmarked black Dodge Intrepid.

Sam pulled the car out into traffic after they exited Chelsea's subdivision; with the Methodist Hospital just a few minutes' drive away. Chelsea easily could have cabbed it the short distance to the hospital, but Sam insisted that he be there during the birth of her baby, along with Beth who would arrive as soon as she finished feeding Sebastian, getting him dressed and into the truck for the forty-five minute ride to Methodist.

****

As Sam guided the unmarked police cruiser to Methodist, Chelsea was mentally freaking out. She did not know what to expect when she gave birth to the child of the monster that had raped her. Would the baby be normal? Or would it be some little scaly monster with fangs? Would she even survive the birth? Having Sam and Beth with her at the hospital was comforting and took some of her fear away.

She and Steven had never been a deeply religious couple, but they certainly considered themselves Christians. The beast might be the father of her baby, but in her heart Chelsea knew that God had chosen this path for her and there was a reason for all of this happening to her. She was determined to stay strong and have this baby and raise it with love till God revealed His purpose for her.

****

Soon Sam was pulling into the parkade of the massive, state-of-the-art medical complex. Seeing the hospital again where Chelsea had fought for her life, and having her right beside him now, going back in to have a baby, brought on an eerie feeling. Looking over at Chelsea he asked, "How are you doing? Everything okay, Chelsea?"

Staring out the windshield in front of her Sam could see her reflection as she spoke.

"Just thinking of Steven and how excited he would have been right now if it was him driving me to the hospital. He really wanted to have a kid. If this baby is a son I will name him Patrick, after Steven's father. He truly was a great man, and Steven would have wanted to name his first son after his father. So that is what I will do to honor my husband. His name will be Patrick Steven Benning. Not sure what I will name the baby if it's a girl. Just always took for granted I'd have a boy."

"That's a wonderful idea, Chelsea. Steven would be very proud. Knowing you, Chelsea, it would just make sense that you have a boy today," said Sam as he climbed out of the car toward the passenger side to get Chelsea out.

Reaching for his hand, she shot back at him, "I know what you were implying, smarty pants. Don't get it in your head, by the way, that when I have this baby I'll become all soft and gooey towards you cops. Post partum can be a bitch!" Chelsea laughed as they headed into the hospital and made their way to the admitting desk.

****

After getting instructions from the admitting desk clerk, Sam and Chelsea made their way to fifth floor maternity, where a pleasant nurse by the name of Janet took Chelsea's information. When Janet asked Chelsea if Sam was her husband, she replied, "No, no, just a family friend," smiling at Sam as she said it. Spotting a look in the Janet's eyes that screamed, "He is your adulterous lover, stupid!" Chelsea put the nurse in her place when she said, "My husband was an LAPD Homicide Detective who was murdered and torn to pieces. This gentleman was his partner."

Janet stared at Chelsea for a few seconds with a look of shock on her face, then just sheepishly said, "I am so sorry, Mrs. Benning. Please follow me to your room." Once they were in the room, she turned to Chelsea, handed her a hospital gown and said, "Please change into the gown, Mrs. Benning. You can use that closet over by the washroom to hang your clothes and place your belongings. Your doctor will be in shortly to see you." As she turned to leave, Chelsea touched her arm and said, "Janet I'm sorry I snapped at you. It's been a rough few months. Thank you for getting me into my room so quickly. And please, call me Chelsea."

Smiling, Janet looked back at her and said, "Thank you, Chelsea, and I do apologize if I implied in any way. I remember now the story of what happened to you and your husband. I am very sorry to hear about your loss." Looking down at Chelsea's stomach, she continued, "I think your life is about to change for the better, my dear. We will take good care of you. Now you get comfortable in that bed and the doctor will be around shortly."

****

Stepping outside into the hallway while Chelsea changed in the bathroom, Sam quickly called Beth to see where she was at; looking around to make sure no staff were aware of him breaking hospital protocol. Beth answered, and he asked her, "Where are you at, honey? Chelsea is all checked in and waiting for the doctor to come around and get everything started."

"Just pulling into the parkade as we speak. I will be there in a jiffy. What floor and room are you in?"

"Maternity. Fifth floor, Room 506. See you soon."

Just as Sam was closing the flip cover of his Motorola 650 cell phone to end the call, he heard a scream come from within the room—"SAAMM!!"

Rushing back into the room, he found Chelsea naked on the bathroom floor bleeding profusely from her vaginal area.

"Oh, my God, Chelsea, you're bleeding!"

Sprawled on the floor, bleeding profusely and in pain, her toughness remained intact.

"No shit, Sherlock. Get the nurses. Now! Hurry! I am having this baby right here, right now, in the next thirty seconds!" she yelled.

He alerted the nurses as he ran down the hallway. There was a flurry of activity as nurses and doctors rushed into Chelsea's room. He thought he heard Code Blue being announced over the PA and for Dr. Jeffrey Burkett to come to Room 506 for an emergency. Sam panicked as he tried to get back into Chelsea's room but was blocked by nurses. He heard the nurse named Janet shouting in a loud but controlled voice, "She is breached. There is no time. We are delivering this baby now."

Suddenly a doctor appeared behind Sam, pushing past him and into the room. He heard Janet call out his name, "Dr. Burkett, she is in full labor. There is no time to move her into the delivery room."

Sam's heart was beating so fast in his chest, he felt it would explode. He watched as Dr. Burkett shouted, "Get me clean towels now and some hot water! She has lost a lot of blood. We may need a transfusion. I need IV pronto!" Sam turned and quietly entered the bathroom to try to catch a glimpse of what was happening. He could hear everything, however. The room was in full chaos. Equipment was being rushed past him, everyone shouting commands. He strained to try to see Chelsea above all the heads of the nurses. Coming around a corner on the opposite side of the room was Dr. Burkett. Sam watched as nurses were pulling gloves onto the doctor's hands. There was far too much commotion amongst the doctors and nurses. Chelsea and the baby were in real trouble. He could feel it.

Through the sea of moving bodies, Dr. Burkett suddenly turned towards Sam and looked directly at him. The room suddenly melted away, with just Dr. Burkett remaining, his eyes locked on Sam's. Sam knew he was about to faint, but before he collapsed to the floor, he could see that the doctor's eyes had turned a bright crimson red as he continued to stare at Sam. They burrowed into him for what seemed like an eternity but was actually only a split second. Sam was not even sure what he had seen, but it jolted him back to reality. Looking back toward the doctor, he realized he was no longer there. He was gone, back into the wave of bodies moving about. *Those eyes!* He couldn't get that image out of his head. It was probably the reflection of some lights emanating from the medical equipment in the room. Didn't matter anyway. He waited to hear what was going on, and then he heard the nurse Janet yell, "Look at this birthmark, Dr. Burkett! It's the strangest thing."

Suddenly, out of nowhere, a gurney with an IV stand came whipping by Sam and into the room. Feeling his shirt sleeve being pulled aggressively, he first thought it had got caught on the gurney as it rushed by, but then realized it was his wife, Bethany, standing beside him, holding the baby seat with Sebastian in it sound asleep. Beth, with panicked eyes staring up at Sam, said, "What the hell is going on, Sam?"

He gathered himself to explain the events to Bethany, knowing it would likely send her into a panic.

"Chelsea all of a sudden collapsed when I stepped out of her room to call you. She was bleeding profusely, yelling at me to get the nurses because she was having her baby. It was crazy. Then I heard the nurse call out about the strange birthm..." Sam didn't get to finish the sentence because suddenly there was a sound that took the breath away from everyone. The sound of a choir of heavenly angels singing. The most beautiful sound Sam had ever heard. There was no sounds of a baby crying, just soft sounds of cooing interspersed by sounds of singing. He heard a nearby nurse whisper, "It is a miracle baby. It's like the birth of Jesus. This room is his Manger."

Then he heard Chelsea sobbing uncontrollably, then cry out, "Patrick, you are an angel sent from heaven! My beautiful little angel!" Sam could then hear Dr. Burkett issuing orders, and the group of nurses crowding around the entrance to the room quickly filed out past Sam and Beth into the hallway as the gurney with Chelsea emerged from the room, being pushed by Dr. Burkett, closely followed by the Nurse Janet, who was cradling Chelsea's baby. The baby was still cooing and singing just loud enough to be heard. Seeing Sam and Beth, Chelsea cried out to them as she was being led away, "It's a boy, Sam! It's Patrick! It is a miracle from God!"

Then just like that she was gone down the hallway with the two of them left standing there as the group of doctors and nurses followed the hospital bed with the miracle baby. As the entourage was about to turn the corner and out of sight, Dr. Burkett, still pushing Chelsea, turned at the last second, and looked back at Sam with eyes so crimson red he would have seen them a block away. Cold chills went up and down Sam's spine. Sam looked over at Beth, who was also staring down the hallway at the now-disappeared group and asked, "Did you see the eyes of that doctor pushing Chelsea when he looked back at us just before he turned the corner?"

Still staring down the empty hallway, Beth, still stunned at what she just witnessed, replied, with a confused look on her face, "No, I didn't. What are you talking about?"

An incredulous Sam looked at Beth and shouted, "You never saw that?! How could you have missed those eyes? I would have seen them from the parking lot outside!"

"Sam, calm the hell down and tell me what you are talking about. What eyes, whose eyes are you talking about, and what does it have to do with anything? Chelsea just delivered a healthy baby boy, stupid!"

A frightened and confused Sam looked over at Beth and said, "Sorry, sweetheart, I'm just overreacting to the situation that just happened. Forget it. Let's just get over to the nurses' desk and see what's going on."

Reaching down, he plucked Sebastian's baby seat's handle from Beth, then grabbed her hand and led her down the hallway.

Chapter 37

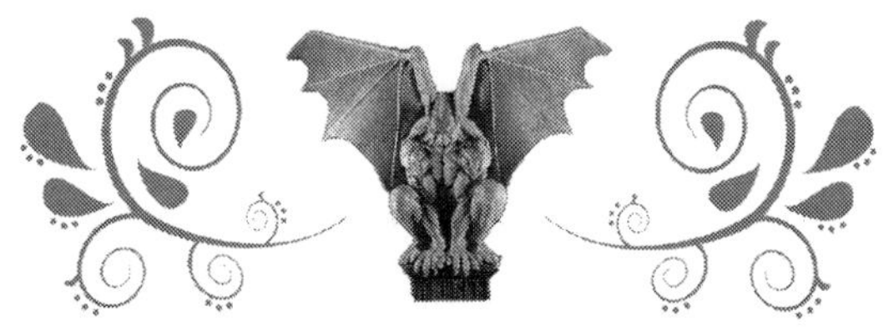

Marie Jimenez had risen to the top of the company secretarial pool through sheer hard work, commitment and the fact she was very good at what she did. It was for this reason that Marie was promoted to Executive Assistant to Antonio José Escalona, VP of Exploration for Heavy Oil at Petróleos de Venezuela, S.A., Venezuela's state-owned oil conglomerate with its head office in Caracas. Her promotion was widely scorned among the company office staff as a lot of more experienced women with longer years in the company had been bypassed in favor of Marie. That soon changed when it became known that the child singing sensation everyone in Venezuela was talking about from the hit TV talent show "Cuanto Vale El Show" was Marie's twelve-year-old son Juan.

Venezuela's version of "America's Got Talent" was the biggest TV show of the year, and the young, cute, extremely talented Juan Jimenez was all the rage. Marie worked long hours and came in on weekends in order to take the time off she needed to take Juan to the studio for rehearsals and the taping of the show. Juan was recognized everywhere, so eventually they had to pick and choose where they would go. Mobs of tween-aged girls would flock to movie theatres or malls if they knew that Juan would be there. It was a surreal experience for both of them. Hopefully things would die down once the show had finished up and people got on with their lives. Marie, with her increased salary from her new position at Petróleos de Venezuela, considered enrolling Juan in a private Catholic school in the fall if his popularity continued.

She was not surprised by Juan's talent; he had been singing since he was in diapers. His beautiful tone was evident right from the beginning, and as he grew it only became more beautiful. Marie would never forget the day when it really hit her just how talented her son really was. Her realization came from the reaction of the people who heard him sing in church when he was just seven years old. At the time Juan was just this cute little boy standing amongst all of the adults in the church choir with his tiny voice blended in with the chorus of the other dozen or so choir singers. That all changed when Father Guerrero arranged a piece wherein Juan would do a solo in one of the choir's hymns. He probably thought it would be cute to have this little boy step forward from the choir and sing the chorus of the song solo. What he didn't expect— nor did anyone else in that church, except Marie, who heard Juan sing all day long every day at home—was this little boy stepping forward in his long flowing robes, opening his mouth and beginning to sing a most beautiful chorus that filled the church. The congregation were speechless, transfixed by this boy with the most incredible voice. Some were moved to tears. From that point forward Juan was a regular solo singer in church. His popularity was such that church membership almost doubled, with members from other nearby Catholic parishes flocking to the Sunday service at Parroquia Dulce Nombre de Jesus, in the eastern area of Caracas known as Petare, in the hope that they would hear the incredibly talented seven-year-old boy.

Through his younger years Marie had restricted Juan's singing to their two-bedroom apartment and church, keeping him focused instead on school and sports. Juan excelled in school sports, especially baseball, a talent that he had certainly inherited from his late father Rafael, once a top major league baseball prospect. Last year when Juan was eleven he had made the Venezuelan national team, and they defeated the national team from Ecuador to represent Central America in the Little League World Series Championship in Williamsport, Pennsylvania, where they lost in the quarter-finals to the powerhouse Japanese.

Entering Juan in the "Cuanto Vale El Show" was due to the insistence of Marie's sister Sophia, who had relentlessly hounded Marie till she finally gave in and entered an audio tape, along with a video of Juan singing in church, to the producers of the show. It was not long until they received a call to bring Juan to the studio for an audition. Once the producers heard Juan sing, he was immediately entered into the competition. When the competition began and the people of Venezuela heard Juan sing, they fell in love with him and he became an instant star. His incredible voice and his good looks were matched by his heart-wrenching life story: his father brutally murdered and his mother attacked, barely surviving, to give birth to him, raising Juan by working several jobs to make ends meet over the years. Marie and Juan were the shining stars in a country weary from decades of leftist and corrupt governments.

The live finals of the "Cuanto Vale El Show," shown countrywide on the state-owned Venezuelan de Television, would be airing in two days. Marie was putting in a twelve-hour day for the third day in a row to earn the time off. She actually welcomed it because it allowed her to get caught up, so that when she came back to work she wouldn't have a mountain of paperwork waiting for her.

When her boss, Antonio José Escalona, opened his office door and summoned Marie into his office, she thought for sure that he had decided he would not give her the time off to see Juan perform after all. Entering Mr. Escalona's office always made her a bit nervous, as he was such an important man. He was strict and demanding but he was fair. Marie had a lot respect for him and she worked hard to please him.

Opening the door wide for Marie to enter, he was smiling ear to ear and could hardly contain himself as he motioned her to sit.

"Come on in, Marie, have a seat. Listen, I just wanted to let you know how proud I am personally and the whole company is of you and your son Juan's success on the show. It has been marvelous to watch him perform, knowing his beautiful mother works thirty feet from my desk."

She dropped her head slightly, feeling embarrassed, uncomfortable receiving praise from Mr. Escalona.

"Thank you, Mr. Escalona, for that. You have been very kind and generous to me and I appreciate that very much."

She looked back up at him and was wondering why he was so giddy. She had never seen him like this before. He was always such a serious man.

"Excuse me for one minute, Marie," José interrupted while he picked up the phone and dialed an extension. "Senta, please come into my office." Looking up at a confused Marie, he just smiled.

The door to the office opened, and in walked the department managers, all nine of them, carrying a cake with dazzling candles burning away. Oh my gosh, thought Marie, it was her birthday and she hadn't even remembered. How nice that Mr. Escalona had all of the department heads joining in to celebrate her birthday!

José came out from behind his desk and stood in front of her and spoke.

"Marie, we all know that you never take time for yourself, that you work so hard to provide for your son, so we thought we would get together and do something nice for you. So please blow out the candles and make a wish."

The cake was monstrously huge and incredibly beautiful. Written on it was "Happy Birthday Marie from your friends at Petróleos," and underneath was a picture of a young boy holding a microphone with the caption written in rainbow icing that said, "Good Luck, Juan! You can do it!"

José motioned to Senta, and taking the cue, she reached over to another manager and handed a box to Marie and said, "On behalf of all of us managers, we all chipped in and bought you something nice for the show this week. Here, Marie, we hope you love it." beamed Senta. Opening the box, Marie lifted out the most beautiful dress you could ever imagine. It was a cross between a formal evening dress and a spiffy office dress. Just perfect for the occasion and certainly something that she had not even put much thought into. The finals of the competition were a little more formal dress.

Stunned at the nice gesture from her coworkers, Marie struggled not to break down.

"Thank you so much, everyone. It is beautiful! I cannot thank you enough. Thank you for remembering my birthday: Marie found herself starting to cry, when Jose said, "Wait, no tears yet. I have something for you!" Handing Marie an envelope, he said, "This is a well-deserved gift for you Marie. Your work here is exemplary and I wanted to reward you. To go along with what is in that envelope I am giving you the rest of the week and all of next week off. On the company and not part of your allotted holidays. I want you to go and relax, enjoy the show with your son, and the two of you go celebrate somewhere, okay?"

Opening the envelope, Marie pulled out a birthday card wishing Marie a happy birthday from Petróleos. There was also a check inside made out to her name for $5,000 US. She thought there had to be some sort of mistake, that he must have added two more zeros than should have been. "Mr. Escalona, there must be some sort of mistake. This check is for $5,000?"

José and the other managers gathered around Marie, hugging her as José spoke.

"There is no mistake, Marie. Take the money and spend it on yourself and your son. Have fun and spoil the hell out of Juan. Now have some cake with us so I can get everyone back to their jobs and you can get the hell out of here for the next ten days!"

Now Marie really cried. Just standing there in front of José, she bowed her head till her chin hit her chest, and bawled her eyes out. This was the most beautiful thing that anyone had ever done for her. Wrapping his big arms around her, José gave Marie a hug and wished her and Juan well and said that he would see her in a few weeks. After Marie received good luck and birthday hugs from everyone else, eventually they all filtered out, including Mr. Escalona, who had a meeting to get to. Leaning against her desk, Marie looked at the dress and then the check for $5,000, and the tears flowed again. She cried for the memory of her late husband Rafael, gone now for almost thirteen years. How proud he would have been for her and Juan right now. She missed him so much, even still.

Two days later she was standing in the front row with her sister Sophia, decked out in her beautiful new dress, waiting patiently for her son Juan to make his entrance on the stage for the first of two songs he would sing tonight. Both finalists were singers, and the other singer, a twenty-seven-year-old mother of two young boys, sang her heart out in a beautiful rendition of Whitney Houston's "I Will Always Love You." The crowd gave her a well-deserved standing ovation for her performance. Then Juan hit the stage and the audience went nuts. Marie was still so incredibly amazed at the reaction when Juan walked out. Here was this twelve-year-old boy dressed in a smart-looking, professionally tailored royal blue suit that made his brilliant blue eyes sparkle and, to top it off, a royal blue-with-yellow striped tie. He looked amazing, he really did. She almost melted when Juan looked down at her and Sophia with a grin and a wink, Then he began to sing. The song they had chosen for him couldn't have been any more perfect, the beautiful Ricky Martin ballad "Private Emotions." Juan's perfect vocal tones made this song soar like a string of balloons reaching for the clouds. His command of the song was that of a seasoned professional, but the fact that he was a twelve-year-old boy made it even more special.

When Juan finished, he waved at the audience, then made his way down the steps at the side of the stage and came to his mom and wrapped his arms around her waist and hugged her. The audience and judges alike were clapping or crying or both. It was an incredible scene. The other finalist did not even stand a chance, and they might as well have called it right then and there. Looking up into his mother's eyes, Juan spoke words that she could not hear, but she easily read her beloved son's lips as he said, "I love you Mom." Juan then turned and ran back up the stairs with the audience screaming, jumping up and down, cheering their young star.

Not long after. as the two finished up their final numbers, with Juan blowing everyone away with the upbeat Enrique Iglesias song, "Heartbeat," the show wrapped, and the country would dial in their votes for the next two hours. Backstage, amongst all of the pandemonium of celebration, Marie and Sophia made their way to Juan's side, and he got big hugs from his auntie. "You were sensational, little man!" cried Sophia as she gave Juan another big hug.

Their celebration was suddenly interrupted by an approaching stranger who had clearly also been moved by Juan's performance.

"Excuse me, ladies, I would like to congratulate young Juan on his outstanding performances tonight. You certainly had the audience fired up, and I am sure the people watching at home were as well. I can't see your country not voting for you. Let me introduce myself. My name is Robert Best; I am a music producer from the United States and a VIP guest of the show. I wasn't in the front row like your mom here, Juan, but certainly close enough to recognize talent when I see it. Congratulations once again, Juan, to you and your Mom on a spectacular evening. I will see you again sometime soon, I hope," and with that he turned and left the three of them a little amused, but more confused, until the show's producer appeared. "I saw you all speaking with Mr. Best. He is one of the most talented producers in the United States. Now that is someone you will want to stay in touch with," he commented as he strolled away looking for the other finalist.

Soon the buzz backstage began to die down and Marie seized the opportunity.

"Well, Juan, I am going to sneak you out of here and home to bed, what do you say to that? Maybe we can talk your Aunt Sophia to hit a drive-through on the way home!"

With a reaction that even the title of "Cuanto Vale El Show" couldn't match, Juan jumped with glee.

"Yes! Awesome, Aunt Sophia, let's go. I am starving!" a jubilant Juan yelled as he grabbed his mother's and auntie's arms and started heading for the exit.

A few minutes later, after pushing through the gauntlet of well wishers and television people, they were all alone, the three of them in the car, eerily quiet after the thunderous noise they had just left. As Sophia pulled into Marie's condo complex, Marie looked back into the back seat and smiled as Juan was sleeping soundly, with his Quarter Pounder missing only one bite out of it and his half-eaten box of fries all over the seat.

Saying goodnight to Sophia, she cradled little Juan in her arms and was heading up to the condo when Sophia called out, "Get ready, sister! Your life is about to change!"

Chapter 38

Nancy and her beautiful twelve-year-old daughter Brittany were quite the team. They looked like big sister–little sister, with Nancy's striking good looks passed down to Brittany, and then Brittany passing her in that department, as she was growing up to be to quite the little beauty queen and easily could be heading toward a career in modeling. Nancy would not have that for her daughter and would beat off the talent agents with a baseball bat, she laughed to herself thinking about it. Nancy had been truly blessed with a miracle, she knew when Brittany was born. She had a best friend, and that was her daughter. Nancy cherished every day they had together. The memories of her attack were long gone.

Brittany, in addition to her emerging beauty, had shown an incredible talent for playing musical instruments. Early on in grade school she was discovered all alone by herself in the school's music room playing a flute that she had discovered in a case on the shelf. The music teacher, Tim Hallworth, was about to march Brittany down to the principal's office for, first, being in the music room where she was not a student and, second, for the unauthorized use of the school's instruments, when he heard her play. He leaned against the doorway and just listened. This little girl was playing the flute as if she owned it; the sound coming from it was beautiful. Upon seeing Mr. Hallworth standing there, Brittany quickly apologized and started to put down the instrument to return it to its case when the teacher called out, "Please, don't stop! Keep going, that was beautiful, please," motioning for her to continue. Seven-year-old Brittany Campbell picked up the flute again, and this time she played it. She pursed her lips and blew the right amount of air to make the instrument literally sing. A seasoned professional would have been jealous. Mr. Hallworth was dumbfounded that this young girl, who had never stepped into his class before, that he knew of, was so accomplished.

"So tell me, little one. First off, what is your name?" a beaming Mr. Hallworth asked.

"Brittany Campbell. I am so sorry for being in here without permission. I will never do it again, I promise," she said as she packed away the flute in its case.

"Don't apologize, Brittany. Anyone who can play an instrument like that should never apologize. You are so young. How did you ever learn to play like that? Have you played a lot?" he asked her.

"Umm, well, this is my third time in here, so three times," Brittany said with a sheepish shrug.

"That is impossible. You must have had professional lessons at some point, or lessons, at any rate."

Still standing and looking at Mr. Hallworth as if she had been caught with her hand in the cookie jar, she replied, "No, just wandered in here a few weeks ago, snooping, when I shouldn't have been, and saw one of the most beautiful things I have ever seen sitting out on this stool, so I just picked it up out of curiosity and started to play it. At first it sounded really bad, because I couldn't figure it out. Then I tried blowing air in it but that just sounded like I was trying to blow out birthday candles," laughed Brittany.

Bewildered and completely amused, the music teacher thought of something.

"Well, I'll be damned. Would you like to try another instrument? Say, a trumpet?" asked Mr. Hallworth.

"Oh yes, could I? That would be wonderful, Mr. Hallworth.

Thank you!" an overjoyed Brittany beamed.

Walking over to the shelves that housed the music class's collection of instruments, he pulled the shiny clean brass trumpet out of its case and handed it to Brittany, "Here, try this, Brittany. You will purse your lips like you would to play the flute, except you are going to place them right into the mouthpiece. Say the letter 'M' but stop at the 'mmm' part. Keep your lips in that position. Now, blow through this position in a buzzing sound. It may sound odd, but that's the basic lip position to use while pla..." He didn't even finish when Brittany was already blowing and the trumpet was playing. Working the three buttons on the trumpet, getting a feel for the sounds it produced, Brittany did not take long to figure out that the number two and three buttons closest to the horn made the sound pitch higher. She was racing up and down the pitch scale, working her breathing and blowing, getting better and better by the minute. She was a natural, thought Mr. Hallworth.

"Why have you never come to my class or signed up for music before, Brittany? You are a naturally talented musician I can see that," he said.

She just looked at her music teacher and shrugged her shoulders.

"I honestly never knew I had a knack for playing an instrument, nor any interest. It just sort of overcame me when I walked past your empty class. It was like something was drawing me in here for some reason."

"Well, guess what, it doesn't matter how you came in here, the important thing is you did come in here. Why don't you come back during the lunch hour and I'll meet you here and we'll crack open all of those cases and see what else you like to play, okay? How does that sound?"

"That sounds like fun! I will see you back here at lunch, Mr. Hallworth, and thank you."

"My pleasure, see you after your next class. You'd better get going so I don't get in trouble for making you late!" laughed Mr. Hallworth.

The lunch hour with Brittany was an awakening of sorts for Mr. Hallworth. Watching Brittany pick up instruments like the saxophone, trombone, and clarinet and play them as if she had been playing them for years was an incredible experience. Soon Brittany was spending more of her lunch hours and after-school time playing and practicing. She was a child music prodigy, thought Tim, without a doubt, and it was a beautiful thing to see and hear.

****

Nancy had heard about her daughter's interest in music class when Brittany came home one day all excited, jumping up and down, elated that she got to play the flute and a bunch more instruments at school and wanted her mom's permission to stay after school on Mondays, Wednesdays and Thursdays to practice with the music teacher Mr. Hallworth. She required a note from Nancy giving her permission.

"Are you sure, honey, that you want to be putting so much time into music class? Shouldn't you be maybe doing some other things as well, like sports?" Nancy asked her.

"No way, Mom, playing music is way more fun than sports. Doing sports is for guys, Mom. I am a girl, and we do more important things—don't you know?"

****

Asked by the school principal why he was working with this little girl one on one and not having her in his music class with the rest of the students, Mr. Hallworth replied, "Dave, come by my class at noon hour, and you will know why. This little girl is showing signs of musical genius, believe me. Three months ago she had never even held an instrument, and now she can play any instrument in my class like a seasoned professional."

So the school principal, Dave Johnson, did stop by that lunch hour out of curiosity, and what he heard, and saw, was incredible. This beautiful little seven-year-old girl was playing a saxophone with such command and professionalism she could solo in a blues club downtown and get a standing ovation. She was brilliant, he thought to himself. Motioning for Mr. Hallworth to step out in the hall, he asked, "Tim, do you know what the hell you've got there? She is incredible, for God's sakes, she should be playing with the Boston Pops! Does her mother know about this? How good her little daughter is?"

"Honestly, I don't think so, because she never picked up an instrument till she strolled in here quite accidentally three months ago. She did get a permission slip from her mother to be here, so I assume she at least knows she is good at it."

"Hell, she's more than good, Tim; you have to get her mom in here to hear her. Do you know who her mother is?" asked Dave.

"No, who is she? Is she famous or something, a professional musician?"

"Not likely. Not sure if you were even around here at this time but seven years ago her mother was viciously attacked by a gang of thugs, and they almost killed her. They did murder her husband during the attack. Her mother has been through hell, and for her to hear what her daughter can do with an instrument would be wonderful. Make it happen, Tim," said Dave as he turned to leave down the hall, back to his office.

Tim called out to Dave before he disappeared into the sea of students flooding the hallway, "My music class is having its spring concert next week, I could have Brittany perform solo for a few songs. We could surprise her mother with a front row seat! What do you think?"

"Sounds perfect, I can't wait!" replied Dave as he turned and joined the throng of students milling in the hallway.

So the next week, Tim made sure her mother knew about the concert, as he was able to catch Mrs. Campbell when she picked up her daughter at the school the following Monday. "Hi. You must be Brittany's mom. I am Tim Hallworth, your daughter's music teacher," he said, extending his hand through the open window of Nancy's car.

Her eyes shielded by dark sunglasses that also masked her 'don't really care' attitude, she replied, "Oh yes, I've heard so much about you. My daughter loves your class and she seems to enjoy playing instruments, because that is all she talks about," said Nancy as she looked over at her daughter in the passenger seat giggling away.

"Well, I haven't even told Brittany this, but my regular music class is having their spring concert on Thursday night, and I would like Brittany to come up and perform a couple of solo songs if she's up for it, and if she is, it would be wonderful to have you there to hear her," said Tim.

"Oh, Mommy, please, can I do it? It would be so cool! Please, Mom!" pleaded Brittany.

"Don't see why not, it would be great to see what my daughter has been up to these past few months," said Nancy, smiling.

"That would be great, you will love it, Mrs. Campbell. Brittany, you can sit with your mom during the concert, and when I'm ready for you, I'll call you up, okay?" said Tim.

Tim watched as a beaming Brittany looked up at him through the window.

"Oh, boy, this will be so cool, Mr. Hallworth! The whole school will be there, won't they?"

"Every one of them," he said. Then Brittany just giggled with excitement.

****

A few nights later, Nancy and Brittany found their reserved seats in the front row of the school gymnasium. The place was filled with several hundred parents and relatives, taking in their children's big spring concert. Nancy was nervous, as she didn't want to see her daughter embarrassed. These kids have been playing all year and Brittany just started, and Mr. Hallworth was having her play solo? Oh boy, she thought. Just go with it, she thought, Brittany is so excited.

The concert began with the Grade One class who really just blew randomly into a bunch of instruments, making some sort of sound. Didn't matter to Mr. Hallworth, though, as he stood in front of them swinging his arm around and around as if he were leading a symphony. So cute.

Then Brittany's Grade Two classes came out, and they were not much better than the Grade Ones but Nancy did at least recognize some sort of a song in that noise. It was so cute to see all those little kids trying so hard and looking so important at the same time. Looking over at Brittany, she saw her smiling away, having a great time watching and listening to her classmates. The Grade Two classes performed six songs and they were quickly followed by a combined Grade Three and Four class. They were again marginally better than the Grade Twos but certainly making progress. Then the Grade Five and Six class also performed combined, and they were much better. They were in tune with each other, and though the songs were simple and easily recognizable, they were advancing along quite nicely. Brittany leaned over to her mom and whispered, "Aren't they fantastic, Mommy! They are so good." She smiled down at Brittany as the Five-and-Sixers were finishing up and then began to stand and file off of the stage, when Mr. Hallworth, the music teacher, approached the podium to the side of the stage that had a microphone, and began to speak.

"We have a special guest here who is going to perform a few solo songs for us tonight. The first song will be on the flute and the second solo will be played on the clarinet. This wonderful little seven-year-old girl I caught all alone in my class playing the flute approximately three months ago. She had never picked up an instrument in her life before. Soon she was playing the clarinet, trumpet, baritone, the French horn and the saxophone. Tonight she is accompanied by her mother, who has never heard her daughter play before, and like you, will hear her play for the first time. Please help me welcome to the stage Brittany Campbell!"

Amid a round of quiet and polite clapping, Brittany smiled at her mother, left her chair and walked up onto the stage and took a chair that Mr. Hallworth had placed in front of her. There were two chairs beside her. One had the flute resting on it and the other had a clarinet. Nancy noticed there was no music stand in front of her. Did Mr. Hallworth forget to put that out? She had to read the music, didn't he know that? Brittany would start to play and she would have no music, she thought. Watching Brittany reach over for the flute, Nancy could only cringe, knowing what was about to happen and how embarrassed her little daughter would be. She was about to stand up and say something, but then Brittany began to play.

To say that Nancy was shocked beyond belief would be an understatement. Watching and listening to Brittany play the flute was breathtaking. It was surreal, and it didn't take long till her lower lip began to quiver and the tears flowed down her cheeks. She was trying to maintain control of her emotions so she wouldn't look like a basket case, but it didn't matter, because glancing around, she noticed that pretty much everyone else was bawling, too. It brought Nancy all the way back to the day she'd given birth to Brittany—the incredible singing and cooing when she was born and how much it enraptured the doctor and nurses. Brittany was fantastic, she was literally playing as if she had been doing it at an exceptional level for years, but she was only seven and had just started! When she finished her song, the people in the audience leapt to their feet and gave little Brittany a thunderous ovation. Looking out at the audience, all she could do was just smile and giggle. Nancy couldn't hide her tears, so when Brittany looked down at her, she could tell her mom had been crying so she blew her a big kiss, which just made Nancy cry even more. Then Brittany sat down again in her chair and picked up the clarinet, and the audience quieted down for the treat they were about to hear again. Listening to her play the different-sounding clarinet, yet with the same passion and control, was simply incredible. Nancy did not know much about a clarinet, having never played an instrument in her life, but the sound Brittany was producing was, quite simply, amazing.

Later that night, as they drove home from the school, Nancy looked over at Brittany and said, "Boy, oh boy, did you ever shock the be jeepers out of me when you played, my dear! I was so amazed at how good you were, I could hardly contain myself, watching you play like that. Why didn't you tell me you were that good, my dear?!"

"I just didn't think I was that good. I guess, after hearing everyone's reaction and the big applause they gave me, maybe I am pretty good, huh, Mom?"

"You're darn right you're good, Brittany. Wow, I still can't believe it," replied Nancy, thinking how incredibly wonderful it would have been if James had been alive, and beside her tonight, to experience what she had just experienced.

"Mom, do you think I could take piano lessons? They don't have one of those in the school. It looks like it would be so much fun," said Brittany.

Dabbing her eyes with a tissue as she drove, Nancy replied, "You certainly can, my dear. I will speak with Mr. Hallworth and get that set up, okay?"

****

In the five years that had passed since that incredible night at the school concert when Nancy got to hear her daughter play music for the first time, Brittany had accomplished so much more in music. She took to the piano like a duck to water, mastering it in just a few short months. Soon she was a regular guest performer with the Rhode Island Philharmonic Orchestra, playing a variety of instruments. Their concerts regularly sold out when they announced that Brittany Campbell would be a guest performer. She was becoming quite the little local star in and around Providence, but when the world-famous Boston Pops asked Brittany to perform with them for a Christmas concert, it attracted quite the buzz. Nancy was deluged for interview requests from CNN, ABC's Good Morning America and NBC

Dateline, to name just a few. Her little local star power had just gone national, and even international.

Nancy's career as one of the country's leading environmentalists kept her busy, and combining it with the rising music career of her daughter made for a serious juggling act. She needed help, so she decided to hire a full-time live-in nanny to help out. Her name was Leanne Reston, and she was twenty-seven years old, working on her college degree online, and needed a decent-paying job that would allow her to continue her school workload, so she answered an ad Nancy had placed online on Craigslist. Nancy felt a good connection with her, and once Leanne spent a few days with Brittany and Nancy saw how well they got along, she knew her search was over and hired Leanne immediately, asking her to move into the guest room and become part of the family.

Nancy felt the need to move Brittany to a more specialized school, so she enrolled Brittany into a special charter school that focused her on other interests besides her music, the Paul Cuffee School, a maritime charter school. Brittany had always shared a love of the environment with her mother, so enrolling her in Paul Cuffee would enrich that part of her life. Brittany's musical training no longer came from her school anyway, as Nancy had her working exclusively with a well-respected classical teacher. He worked with Brittany on the piano most of the time now, as she continued to excel.

Picking up Brittany from school, Nancy said to her, "Guess who is going to be picking you up from school the rest of the week?"

"Leanne!!" Brittany yelled ecstatically.

"Yes, she is. I hired her to be our new nanny to help me look after you while I'm away working. What do you think of that? Would that be okay? Because if it isn't, I can take another job, sweetheart, okay, if you prefer your mommy. Most of the time it will still be me, honey, and other times it will be Leanne, and then some of the time it will be both of us."

"She is so cool, Mom, this is awesome! Thank you so much,"

giggled twelve-year-old Brittany as she leaned over to her mom and squeezed her arm tightly.

"Remember, she's taking university full-time on the computer, so keep that in mind and be respectful of her time, okay? I think it will be fabulous, you'll really like her, and knowing that will make me feel so much better when I have to travel for work."

"I know, Mom, don't you worry, we'll be fine. You are such an awesome mom. I love you so much!"

"I love you too, sweetheart."

Meanwhile, the newly hired nanny Leanne Renton was busy putting away her things in her bedroom closet at the Campbell residence. Another step, thought Robert Best, in ensuring his master plan would continue to stay on course. Everything was on track, with all of the seven prodigies. As Leanne Renton/Robert Best's eyes burned crimson red, almost in glee, she gathered herself, as she heard the Campbell car pull into the garage.

Chapter 39

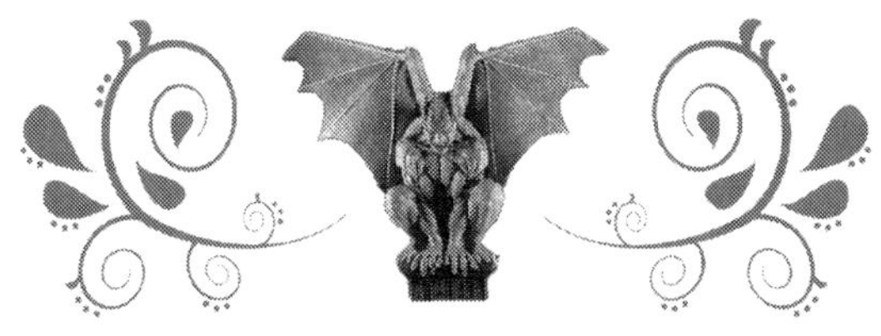

Finishing up his evening service for another Sunday at his St. Colmcille's Parish Church in Swords County, Thomas was tired and decided he would pass on visiting with church members tonight over dinner. Now seventy years old, he just didn't have the energy for it tonight, opting instead for some leftover stew from Friday that he would nibble on over a cup of hot tea, as he was not very hungry either. He had lost his zest for Sunday night visits over dinner with members from his congregation, something that he used to cherish. Ever since the slaughter almost thirteen years earlier of the McClosky's, whose home was his favorite dinner destination on Sunday nights, he only went out if it was a special occasion. Patricia McCloskey's stew was award-winning in his judgment back then, and oh, how much he had loved it! He sure missed the McClosky's; they'd been more than just church members, they'd been his friends.

The dark and evil forces that had wrought so much havoc, death and destruction that very fateful Sunday so many years ago still followed Thomas to this very day. He had met his enemy on numerous occasions over the years and he knew his life was in danger, as so was everyone else in this world in danger. Satan was active among us and he had a plan for our ultimate destruction, Thomas was sure of it. His work on SOSL over the years in Rome had taught him many things about God's plans for this world, but very few of his fellow clergy in the priesthood had had the opportunity to see Satan 'up close and personal,' and to actually feel the terrifying fear that he represents for mankind. Satan's plans for little twelve-year-old Chloë McCloskey had yet to reveal themselves, but Thomas vowed that he would use whatever life he had left on this earth to ensure she had the protection of God Himself.

Since Chloë's birth she had been under the careful care of Sister Beatrice McGarrigle, most recent of the St. Patrick`s Academy in County Mayo, Ireland, sixty-two miles west of Dublin. He had overseen Chloë's care very carefully over the years through Sister McGarrigle. Upon the traumatic death of her mother Katherine, the newborn Chloë was quickly moved into the full-time care of the Church, with Katherine's parents Kenneth and Joanne Kearney giving their blessing to baby Chloë's adoption by the Church. Sister McGarrigle, handpicked by Thomas, had been Chloë's main caregiver since her birth.. She was young and enthusiastic, and her love of God and Jesus Christ was palpable, something that Thomas wanted to ensure Chloë would always be surrounded by. Sister McGarrigle's knowledge of Chloë's birth and the circumstances surrounding it were kept to a minimum; she knew only that Chloë's mother had died during childbirth. Her father had been murdered months earlier by a gang of thugs in a robbery attempt that also took the life of her father's parents. A tragic beginning for the orphaned baby, and when Thomas chose Sister McGarrigle for the role of Chloë's caregiver, she took the responsibility very seriously and soon they became very close, almost like mother and daughter.

Chloë, for the first ten years of her young life, was raised by Sister McGarrigle in the St. Brigid's Orphanage in Dublin, a Catholic convent that had been built over one hundred and fifty years ago and was steeped in history. The convent had housed and raised some well-known Irishmen over the years, including members of the Irish Parliament, professional soccer players and some famous, not-so-good Irishmen, like the legendary Celtic Caper. The Celtic Caper was a deft bank robber from the late 1800s who turned to a life of crime when he ran away from the orphanage at the tender age of thirteen.

Chloë was moved to the more modern St. Patrick's Academy in Mayo, a ninety-minute drive west of Dublin on the N7 that allowed Chloë more opportunities to receive advanced education than the stuffy and traditional St. Brigid's. Plus, with word now getting out into the general population about the child singing prodigy at St. Brigid's, the move out into the countryside at St. Patrick's provided the necessary insulation Chloë still needed from the curious public, who had never forgotten about the surviving child from the tragic death of Katherine McCloskey. Newspaper stories on Baby Chloë, as she'd been called early on in her life, tried to keep track of her and continue to update her story, but eventually the public would forget about her until a reporter, on some slow news day, would fill his column with a 'where is she now' article.

Chloë, like the day she appeared for the first time in this world singing like an angel, could sing. Really sing. Her voice was unique, sounding like no other. It was soft, gentle, smooth, beautiful and powerful when needed to be, and only became richer in tone and maturity as she grew older. Chloë, as a five-year-old, would entertain staff and children for hours, singing Christmas carols and hymns during the holidays. Sister McGarrigle would take her to other orphanages, both Catholic and non-Catholic, to entertain children, and she brought tremendous joy wherever she travelled. It was hard to believe, thought Thomas, that Chloë was the child of The Lord Almighty's biggest enemy. He knew in his heart that he loved Chloë as if she was his own and would protect her with his life. Through God's grace she would be saved. Thomas believed it with every fiber in his being.

The St. Patrick's Academy, with its countryside isolation, was a sprawling complex, housing gifted students from the Catholic faith from all parts of the world. The academy was well known for its yearly stage productions under the tutelage of Father Joseph McKracken, and this year the big musical production was *Annie*, starring, of course, Chloë as Annie. Public anticipation of this year's musical with the young Chloë McCloskey was drawing attention once again to the story of Chloë and her life, something that Thomas and the Church worked very hard to avoid. But Thomas knew that he could not shield her forever, especially with her incredible singing ability. Tomorrow was opening night, and members of the Dublin press were expected to be in attendance. Father McKracken's musicals were always eagerly awaited, and the surprise choice of the production *Annie* had the public and the press scratching their heads. Thomas knew exactly why Joseph had chosen *Annie*. He wanted to showcase twelve-year-old Chloë McCloskey in the lead role because he knew she would be perfect.

Thomas had settled in his big armchair to tackle a crossword before he called it a night, when he began thinking about his next encounter with the Beast or, in his human form, Robert Best. Would it be tomorrow night at the opening of *Annie*? He suspected it would. He felt the now familiar feeling of dread creep its way into his stomach, where it would continually build till the production tomorrow night. Best, or Satan, for that matter, did not frighten him. The fear that he felt was for Chloë. What were the Dark One's plans for her, he wondered. How could he possibly use a little child for his intended plan to destroy the world, as Thomas knew he was planning? Maybe tomorrow night a piece of that plan would reveal itself.

****

Monday morning arrived, and as always, Sister McGarrigle, before she dressed for the day, usually in her normal habit, took time for prayer. Ever since she'd been just a little girl she would kneel beside her bed and speak to God through prayer, a routine she continued to this day. Serving God and the Catholic Church full-time was something she had always wanted to do. Her calling had been strong when she was just a teenager, and she followed her instincts right into the convent when she was only nineteen years old, completing her postulancy six months later. She was serving God full-time and was as happy as one could possibly be when she began her novitiate, which would last for the next eighteen months. Three years later, after declaring her temporary vows, Beatrice was ready to take her solemn vows, and so, at the age of twenty-five, Beatrice McGarrigle became Sister McGarrigle.

Three years later, at the age of twenty-eight, she was summoned to the offices of Abbess Sister Agnew, in charge of the Killeenatrava Nunnery in the County Mayo. Never having been summoned in front of Sister Agnew before, Beatrice was quite nervous, wondering why she was being called in. When she arrived, there were two priests with Sister Agnew in her office. My dear, she thought to herself, what could they possibly want. Sister Agnew greeted her, saying, "Thank you for coming, Sister McGarrigle. Please have a seat. Let me introduce to you Father Thomas O'Sullivan, of St. Colmcille's Parish Church in Swords County, and Cardinal Kevin Zorn from Rome." Sister Agnew waited for Sister McGarrigle's shock at having a Vatican Cardinal in her presence to subside before she continued, "Sister McGarrigle, they are here to speak with you about a very special little girl." Sister Agnew motioned towards Father O'Sullivan.

"Thank you, Sister Agnew. I know you must be surprised at our presence, Sister McGarrigle, but let me assure you that you are here for a very special reason and that you have been chosen to perform God's work in a very special way," Thomas stated.

Fidgeting uncomfortably in her chair, Beatrice spoke.

"Most certainly Father, whatever God has decided for me is what I will do. How may I serve thee?"

Thomas continued, glancing first at Cardinal Zorn, who nodded his reassurance.

"Have you heard about the McCloskey family from Balbriggan that was brutally attacked and murdered by a gang of thugs last year?"

Sister McGarrigle sat up straight in her chair and leaned slightly forward and towards Thomas when she spoke.

"I do not care to read the news, Father. My commitment to

serving Him keeps me busy enough."

"Very well. Grew McCloskey and his parents were murdered. Grew's wife Katherine barely survived, but lived long enough to give birth recently to a baby girl, called Chloë. Katherine did not survive. Baby Chloë has been adopted by the Church, Sister," explained Thomas.

Sister McGarrigle gasped, "Oh my word that is so terribly tragic Father. That poor little girl growing up without her parents!"

"Indeed it is, Sister. Baby Chloë is a very special little girl, and we have chosen you to be her everyday guardian and spiritual provider. You will raise this little girl into adulthood, Sister, under the watchful eye of Sister Agnew and myself. This is the path God has chosen for you, Sister McGarrigle."

She now stood and faced him, her voice louder and more confident. "I will do everything I can to raise her in the eyes of the Lord, as you command, Father."

Thomas found himself smiling, knowing Sister McGarrigle was the right person to look after Chloë. "We know you will, Sister, and so let me inform you that your duty with baby Chloë begins right now," stated Thomas, watching Sister Agnew leave the room and return a minute later, holding an infant baby wrapped in blankets, cooing away, a sound so incredibly beautiful that it took the breath away from Sister McGarrigle. Sister Agnew approached her, placing Chloë in her arms, and they all awaited the reaction between the two. It was exactly what they expected, an instant bond.

Sister McGarrigle was beaming, her smile radiating a love that caused Thomas to feel relief wash over him.

"She is beautiful, Sister Agnew. Her sounds are so incredibly beautiful, she sounds like an angel," Sister McGarrigle commented as she cradled Chloë in her arms.

"We told you that she was special and we meant it. She has been singing like this since her birth last week. Her birthmark reflects that. Let me show you, Sister," said Thomas as Sister Agnew stepped forward and peeled back the blankets, unsnapping Chloë's cotton outfit, exposing her birthmark of three musical notes on her right inner thigh.

Sister McGarrigle's eyes opened wide in amazement. "Oh my, look at that birthmark, how unusual is that?!"

"Unusual, indeed Sister, but very appropriate, wouldn't you agree?" asked a smiling Thomas..

****

A short time later, when Father O'Sullivan and Cardinal Zorn had left, and Beatrice was holding Chloë in her arms, she asked Sister Agnew, "May I ask, Sister, what was a Cardinal from the Vatican doing here accompanying Father O'Sullivan? He never said one word the entire meeting. I thought that to be very strange."

"His presence should reinforce in you the importance of the well-being of this child, Sister McGarrigle. Do well, by God, take good care of this baby!" said a smiling but stern-looking Sister Agnew.

So over the next twelve years Sister McGarrigle never left Chloë's side. Beatrice was Chloë's surrogate mother, big sister, friend and spiritual leader, shaping a deep faith in Jesus Christ inside Chloë. Thomas often stopped by the Killeenatrava Nunnery to check in on Chloë and, delighted to see how well Sister McGarrigle and Chloë were doing, he would congratulate Sister Agnew for her guidance and leadership. When Chloë was three years old, Sister Agnew said goodbye to Sister McGarrigle and Chloë as they transitioned to St. Brigid's Girls National School in Dublin. Chloë flourished at St. Brigid's after her fifth birthday, when she began elementary school. She was a naturally gifted student, very intelligent. Her singing ability had everyone at St. Brigid's talking about this wonderful little five-year-old with the voice of an angel.

****

When Chloë had turned twelve this year, Thomas had her moved from St. Brigid's in Dublin to St. Patrick's Academy in County Mayo. He could not get out there as often to see Chloë as he would have liked because of the distance, but tried to stop in every few weeks. Tonight was the opening performance of the academy's *Annie*, so everyone was excited. He had been informed this morning that Cardinal Zorn would be flying into Dublin this afternoon for the performance and to see first-hand the progress of Chloë. The academy was all abuzz at the news that a Vatican Cardinal would be attending the performance tonight. When Thomas arrived at the airport to pick up his good friend, he was dressed in his usual clergy dress of black pants, black buttoned-up shirt and clerical collar. When he saw Kevin appear from the customs gate from his flight from Rome, wearing virtually the same clothes, he realized they could have been brothers, they looked so much alike. Once athletic young priests, they both had now reached their seventieth birthdays, but both still carried themselves with a youthful step.

They exchanged pleasantries and hugs inside the airport and then made their way to the parking garage. Climbing into Thomas's comfortable BMW 316 for the drive to St. Patrick's, they made small talk on the way, with Kevin updating him on SOSL and the latest developments around the world that he was analyzing for his next report. Having just completed a SOSL conference at the Vatican just a few months ago, he was fairly up to date on SOSL progress. Soon, however, the discussion turned to Chloë.

"Tell me, Thomas, how is she doing at St. Patrick's? She grew so much, both spiritually and as a young girl, at St. Brigid's, didn't she?" Kevin asked.

"She is doing incredibly well under the care of Sister McGarrigle. Her singing ability is truly unbelievable, Kevin, as you will see tonight. She is starting to attract a lot of attention to herself. We can still contain it, but word is getting out about this child phenomenon who can sing like an angel. She was born to sing and she loves it so much. Eventually it will be her singing that will take her out into the world," a solemn Thomas explained to Kevin.

"What is it, Thomas, that bothers you so about that reality?"

Deciding at the last second to stop for a yellow light, causing the car to stop suddenly, he looked over at Kevin and said, "I just don't understand why Satan chose Katherine and her child for whatever he has planned. It just does not make any sense. Chloë is like an angel, but yet…." Thomas couldn't finish what he wanted to say.

"Maybe that is it, Thomas. Satan wants everyone to think she is an Angel of God, and then he will unleash her true power. We must guard against that, we must watch her always, Thomas, as difficult as that will become," said Kevin.

They arrived a short time later at St. Patrick's Academy. Thomas and Kevin spent time with the staff of the academy, offering words of encouragement and prayer for the great work that was done here with the children. Kevin spent a few minutes with Father Joseph McKracken, praising him on his commitment and dedication to the academy and to God. To have a Vatican Cardinal visit was a very big deal for St. Patrick's, and the top clergy in Ireland would also be in attendance at the performance of *Annie* tonight, including the Bishop of Killala, Bishop Henry Fitzpatrick. When Sister McGarrigle arrived with Chloë, it was the first time in many years that Kevin had seen her, and it was a shock to see how much she had grown into such a beautiful young girl.

Soon Kevin was tiring, and he and Thomas excused themselves to their quarters to get some rest before the academy served them dinner and they attended the performance. Kevin having informed Thomas he would rest for an hour and see him soon, Thomas returned to the offices of the Abbess and Sister Agnew, who now, getting up in age like him, was content in serving her Lord right to her last day. He asked Sister Agnew for a few minutes to speak alone. The two of them walked to the corner of the room, away from the other staff of the academy, where he asked her, "Sister, how has everything been with Chloë?

Have there been any instances where she has been in trouble, out of line, anything at all that would seem out of her normal character?"

"No, nothing whatsoever, Father. She has been a model student, a wonderful child in every sense. Sister McGarrigle has never mentioned anything negative to me about Chloë. Why would you ask Father, if I may?" Sister Agnew asked with a curious look.

"She seems so perfect, I was just looking for any indications there could be any underlying flaws. Never mind, Sister, it's just the psychologist in me, always probing the human psyche," said Thomas, deflecting the conversation away from Sister's concern. He was expecting that response, as he knew Chloë had been a model student and child at St. Patrick's. He also knew that if indeed Satan had plans for her, Chloë was in very grave danger.

After the academy treated him and Cardinal Zorn to a hearty meal of traditional Irish bacon and cabbage, Colcannon and fresh bread, they made their way down to the academy auditorium where Thomas, Kevin and Bishop Fitzpatrick were all seated in the very front. Opening night for the musical was packed, as it was always a highly anticipated event for the locals in County Mayo and surrounding counties. The audience was abuzz about the little girl who was playing the lead role of Annie. Thomas overheard one lady say to another sitting behind him that the young girl playing Annie was an angel sent from Heaven to the academy, she was so gifted a singer. He truly wished in his heart that this was indeed the case. Soon the lights dimmed, and Father McKracken walked onto the stage and up to the podium with a microphone at the far right of the stage.

"Ladies and Gentlemen, welcome to St. Patrick's Academy. We are very honored to have with us tonight some very special guests, including Bishop Fitzpatrick of Killala and Cardinal Zorn from Rome. I would now like to ask our beloved friend and supporter over the years, Father O'Sullivan, to say a prayer before we get started. Father O'Sullivan?" Father McKracken motioned towards Thomas.

Crossing the stage from the left over to the podium, Thomas thanked Joseph and asked everyone to bow and join in him in prayer.

"Dear God, we give thanks to You, our blessed Almighty, for the wonderful blessings You have Bestowed on Father McKracken and this wonderful school. We, the audience, have the pleasure of enjoying the fruits of your labor here tonight. We give thanks to you Lord, for honoring us with the presence of Cardinal Zorn and Bishop Fitzpatrick here tonight at the academy. May you grant Cardinal Zorn safe passage upon his return to Rome. In the name of the Father, the Son and the Holy Spirit, Amen."

When Thomas returned to his seat, Father McKracken continued, "Thank you, Father O'Sullivan. The academy is very proud to do something completely different this year and present the timeless musical *Annie*! We would not have been able to choose this production if it weren't for our young star Chloë McCloskey, whom you will enjoy here tonight. The group has worked very hard all year long for this night, and with God's Grace it will be worth it. So please, if you will, sit back and enjoy the show."

The curtain opened, and there was Chloë, dressed as Little Orphan Annie, with her dog (a well-behaved mutt borrowed from one of the academy landscapers), looking out at the audience with a wide smile. Then she began to speak the role she had been practicing all year. She is such a confident and beautiful young girl, thought Thomas, and everyone in the audience will see how special she really is. She was a natural performer the way she moved about the stage as the show carried on, interacting with the other actors. The audience was completely enthralled with the production. It was wonderfully done; the sets and the choreography were perfect, the acting and singing excellent.

It was when Chloë stepped forward to the front of the stage with her dog and sang the solo "Tomorrow" that the audience was completely blown away. Chloë sang the song with conviction and power, and when she reached the chorus, her incredible voice, with its amazing range, shone through, the audience thoroughly enjoying every second of it. Her talent was way beyond that of a twelve-year-old. Looking over at Kevin, Thomas could see he was truly amazed at Chloë's performance. Who wouldn't be, he thought. It was spectacular.

The show ended, leaving everyone with the feeling it was over too early, as the audience leapt to its feet as one and gave the production a standing ovation that could have been heard back in Dublin. When Chloë and her dog stepped forward and she executed her little bow to the audience, they screamed with delight and more rousing ovation. She was definitely the star of the night, and Father McKracken was right when he said this musical could not have been made without the talent of Chloë. For the next thirty minutes, Thomas and Kevin, along with Bishop Fitzpatrick, spent time having refreshments and dessert in a reception room set up for the production staff and guests, where they congratulated everyone on a job well done. Soon Thomas and Kevin excused themselves to return to their rooms for the night. Kevin needed to be back to the airport first thing in the morning so they would both have an early morning, as Thomas of course, would take Kevin to the airport on his way back to St. Colmcille's.

Standing in front of Kevin's dormitory room door, Thomas wished his good friend goodnight. "Sleep well, my friend, it has been a very long day for you."

"That it has, but I thoroughly enjoyed the show tonight. Chloë was truly magnificent, don't you think, Thomas?"

"She certainly was the star of the show. Goodnight, Kevin."

****

Saying goodnight to Thomas, Kevin entered his room and was shocked to see Sister McGarrigle there. "Cardinal Zorn, I wanted to stop by and see what you thought of the production tonight and Chloë's performance," said a beaming Sister McGarrigle.

"I thought the musical was wonderful, Sister, and Chloë was

simply amazing. You should be very proud, Sister McGarrigle. Now, if you don't mind, I must get some rest," replied a startled Kevin.

"Certainly, Cardinal Zorn. Can I help you with those robes, Father? They must become very heavy after a long hard day," said Sister McGarrigle as she stopped to reach up to help Kevin with his clothing as she walked past.

Shocked and alarmed at her behavior, he demanded she leave his room at once.

"Excuse me, Sister. What is the matter with you? How dare you talk to me like that! You leave my room at once, and I will have Sister Agnew throw you out of here first thing in the morning, do you hear me?!"

"Oh, come on, Father, don't tell me you aren't interested in a little temptation," laughed Sister McGarrigle, pulling the tunic of her habit upwards exposing her naked, panty-less crotch.

"Damn you to hell! You are no Sister, you're just some whore off of the street!" bellowed Kevin.

"Oh, I am much more evil than that, Father!" laughed Sister McGarrigle, lashing her tongue at Kevin's neck as he backpedaled for the door. Hearing the lock snap into place before he reached the door, Kevin turned back toward Sister McGarrigle to see that she was transforming in front of his eyes. Her face had turned to pure evil, dark scars appearing on her face, her teeth rotting and her tongue lolling and licking her now cracked, bleeding and purple lips. Her eyes then turned pure crimson red, shining brightly. Her voice had turned to a howl, like a madman trying to get out of a straitjacket. Kevin was in the presence of Lucifer himself, he had no doubt, but he was not afraid. In all of his years serving the Lord and the Church, he had never encountered Satan in such a purely physical state, and all he could feel was a profound sense of sadness at the misery he projected.

"You do not scare me, whoever you are. You are a coward, too afraid to live in the light of day, a deceiver and a liar. You run from God and his Almighty power because you are the one who is afraid!" spoke Kevin with a forceful voice.

"Silence, you pathetic little sheep! You serve God and His people because you are weak and afraid to die. Well, be prepared, Cardinal, because tonight you will die!" A hysterical Sister McGarrigle laughed uncontrollably in a demonic voice that boomed and echoed throughout the room.

"Tell me, why are you here tonight? It is because of the girl Chloë, isn't it? You are watching over her, aren't you, you coward?" sneered Kevin, now grasping the cross he had pulled from his robe pocket, holding it out directly in front of him.

Suddenly, out of nowhere, the transformed Sister McGarrigle , now a hissing beast-like creature, punched Kevin squarely in the face so hard it send him flying back into the wall. The shards of light danced in Kevin's brain as his broken nose bled profusely down the front of his robe.

Spitting blood from his shattered mouth, Kevin yelled, "Go ahead and kill me, beast! I am just an old priest who has come to the end anyway. Chloë will be saved, and there will be nothing you can do about that, coward! God's mercy will save her soul and tear her from your talons!"

"You are no old and worn-out priest, Zorn! I know exactly who you are—a useless and used pawn of God. He has had you chasing a lie, cooked up by your Church, that He will end this world through an Armageddon. What is this stupid little Vatican SWAT team called again, SOSL? That is pathetic," laughed the Beast so vehemently into Kevin's face he could smell the rotting flesh of Sister McGarrigle and her damned soul. The Beast stood up, half of it some evil monster creature and the other half, the rotting flesh of what used to be Sister McGarrigle. The Beast grabbed Kevin by his throat and lifted him up into the air, choking his air supply completely with a grip so powerful and unyielding that Kevin knew he would die in just a few seconds.

Wrenching the metal eight-inch cross from Kevin's unresisting hands, the Beast drove it right through Kevin's throat till the bottom of the cross poked through the back of his neck. His eyes bulging and trying to suck in one last breath through his nose, Kevin closed his eyes and tried to think of another image that he would take with him to Heaven. He thought of his sister from South Dakota that he had not seen for over forty years, dead from an overdose of drugs, living on the street as a whore at the age of twenty-eight. How they used to be the best of friends playing in their parents' backyard. Taking turns pushing each other on the swing set. He missed her so. He hoped that he would see her soon.

****

The next morning at 5:30 a.m., Thomas, fully dressed and working on his second cup of coffee, wondered where Kevin was. He needed to get down here in the next few minutes if he wanted some breakfast before they left for the city. Getting up from the table, he excused himself from Sister Agnew and Sister McGarrigle. Thomas had a sinking and overwhelming feeling of dread overcome him as he approached Kevin's door. Leaning against the door to listen for any sounds, he heard nothing. Tapping on the door, he called out, "Cardinal Zorn, it's Thomas. Just wondering if you were almost ready to go, as breakfast is on the table and we must be on our way to catch your flight." Again, silence and no response. Fearing that maybe Kevin could have had a heart attack or something awful like that, he tried the door and found it was open.

Entering the room, Thomas felt himself automatically repulsed into a hunched position as he looked up at the corpse of Cardinal Kevin Zorn, his friend for over forty years, impaled by the throat with his own cross, which had been driven through his throat and into the wall. His feet dangling a foot off the ground and his head, with its bulging eyes, leaning to the left. Thomas winced, as he could see his tongue hanging loosely over his bottom lip. He had almost forgotten about whether or not he would see Best for Chloë's performance. His dear friend and champion of God now gone, and he had never even heard a sound. Satan was a coward, Thomas knew for certain. As he turned to leave the room, his body shaking with anger, he looked back at his friend one last time, prayed for him and then did something else. He vowed that he would kill this demon. For the McClosky's, Kevin, and for Chloë.

Chapter 40

Bentley Paxton reached down to the end of the couch to cover her feet with the blanket, as the cool air coming through her opened window was getting chilly. Now the senior writer for *Music Talks*, the leading music industry publication, she was settling in for the night to watch the semi-finals of "America's Got Talent," one of her favorite shows of the summer, sipping a green tea, waiting for the show to start. The show this year was all about the kid from South Dakota, Connor Asker. He was the talk of the country with his performances on the show as the twelve-year-old child prodigy whose singing could reduce a mountain peak to tears and whose voice could melt the snow-packed glaciers. Bentley knew the music industry better than most people, and she had seen raw talent over the years, but it was very rare to hear someone so young with such a mature voice that resonated with such a melodic beauty that captured you and wouldn't let you go. Winning the "America's Got Talent" competition was a foregone conclusion, but more importantly, the show provided a young budding superstar a platform for a coming-out party.

As the show ended, Connor blew the judges and the TV audience across America away with a stunning rendition of Coldplay's "Fix You." His voice captured the soul of the song as if he had written it himself, and as his voice soared through the chorus of the song, Bentley felt chills run down her spine. This little boy was the real deal and would be a household name before long, if he wasn't already.

Now living in Los Angeles, after moving there from the bay area almost six years ago, she was in her late thirties and a seasoned veteran of the music industry. She loved her job still, no burnout factor yet, but nothing much more than that. She had still not entered into any serious relationship but had come close over the years, especially with music producer Avery Johnson. She found dating difficult, as her job took her away so often, but she had dated sporadically over the years, as her beauty and position always attracted men hoping to charm her. But the music business is cutthroat, and she just found it easier to go it alone with no commitments. It allowed her the freedom to just pick up and go to cover a story or an interview with no guilt or responsibilities. It just worked for her, but it was lonely at times and she longed for a meaningful relationship someday. She had almost found herself heading in that direction with Avery over twelve years ago when they met while she was interviewing him during the Grammy Awards. There was chemistry between them, they had both felt it, and they'd both wanted it. They dated, or tried to date, for two years, but eventually it ended as the distance between their two cities, and their careers taking off, left little time for each other. She found herself missing him whenever she would see him on TV at an awards show or would read an article about him in the paper or a industry magazine. Avery had grown into one of the most powerful people in the music industry, a real heavyweight.

Her thoughts were suddenly pulled away to the familiar Beyonce ringtone of her Blackberry. Reaching for the phone on the coffee table, she saw that it was her boss, Jonathon Green. Hitting the send button, she said, "Hey, it's after 10 p.m., why am I answering a call from the office, I ask myself.", knowing full well she would answer even it if it was three in the morning.

"Nice try, Paxton, we both know you have that Crackberry within arm's reach twenty-four hours a day waiting for me to call," a sarcastic Green said.

Reaching down to the remote, she turned down the volume on her TV.

"Let me guess—the magazine found a singing giraffe in the African jungle and needs me to kayak down the Congo through hordes of starving crocodiles, poisonous snakes and horny natives to get the story, is that about right?" laughed Bentley.

Jonathon had the stupidest laugh, which made her laugh even more, and it was cackling through her phone into her ear. "Shit. Now on top of your perfect looks you're clairvoyant. How did you know?" Green deadpanned.

"Okay, okay. It's late on the east coast, what's up that you need to crawl out of bed to make this call, Jonathon?" asked Bentley.

His voice normalized without the stupid laugh. "Did you watch America's Got Talent tonight?"

"Of course I did. Who wasn't tuned in to see that kid sing?"

"*Music Talks* has an exclusive interview with him next Wednesday night after the taping of the finals, whether he wins or loses."

She instinctively leaned forward off the couch when she heard that. This was big, and she couldn't contain her excitement. "Really!! Jonathon, that is wonderful news, it is a great story. Thank you for letting me do it!"

The annoying cackle returned. "Wow, Bentley, he's just a twelve-year-old kid with a set of pipes. Here today, gone tomorrow. Plus the interview is in your backyard, in Hollywood. You'd think I was asking you to cover the final interview granted by Mick Jagger before he retires for good."

"Oh, I would take the interview with the Asker kid over Jagger any day, Jonathon. This kid will have an incredible career in this business, and that first interview will be played for generations, you just wait!"

"Okay, whatever, Bentley, just get the story. There are a couple of things you need to be aware of. First, the interview is being taped by NBC Dateline to be aired on Sunday following the final. So this is a camera interview, but we get our story, and the credit as the lead, and NBC's cameras were invited by *Music Talks*," instructed Jonathon.

"Great, now I have to wear makeup. Okay, what's the second thing?"

Jonathon's voice once again was serious. "Absolutely no mention of Connor's birth parents and the circumstances surrounding their death. Stick to his childhood growing up and where the music came from, okay?"

"I'm not aware of the circumstances surrounding the death of his birth parents."

"Well, you would be about the only one in America who isn't. Google it, it's all there, just don't talk about it, okay? Are we clear?"

Wondering why she had never heard about the death of Connor's parents when it sounded like everyone else had, she said, "You got it, boss. Thanks again, Jonathon, and get some sleep. Talk soon."

After hanging up with Jonathon, she opened up her laptop and refilled her cup with another green tea. She did a Google search on Connor Asker, and it came up with a plethora of "America's Got Talent" links till she scrolled down to almost the bottom of the page, where she read a link describing the tragic deaths of Brent Asker and his pregnant fiancé Lori Weston. Reading through the articles, Bentley was numb. Connor's parents had been through so much, the brutal murder of Brent's father and Lori's parents, then the awful car accident on the way to the hospital that killed Brent, and a barely alive Lori giving birth to Connor before she expired. Then Lori's sister and her husband from South Dakota adopted Connor as a newborn child and, as a tribute to her sister and her fiancé, kept Connor's last name Asker intact. They recognized his singing talent early on and helped foster that gift. A tragic and sad story, she thought. Connor's story would make the basis of an Oscar-winning film. It had all the marks of tragedy and triumph. The journalist in her ached to probe this story with Connor's adopted parents during the interview, but she knew that was impossible. Hopefully another time she would have that opportunity.

The next night Connor Asker was voted through to the finals of "America's Got Talent"—as if there had ever been any doubt whatsoever. He was up against a magician in the finals whose incredible displays of illusion and disappearing acts were absolutely amazing and who might have been able to win in the finals if he weren't up against Connor Asker. The magician didn't stand a chance.

The following week a Fed Ex package arrived from the studio with her press credentials for the final show live broadcast that night in Hollywood at the Kodak Theatre. Her interview with Connor was not till after the final results show the following night. Given the chance to watch the final performances live, she was happy to be just a fan that night, and she couldn't wait.

She arrived at the live final show, found her assigned seat and settled in to watch the spectacle unfold. NBC produced a fantastic show, and the first performer was the magician. Using a combination of great theatre, special effects, and whizzy props, he made a female assistant appear in two places at the same time with such realism that the studio audience was completely fooled and had no idea how he had done it. Had to be mirrors, thought Bentley, but where the hell were they, then? She found herself cheering wildly for the magician, his act was great.

After the television commercial break, little Connor Asker was being introduced by the host. The audience began to cheer like wild animals as soon as the host began his introduction. Everyone was on their feet and the noise was deafening. Walking out on stage, dressed in a cool, graphic printed t-shirt, with a black vest combined with a pair of faded blue jeans, Connor was a scruffy unshaven beard and some tattoos away from looking like the lead singer from Maroon Five. He was so mature-looking, it was spooky, thought Bentley, seeing him in person. Then he began to sing, and the audience stopped cheering and returned to their seats to take in the performance. It was as if the show's producer had turned a switch backstage that made everyone stop cheering and sit down all at the same time.

Connor's singing style was fresh and current, and he was not going to deviate from that formula for the finals. Choosing the Justin Bieber hit "Baby," Connor had the crowd in a frenzy, especially when he was joined on stage by Ludacris to complete the hip hop arrangement. Connor was slaying the song, and his stage presence and command of the audience was mature far beyond his twelve years. America was witnessing the birth of a major star. The song might not have showcased his incredible singing pipes, but he sang it on stage in such a way that Justin Bieber himself could only have watched and saluted. When the song ended, there was pandemonium in the Kodiak Theatre. Screaming pubescent girls rushed the stage to get a piece of Connor, with their mothers almost joining them. The show's host was nearly crushed by the rushing girls. Security people jumped onstage to separate the girls from Connor, and the producers and stagehands joined shortly thereafter to lend a hand. It was crazy, a spectacle, but an indication of what to expect in this young man's career, thought Bentley to herself, watching it all unfold onstage in front of her. It's going to be a great interview for *Music Talks*, without a doubt.

The next day arrived, with all the hype from Connor's performance on all of the entertainment shows and showbiz clips on the news channels. Connor was the talk of the country, everyone was talking about him. NBC had already started advertising their exclusive Sunday night Dateline interview between *Music Talks* magazine and Connor Asker. It was a coup for *Music Talks* and Dateline NBC ratings for the show would be spectacular. The final show that night, where the winner would be announced, was almost anti-climatic because no one really cared if Connor won; he was a star regardless, and America loved him. One of the surprise announcements NBC made for the final show broadcast was the American debut of twelve-year-old Juan Jimenez from Venezuela, the winner of the South American version of "America's Got Talent." Juan was quickly becoming a major star in Latin America.

The final show was a choreographed spectacle the likes of

which had never been seen before. NBC put everything into this final, knowing most of America would be watching. The show's opening act was Juan Jimenez. The live audience and most of America did not see this coming. The little Latin heartthrob sang the hell out of Enrique Iglesias' 'Takin Back My Love'. Where are these kids coming from, thought Bentley. This kid was as talented as Connor Asker. The audience was going bonkers, the judges were standing on their feet, and the host was forced to wait out the deafening noise from the audience before he was able to get things back under control. Wow, what a performance!

Soon the show was reaching its end, and the announcement of the season's winner was at hand. When Connor was announced as the winner, the theatre exploded in celebration. The excitement Connor was creating in America was eerily similar to the impact Elvis had on the country's youth in his early years. His swinging hips drove women mad. Well, not only were the girls going mad over Connor, but so were the mothers. The show ended, and Bentley made her way backstage with her VIP pass and took in the celebration with Connor, his adopted parents, the show's producers, hosts, judges and a million other people, it seemed.

She glanced at her watch and noticed it was starting to get quite late. She approached the Dateline producer who was nearby and mentioned that they should get going on the interview as it was getting late for a twelve-year-old and the last thing anyone wanted was for Connor's parents to kill the interview for another day because it was too late for their budding little superstar. Turning to rejoin Connor to get him to start getting ready for the interview, she stopped dead in her tracks. Standing beside and talking with Connor and his parents was Robert Best, an arrogant jerk, but now one of the hottest music producer/managers in the business. What the hell was he doing here? The guy was a complete creep and she didn't have time for this. She needed to get moving on the interview. Joining the entourage, she did not even acknowledge Best, but instead looked at Jocelyn and Ben and said, "Sorry to interrupt, but we need to get started with Connor's interview. The producers for Dateline are ready and so am I."

"Ms. Paxton, so nice to see you again. You are looking as lovely as ever. Robert Best, if you have forgotten," Best extending his hand to go along with the sarcastic remark.

"Mr. Best, I would offer you some interview time, but *Music Talks* is a little busy at the moment with someone a little more newsworthy, so if you will excuse us. Thank you," shot Bentley right back at Best.

"Ouch, that was a stinger. Ben, Jocelyn, it was a pleasure. Connor, you and I will see a lot of each other in the years to come. Congratulations on the victory," said Best, shaking everyone's hand as he departed, except of course, Bentley's. He didn't even try.

"I presume you two don't like each other much, huh?" Connor asked her as they watched Best disappear out of sight.

"Well, let's just say I have some professional standards that I try to maintain and adhere to. I am not sure he does. Anyway, enough of him. Let's get you prepped for the cameras one more time, young man," replied Bentley as a Dateline producer took Connor and his parents off into a room to get him ready and Bentley headed to the interview room. Seeing Best had unnerved her, and she struggled to get him out of her mind so she could concentrate on the interview. She suddenly thought of Avery for some reason. Maybe it was because he also was creeped out by Best. Oh well, she thought, time to work.

A few minutes later, they were in front of the cameras, the lights being adjusted around them, Connor and his parents ready to go. She began the interview with some questions about the victory in the show that had just finished.

"Connor, you are twelve years old, you just won one of the biggest competitions in the world. How are you feeling right now?" she asked.

Smiling and exuding an air of confidence and maturity, Connor stated, "I feel really good, you know. When this all started I had no idea I could have won this thing, I just wanted to sing and show America that I could sing. I think I accomplished that in this show."

"What will you do with the million dollars?" asked Bentley.

Looking at his mom and dad, he said, "I have the best parents in the world, and this money is for them. I don't need any money, I'm twelve years old. I can barely spend my monthly allowance of $40, what am I going to do with a million dollars?" replied Connor.

"Do you know how much a million dollars is, Connor?" asked Bentley with a smile.

"Yeah. About $500,000 after taxes," laughed Connor.

That was how the interview went. People of America would see that this little superstar who was about to become a household name very shortly was a charming, honest and well-spoken young gentleman. It was obvious that Ben and Jocelyn had raised Connor very well, as he was simply a joy to be with. Bentley thoroughly enjoyed the interview, and when it wrapped she was almost a bit sad. She felt as if she had known Connor all his life, he made her feel that welcome and comfortable.

It was almost midnight when she climbed into her Beetle convertible and headed for home in Santa Clara. What a week she'd had. The Dateline interview would come out in a few days, giving her some incredible exposure as the woman who interviewed Connor Asker. Time to hit up Jonathon for a big raise, she laughed to herself, as she gunned it when she merged onto the 680. Feeling the warm breeze blow through her long hair, she felt unstoppable. Her career was going great and she loved her job. She reminded herself again that she was still missing something in her life. She knew what it was, but she hated to admit it. She was lonely. Maybe someday. Maybe someday it would happen for her.

Chapter 41

Daniel and Michelle Leroux of Rigaud, Quebec, Canada, had no idea, when the adoption agency granted them the sweetest little three-month-old baby girl one could imagine, that they had become the parents of what would grow up to be a darling twelve-year-old who was the talk of the nation.

Daniel, a retired and fully pensioned Canada Post employee at the age of fifty-three, with thirty-two years of service, was in a position to manage their daughter Elizabeth's burgeoning career as an opera singer and accomplished musician. Michelle, also a Canada Post employee, still had another three and a half years to go before full retirement, and she was determined to get there rather than pull the plug now after twenty-three years and accept only a partial pension.

The Children's Adoption Agency, a provincially regulated government body, allowed the Leroux to give the baby girl a name of their own, as she was young enough to easily adapt to a new name, so they called her Elizabeth after Michelle's grandmother. The agency case worker who had been working with the Leroux for several years in their quest to adopt a child informed them that the baby was a survivor of a tragic accident that had claimed the life of the mother and the baby had been born while the mother was on life support. There was no record of the father, so the links to the baby's past were gone. The health of the mother was clear of any past drug or alcohol abuse, so the Leroux felt extremely blessed to have such a young baby but also a very healthy one. Little did they know how famous this infant would become.

From the minute they brought her home, Elizabeth had shown an unusual affinity for music. Whenever music came over the TV, or if they were in the car and the radio was on, Elizabeth would instinctively listen intently, and at five months she was regularly bobbing her head and moving her hands perfectly to the beat of whatever music was playing. She was a delight in every sense, but to assure themselves that her amazing connection to music was not in any way connected to autism they had her tested by specialists. The doctors advised the Leroux to invest in her own CD player because their little girl was showing signs of high intelligence and her penchant for music was her way of funneling that intelligence towards something that would satisfy her curiosity.

And so it went for the Leroux over the years, watching and enjoying the talents that their daughter displayed more and more the older she became. Elizabeth had a beautiful voice, and at the age of seven was profiled in a special documentary by the Canadian Broadcasting Corporation on super-intelligent and talented kids in Canada. Not only could Elizabeth sing like an angel, she was also an accomplished pianist and guitarist and proficient on just about any other instrument. Her IQ was through the roof, over 140 with advanced cognitive abilities and heightened intensity that produced the ability to quickly adapt to various types of musical instruments.

Daniel and Michelle enrolled Elizabeth in St. George's School of Montreal for gifted students when she was in grade six, on the advice of her public school councilors. The Leroux transferred to Montreal and moved into the city to support their daughter's growth. They settled into the Rivière-des-Prairies–Pointe-aux-Trembles neighborhood of Montreal, a well treed and lovely area of the city, Elizabeth continued to flourish. As Francophone, the Leroux's first language was French, which they spoke at work and at home. St. George's School was an English-speaking school simply because of the linguistic diversity of the students enrolled there. Elizabeth was a popular student because of her diverse musical talents and her high intelligence. One of her best friends, a Korean immigrant named Ae-cha Lee Kim, loved to listen to her sing and play music and would sit in the back of the music room on numerous occasions by herself just to listen to Elizabeth play. Ae-cha did not have a musical bone in her body, but music inspired the highly intelligent young girl, and she thought her new friend Elizabeth was the best.

By the time Elizabeth turned eleven, the demands of her performing and singing were starting to become a little chaotic, so the Leroux decided that Daniel would retire in order to bring some normalcy and organization to their child's life. Now that her father was able to drive her to school and then pick her up afterwards, Elizabeth would often invite Ae-cha to come over after school and study with her. Ae-cha's Korean father, who spoke very little English, would then pickup Ae-cha on his way home from his job as an accountant with Revenue Canada Taxation. At the age of eleven, both Ae-cha and Elizabeth were studying at a university level. Daniel would watch the two of them interact together and marvel at the intelligence level when they were in the same room. One minute they would be studying, sounding and acting like fourth-year university students, and then the next acting silly and goofy like eleven-year-old kids. Both Daniel and Michelle loved their daughter so and felt incredibly fortunate. They also wondered what kind of mother and father Elizabeth had been born from to have such incredible natural talents and abilities.

When Elizabeth was profiled by the CBC in their documentary about gifted and super-talented kids in Canada, she became a celebrity of sorts, not only at her school amongst her peers but within the entire city of Montreal. News channels interviewed her, she had camera crews interview her when she was singing, and clips of her playing the piano or the guitar would show up on the news. It was getting crazy, and having her father nearby to manage the chaos was a big reason Elizabeth had not only the space to continue to grow and expand her musical talents but also the space to just be a twelve-year-old kid. For Daniel and Michelle, allowing her to be a kid was a top priority, and they never lost sight of that.

Everything changed, however, when the Montreal Symphony Orchestra invited Elizabeth to perform at their summer concert series in the acoustically perfect brand new Place des Arts concert hall. News channels began to report on the invitation, and the hype about her upcoming performance began to spread. This would be Elizabeth's coming-out party to the world, everyone said. Rumors were flying that international singing superstar Celine Dion, a native Quebecer, would be in attendance. Knowing this would change everything in Elizabeth's life, as the world would discover how truly gifted of a musician she really was, Daniel and Michelle struggled with the decision to let her perform. It was a tremendous opportunity for their daughter, they knew, but they also wondered if this was too much for her right at this time. Perhaps instead they should continue to keep her out of the spotlight to avoid the accompanying distractions so she could focus on just being a damned smart and talented kid. It was Elizabeth's insistence that she wanted to perform that made Daniel and Michelle decide to go ahead and let her. They knew they could not keep this mega-talented child hidden much longer. It was just a matter of time.

As the big day approached, the MSO decided that having Elizabeth perform on opening night would be a great way to launch their summer concert series, with all of the media attention she would generate. Posters for the concert series advertised guest appearances by some of Canada's most renowned artists for each show during the summer, with the opening show featuring twelve-year-old Elizabeth Leroux, billed as 'Canada's Little Darling.' The plan was to have Elizabeth come on stage after the orchestra took its break at the halfway point of the show. She would sing three songs, accompanied by the MSO and by herself on piano. The three songs that she and her parents, along with the MSO director, had chosen were kept a secret, so as to surprise everyone. Daniel and Michelle, as well as Elizabeth's best friend Ae-cha, were asked to join Celine Dion and her husband René plus their three kids in their private suite for the concert. Elizabeth, who had always idolized Celine Dion, would not be left out, as she would get to join them after her performance was done.

The Place des Arts had been built by the cash-strapped Quebec government amidst a tremendous backlash by the taxpaying public, who felt that the last thing the government should be doing was spending money on concert halls when the country was in the grip of a deep economic downturn. The building, however, did get built, and was the home base for the world-class Montreal Symphony Orchestra. Attending a concert by the MSO in the new building, with its great attention to detail in design both architecturally and acoustically, was a treat for the senses. When the lucky enough people who were able to get tickets to the 3,000-seat concert hall started to arrive and find their seats, there was a buzz in the building that could be felt as well as heard. The general feeling, it seemed, amongst the concert goers, was that they were in store for something very special tonight. When word began to spread that a top US music producer was also in the audience to see Elizabeth perform, it added to the hype that Celine Dion had already brought to the show when she announced that she would attending. In her statement to the press, she said, "I am a big supporter and fan of the MSO, and to hear and see them in their brand new state of the art concert hall is going to be fantastic." Then with a big smile she told reporters, "To be honest, my kids insisted we take them tonight to see Elizabeth Leroux perform, they are huge fans."

Soon the lights dimmed over the audience, indicating the show was about to begin, silencing the crowd almost immediately. The stage glowed brightly, revealing the MSO as they launched into a stirring rendition of Beethoven's Ninth Symphony that showcased the new concert hall's stunning acoustics. The MSO continued on with pieces from their Russian repertoire, Borodin, Tchaikovsky, and Shostakovitch, bringing the first half of the concert to an end. With a twenty-minute break before the second half, people rushed to use the facilities, get refreshments or gather to chat and stretch their legs. Milling about almost unknown amongst the concert goers was Robert Best, the hotshot music producer with some of the top Hip Hop, R & B and pop artists in the world as his clients. Certainly no one attending a symphony concert in Montreal, Canada, would have known who he was, except of course Celine Dion, one of the biggest-selling female pop vocalists of all time. Strolling through the main foyer with her entourage, which included her three kids and husband René, she recognized Best and stopped to say hello.

"What a surprise to see one of the music industry's hottest producers here in Montreal at a symphony. What brings Robert Best to Canada?" asked Celine.

"I am a huge fan of classical music, and it's an opportunity to see the new building and to see what all of Canada is talking about, this Elizabeth Leroux," explained Best, using his hands to point at the building, then gesturing with his hands to mimic a small child when he mentioned Elizabeth's name.

"It was nice to see you again, Mr. Best. Enjoy the concert and this beautiful city," smiled Celine as she nodded at Robert and then strode away with her herd. Looking at her husband René, she commented, "Who's he kidding? He probably has a contract in his suit jacket for Elizabeth to sign before he leaves tonight." Watching Dion's entourage disappear through a doorway leading to what would be her private box, Best thought to himself what a bitch she was. He could have ripped out her heart from her chest before her fat husband even had a chance to take his next breath. Soon the music industry would not know what hit them when he unleashed his plans. He would be the biggest music mogul the world had ever seen, and divas like the lovely Ms. Dion would bow down to him as if he was a God. Wouldn't that be funny, he thought to himself, but really he could care less. *They will all be dead anyways*, he laughed, as he made his way back to his seat and sat back to enjoy the show. He was here for one reason only, and that was to see firsthand the reaction of the audience to the coming-out of his creation, Elizabeth Leroux. The love affair this country had with their Celine Dion would officially end tonight.

Once again the lights dimmed, and the PA announcer asked the audience in both English and French to welcome to the stage five-time Grammy award winner and Canada's own Celine Dion. This was definitely an unexpected welcome surprise, and the audience showed their appreciation with thunderous applause. Putting her heart and soul into two of her classics, "Power of Love" and the French ballad "Les oiseaux du bonheur," backed by the MSO, she gave a spectacular performance. The audience, subdued but appreciative in the first half of the concert, were now loud, boisterous and on their feet trying to get Celine back on stage for a third performance as the stage grew dark. After about a minute, a spotlight shone on Celine once again standing at the podium, asking for quiet. The audience obliged and Celine continued, "Thank you so much everyone, I love you all. It gives me great honor to introduce to you one of the most talented singer/musicians this country has ever produced, Elizabeth Leroux," and with that the spotlight on Celine went dark and another light shone out of the dark and focused on twelve-year-old Elizabeth Leroux dressed in a lovely navy blue shimmering sequined dress sitting at an enormous black grand piano. Smiling from ear to ear, she began playing the piano with the grace and talent of a world class virtuoso. It was breathtaking to hear, and she was quickly joined by the MSO, accompanying her in an upbeat version of the classic Well-Tempered Clavier by Johann Sebastian Bach. This would be a difficult piece for anyone, but to change the arrangement ever so slightly made it even more difficult, so seeing and hearing Elizabeth rip through it with ease was astonishing and beautiful. The song showed the audience what an incredibly accomplished pianist that she was, and when she moved onto a stool in front of the stage holding onto a flute for her second piece, the crowd braced. When Elizabeth began to play the flute, producing a dreamy, fluttering sound so lovely she had the audience spellbound, the MSO joined in to accompany her with its full string section, then paused to allow Elizabeth's flute to work its magic. The piece was truly amazing and had the audience on its feet roaring its appreciation.

For Elizabeth's third and final piece, she would sing her idol Celine Dion's famous song from the Titanic movie soundtrack "My Heart Will Go On." Backed by the MSO, her performance was simply a masterpiece. Elizabeth's vocals were incredible, and she matched and exceeded Celine's vocal range with such ferocity and power it was magnificent to behold. The emotion she generated in the song touched everyone in the audience on a level that brought some to tears. When it ended, the audience were numb from the experience, and the deafening roar of the crowd almost brought down the newly installed acoustic panels from their ceiling brackets to the floor. When Elizabeth turned towards Celine's private box to bow down in appreciation to her idol, the crowd went crazy. Straightening up again, addressing her appreciation to the audience into the microphone, she waved and blew kisses. Looking back again at Celine's box, she waved at her best friend Ae-cha, who was jumping up and down, screaming her lungs out.

****

Leaving his seat in the middle of the concert hall, pushing past all of the clapping and cheering audience, Robert Best made his way to the exit. Nobody even noticed the gleaming bright red eyes of the Beast as he made his way out of the building, completely and utterly satisfied at the way events had unfolded tonight.

It had gone exactly as he had hoped. The press would have a field day with the reviews, and soon Elizabeth would be as popular as the other twelve-year-old music prodigies who were popping up everywhere around the world.

The power coursing through the soulless body he occupied

was immeasurable. The cauldrons of hell would soon be overflowing with the empty souls of a lost mankind when his plan was unleashed. The tears from Heaven on His loss would cleanse this earth of His memory forever.

Walking out onto the street, and before he vaporized into the mist of the night, Best felt mega-powerful, with an energy wave that was cascading through his mind like a powerful drug. He needed to kill a few humans before he disappeared with the breeze, simply because he felt like it.

He knew that God could feel his power surge right now and would be investigating as to the source, but he would confuse and anger Him with a brutal attack and murder of some unfortunate Christian souls across town.

He loved to kill humans, especially the Christians, because it pissed off God even more, but nothing satisfied him more than stealing the soul of a human. Soon he would have them all and there was nothing that the Almighty could do about it. To protect his Robert Best character he would morph into a reptilian monster creation again when he killed tonight. He liked that one a lot, it scared the shit out of his victims. It was time to have some fun.

Chapter 42

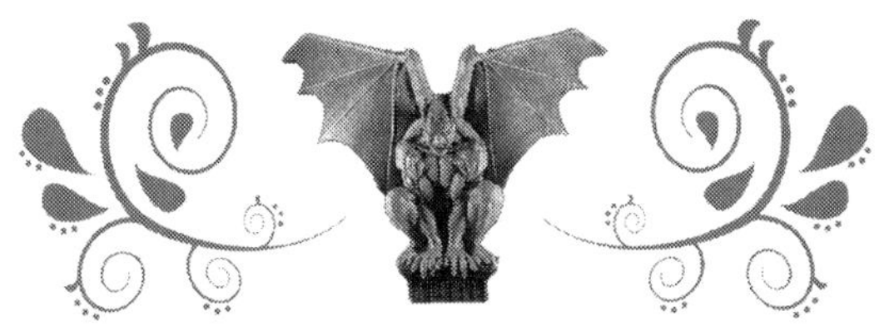

Sam and Bethany prepared for their son's twelfth birthday party that afternoon and were busy getting the house ready for the kids who were coming, and their parents, family and friends. This would be Sebastian's last birthday before his bar mitzvah. Coming over today, and only three months younger than Sebastian, was his best friend Patrick Benning. Their moms were also the best of friends. The older the two boys became, the more different they were. Seb, as he was called at school and now at home, was going to be tall like his dad, already a whopping five foot ten at just twelve years of age. Athletically gifted, Seb was very good at basketball and football, as well as track and field. His marks were top notch, and he had high school basketball star written all over him. If he continued to develop physically, football would be a natural, but his first love was basketball, and he routinely kicked his dad's butt in games of twenty-one on the driveway court.

Patrick Benning, on the other hand, did not have an athletic bone in his body. Not that he was uncoordinated or anything like that; he was just not very good in sports. Patrick was physically filled out for a twelve-year-old but was not into sports. Patrick had showed early, since he was a toddler, a tremendous love for music, especially percussion. He was in the mall one day with his mom, Chelsea, as they were walking past a music instrument store. On display in the window was a drum set. Six-year-old Patrick began to vigorously pull his mother's hand in the direction of the music store. He continued to yank and pull and ask his mom to take him inside, and when she did, he made a beeline for the drum set in the window display. As he stood beside the drum set with a look of wonder on his face, a salesman approached them and asked Patrick if he played the drums. Chelsea replied that no, he did not, and Patrick just continued to stare at the gleaming stainless steel-trimmed drum set. The salesman retrieved a set of drum sticks and brought them to Patrick, asking him if he would like to play the drums, to which Patrick replied, "Yeaaah!"

Helping him up onto the drum set and adjusting the stool so his feet would touch the bass drum pedal, the salesman handed the sticks to Patrick, thinking he would bang away and then cry and scream to his rich mom to buy them for him and he would make a sale. What he did not expect was for this little six-year-old to bang the sticks at random for a few seconds and then all of a sudden begin to work the drum set in a controlled beat. Soon, within a minute, Patrick was pounding away on the drum set like a pro, his little hands working the sticks over its face, backed by a continuous thump of the bass that was perfectly in time. It was incredible to hear and see. Soon two large crowds were gathering, one in the hallway of the mall in front of the store display watching Patrick perform and another inside the store that had come over to see what all the fuss was about. Even a drum solo by a professional is barely listenable, and to listen to a six year old bang away should have been a nightmare, but Patrick, wide-eyed with complete enjoyment, pounded the drums to a crescendo, then back down again, then back up followed by a smash of the cymbals.

Chelsea just stood there astonished, watching her little son entertain dozens of people, who were all as stunned as she was. The only thing missing, it seemed, was Patrick twirling the sticks in his little hands like those rock drummers do. *Jesus,* Chelsea thought, *this was crazy.* Finally, Chelsea decided that enough was enough, already, of this sideshow and stepped up onto the window display to let Patrick know he had to stop playing as they had to get going. Looking over at his mom while still working the sticks over the drum set, beads of sweat on his little forehead and his long blond hair beginning to stick to the side of his face, and with his tongue hanging out the side of his mouth, he looked at his mom and said, "Oh, please, Mom, can I keep playing, this is so much fun! Please. Please!"

Then the crowd began to chant, "Patrick! Patrick! Patrick!" This fuelled Patrick and he began pounding away with even more vigor.

"Okay, Patrick, enough already, son, we must go. Maybe we can talk to this nice man who gave you the sticks about getting this set. What do you say about that, huh?"

Abruptly ending his drum playing, Patrick climbed off the stool and wrapped his arms around her waist and screamed, "Will you buy this for me, Mom? Oh please, can you buy this, please? Pleassee!"

"I said I would, didn't I? Let's go, little man," said Chelsea as she helped Patrick down off of the windowsill to the roar of applause from the people who had gathered in the store and out in the hallway. Looking at the salesman who was smiling from ear to ear at the attention Patrick had brought to the store, Chelsea pointed to the drum set and said, "How much?"

"Why don't you come down to my office and I will price that set out for you. There are different options you can add or remove that will affect the price, so let's go sit down and I'll work all that out for you."

She gave the salesman a look that said, "I'm not stupid, so don't even try," before telling him, "By the way, you can take off ten percent right off the top for all the free publicity your store just received from my son's lively little performance."

Thirty minutes later and $2,000 poorer, Chelsea and Patrick left the mall. The drum set would be delivered in a few days, and it included professional setup, but something told Chelsea that Patrick could put together the drum kit in his sleep if he wanted to. It seemed he was a natural-born drummer, and she wasn't sure why. Then again she'd always known he would be a very special little boy, ever since his miraculous birth, when the cold, hard fear she felt as she was lying on the bathroom floor in the hospital delivering Patrick that she was about to give birth to a monster was then replaced by the joy of a miracle. The miracle of God's intervention by casting out the demonic seed that had grown inside her and His replacing it with the gift of His love. The gift of Life. The gift of Patrick.

****

Patrick and Seb were the best of friends because they just got along and showed a mutual respect for each other's interests and talents. When he was nine years old, Seb began to ask his parents why his best friend had no dad. Sam and Beth explained to him that Patrick's father was a policeman just like his dad was and that he and dad had been partners. They decided to tell Seb that Patrick's father had been shot to death in the line of duty and was a hero.

Chelsea and Patrick arrived for the birthday party, and after hugs were exchanged between everyone, Patrick quickly disappeared to join Seb and the other kids from the party. Beth grabbed Chelsea by the arm and led her into the family room to meet some other parents as well as Sam's brothers and their families. Sam's brothers, all three of them, were Orthodox Jewish rabbis. It was a calling that had also been expected of Sam, but instead he had broken away from the traditional Orthodox way of life and decided to join the police academy after college, much to the great disappointment of his father. Sam's three brothers were great men whom he respected and loved very much, and they loved Sam the same and had never judged him for the path he'd chosen in life. They frequently got together to talk and share, shoot baskets in the driveway with their kids, and just do what families do. The only thing with this family that was kind of different was that three of them wore their hair funny and wore funky clothing, and the other guy carried a gun and a shield on his belt. No big deal. Later on, after the cake was eaten and Seb opened his presents from the other kids and from his aunts and uncles, things began to wind down. Soon everyone started to leave until finally it was just Chelsea and Patrick. With Patrick and Seb in his room playing Xbox, the three of them, Chelsea and Sam and Beth, relaxed in the living room. Beth wanted to know how Patrick was doing lately with his drumming and if the KISS reunion tour had recruited him. Laughing, Chelsea just said that when she could afford it she was going to remodel the garage to move his drum kit out of the house because the noise of his playing was driving her crazy.

Excited at the opportunity to help Chelsea out, Sam volunteered his time.

"Maybe I can spend a weekend over there getting that done for you, Chelsea. It's more cleaning up than anything else. What do you say I come over next weekend and take care of that for you?"

Sam noticed a change in Chelsea's voice, detecting an underlying sadness.

"Thank you, Sam, but you know that garage is where I moved all of Steven's stuff, from his clothes to his hunting equipment and everything in between. I just didn't know where to put it all, and I wasn't ready to get rid of it. I know if I got rid of most of his stuff then I would be able to use the garage, Sam, I just don't know if I'm ready yet," Chelsea explained.

Beth glanced over at Sam, for reassurance, before she replied to Chelsea's concerns.

"Chelsea, you just have to make that decision to let it go. I know how hard it must be for you to make that decision, but you must. It's been a very long time now that Steven has been gone. Excuse me for saying this, honey, but you need to meet someone in your life. Start a relationship. You are a beautiful woman, Chelsea, and having a good man to start your life over again with would be so wonderful for you."

Leaning forward in her chair, holding her hand up like a stop sign in Beth's direction, Chelsea replied.

"Whoa, not ready for that yet, Beth, let's focus on Steven's stuff in the garage first. Besides, I have Patrick, and he's all I need right now." Looking at Sam, she continued, "I think I will move Steven's stuff out of the garage Sam. If you could come down and help me go through it, and if there's anything you want for yourself then take it, otherwise I'll donate it, or throw it away."

"I think that's a great idea, Chelsea. Then let's do that next weekend. Patrick can spend the day here with Seb while we go through that stuff and haul it away."

A few minutes later, after more discussions on Steven's belongings, Chelsea declared that they should get going as well, since Patrick had school in the morning. After she summoned Patrick downstairs, he tried his best to convince his mom to stay longer as he and Seb still wanted to play. Chelsea reminded him that it was a school night, and they said their goodbyes. Sam walked them out to their car, and after Patrick jumped into the front passenger seat, Sam looked at Chelsea in the eye and asked her, "Is everything okay, Chelsea? You holding up okay?"

"I'm doing fine, Sam, really I am. Patrick has been such a blessing for me, and he keeps me fulfilled, you know. Beth was right, Sam; I would like to meet someone someday. It gets lonely sometimes, I'm not going to lie."

Sam instantly thought of a widowed cop he knew, a great guy.

"I know a wonderful guy in Commercial Crime. Works Monday to Friday, no shift work, he would be good for you."

"Please, no policemen, Sam, that would be too weird. I'd find myself comparing his stories of his work days to Steven's. No, a clean break completely, Sam. Maybe I'll put my profile online, catch me a rich doctor or something," laughed Chelsea.

He gave Chelsea a reassuring hug and said, "You are a beautiful woman and you deserve someone, Chelsea. It will happen for you now that your heart is open to it."

The car door swung open and Patrick yelled out, "Hey, can we get going, Mom, you were the one that wanted to leave!"

"Okay, I'm coming, son. Thanks, Sam, you and Beth are

awesome. Love you guys. Talk soon." Chelsea gave Sam a peck on the cheek, then climbed into the car and sped off.

Sam watched as her car disappeared down the street. He flashed back to the days before Patrick was born, when Chelsea would have spent the afternoon chewing his ass off for the lack of progress on her husband's murder investigation. Something was not right, he said to himself, standing there on the street, deep in thought. The case still haunted Sam; he could never not stop thinking about it. The brutality, the lack of forensic evidence, the abrupt change in attitude from Chelsea, the desire by department heads to completely shut down the investigation – it all left a pit in Sam's stomach that could never be filled. Steven had been his best friend and his partner. His wife, almost thirteen years later, was still a widow, still living in the shadows of her dead husband, unable to move on. Sam felt a deep sense of loss standing there. He felt a feeling that he had let his best friend down, his wife and his unborn son. It was time to investigate Steven's murder once again. Sam felt a strong urge that he could not explain to look in the investigators' files once again. Search for clues he might have missed. It must be there. The key to unlock Steven's death had to be hidden in those files. Turning to walk up the driveway to the house, Sam felt a compelling responsibility to solve this case. For Steven, for Chelsea, and for their son Patrick.

Chapter 43

Over the last twelve years since the birth of Michael, a lot had happened. Then again, not very much at all had happened. There were many things that had not changed in Ann's life, for instance her entire family shunning her completely. She had been ostracized from them as they still thought she was stark raving mad. That was completely fine with Ann, she certainly didn't need them. Ann's lawyers had ensured that she and Michael would be taken care of financially for the rest of their lives. Her family's wealth was measured in the billions, so in addition to a sizeable inheritance transferred to Ann's estate, she had insisted that her charities also be well funded for years to come.

What had changed, of course, was the birth of Michael. Ann had not expected the birth of such a wonderful and beautiful child. What she had really expected was to give birth to a demonic and evil baby. She had accepted that in her mind as a fact, along with her determination to raise the baby with all of her love regardless. The fact that Michael was so special was difficult for Ann to comprehend, but she embraced it as God's plan for her. Therefore, she would stay the course for Him and raise Michael with unconditional love. Ann never had found out what happened to Karen, her assistant and friend during the year leading up to the birth of Michael. She had completely disappeared and Ann had never seen her again after she was rushed into emergency, bleeding and in labor. Something inside of her told her that Karen was a guardian of the Devil, assigned to watch over Ann to ensure the healthy birth of its child. Ann did not care, because her faith in Jesus Christ would show her a path through this, and she held onto that belief with every fiber in her being.

Michael was an exceptional baby, a very gifted child right from the very beginning of his life. This did not surprise Ann; she had expected him to be special. She was surprised, however, when he gravitated towards music as his outlet for showcasing his incredible abilities. Music came super-naturally to Michael. He could play any instrument but really liked the guitar and the piano. His voice was beautiful, and by the time he'd reached the age of eleven it was already maturing into its own and had already gone through the normal changes. All through grade school, Michael, was very popular, not only because he was such a talented musician, but because he was a very handsome lad, incredibly so, actually, and of course very popular with the girls. This popularity made all the other boys want to be Michael's friend. Through it all, Michael was able to stay grounded and focused. He never let all the attention go to his head or distract him. He came early to the school's music class and stayed late. On many days Michael would ask to stay late so he could practice. He was not practicing for any particular reason or concert; he did it because he loved it so much. When he would master one instrument he would beg the music teacher to let him try learning another and then another, until soon he could play any instrument in the music class with ease. He was a musical child prodigy, Ann was told by the music teacher. He was a child who should be put into a special school for music so that his natural, God-given talents could be nurtured. The teacher was partially right, thought Ann, in that Michael's talents needed to be nurtured in an environment that would grow them and not slow him down. But his talents were not God-given, that was for sure. Michael had reached a plateau at his private school, so Ann, at the advice of his music teacher, enrolled Michael at the age of eleven in the Richmond School of Music in West London, a school for the very talented and gifted in music for children of all ages.

Michael loved it at Richmond, and the school embraced his incredible talent and personality. Further expanding his love of string instruments, Michael soon mastered the violin, harp, cellos, and electric, bass, and acoustic guitars. Michael did not need to read sheet music to learn; it came naturally, and with the music teacher showing Michael different techniques with finger placement and pressure points to create different sounds, he excelled. Once in a while, Michael would take some time by himself with the acoustic guitar or the piano along with paper and pen and draft out some songs that were swirling around in his head. It was at Richmond that Michael discovered his ability to write music and compose. It was soon after this that Ann was summoned to the school by the school administrator. Worrying that Michael had finally cracked and his inner demons had emerged and some violent episode had happened at the school, she was happy to hear that wasn't the case. In fact, the Administrator, Kathy Ovens, was very happy to see Ann and welcomed her into her office.

"Thank you for coming down, Ms. Lockwood. I must say you have a very incredibly talented and charming child. When he first came to us at the age of eleven, he truly was a very talented young boy. Over the past year, not only has he has proven that he is very talented, but he has shown clear signs of musical genius, Ms. Lockwood. Your son is a gifted musical prodigy," smiled Kathy.

Ann was instantly impressed with Kathy.

"Thank you, I think so, too!"

Kathy stood up from her desk and came around and sat in the empty chair beside Ann.

"I hate sitting behind a desk when I am meeting with someone. Feels too formal and authoritarian. I hope you don't mind. The reason I asked you here today, Ms. Lockwood, was to see if you would be open to allowing us to let Michael perform with the London Symphony Orchestra. Rarely does the symphony bring in a student from the school to guest perform, and your son is by far the youngest student who has ever been requested by the LSO to do so."

Ann was stunned to hear this news. The symphony wanted Michael to perform? He was only twelve years old. This was unbelievable.

"Oh my gosh, the symphony? What an honor for Michael! What does he think?" asked Ann.

"It is an honor for him, Ms. Lockwood. You should be very proud. Do you mind if I call you Ann? You can call me Kathy."

"Certainly, please do call me Ann," she replied. She could tell Kathy was very proud of her Michael and his accomplishments. Her heart was in the right place, namely the well-being of her students.

Leaning forward in her chair, Kathy patted Ann on her knee before she spoke. "Let's bring Michael into this meeting, shall we, so we can get his input as well. Would that be okay?"

"Good idea, Kathy, let's do that."

Soon Michael was brought in, and after giving his mom a hug he settled into the chair beside Ann where Kathy had sat, as Kathy returned behind her desk. Kathy explained to him that she'd just been telling his mom that the London Symphony Orchestra had requested that he guest perform at an upcoming concert. Michael squealed in delight, "Are you serious?! That is so awesome! Mom can you believe it, the London Symphony Orchestra?"

"Yes, son, you should be very proud. It is a tremendous honor for you. You deserve it, Michael, you have worked very hard," smiled Ann, looking at her son.

"Your mom is right, Michael, this is a huge honor bestowed on you and on our school. Not very often does one of our students get to perform with the LSO, and especially someone so young like yourself. You are an incredibly gifted and talented musician, Michael, I hope you know that. Cherish this talent, Michael, and always allow the love of music to grow inside of you. Will you do that for me? For yourself and for your mom as well?"

Ann watched her son as Kathy spoke and couldn't help but notice how mature he looked for his age. She warmed inside as she saw how excited he was at this opportunity.

"I will, Mrs. Ovens, thank you so much for this opportunity and thank you, Mom, for enrolling me in this school," beamed Michael, clearly thrilled with what was transpiring.

The London Symphony Orchestra had decided to have Michael perform during the entire second half of their concert and to introduce Michael to the audience after their halfway break. He would play mainly in their string section, alternating between the violin, cello, and harp, showcasing his talents to the audience. The plan was for Michael to end the show by playing a solo piece on the piano while singing. The LSO were being very gracious in giving Michael this opportunity, but they were as thrilled as anyone to have him perform.

Michael had become, much to Ann's surprise, quite a fan of American Christian music legend Michael W. Smith. Ann would often hear him sing or hum Smith's songs. It was a bit of a surprise, however, that Michael had chosen to sing a Michael W. Smith ballad, "Rise," a song that encourages people to rise up, reach up to God, and leave it all behind. It seemed to Ann as if the demonic spirit that lived in her son's soul was mocking the Lord. Raising Michael with love was easy and natural for Ann; she was his mother. But Ann was acutely aware of his bloodlines and prayed daily for God's love and mercy and that Michael's soul would be saved. Ann knew that He would not forsake Michael, that His plan for him would reveal itself at some point. She needed to remain strong and have faith that God's love would prevail. All alone in this journey, she sometimes felt as if she was stranded on this tiny little island all by herself with Michael, and with nowhere to go or no one around to help. It was hard, but she loved him so much and knew that his birth was planned and that God had always known about his birth.

When word broke out at Richmond that twelve-year-old Michael Lockwood had been picked by the LSO to guest perform, he became a bit of a celebrity at the school. Then they discovered he would be playing an entire half of a show, not just one song like the few people before him who had been lucky enough to have been chosen. Everyone knew how talented Michael was, and the news of his selection by the LSO just confirmed it. Everyone wanted to hang out and be seen with the young music prodigy from Richmond. Girls from neighboring schools were seen hanging out at Richmond just to get a chance to meet the very handsome young Lockwood boy.

When the night of the concert arrived, the Richmond School rented a limo to pick up Ann and Michael at home. Ann could have bought the entire limo company with her credit card, but that wasn't the point. The point was that they were being treated like celebrities and Michael was the star of the show. When they climbed in, they discovered that Kathy Ovens, the Richmond school administrator was already in the limo. "Hi, guys! I thought I would tag along with both of you, if that is okay?"

"This is wonderful, Kathy, great to see you. I'm so glad you will be with us. I'm kind of nervous, so having you here is perfect!" laughed Ann.

Kathy beamed as she saw how handsome young Michael looked in his tailored tuxedo. "How about you, Michael, are you nervous?" asked Kathy.

"No way, Mrs. Ovens, I'm so excited I can't wait to play with some of the best musicians in the world," smiled Michael with utter confidence.

"Well, you look very handsome in your tux, young man. Ann, you must be very proud!"

"Yes, I am proud of him, Kathy, but I would be even more so if I could only get him to unload the dishwasher," commented Ann, poking Michael in the ribs.

Having a good laugh on Michael's expense, thinking it might loosen him up, Ann knew he did not really need any loosening up. She did it more for appearances in front of Kathy. Michael was born for this, she had always known that. This concert was his coming-out party, in a way, to let the world know that

Michael Lockwood had arrived. The confidence and talent that oozed from his little body was palpable. Pulling up in front of the Barbican Centre on Silk Street in London, Michael, Ann and Kathy climbed out of the limo and made their way into the concert hall. With Kathy's direction, they made their way towards the LSO producer, Lawrence Green, who greeted Michael and Ann and welcomed them to the LSO at the Barbican. He let Ann know that he would take Michael backstage so he could warm up with the LSO and also practice while the LSO were performing during the first half. Giving Michael a big hug and wishing him well, Ann watched him walk down the plush carpeted hallway that led to the backstage studio. This was almost a surreal moment for Ann, watching little Michael depart. She flashed back to an image of Dalton, how much in love they had been, and how they had often spoken of having children in the future. This should have been our moment, Dalton, she thought to herself. That should have been your son going onstage with the London Symphony Orchestra tonight. Ann was brought back to reality when she heard Kathy say, "Are you all right, Ann? I know this is very exciting and nerve wracking all at the same time," offering Ann a Kleenex. Ann had been crying, and she realized she likely had mascara running down her cheeks, so she excused herself to freshen up in the ladies room.

She gathered herself a few minutes later, exiting the ladies room, and joined Kathy, who was such a nice and caring lady that Ann felt a strong friendship growing between the two of them. They made their way to their reserved seats in a VIP box up in the second tier of the concert hall, where they had a perfect view of the entire stage so that no matter where Michael would be performing they would be able to see him. The first half of the concert began with some familiar pieces that Ann recognized from the soundtrack of one of the Harry Potter films that she and Michael had watched together. The LSO, with a reputation as one of the finest orchestras in the world, did not disappoint. Ann had had the opportunity see them often, both at the

Barbican and St. Luke's, and she always thoroughly enjoyed their performances. Little had she known that someday her twelve-year-old son would be performing with them. When the break came, the audience stood and stretched and made their way to the lobby for refreshments or the restrooms. Kathy and Ann decided they would make their way to the bar and see if they could get through the line in time to get a glass of wine before the concert resumed. Making small talk, Kathy said, "My husband Richard and I would be delighted, Ann, if you and Michael could join us for dinner some evening at our home. We would be honored to have you. Richard is a huge fan and collector of Elvis Presley memorabilia, so he would love to show you all of his stuff!"

"That would be so much fun. I would like that, Kathy, thank you. Michael is a massive fan of Elvis Presley, so he would be thrilled. That is so kind of you and your husband."

"Then that's a date. Be prepared when you come, as Richard will likely greet you at the door in one of his white sequined outfits, I'm sure of it!" laughed Kathy.

Finally getting to the front of the line, they each chose a glass of house Merlot. Hearing the PA announcing that the concert would resume in five minutes, they laughed, knowing they would have to gulp down their wine. Ann asked Kathy while they were finishing up, "How long have you been married Kathy, you and Richard?"

"It will be twenty-seven years this September. It's crazy how that sounds when I say it, it sure does not seem that long."

Taking a final sip of her wine, Ann did not know how to comment back, as she was still thinking of her husband Dalton, and to hear Kathy say twenty-seven years made her a little choked up. Sensing this, Kathy said, "Oh, honey, I am sorry if I made you sad. You still miss him, don't you? You poor thing."

"I'm fine, Kathy. Just thinking of Michael and his big day and how wonderful it would have been if Dalton could have been here to see this. Anyway, enough of this sad talk, we'd better get back to our seats or we'll miss it."

They found their way back to their seats just in time, as the concert host walked out on to the stage and announced, "Ladies and Gentleman, you are in store tonight for a rare treat. On occasion, the LSO welcomes a guest performer. Tonight we are introducing to you a talent so special I am sure you will be very excited to hear him. This young man came to us through the Richmond School of Music, and he is, I can tell you, one of, if not the most, talented musicians I have ever heard. Please welcome twelve-year-old Michael Lockwood!" The curtain rose to an appreciative and polite audience, giving Michael and the returning LSO a warm round of applause.

The stage was darkened with the exception of the spotlight on Michael, moving the bow of his violin over the strings of his instrument, his left hand working, squeezing and stroking the strings of the violin as if he owned it. The song was a hauntingly beautiful one that Ann did not recognize, but it was captivating and had the audience spellbound. Soon the rest of the violin and string section worked their way into the piece and were joined in varying degrees by the entire orchestra. The song then slowed, and again the lights darkened with the spotlight illuminating Michael once again as he wowed the audience with his beautiful and skillful playing. When the song ended, the audience broke into a roar and gave Michael and the LSO thunderous applause. As Michael approached the front of the stage and bowed, the audience again roared their approval. Michael then made his way to the cello section and, finding his seat, picked up his huge instrument that almost dwarfed him. The song this time was more of a dark, brooding kind, with rich, deep undercurrents that carried the audience to an imaginary place in their minds. The audience were then taken to another more exhilarating place with Michael's aggressive strumming of his cello, backed by the orchestra. It was simply brilliant. When the song ended, the audience leapt to their feet and roared their approval at the masterpiece that had just been laid down by Michael and the LSO. The second half finished with Michael and the orchestra playing classic songs from movies that everyone could recognize but had never enjoyed as much when performed by the LSO alone.

When the show finally closed, it was clear the audience had loved every second of it, and the place resembled a rock concert. The audience refused to go home, continuing instead with their thunderous applause and cheering. The LSO listened, and they returned to the stage, where a grand piano was spotlighted in front of the orchestra with little Michael sitting in front of it. It was the opportunity that Michael had been waiting for. He wanted to showcase his singing, and now was his time. Performing "Rise" by Michael W. Smith, Michael let his voice fill the huge concert hall, stunning the audience into complete quiet as their ears tried to let their brains know they were listening to a musical genius. His piano playing was superb, and his voice was out of this world. The audience was mesmerized, including Kathy and Ann. His vocals were so hauntingly pure, the song so emotionally powerful, that the hall was bracing for applause that would blow the roof off. When Michael, along with the soft, caressing backdrop of the LSO, finished the song, the place turned into chaos. Regular LSO concert goers were all gaga and speechless. Almost to a person, felt they were witness to the advent of a future superstar of huge magnitude. Ann was overwhelmed at the effect Michael had wrought with that song. It was magnificent. Stepping away from the piano, Michael bowed to the audience several times. He turned and faced the LSO and bowed to them. Waving to the crowd, Michael made his way off the stage. Kathy, turning to Ann, was beside herself; she had not seen this coming either and was speechless. Leaving their seats amid the chaos to locate Michael, they did not notice the satisfied expression on the face of the stranger just two rows directly behind them.

Robert Best, still standing along with everyone else, cherished the moment. The reaction was far more than he'd expected, but he had come to expect the unexpected with the seven children. *The reaction they are generating at just twelve years old was simply incredible*, he thought. Just wait till they reached sixteen or seventeen! The world will go ballistic over them. *Just watch*, he thought, *just watch what will happen.* Making his way out of his seat, he almost bumped into the woman from the school and Michael's mom, Ann. He wasn't worried she would recognize him, but she might feel his presence if they were to make physical contact. That would spook her, as she was wary as it was. He needed to be a little more careful, he thought. Ann Lockwood was dangerous, and his patience with her was running out. He needed her for a while longer, and then he would get rid of her for good. Soon, he said to himself. Soon.

Chapter 44

Driving away from the Showensteins' home, Chelsea and Patrick rode in silence. Patrick was still a little miffed at his mom for making a fuss about leaving and then standing at the car for fifteen minutes while she talked. He could have just stayed inside with Seb and played longer. Playing video games for him was a release that he needed; it was like a drug that took him away from the stress and pressures of life. He had a creative flow coursing through his brain that was all-encompassing, always turned on high, and the tension it created in his regular life was stressful. It affected his relationship with his mom and others at school. He tried to control it, and for the most part he did, but it was hard, his mind was churning and churning, ideas and information on song writing, lyrics, and instrument arrangements jammed into it as if a boxer were trying to pound it into his head even though it wouldn't all fit. He would let the information swirl around inside until it was full and he couldn't think anymore. He then had to sort through it all to make sense of it. The older he became, the easier it was to assimilate the barrage of creative energy that continually flowed through his head.

What scared Patrick to death was another energy, one that had an even stronger control over his mind and that he had not yet figured out how to manage. He loved to kill things. A lot. Mostly domestic animals around the neighborhood, but the urge to kill a human was all-consuming, and he knew in his heart that he would kill someone soon. Very soon, maybe even tonight. He had slipped out of Seb's birthday party earlier this afternoon and sneaked across the street and into the backyard of their neighbor and broken the neck of the golden retriever that he could hear barking when they arrived for the birthday party. He had wanted to kill that stupid mutt for months.

Looking at his mom while she drove, he knew he would never kill his mom. He loved her so much; she was the best mom in the world. Then there was that dark energy that did not differentiate between moms and strangers. He had to find a way to control this dark and terrible urge that was controlling him. The only way he could keep his mind from thinking about snapping the neck of someone was to focus all of his thoughts on music. *He would write some songs tonight, that will work,* he thought. He would, however, kill some cats or birds or something first, so he could focus. *Oh, he was so confused,* he thought. Focus on this, focus on that. Kill this, kill that. His head hurt so much he just wanted to get home and figure out his energies.

****

Watching Patrick sleep at a red light, Chelsea thought how blessed she was to be given such an incredibly talented and wonderful son. He was so gifted, so considerate, and so giving. Already at twelve years old he has heart throb good looks. *He is going to be a stunner that's for sure. He has an incredible future ahead of him,* she thought. He could be anything he wanted to be, he really could. Music is what seemed to have laid a claim to the gold buried within him. When he gets older that could all change, he might get bored with music, he was just so incredibly intelligent. Hearing the honk behind her, Chelsea, daydreaming still, stepped on the gas as the green light turned to yellow. She couldn't believe she'd told Sam that she was ready to meet someone. Knowing him, there probably was someone from the station waiting for her in her driveway with flowers and a box of chocolates to ask her out. She giggled out loud to herself at what a stupid thought that was. It would be kind of neat, though. It had been so many years since she'd been out on a date, it was crazy. She'd read an article in a women's magazine once that said when someone is not ready for a relationship and is closed to it, they walk around in life with a neon message written across their forehead that says 'Bitch.' Checking the rearview mirror quickly, she checked to see if that was what her message said. Yup, that is what it says, she laughed at herself, looking at her forehead in the mirror. What a dope she was. Maybe she should change that message on her forehead. Yeah, time to change it.

The next morning, after Chelsea watched Patrick get onto his bus for school, she picked up the phone and called Beth Showenstein. "Good morning, Beth, sorry for calling you so early. Are you still getting Seb off to school? I can call you back or you can call me after he's gone. Are you sure? Okay, well, I'll be quick anyway. I just wanted to invite you over for coffee this morning if you were up to it. Feel like being with a friend today. Yeah, you don't mind? Great, then, Beth, see you in a few hours!" Chelsea was happy she was able to catch Beth with no plans this morning. It would be fun for the two of them to connect.

Soon Beth arrived over at the house with a box of Dunkin' Donuts and a mischievous look on her face. "Thought we would treat ourselves, Chelsea, what do you think?" Beth asked, thrusting the box of sinful treats towards Chelsea.

"Oh, Beth, you know I have the worst time in the world trying to resist Dunkin' Donuts, why did you have to do this to me?" said Chelsea, a look of complete defeat on her face.

Beth walked around Chelsea and into her kitchen, where she placed the box of donuts on the counter.

"Come on, silly, just have one then, the sugar is a great trigger to open up your mind to what's in it that's bothering you this morning, which is why I am here, girl. Let's talk, sweetheart. What's on your mind?" asked Beth. She was a successful plastic surgeon, had her own business that was doing very well and had recently brought in a new surgeon as a partner, allowing her to reduce her workload and her hours. Now she was down to working Tuesday to Friday instead of Monday to Saturday.

Settling into the kitchen, Chelsea, in her Lululemon, and Beth in shorts, grabbed a donut each, savoring the incredible taste, when Chelsea said, "I'm glad I passed on cake at Seb's party yesterday." Beth added, "Yea, well, I didn't," and she laughed, grabbing her second donut right after she finished her first.

Taking a seat at the kitchen table across from Beth, Chelsea steered the conversation in a more serious direction.

"When I left your place yesterday, Beth, I confessed to Sam in your driveway when I was leaving that I'm ready to meet someone in my life now, I am open to it. As much as I miss Steven and everything he meant to me, I need to move on and find someone I can share my life with before I'm too damn old."

"Sam told me that, and that's why I wasn't surprised when you called. In fact, until you called and invited me, I was going to show up here myself uninvited just to chat. I think you're long, long overdue to meet someone, Chelsea. I'm so happy to see you coming around to the idea of opening yourself up to a new relationship."

"Thanks, Beth, you're a great friend, both you and Sam are. Not sure how I ever would have made it through everything without you guys."

"Nonsense, Chelsea. Your wonderful son is the blessing that has sustained you, my dear. Without him you would have had a much tougher time."

Chelsea glanced down at her coffee, lingering for a few seconds, then looked up at Beth, tears rimming her eyes, threatening to spill over.

"Yes, I most certainly would have. Did you know he is writing music now, composing music and lyrics? There just doesn't seem to be an end to the talent for music he has. It's incredible."

"Your son is incredible, plain and simple, Chelsea. He is a

gift from God to you. Sam and I are so happy for you and for Patrick."

So for the next few hours Beth and Chelsea talked about relationships and Chelsea getting back into the dating scene somehow. Chelsea howled when Beth said, "Tell you what, my gift to you. Come down to the clinic and I will give you the biggest set of boobs your back can handle, and your dating problems will be instantly solved!"

After Beth left, Chelsea spent the rest of the day doing household chores, often laughing at Beth's jokes, especially the boob one. Maybe she should take her up on it, she laughed to herself.

Later that night, after tucking her son sound asleep into bed, she stood in front of her bathroom mirror, completely naked, staring and evaluating every square inch of her body. At forty-one years of age, there were parts of her that still had not succumbed to the years. Her breasts were not big, nor were they small. They were beginning to droop but still decent, she thought. A good bra would always make them look dynamite, she laughed. Standing sideways in front of the mirror, she stared at her stomach. No way was it a flat belly anymore, but like her breasts, it was hanging in there, swollen slightly. She came from athletic genes; both her mother and father had met in college on athletic scholarships. Her mom was a swimmer who was nationally ranked at one time but never could crack the women's Olympic team. Her father was all about baseball and football, eventually attending college on a football scholarship, when a serious knee injury in his freshman year ended any chance of a professional career.

After completing her body examination feeling silly – why did she even think she needed to do that? – Chelsea ran a hot bath. Immersing herself in the steaming hot water and suds, she laid her head back against the tub and let her mind drift off. Thinking about Prince Charming sweeping her off her feet, she found herself thinking about Steven again. She missed him terribly, always would, but it was time to move on. She had made up her mind. Her son was twelve now, less dependent, and it was time for Chelsea to grab some of the wonderful nuggets life had to offer, and the one she wanted was companionship. She would open her heart to it, replacing the neon 'Bitch' sign with 'Hi, I am a nice person,' followed by 'I am also horny'. Chelsea laughed out loud thinking of that message written across her forehead.

****

Twelve-year-old Patrick silently, but quickly, slithered down the hallway to the stairway, swearing he just heard his mother laughing in the bathroom. *What was up with that*, he thought. He locked his bedroom door behind him, as he did every night so his mom would think it was because he did it to be safe. But he did it to keep her out and from discovering he actually wasn't home at all. The creative and dark energies that wreaked havoc on his mind did not afford him the luxury of sleep. Patrick had not slept a wink in years, for as long as he could remember, actually. He didn't know how his body functioned without sleep, but he never thought much about it. When the house was still and quiet during the night he would practice the drums or other instruments, just using his sticks pounding away on his mattress. Other times he would silently work his fingers furiously over the strings of his Peavey bass guitar. Often, over the past year especially, he would compose and write music. He had written reams of songs, and they filled so many boxes that he could no longer hide them all in his closet. He knew he had to find a secret storage place, and he found that in the attic space. When his mom was not home he would carry and then lift the boxes up the ladder and into the attic that was located in the hallway outside of his bedroom door. He kept this huge library of music that he'd written a secret, as it would startle most people he knew. He would wait to show the songs. Timing.

As he made his way down the stairs and to the back door, the dark energy blasting Patrick's brain was thumping inside his head like a drum solo. He would kill big tonight, he knew, a very large animal or maybe a real person. *Whichever he came across first*, he thought. Opening the back door, hearing his mother laughing hysterically, he disappeared into the dark night. The dark energy pulsating through his brain was creating a desire to kill so intense that Patrick could not wait, nor stop. He went right to his neighbor's house on the other side of their backyard fence. Scaling the fence was a piece of cake, but the noise caused the only dog on the block that Patrick had not yet killed to start barking as if someone had just stolen a cooked piece of roast beef from its jaws. Quickly grabbing the medium-sized Heinz 57 dog in a head lock, he squeezed its neck hard enough to muffle it quiet, and then slammed its head to the ground, breaking its neck and killing it instantly. The dark energy was pleased, but wanted more, pushing him to keep moving. Get into the house and do a real kill, instructed the powerful energy source. Dropping the limp and silent dog to the ground, Patrick jumped up onto the back step. The knowledge that he was going to kill the neighbors he had grown up with was like an electric current zapping his bloodstream. His mind a blur, he opened the back door. It was unlocked, and he realized it was not even ten o' clock at night yet. Opening the door made an audible creaking sound, drawing the attention of Bill Crittenden, the neighbor.

"Honey, sounds like someone is at the back door. Can you get it, please?"

Patrick could hear Mrs. Crittenden yell down from upstairs, "Bill, for Christ's sakes, I'm in the bath. Get off your ass and get the door!"

"Alright, alright, I got it." *What a bitch*, Bill thought to himself as he rounded the corner and saw a kid standing at his back door. The kid's eyes were glimmering a bright red, what was up with that? Then he realized it was just his backyard neighbor, Chelsea Benning's son, Patrick. What the fuck is with those eyes?

"Patrick, what are you doing in here, a knock would have been nice don't you think?" snarled Bill.

"Really, Bill, why is that? I thought we were neighbors," hissed Patrick, his eyes glowing a bright, beacon red.

"You break into my home to get mouthy with me, you little shit? What the hell is up with your eyes, kid?"

With a speed that surprised even Patrick, he punched Bill Crittenden so hard in the Adam's apple he could feel the cartilage in his throat explode. With eyes wide open in complete and utter shock, Bill was falling backwards, first bouncing off the kitchen wall, then out into the hallway separating the living room from the kitchen. Patrick moved towards him again, smashing his powerful little fist so hard against his nose the bone and cartilage split and shattered like a dry log being smashed by a powerful blow from an axe. Bill was dead before his head ricocheted off the end table and his fat body hit the living room floor, the lamp falling on top of him illuminating his blood-spattered, smashed-in face.

The bitch wife cackled from upstairs.

"Bill, what the hell are you doing down there?!" yelled down his wife Evelyn, standing at the top of the stairs with a towel wrapped around her wet body and another wrapped around her head. Cautiously walking down the stairs when she heard no response, she then saw Patrick in the hallway at the bottom of the stairs.

"Jesus, you scared the hell out of me, Patrick. What are you doing here – and where is Bill?"

She cautiously walked down the stairs. Then she saw Bill sprawled on the living room floor with his pulverized face still seeping blood everywhere.

The cackle turned to a blood-curdling scream.

"Oh my God, what have you done?! What have you done! You killed him, Patrick! Jesus Christ – you murdered my husband!" she screamed hysterically, backing up the stairs, her voice filled with terror, "Your eyes, Patrick! What the fuck is going on here?!"

Before she even had a chance to run, Patrick leapt up the stairs so fast it was as if he was flying. Maybe he was. When he reached Evelyn, he flung her so hard down the stairs that she didn't land until the last step before the floor. She hit with a sickening thud that knocked the air out of her lungs. Her shoulder was broken and her arm was twisted grotesquely behind her back; all she could do was moan. Her towel that had covered her body was somewhere on the stairs, her naked body still wet, exposing a middle-aged woman whose best years, if she ever had any, were long gone. Patrick did not waste any time, the dark energy was overjoyed, leaping around inside his head like a pinball being smacked by the little rubber flippers. Face down on the carpet hallway at the bottom of the stairs, Evelyn moaned, trying to get up, the towel on her hair unraveling and about to fall off. He reached the bottom of the stairs and kicked her hard in the middle of the back, sending her face down against the carpet again, sobs of pain escaping her. He then drove his boot violently into her broken shoulder, her cry of pain muffled by the carpet. Patrick returned to the kitchen and grabbed a large kitchen knife from the countertop rack and made his way back to Evelyn, who had not moved. Throwing the towel on her hair off to the side, he grabbed her wet hair and yanked it back as far as he could, causing her to scream out in pain. Taking the large kitchen knife, he plunged it deep into her neck, severing the arteries, forcing the blood to explode from her, spraying him and the surrounding walls. Intoxicated by the sight of all of the blood and the wet, warm sensation of it on his skin, Patrick, with the dark energy source firmly in control of his mind, finished her off by slitting her throat her from right to left with the large and surprisingly sharp kitchen knife. The watershed of blood cascaded over the carpet in front of her. Her neck muscles and tendons had been stretched by Patrick pulling her wet hair all the way back and then loosened when he stabbed her in the neck, which made cutting her neck easier and cleaner.

He dropped her almost-severed head to the floor and stood up and surveyed the carnage. He'd killed two people, his neighbors he had known all of his life. *What an incredible rush he had just experienced*, he thought. He'd expected to feel sorrowful and remorseful when the dark energy in his mind began to subside, but instead he was alarmingly calm and at peace with what he had just done. He was blown away by the amount of blood that had come out of Evelyn. He was a mess, however, and he needed to clean up before he made his way home. "Hi, Mom, sorry I'm covered in blood but I just slaughtered our neighbors, the Crittenden's, so I'm going to have a shower now, okay? Oh, and do you mind washing the blood off of my clothes? Thanks, mom." No, that wouldn't do.

He made his way to the Crittenden's basement, where he found the washer and dryer. Patrick stripped everything off, including his boxers, and threw it all in the wash. After spending a few minutes figuring out how to run the washer, he added the detergent, adding a little more than the bottle called for. He then made his way up the stairs and into their bedroom. He entered the ensuite bathroom to take a shower. Noticing the bath was still full of Mrs. Crittenden's warm bath water, he drained it and cranked up the hot water, pulling the pin to turn the shower on. Adding a little bit of cold water to the mix so he wouldn't burn the skin off himself, he climbed into the shower, the steam already filling the bathroom, fogging over the mirrors. Scrubbing himself clean of all of the blood, he allowed the steaming hot water to pour over him, pushing what was left of the dark energy source to the back of his mind. The creative energy source was returning, taking over now, spinning his head with thoughts and ideas for songs. Patrick began to put together, standing in the hot water from the shower, a song he would write, reflecting the rush of his first kill of another human being and the raw thrill and excitement it had created.

Twenty minutes later he was sitting in the Crittenden's living room. He watched TV while waiting for his clothes to finish drying. Looking down at Bill's corpse, his skin purple, the blood on his face turned black, Patrick thought about the line he had just crossed. He knew he would never be satisfied killing an animal again. He would kill humans from here on. The dark energy source in his head, when it returned, would want that incredible thrill again and again. He thought about what Bill had said when he first saw him at his back door. He'd asked about his eyes and why were they so red. What was that about? Not sure, and not important, Patrick surmised. He glanced at Evelyn down the hallway, crumpled in a heap at the bottom of the stairs, naked, her face buried in the carpet now turned black from the blood. The cops would have to peel her face off of the carpet to get her off the floor. Her face and the carpet had become one.

Hearing the buzzer from the dryer indicating his clothes were dry, he got up from his chair, turned off the TV and went downstairs to get dressed and get home and settled before the cops descended on this place and began to comb the neighborhood looking for someone who might have seen or heard anything. His bedroom faced out his backyard, while his mom's faced the street. He would tell investigators tomorrow that he did hear something last night. He heard banging and shouting, sounded like a bunch of people. They sounded mad, he would say. He was scared, so he just tried to go back to sleep, and he must have done so, because he never heard anything more after that.

Back at home, Patrick was making his way up the stairs on the way to his bedroom when he stood and paused in front of his mom's bedroom. Hearing her familiar breezy, light wheezing or snoring, Patrick went to his room where he retrieved his key from his hiding spot in the main bathroom. He hid a key in the bathroom so that if his mother ever woke and caught him up he would just say he had to go the bathroom. Back in his bedroom, he sat on his bed and loosened up his creative mind by air drumming on the bed. Often he would pretend that he was Peter Criss from his favorite rock band KISS. Pounding his bed with the sticks, moving his head up and down to the beat of the song "Detroit Rock City," he began to twirl the drum sticks in his hands, just as he'd seen Peter Criss do on all the Kiss videos on MTV. Wow, he'd never known he could do that, he thought. Spinning the sticks like a professional baton twirler, he was having a blast when the creative juices in his mind started to let him know it was time to write that song he'd thought of in the Crittenden shower.

****

The next morning, Patrick, sitting at the kitchen table eating his favorite cereal, Honey Nut Cheerios, while his mom rushed around getting his stuff ready for school, said, "Mom, why don't you relax? I can pack my own backpack, you know. I can even make my own lunch. You seem to forget that I am twelve now."

Smiling at Patrick, still in her housecoat, Chelsea said, "You're right, honey, you are twelve. Tomorrow morning you are on lunch detail, okay?"

Before Chelsea could continue, the front doorbell chimed. As she turned to walk towards the door wondering who could be here at 7:30 in the morning, there was a loud rap on the door. *Jesus, what is your problem*, thought Chelsea, unlocking the door latches, yanking open the door only to see Sam Showenstein standing on her front step.

"Sam, what are you doing here? Is everything okay at home?" asked Chelsea, and then noticed all of the cop cars on the street with their lights flashing. "What the hell is going on, Sam?!"

"Chelsea, may I come in? It's your neighbors, the Crittenden's. They've been murdered," explained a somber Sam, stepping into the front hallway.

Her hand instantly went to her mouth, stifling a gasp.

"Oh my God, Sam! What happened, what happened to them?!"

****

Patrick heard the conversation between Sam and his mom, and knew shit was about to hit the fan in this neighborhood. It made him think of some lines he would add to the song he'd composed during the night.

Chapter 45

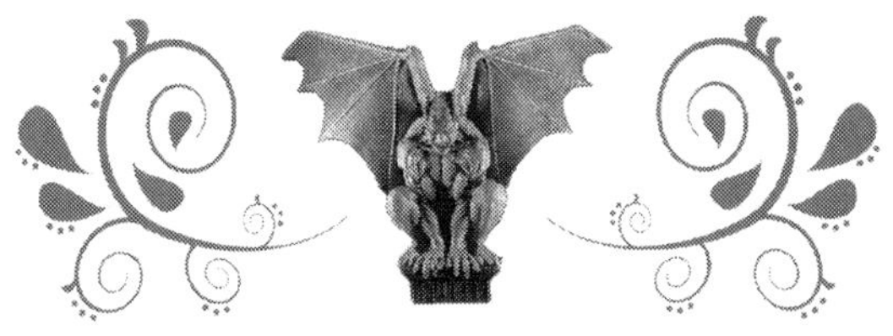

Robert Best was the hottest music producer in the business, boasting a stable of the hottest acts in hip hop, pop, and country music. He was the king of the hill and everyone wanted a piece of him.

Everyone, that is, but Avery Johnson from Alive Records. The only piece of Robert Best Avery wanted was something to grab onto while he drove his fist into his face. Avery, himself one of the most respected and busiest music executives in the industry over the last dozen or more years, had never liked Best. This went right back to his first chance encounter with Best almost thirteen years ago in that LA nightclub when Best ran into him, introducing himself as a new music producer and manager and asking if he could bring his client by Avery's offices to talk about a recording contract. Avery had politely said no amidst the pounding music of the club and the lights from the dance floor. He'd just wanted to stop at the club for a drink before making his way home, and this Best dude had been a major, in-your-face pain in the ass.

The next morning he had discovered Best and his client, Devon Devine, a droid if he'd ever seen one, were in his office waiting for their 'scheduled appointment.' Blowing him off and out of his office, Avery would nevertheless run into Best again over the years as the creep actually built quite a reputation for himself in the industry and attracted a lot of new talent. Best approached Avery on numerous occasions over the years to lease his recording studio to produce records, and Avery told him to get lost. Let him build his own damn studio with the money he must be making, thought Avery. The guy was a creep, very weird, and Avery thought he was an asshole, but he also had to admit he was a talented producer; how else would he be getting the talent he was attracting? His clients were winning Grammys; Best had also won some statues, so he was good, no doubt.

Picking up from his inbox the latest issue of *Music Talks* that Jenn had left for him, he flipped through it, then returned to the front cover. His jaw almost dropped to the floor looking at the cover. Gracing the front cover was a picture of Robert Best dressed smartly in a dark suit, with purple tie, looking very successful with both of his hands placed on the shoulders of the young twelve-year-old phenom of *America's Got Talent* fame, Conner Asker. The tag line on the cover read, "America's new hot shot producer takes control of the career of child prodigy Conner Asker." The piece was written by Bentley Paxton, the beautiful journalist for the magazine whom Avery dated briefly many years ago. Flipping to the article, Avery went on to read the piece. It was interesting to him because he remembered that Bentley disliked Best as much as he did. Covering the incredible story of Conner Asker and his from-out-of-nowhere entrance onto the music scene at a very young age, Bentley did an interview that was aired on TV by *Dateline NBC* right after the little kid won the competition. It had been great watching her expertly peel back the layers of this raw young phenomenon. Plus she looked absolutely gorgeous, causing Avery to pause and think about what could have been. Mostly he did not even bother reading *Music Talks*. It bothered him to see Bentley, so he avoided the mag. Jenn, of course, would make sure that he did not discard the magazine without reading it because she knew that it was important that Avery keep current in the industry and in what everyone else was doing and reading. Reading *Music Talks* was part of the process for keeping current, just like making appearances at concerts, charitable events, and so on. All in the name of schmoozing, so the artists' agents would continue to call him when they had a new client.

Seeing Best's mug, though, still pissed him off, especially on the front cover. Avery had been on the cover of *Music Talks*, the largest circulation and online music industry publication in the business, only once. It was the interview that introduced Avery to Bentley. Best was the wrong producer and manager for that young Asker. Best was a dickhead, and this young kid needed someone who truly cared about him, ensuring the success didn't get to his head and keeping the young man grounded. One only had to look at the career of Justin Bieber, the latest example of a great, young, and talented singer, being swallowed, then spit out by the sharks that swim in the waters of music. Best would use this kid and squeeze everything he could from him, and then discard him like yesterday's garbage.

There were a lot of incredibly talented kids coming into the scene all of a sudden and in many different ways. The kid in Venezuela who'd won the Latin American version of *America's Got Talent*, the Leroux kid from Canada, and Avery's contacts were raving about two young phenoms in Ireland and England. The most amazing thing about these kids was their ages. They were all exactly twelve years old. How crazy is that? He wondered how long it would take before Best represented the rest of these kids, he laughed. Avery preferred to stay away from young talent like these kids. Sure, they were great, but like Bieber, very short shelf life. If they were still around when they reached the age of twenty and wanted to take their careers to the next level, then he would take them on. *Who is he kidding*, he thought to himself. If his phone was to ring right this second with the mother of one of these kids, Avery would be on the next plane out. He would take a shot at steering these kids the right way and giving them every chance to have a long and successful career.

Almost on impulse, Avery thought he would dial up Bentley to touch base with her, see how she was doing and what she had thought of Best during her interview. Nervously calling her number, he was taken aback when she answered almost immediately. *Guess there's no turning back now*, he thought.

"Bentley Paxton speaking," she answered.

He felt the nervousness swell inside of him when he heard her voice. What is he doing? Keep it strictly business, he reminded himself.

"Bentley, its Avery, how are you?"

He was sure he could detect real excitement in her voice when she spoke.

"Oh, hi Avery, long time no hear. I'm doing great, how about you?" she asked.

"Like you, I'm doing well. Listen Bentley, I don't mean to bug you, but I just read your piece in *Music Talks* regarding the Asker kid and Best. How the hell did he get his tentacles into Asker? I didn't see that one coming did you? How was that interview? I mean, I know how much you dislike him."

"Like talking with the devil himself is the best way to describe it, Avery. The vibe he gives off, it's hard to explain, but simply put, it is creepy scary. Like he sleeps during the day in a coffin and comes out at night," chuckled Bentley.

Talking about Best always pissed Avery off, and he found himself getting angrier the more he talked about him.

"Wow, I don't get how clients gravitate to him like they do. You can't argue with his success; he does turn out great records, but Jesus. Doesn't anyone else see the guy is a freak besides us?"

"Apparently not. There's something about that guy that's sinister in some weird way, it's hard to explain. When I first interviewed Conner Asker the night he won *America's Got Talent* he was such a delight, a mega-talent about to explode, but yet still such a grounded boy, very nice and very considerate. The second interview he was definitely different. His attitude was changed, no longer the aw shucks kind of kid, I'm just the kid next door who got lucky, but more the 'Look at me now' kind of kid. His answers seemed scripted, as if he knew what I was going to ask. They were short and simple answers to my leading questions. No doubt he had been schooled by Best. He has lost his sweetness and I know it's because Connor is being handled by

Best," explained Bentley.

Finishing his earlier thought, Avery continued.

"I thought a guy like Best would eventually get eaten up by the system and never be heard from again. That was what I thought thirteen years ago when his only client was Devon Devine. I was completely off the mark. The guy has not only grown to have staying power but continues to churn out talented stars and hit singles."

"You know another weird thing about Best? I asked him during the Asker interview, off the record, whatever happened to his clients that I interviewed so many years ago when he was just starting out, a band called Watermark," said Bentley.

"Yea, I remember them, had a few hit singles before they were dispatched to the scrap heap. Pretty good songs that got a lot of airplay, if I remember, in the late nineties," said Avery.

"Yeah, well, Best didn't remember them, or at least acted like he didn't. Quickly changed the subject by saying that it was too many years ago and he had lots of former clients he no longer associated with."

Avery gripped the phone cradle even harder, his blood rising.

"Are you kidding me? You manage and produce a band with hit records and you can't remember them? Now that is bizarre and bullshit."

"It gets even more bizarre. I decided to track down the band under the 'Where are they now' banner. It took me a rock pile of stones to upturn, but I finally found what happened to them," Bentley explained.

"Let me guess, the headlining act at a casino on some Indian reservation in Minnesota." "They're dead. All of them. All five of them, Avery."

"Jesus, Bentley, how did they die? Did their tour bus crash or something?" asked Avery.

"Every one of them died individually and tragically. The lead singer Randy Sims was the first to die. He killed himself with a shotgun in his mouth. One died by what they call death by cop, meaning he stood in the middle of Las Vegas Boulevard waving a pistol in the air. SWAT members moved in and he refused to drop the gun. When he pointed it at one of the cops, SWAT opened up and tore him to pieces with automatic gunfire. The other three members died in ways just as bizarre. One was trampled by a herd of cattle while working in a feedlot, witnesses stated he just jumped in randomly in front of the stampede. Another died overdosing on pills given to him by his mother, who gave into his wish to end his life. His mother was charged with assisted suicide. The final member of Watermark jumped in front of a speeding subway train in New York City."

The tragic suicides by the members of Watermark shocked him.

"Every one of them killed themselves? That is fucking awful. Pardon my French, Bentley. Best actually never remembered who they were when you asked him. That guy is a bloody monster. Once he sucked every ounce he could from those kids he cast them to the side like trash."

"I remember my interview with them, Avery. They were like zombies. Never said a word, Best answered every question I asked, not allowing the boys to even speak. I had the feeling that if they did speak up they would feel his wrath, whatever that would be. When Best discarded them they probably had no clue what to do with themselves or how to cope with life. Best likely had them so doped up most of the time."

"Now you are already seeing a shift in Asker. What about Asker's parents, what do they think of all this? Is there any concern about the changes in their son since he has been with Best?"

"To be honest, I haven't been able to reach them. I've left them numerous messages. I will get them eventually, though. They could be completely oblivious to the control Best might be exerting over their son."

"Could be a story within a story. Successful music producer sucking the life blood out of his clients, and when their careers are over they commit suicide. Might be a good story for 60 Minutes. Anyways, enough of that Best. Anymore and I'll have to down a bottle of Tums to settle my upset stomach. Tell me about yourself, Bentley. How have you been? Still driving a ragtop bug?"

"I'm still driving my bug, Avery, not very often with the top down, though. Too hard on the hairdo you know," laughed Bentley.

Sensing the conversation was heading into an uncomfortable direction, Avery chose to end it before he said something he shouldn't. "I better let you go, Bentley, I know you're busy. It was great talking with you again, it really was, even if it was mostly about that loser Best."

He sensed in Bentley's reply that she didn't want the call to end.

"Good to hear from you again, Avery, as well. Keep your head up when swimming in the same waters as the Great White Best."

"Would you be up for dinner again sometime, Bentley? Maybe I'll give you a complimentary interview," joked Avery.

"That sounds like a good idea. I'll wait for the call, Avery. Take care," said Bentley, hanging up the phone, wishing Avery had asked her out for that dinner tonight. She missed him and she felt it even more when she heard his voice.

Hanging up the phone with Bentley, Avery leaned back in his chair and cursed himself for not having the guts to just ask her out again right now, rather than leaving it hang out there. His heart leapt around like a lottery ball floating in the cage with the other balls before it fell down the chute. Jesus, she had a control on his heart strings. No other woman could do that.

Alive Records had season's tickets to the Dodgers that they gave out to clients, friends, and family. This afternoon Avery was going to use them, and he had asked Jenn to arrange, through one of the foundations Alive Records supported, for a kid who was a huge baseball fan to come along. It was Saturday, and the Dodgers' afternoon game was at 2:30 p.m. against the Atlanta Braves. Jenn made arrangements for Avery to pick the boy up at noon so they could grab a bite to eat before they had to fight the traffic to get to the stadium. Reading the email on his Blackberry from Jenn with some background on the kid, he typed in the address of the pickup stop into the GPS of his BMW. The kid was from the notorious gang-controlled east side, a place where Avery would never drive this car to if he wanted to live, or at least keep the car in one piece. Driving down one-or two-lane roads in gang-infested East L.A. was suicide. Meeting in a public place on a major thoroughfare in this area, however, was safe and that was where Avery was picking up the kid. According to Jenn's email, the kid's name was Michael Jackson Williams, age eleven. The kid was a regular along with his momma at the Kate Brown House, a shelter for battered women in East L.A. that Alive Records supported. Mikey, as he liked to be called, would accompany his mother several times a week to help out at the shelter. She herself was a former resident of the center. Pregnant and beaten, Mikey's momma would show up at the center only to return again and again to her boyfriend, who would use her face and body as a punching bag. It wasn't till Mikey's momma took repeated blows to her stomach from the boyfriend, in a drug and alcohol–infused rage that almost ended the pregnancy; Mikey's mother was convinced to stay in the shelter for good. Once she sobered up and kicked drugs for good, she was able to take her newborn baby and get an apartment of her own nearby with the help of the shelter. Giving back to the shelter was her way of saying thank you, and the shelter needed volunteers badly, running strictly on the private donations and staffed by volunteer women who had been helped in the past get their lives turned around.

Avery was meeting Mikey and his momma at a Wal-Mart location on Main Street, the major thoroughfare connecting east and west L.A. He was to meet them at noon in front of the customer service counter. Making sure he was early, Avery parked and pulled $300 out of his wallet and balled it in his fist as he made his way into the store. Noticing a younger black woman who looked to be in her late twenties standing with a young boy who had to be Mikey, he approached them and asked the little boy, "Are you Mikey?"

"Yes, sir, that's me. Are you Mr. Johnson?"

"That's me, but you have to call me Avery, okay?" Avery instructed while he shook his hand. Looking up at his mother, Avery said, "Good afternoon, Ms. Williams, I'm Avery Johnson, nice to meet you."

"Nice to meet you, Mr. Johnson, my name is Cecile Williams. I have heard so much about you. Thank you for taking time away from your very busy schedule for my son. He is thrilled about today. It's all he's talked about since he found out he was going."

"Thank you for giving me the opportunity to spend some time with your little guy. I have been told he is a great kid who loves baseball. That will make two of us who love baseball, so we'll have a blast. What do you say, Mikey, should we get going?" Avery looked down at the eleven-year-old whose head was bobbing up and down in anticipation. Looking back up at Cecile, Avery continued, "I will have him back here in this spot at 6:00 p.m., okay? Here is my card in case you need to reach me at all while we're at the game. I have your contact info in case I need to reach you."

After Mikey said goodbye to his momma, he and Avery turned to leave when Avery turned around and extended his hand towards Cecile and said, "Please take this and do something nice for yourself while we are at the game." Before she could even react to what Avery had just done, which was to plop $300 in her hand, they were gone out into the parking lot.

Climbing into Avery's BMW 740, little Mikey was all wide-eyed at the beauty of the car and all the cool electronic stuff on the dash. Avery wondered if the kid had been in much nicer cars than this one that the gang boppers drove. Making their way to the stadium, they chatted about the Dodgers and Mikey's love of the game. The little kid knew everything about the Dodgers, the players and their stats, just as Avery did. Avery loved baseball, especially the Dodgers, and read the box scores daily from the night before. Stopping for a burger and fries at the In-N-Out

Burger, they continued to chat. Avery was impressed at how nice the little man was, always saying thank you and very articulate when he spoke. A smart kid and his momma had done a great job raising him in what he was sure must be very tough conditions. Getting to the ballpark, Mikey was in complete wonder. This was the first game he had ever attended, so it was a very big deal for him. Avery bought Mikey a Dodgers jersey and hat, making the kid squeal in delight. He was having as much fun as the kid was. The kid almost passed out when he discovered Avery's seats were right on top of the first base dugout, two of the better seats in the entire stadium. When the game began, Mikey wanted to keep a score sheet, which kept them both into the game at all times. On a couple of plays that were bobbled, Mikey and Avery would argue about whether it should be scored an error or a hit, which would eventually be decided for good when the official scorer posted his decision on the scoreboard.

As the game progressed, the two of them were having a blast. Mikey was into every pitch and every at-bat. He was a true baseball fan, and Avery was impressed. Feeling his Blackberry vibrate, he checked the caller ID and saw it was Jerry Wagner, manager of his top country singer, Annette Worth. Letting Mikey know he was just going to retreat to the mezzanine to take the call and would be right back, he made his way up the stairs while taking the call from Jerry.

"Where are you, Avery, sounds like you're at a ball game or something?" asked Jerry.

"Good call, Jerry, I'm at the Dodgers game. What's up?"

"We have a problem with Annette. She's sicker than a dog Avery, and she's scheduled to record with you Monday morning. Can we reschedule?"

"Jerry, it's Saturday, Monday is two days away. Just stick to the schedule, she'll be better by Monday, I'm sure. There are no dates to reschedule to, Jerry. I'm booked right through the summer."

"Can we swap studio time with another one of your clients?

Someone who isn't violently ill, maybe?"

"Call me tomorrow night and give me an update on her condition and we'll make some decisions then, okay?" Avery instructed Jerry before he hung up the phone.

When he returned to his seat beside Mikey, it was as if he had never left. Mikey was still right into the game. Glancing down at the scorecard, he could see the little diamond-shaped icons all covered in scratches from Mikey's pencil as he filled them in as the game progressed. The card would be a great memento from the game for him to keep. All of a sudden there was a huge commotion not far from where Avery and Mikey were sitting. When Avery looked over to see what was going on, he couldn't believe his eyes. Finding their seats, just a few rows away, were Robert Best and his client, Conner Asker. Making eye contact with Avery, Best winked and nodded his head in Avery's direction. Pompous bastard, thought Avery. Of all the places in this city, Avery runs into Best again at the ball game. Not wanting to ruin the fun for Mikey, Avery turned back to the game and focused on the batter, the Dodgers' cleanup hitter, Matt Kemp.

"Who was that?" asked Mikey, referring to Best and Asker and the commotion they had caused when they sat down.

"You mean you didn't recognize them? You don't know who that kid is?" asked an incredulous Avery.

"Nope, never seen him before. Should I? Who is it?"

"Never mind, Mikey, let's just enjoy the game."

As the game wore on and entered its final at-bats with the Dodgers holding a slim 3-2 lead and the Braves coming up to bat, Avery heard a voice he did not want to hear, and it was coming from directly behind him.

"Hi, Avery, enjoying the game? Who's the kid?" an amused Best asked as he leaned over from the seat directly behind Avery and Mikey.

"Shouldn't you be over there with your client, Best? I'm sure all of the network TV cameras are focused on the kid between innings. You wouldn't want to miss out on all that free publicity, right?" chided Avery. He thoroughly disliked Best and just wanted him to leave.

"I could move him over here behind you, as these seats are empty. Maybe you and your young client here could get some free face time as well. From what I've been hearing, you could use it," Best sarcastically replied.

"I have no problem dealing with the onslaught of security and police after I punch you right in the middle of your face, Best. Now take your sorry ass back to where you came from before I rearrange that smug look of yours."

"Someday you will see where I came from, Mr. Johnson, and that will be a great day for you."

Seeing the sneer spread across Best's face, Avery decided he'd had enough.

"What's that supposed to mean?" An angered Avery began to stand up.

"Whoa, big boy, I'm leaving. Sit down and enjoy the game. Nice meeting you again, Avery, and I hope you're enjoying the game, Mikey."

Avery watched Best return to his seat, where he motioned for Asker and they began to climb up the stairs and out of the stadium before the crush of the crowd. Then he realized Best had just called Mikey by name. How the hell could he have known that? He was too far away for him to have heard him call his name, and even when he was behind him, Avery was sure he had never mentioned Mikey by name. The guy gave off a vibe that just screamed, 'I am a moron.' Someday Avery hoped he would get the opportunity to rearrange his face. Even in front of a live television audience. Jenn would love that publicity exposure: 'Rival music producer mogul punches out his competition in a jealous rage.'

Looking down at Mikey and enjoying the innocence of his love for the game of baseball, Avery rubbed his hand on Mikey's head, almost causing his new Dodgers hat to fall off. They both laughed and watched as Jonathan Broxton, the Dodgers' closer, came into the game to try to finish off the Braves.

Chapter 46

The day after Seb's birthday party, Sam was back at work at his desk in Homicide. The horrific murders of the Crittenden's next door to Chelsea and Patrick's home sometime during the night were a shock. One of the detectives assigned to the scene was a veteran of the department who had also known Steven Benning. When he realized that Chelsea Benning lived across the back lane from the murder scene, he called Sam. Sam hardly slept a wink anyway, his sleep still blocked, churning the murder of his partner Steven around and around his mind, desperate for a clue as to the perpetrators. His wife Beth gave up during the night trying coax him into relaxing and letting it go before he made himself sick worrying about it. It was long over, and there was nothing that he could do anymore to change that. It was not a fight at three in the morning, but clearly Beth no longer saw any benefit in hanging onto the notion that the department would suddenly reopen the case. There were no clues, it was closed years ago, and most importantly Chelsea had moved on. Worrying about it or, even worse, lobbying the department to reopen the case would bring back painful memories that did not need to be retriggered for Chelsea. Her life had moved past it, and she had a wonderful son to be thankful for. so why would Sam want to dredge this up again? Sam could not answer that other than to say that he had a knot in the pit of his stomach that was not going to go away until he solved Steven's murder. He promised

Beth that he would not obsess over it and it would strictly be on the Q.T. Before rolling over to go back to sleep, Beth made Sam promise that Chelsea would never know that he was secretly investigating the case.

Sam was not assigned to the Crittenden murder case, but felt he should be the one to go and see Chelsea to break the news to her. He convinced her to take Patrick and spend a few days at Sam and Beth's home until the police felt the neighborhood was safe again.

So many years had passed since that day in the hospital when Patrick Benning was born. Sam would never forget that day for as long as he lived. He could never shake the memory of the deliberate stare by the doctor and his burning red eyes. Nor the other circumstances surrounding the boy's birth, the beautiful sound of his coos like singing filling the room where he was born. He revisited the reports of Chelsea's attack and Steven's death over and over again trying to make sense of them. Why had Chelsea suddenly and abruptly stopped referring to the attacker as a demonic beast? She had been so insistent, so determined that Sam and the LAPD investigate that angle. The department cast aside her reports as that of a traumatized victim who had also witnessed the brutal murder of her husband. Who could disagree with that? These factors were weighing on Sam. Those damned crimson red eyes that Sam had seen when he looked into the eyes of that doctor! Now that *was* demonic, he thought. Maybe there was something to Chelsea's original story. *Nah, that was crazy*, he thought to himself. Stay focused, he told himself. Read her reports again. Find the connection. He was remembering Dr. Burkett and how he looked at Sam as he turned that final corner and how a split second before he disappeared out of sight he glanced at Sam for just a nanosecond. Long enough, though, to strike a bolt of fear through him.

Reading the reports again for the umpteenth time, Sam found the connection, and it hit him like a thunderbolt. Shock waves resonated down his spine like a tsunami, but there it was. As bizarre and unbelievable as Chelsea's story was, it was true, and Sam had found the proof. Sam cursed himself for not finding it sooner. It was right there, and he'd missed it.

Sam knew he had missed it because he had just skipped over it when he read it because to him it had been just fantasy, never to be taken seriously. It was unmistakable now. Chelsea, in her description of the attacker, said very clearly, *"It was his eyes that I will never forget.* They were fire red and glowing like a demonic beast."

Swinging his chair in front of his computer screen, Sam began to Google "demonic beast with glowing red eyes" and other variations, all of which led to references to the devil, Satan, Lucifer, evil one, Beelzebub. It was insane to even think about this connection, but Sam continued reading. He read Chelsea's statement in which she'd told investigators, including himself, that she'd been chosen. She continued to claim she was the lineage from an enemy of the Beast from 400 A.D. Sam then Googled battles involving the devil in and around 400 A.D. and came up with no useful hits, just a bunch of extraneous junk. Chelsea said in her statement that the Beast spoke in Latin. He needed more information on that. Sam knew he would have to interview Chelsea once again about the day of the attacks and press her for the details of the Beast that she had described so many years ago. He did not know how he was going to do this. The subject matter was crazy, and he had made a promise to Beth that he would not disclose to Chelsea that he was still investigating Steven's murder. Sam then had an idea, and he picked up the phone and called his oldest brother Jacob, a Jewish Orthodox rabbi.

"Jacob, it's Sam. How are you, my brother?"

"Doing fine, Sam, what's up? Sebastian wants to exchange his gift or something?"

Sam gripped the phone tighter, knowing what he was about to reveal to his brother would be difficult.

"Jacob it's work related. I have a murder investigation with some strange twists, and I need your expertise if you can help me."

"Hmmm, murder investigation, strange twists, sounds like fun. What can I do to help my little brother?"

To give Jacob some background, Sam went on to explain the details of the attacks as described by Chelsea, the murder of her husband and the brutal attack and rape. Describing the monstrous beast and the rape of the victim, he found himself feeling kind of silly hearing himself describe the details to his rabbi brother. Then Sam explained that the words spoken by the Beast before he raped the victim indicated that she had been chosen. He further explained how the beast then continued in Latin that the victim would not be able to recall.

"Sam, you just described the plot for the movie that is playing downtown. What are you asking of me? Do you need an exorcism? Because if you do you will have to get a priest," a confused Jacob explained.

"If I could get the victim to recall what this Beast said in Latin could you translate it for me?" asked Sam.

"Of course, little brother, but you already knew that I would and you would have asked me when you had that information. Now why don't you tell me why you really called, Sam?"

"Does this sound completely nuts to you, Jacob? Is the victim so completely traumatized that she would have made this up?"

"Yes, it does sound nuts, but you obviously are not convinced. You are talking about Chelsea Benning, aren't you, Sam?"

"Jacob, you know I cannot tell you that, and besides, what does it matter if it was her I was talking about?"

"Because, Sam, it happened over twelve years ago, the case has been closed for years, and you cannot forgive yourself for not solving your friend and partner's murder. I never knew the details of the Benning murder and attacks, but it was pretty simple to connect the dots after watching how you acted in front of her at Sebastian's party on Sunday."

"What is that supposed to mean, how I was acting?"

"The burden of that investigation, when you are around that

woman, is like seeing you walk around with a Buick strapped to your back."

"Jacob, please."

"I'm telling you, Sam, I could see it on Sunday, and I have been seeing it at every one of Sebastian's birthday parties for twelve years. You have to let it go, Sam. It will, if it isn't doing so already, affect your marriage, your job and your health. You have nothing to be ashamed of, Sam; you did not fail Chelsea or your partner. There is nothing that you could have done outside of what you have already done to solve that murder. Your own department has closed the case, Sam. I am sure what Chelsea experienced was horrible, but seeing her now it looks like she has moved past it, and has a wonderful son to live for. Why can't you move on from it, Sam? You cannot solve them all, you know, including Steven Benning's," scolded Jacob.

Here it was, the moment when he would reveal to his brother that he was nuts.

"You don't understand, Jacob. I believe her story."

"You what?! You believe she was attacked by some monster, Sam? I can't believe I am hearing this!"

Sam explained the strange stare he had got from Dr. Burkett amid the chaos in Chelsea's hospital room when she went into labor. The doctor had looked through and above all the nurses and staff crowded into that little room, and when he looked at Sam his eyes were glowing a crimson red as if they were on fire, and it had spooked Sam to the core. When Chelsea gave birth to Patrick, the room went from complete bedlam to such quiet you could hear a pin drop. The silence was then filled with the most beautiful, melodic sounds from a newborn Patrick that were breathtaking. There were none of the cries you would hear normally when a baby is born – only these incredible sounds as if an angel was singing. Then the head nurse interrupted by announcing the strange birthmark on the baby that looked like three musical notes.

"That birthmark could easily be read as three sixes, Jacob – the mark of the beast."

"I don't know about that, Sam. Have you ever seen the birthmark again on Patrick since his birth? It could have disappeared by now, like a skin blemish at birth that he just outgrew."

"No, I haven't. The birthmark is on the inside of his left thigh. I could ask Chelsea." Sam then finished telling Jacob that when Dr. Burkett and the nurses transferred Chelsea out of her room and down the hallway to a recovery room and just before they disappeared around the corner, the doctor had glanced back at Sam, staring at him for one last second as if to warn him, his eyes growing bright red, it was unmistakable, Sam said. He knew what he'd seen. It matched exactly what Chelsea had told the original investigating team about the eyes of the beast that had raped and attacked her, that they had shone a deep crimson red.

"After twelve years, why now, Sam? Why didn't you get this out of your system at the time, when Patrick was born? Why now?"

"I had completely missed it in Chelsea's statements where she described the beast that attacked her as having burning red eyes. Just wasn't a plausible story, so it was dismissed and never taken seriously by any of the investigators. The circumstances surrounding Patrick's birth and my own encounter with Dr. Burkett have gnawed at me for the last twelve years. It was when I went back into the reports this morning and began to read through them again and again is when I made the connection and it scared the hell out of me."

"Not trying to sound like your commanding officer or anything, but before you sit and talk with Chelsea and open up a can of worms that cannot be closed, do some more research, will you? Whatever happened to this Dr. Burkett? Have you talked to this guy? See where that takes you. Tie up some more loose ends before you stampede towards this 'devil did it' theory, okay? Just looking out after my little brother, you know what I mean, even though you are a seasoned LAPD Homicide detective," chuckled Jacob.

"Great idea, Jacob, never thought of that. Wow, I think I'm a little too wrapped up in it. It's clouding my decision making. You want to change professions, brother?"

"Enough already. You probably already had him in your calendar to see him after what you discovered this morning. Sam, be careful, take it slow. You have lots of risk going down this road, okay?"

Hanging up with his brother, Sam felt a boost of energy. Tracking down Dr. Burkett and speaking with him and being able to look into those eyes again was something he should have done years ago. Not quite sure how to track down a doctor he'd met twelve years ago, he got up from his desk and headed out of the office. His destination was the Methodist Hospital of Southern California. An hour later he was standing in the administration offices of the Methodist, showing his badge and telling the receptionist, "I'm investigating a cold case murder from twelve years ago and I need to know if a doctor that was on your staff that many years ago is still around."

"I will have you speak with Mrs. Oliveira, our Administrative Director. Please take a seat, Detective Showenstine and I will get her for you," instructed the secretary.

Feeling her disdain for the police coming through her voice, he shot right back at the receptionist.

"I will take a seat right over here, okay, and glance through your magazines that are likely three years old or more. Oh, and by the way, the name is Showenstein, not Showenstine."

"My apologies, Officer. It sounds like you're a veteran of reception areas. I think if you look we have a current edition of *House & Garden*. Excellent read, talks about getting the most out of your spring annuals," smiled the secretary.

About ten minutes later, a woman entered the reception area, and as she was walking towards her office the secretary called out to her and said, "Mrs. Oliveira, there is someone here to see you."

Turning back towards the reception area, she approached Sam with her arm extended. Mrs. Oliveira, a middle-aged woman, still quite attractive and professional-looking, asked, "Do we have an appointment?"

"My apologies, ma'am. My name is Detective Samuel Showenstein of the LAPD. Homicide. May I take a few minutes of your time, please?"

"Homicide. Well, this is quite interesting. What would Homicide want from Methodist in a homicide investigation? Please, come into my office."

It was obvious that Administrative Director of Methodist was an important position if the size and luxury of her office was any indication. Sam got right to business. "Mrs. Oliveira, I am investigating a cold case from twelve years ago. There is an obstetrician who was on staff at that time who delivered the baby of a woman whose husband was murdered. There are some loose ends that I'm trying to tie up in this investigation and I would very much like to interview this doctor," explained Sam.

"Twelve years is a long time ago, Detective, but tell me the doctor's name and I will see what I can do."

"Dr. Burkett was the doctor's name."

"Can you leave me your card and I will contact you when I have some information for you? This may take me a while."

"I am in no hurry, Mrs. Oliveira. I can wait. If you prefer I can go back out to the reception room till you are done. I kind of was just getting into the newest edition of *House & Garden*. Fascinating stuff on increasing the life of your spring annuals."

"Alright, Detective, point made. Wait right here," huffed an obviously annoyed Mrs. Oliveira as she left the office.

Returning less than ten minutes later, she looked overjoyed stating boastfully, "Sorry, Detective, there was no Dr. Burkett who was employed here twelve years ago or ever performed surgeries or delivered any babies here. I'm sorry this was a dead end for you."

"Are you sure? Maybe his records go back further. Can you check further back, please?"

"Detective, I went back to when this hospital was built in 1988 and there never was a Dr. Burkett here. I am sorry. Now if you will excuse me, I must get back to work."

"Do one more thing for me, please. Can you check to see if there has been a Dr. Burkett licensed in the State of California during the past twenty-five years?"

"Detective, I cannot do that. I am not authorized to do that. I am sure you can respect that," she answered.

"Mrs. Oliveira, I can just as easily go back to headquarters, obtain a search warrant, return with a fleet of detectives and go through every filing cabinet, every hard drive of every computer in this office till we find what we are looking for. This is a murder investigation of an LAPD Detective; you don't want to make this difficult, if you know what I mean."

With a look that could have been shooting deadly daggers at him, she relented.

"I know what you mean. Follow me, Detective; let's just get this over with."

He followed Mrs. Oliveira out of her office, down the hallway and into a large room full of cubicles with women and men, probably entering data like robots all day long. Approaching one of the cubicles, Mrs. Oliveira instructed a lady by the name of Leona to log into the California State Medical Licenses database and query a doctor with the last name of Burkett. Watching Leona's fingers flash across the keyboard like a blur was amusing. There were six doctors who had held medical licenses in the past thirty years in the database with the surname of Burkett. Three of them were female, two had retired in the 1980s, a husband and wife duo, and the sixth was deceased in 1998.

Sam asked the clerk, "What was the name and age of the deceased doctor in 1998, please?"

"Dr. Brian Burkett, Obstetrician, died in a car accident the evening of May 23, 1998, by this report."

Sam was shocked when he heard that date. It was the day Patrick was born. This was the doctor, without a doubt. His adrenaline pumping, he told Mrs. Oliveira, "I need the personnel file on this Burkett right now."

Following her back down the hallway, he waited in her office while she retrieved the file. A few minutes later she reappeared with a stack of printed computer files. She laid it out in front of Sam and said, "Read it, then I have to return it, otherwise you'll need the warrant."

Reading the file in front of him, Sam saw that Dr. Burkett was forty-two years old at the time of his accident. He graduated from UCLA medical school in 1982 and took various internships at hospitals around the Los Angeles area. His whole file was very run-of-the-mill. Came from a good family, graduated near the top of his class, good reports from his bosses at his internships. All nice and perfect. Closing the file, he then stood and looked at Mrs. Oliveira and said, "Thank you very much for your cooperation, Mrs. Oliveira, you have been most helpful."

Leaving the hospital, Sam headed back to the office to look into the death report and accident scene reports from attending officers in the car accident of Dr. Burkett back in 1998. The pit in Sam's stomach began to churn. It was a feeling of dread with an uneasy feeling about where this investigation was going to take him. He would be alone in this, he knew. The department would suspend him if they found out what he'd just done at Methodist was connected to the Benning case. His wife would not be happy whatsoever, especially if she knew that he was going to speak with Chelsea. How he was going to cross that bridge with Chelsea, he had no idea. He would have to be very careful, tread softly, but he also knew he had to speak to Chelsea regarding her encounter with the Beast and, if she would agree to be hypnotized, to recollect the Latin spoken by this Beast.

Sam took a minute to pray before he started his car. He would need His strength and His guidance, because Sam knew he could not do this by himself. He started his car, took a big breath and put the car into gear.

Chapter 47

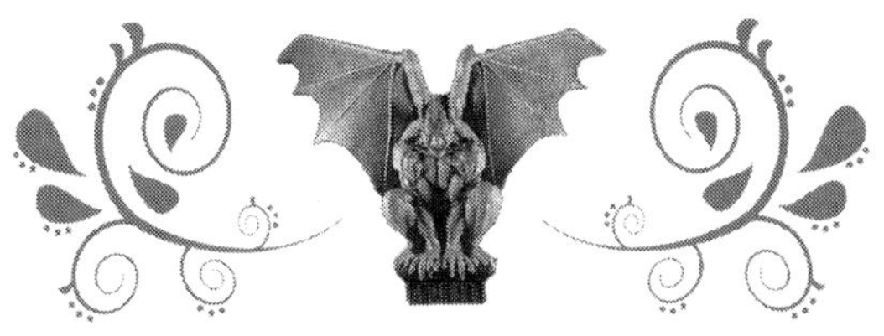

Robert Best left Dodger Stadium with Conner Asker and headed back to the L.A. condo he owned and used when he was in Los Angeles on business. Tonight he was sharing it with Conner and his adopted parents from South Dakota. The condo was bigger than most houses, almost 4,000 square feet, lavishly decorated and appointed. Great for entertaining when he was in L.A., and he allowed clients to use the condo when they were in town themselves. He gave all of his clients a key to the place. He never really entertained people, he thought to himself. He appeared to people as if he was entertaining them. There is a difference. He did it because it was a necessary tool in the business he was in. Appearance meant everything. He had to project success to his peers, the media and the friends and family of his clients who were still alive.

He killed just about everyone closely associated to his clients. It was easier and safer that way. He was never suspected in any of the homicides. Why would they suspect him? Plus he was never in the same city at the time when the murders or deaths occurred. He was the mist of death that swirled through their soul just before they died. He enjoyed having a bird's eye view of a human's soul when they died. He could feel the profound sense of loss when the body died, followed very quickly by their soul. He could sense the agony of God's life mist as it disappeared when the soul died.

His human persona, Robert Best, was a well-conceived and well-planned character he had created hundreds of years ago after his defeat over sixteen hundred years previously in his battle with God over the souls of mankind. Satan, as he was called in the Bible, portrayed in Man's movies or written about in their books, would soon finish what he'd started so long ago. The complete and utter destruction of mankind on this earth was near, very near, in fact, and to know that soon his cauldron of souls in hell would be filled to the brim, making the Prince of Darkness, or whatever people liked to call him, very, very satisfied indeed.

His plan revolved around the seven musical child prodigies he had spawned to help weave the net he needed to capture the millions of human souls he planned to take from God and thereby ruin His plans for an everlasting Kingdom here on Earth ruled by the reappearance of His Son, Jesus Christ. The plan was right on schedule in its development, just as he knew it would be. The seven children were quite remarkable, even better than he had hoped for. The nasty little Benning kid was a real treat, a chip off the old man's block, he chuckled to himself. For the next five years, these children would be the source that he would use to reshape human history forever, and the thought of how close he was coming to unseating God as the true ruler of man was intoxicating to his all-encompassing dark and evil mind.

There was one little wrinkle he needed to take care of before it came back to bite him, and then he would be ready for the next phase of his plan. He would oversee the next five years of the children's lives to ensure they all stayed on the right path and on schedule. His human form Robert Best would then bring it all together to foster the ultimate control he needed. Now back to that wrinkle, he thought.

****

Ann Lockwood of London, England, and her son Michael, the incredibly talented musician fresh from his performance with the London Symphony Orchestra, were the talk of the country. The story of her life as the heir to the Oakley Steel fortune, of her tireless work in the many charities supported by the Oakley Foundation and the tragic murder of her husband and her mother, was dredged up in the papers and media all over again. She did everything she could to contain it, but it was impossible; the media hounded her and Michael relentlessly. She had been almost ready to take Michael far away from London, completely out of the spotlight where he could have some sort of normalcy. That all changed, however, with his performance on stage with the LSO. It would not be fair to take Michael away from what he loved and what he was born to do – make and play music. How music had become his calling she did not understand, nor did she try to. She had decided just to go with it as best as she could, knowing the truth would reveal itself eventually. The beast that had beat and raped her and killed her husband and her mother had also threatened to return if she did not care for Michael at all times. What the latter meant, exactly, she had no idea, but she was pretty sure it meant growing and protecting his musical genius.

Ann had heard the buzz of the Irish girl from Dublin, Chloë McCloskey, who had the voice of a thousand angels, she was told, and the similarities between her and Michael were eerie. Researching the girl's life story, she discovered right away that very little of it existed. It took some of her connections, including her friend, the one-time investigator of her husband's murder, Detective Jeremy Cookston, to help open some doors to learn more of the background of Chloë McCloskey.

"Why would you want information on this Irish girl, Ann? What does she matter to you?" Jeremy asked Ann when she called him on the phone.

She knew she had to be careful with Detective Cookston, as he would view her request as suspicious.

"Well, I'm thinking of bringing her to London to work with Michael but I'd like to know more about her before I get involved. The press will be all over this, of course, so I don't want any surprises."

"Okay, I get it. What do you want me to do exactly, Ann?" asked Jeremy.

No sense sugar coating it, she thought. Might as well get right to it.

"Birth records, school records, background on her parents, and so on."

"Wow, not asking for much, are you? I have a connection with the Garda, Ireland's National Police. I'll see if he can pull her records. Give me a few days, okay?"

"Thank you, Detective."

A few days went by and then Ann got a call back from Detective Cookston, who said, "Ann, I have nothing to tell you. There are no records that exist for the birth or existence of Chloë McCloskey. I ran my checks through my contact in Dublin as well as doing my own in all of the U.K., and there are no records that exist. All I can tell you is it looks like she's been raised in a Catholic convent outside of Dublin, and most recently in St. Patrick's Academy in Mayo County, sixty-two miles west of Dublin under the careful watch of Sister Beatrice McGarrigle and Father Thomas O'Sullivan. The only reason I was able to find this out is apparently she's as popular in Ireland as Michael is in England, so it wasn't difficult to track her down. It is very unusual for no birth records to exist, but you might get the answers you seek if you were to make contact with Father O'Sullivan."

Listening to his story, Ann was not surprised that the birth records did not exist. She thanked Jeremy, "Thank you, Detective, for your help. I will take it from here. You have been most helpful."

"My pleasure, Ann, take care of yourself and let me know if I can be of any further assistance."

Already thinking about booking a flight to Dublin, she found her thoughts interrupted when her cell began to ring. Picking it up and answering, she was happy when she heard her friend Kathy Ovens from Michael's school on the phone.

"Good morning, Ann, sorry to bother you, but I was

wondering if you had any dinner plans for tonight, it being Saturday and all."

"No, I don't think so Kathy. I know I don't, what have you got planned?" asked Ann.

"Well, Richard and I would like to have you and Michael over for dinner so he can show off his Elvis collection to your son."

"That sounds wonderful Kathy, Michael will be thrilled!"

"Oh, that's great then, Ann. I, on the other hand, have another reason for you to come over, and I hope you won't get upset with me."

Here we go again, Ann thought. A blind date.

"Kathy, please not again. Remember the last time I agreed to this with a friend of your husband's from work? The guy was a loser and a drunk. He tried putting his hand down my blouse when he dropped me off at my home."

"I know, I know, Ann, both of us were disgusted. Richard hasn't spoken to that guy since. This guy is a music instructor from the school, Ann. He is not rich nor is he a braggart. A simple man, but very intelligent and a real gentleman. There is no pressure or expectations, just the four of us and your son relaxing over dinner and a few cocktails. What do you say, girl, huh? Nothing to lose, right? You know I wouldn't steer you wrong."

She was about to cancel. She truly hated blind dates. She was in no hurry for a relationship, choosing instead to continue to take it slow. But she could feel the excitement in Kathy's voice so she agreed to do this for her.

"Alright, for Pete's sakes. But no more, Kathy, don't do this to me anymore. I'm in no hurry to meet a man, okay? I'm not going to bring over Michael, though; he'll have to wait to see the Elvis collection. He will be bored to tears, sitting around, watching and listening to a bunch of adults. I'll make arrangements to have a friend of Michael's stay for the night. I'll bring in my babysitter to watch over them."

"Okay, sorry to put you out like that, 'cause you know

Michael is certainly welcome. Dinner is at six, drinks and appies at five, okay?"

"See you then, Kathy."

Wondering what she was getting herself into again, she thought, as she informed Michael he could invite a friend over for the night as she was going out. Grabbing her list of babysitters, Ann tried Michelle first, as she liked and trusted her the most. Michelle said she was available and would be over by 4:00 p.m. as Ann requested. She was not against dating or even starting a relationship, but right now she did not have time for this, especially with all the digging she was doing into this McCloskey girl's background and having to fly out there. Oh well, she would do this one for Kathy.

Arriving a little late at about 5:20, Ann was met at the door by Kathy. After they exchanged hugs, Kathy led Ann into the living room of the very spacious Ovens home and introduced her to their guest, Robert Best, a music teacher from the Richmond School of Music.

Shaking his hand, Ann felt an odd sense that she had met him before or had seen him before somewhere. Maybe they'd met at the school but she couldn't pinpoint it yet. He was a good-looking man, in good shape, who looked to be in his early forties. As they sat down to drinks and small talk, Robert broke the ice with Ann by asking, "Have you seen the Elvis collection, by chance?"

Glancing over at Richard, Ann replied, "No, I haven't. I've been looking forward to seeing what Richard has. Did you get to see it?"

Jumping into the conversation, Richard said, "Nope. Keeping you all in suspense till after dinner. You'll get the royal tour then. I know you're having a hard time containing yourself, but you'll have to be patient. You know what they say, 'Good things come to those who are patient.'" Richard was clearly enjoying the attention his Elvis collection was getting.

After another hour or so of visiting and chatting, Ann was certain she had met Robert before; the feeling of déjà vu was overwhelming. She was just not sure where, but the more they talked the closer she seemed to come to figuring out where she had met him. The name meant nothing to her, but there was something about him that began to touch off some of the early warning defense systems built into the psyche of every woman. Looking at Robert, the sensation of pure danger that began to suffuse her body caused her to shake, and the urge to get up and run out the door was lifting her off the couch, as the realization of who he was hit her like a cold hard slap in the face. She hadn't realized that she had dropped her glass of wine when she heard, as if in the distance, someone addressing her urgently., "Ann, are you okay? Ann, for God's sake, you're scaring me!" Kathy called out to an unresponsive Ann, who was fixated on her guest Robert Best. What the hell was going on with her, Kathy thought. She looked as if she had seen a ghost!

Ann was trying to get up, but she was frozen and couldn't move. The white-hot fear was making it difficult to breathe. The beast that had raped her, torn her husband to pieces and later decapitated her mother was right in front of her. Picking up on her sudden recognition of him, Best stood and smiled at Ann. His eyes glowing an incandescent red, he spoke in a demonic and satanic voice, "Your sixth sense is very sharp, Ann. I am impressed."

Then Kathy's screams filled the room as Best picked up the fireplace poker beside him and turned and jammed it into the right eye socket of Richard, still seated on his recliner beside Best, unable to speak or even react at the bizarre turn of events. Well, he would not be reacting to anything anymore, because he was dead, the two-inch hook of the poker fully embedded in his skull, the blood spewing all over him and his wife Kathy.

Kathy was screaming like a wild beast, unable to control herself after witnessing her guest and co-worker brutally murder her husband in front of her eyes. Backing away from Best, still in shock but no longer frozen in place, Ann shouted at Best, trembling, "Why are you here, what do you want this time?! Why can't you leave me alone?!"

His demonic eyes were burning into her as he screamed, "You stupid bitch! I warned you when I ripped the head off your mother that I would be back! I know what you are doing Ann. Detective Cookston left behind a widow and two small children with not even a pension because he shot himself in the mouth with his own weapon. I know about your inquiries to Ireland and the McCloskey kid. I know everything you do, every minute of every day I know what you are doing! I thought you knew that! Well, I guess you will know now, won't you, stupid bitch!"

Before Best could continue, the loud bang of a firearm echoed in the room. Looking towards the sound, Ann saw Kathy holding a revolver in her hands pointed at Best. Looking back at Best, Ann could see he had been shot in the back. Blood was pooling on his white polo shirt, but it did not seem to faze him. Kathy screamed out, "Get the fuck away from her, you fucking maniac, or I swear I will fill you full of holes!"

With speed that Ann could only sense as a blur, Best picked up a heavy glass dish from the living room coffee table and threw it so fast and hard at Kathy that it hit her square in the mouth, exploding her teeth and gums in a bone-crushing blow. Crashing against the wall and then onto the floor, Kathy tried to get back up but Best was right on top of her. There was nothing Ann could do to stop this monster, so she just turned her head away from what he was about to do. Digging two fingers deep into a screaming Kathy's eyes, he pulled back and put his other hand into her mouth and yanked. All Ann could hear was the sound of bones snapping, tendons ripping and the laughter of Best as he squealed in delight while he dismantled Kathy's face piece by piece.

Dropping the lifeless and mangled body of Kathy Ovens to the floor, Best, himself now covered in blood, walked up to Ann, his eyes burning bright, a maniacal look on his deranged, demonic face. He grabbed Ann by the throat and screamed as he choked, "Next time you see me will be your last day on this earth, you stinking stupid bitch! You will join the others to burn in my furnace of misery for an eternity! Your son will be left to figure his place in this world on his own! Is that what you want? Because that is what you will get! I will start with Michael's friends at school, killing each one more horribly than the last! It's what I do, Ann; I kill, and I will take your soul for eternal damnation! Remember that when you want to play detective again!"

Dropping her to the floor seconds before she would be unable to draw another breath in this world, he picked her up again and threw her across the room to crash into the wall unit with all of the ornaments and books cascading down on top of her. Near death, she asked God in her prayers to take her now, and to do what He felt right with Michael. There was nothing more she could do to protect him. Best, in an unstoppable rage, reached down and grabbed her hair and yanked her off the floor, pulling her hair out of her skull as he did so. Yanking her head back so she was forced to look into his eyes, he screamed once again, "You can pray all you want, you stupid whore bitch, He can't hear you here, it's just you and me! Reaching back, Best slugged Ann one last time with a pulverizing blow that smashed her nose and her teeth, sending her crashing to the floor with a sickening thud.

Her eyes filled with blood, and very close to death, Ann, watched the front door open and Best depart, laughing hysterically as he did. Closing her eyes, waiting for the dark shadows to take her away for good, all she could see was a light and a voice in her head. She couldn't be certain she was hearing it correctly, but as the light in her head began to fade, she swore she heard the words.

"Fight, Ann, fight. Live. I will not abandon you."

About the Author

Errol Barr lives in High River, Alberta, Canada and is busy completing work on book two of the Superstars trilogy, *Vasallus.*

Feel free to contact Errol at errolbarr@gmail.com
Twitter: @errolbarr
Facebook: Errol Barr
Blog: www.errolbarr.blogspot.ca

Made in the USA
Charleston, SC
20 June 2012